CITY AND CITADEL

About the author

I learned to read before I was four, and haven't stopped since. When I taught five to seven-year-olds and had three children of my own, I hadn't much space left for writing, but I managed short stories and poems from time to time. Later I was able to join a writers' group and found it ideal for making me work to improve technique, style, plotting etcetera. Tamlyn jumped out of a short story and demanded I do more. I've so enjoyed the experience, especially finding that plots and characters develop minds of their own and insist on doing their own thing as you go along. I can't imagine it, but if anybody should ask me for a piece of advice about writing it would be, "Don't say 'I could write a book' – do it." It's great fun.

Heather Newby

CITY AND CITADEL

Vanguard Press

A CIP catalogue record for this title is
available from the British Library.

ISBN 978 1 784659 29 5

*Vanguard Press is an imprint of
Pegasus Elliot MacKenzie Publishers Ltd.*
www.pegasuspublishers.com

First Published in 2021

**Vanguard Press
Sheraton House Castle Park
Cambridge England**

Printed & Bound in Great Britain

Dedication

To K.P. and D. with my love.

Chapter 1

Tamlyn stabbed a full stop at the end of his essay on 'plants that heal'. He did it so hard that he nearly broke his pen, but he flapped the page gently to dry the ink, shuffled the pages together and patted the pile with satisfaction. Master Greenwell should be pleased with that, he thought. He grimaced at another scrap of paper containing the title set by Master Garrid. He should have got on with these essays at the start of the summer's break, but there had been so many more interesting things to do. Now here he was, stuck in his room and scrambling through work instead of enjoying the last free hours of summer outside. Oh well!

He sighed. He knew without reading them what the words in Master Garrid's crabby writing would say. 'Give three main methods for recognising evil enchantments and discuss ways to avoid and overcome them.' They'd been given exactly the same title every year since he'd been promoted to the Citadel Academy almost six years ago. In the second year they'd looked at each other, wondering if perhaps the old man had forgotten they'd done it before, but only Willan had dared to mention this fact,

"I am well aware of that," Master Garrid had replied. "This subject is the most vital in your training, and my intention is to see whether you have actually learned anything in the past year. Perhaps you thought you knew it all then, did you boy?"

"N-n-no... of course not, Master. I just thought... well..." Willan had stammered into silence.

"It occurs to me that in fact you did *not* think at all. If you did, and that is the level at which your brain works, we might have to reconsider your position here."

Scarlet faced, Willan had shrunk back behind his desk. He'd vanished from the Citadel a few days later and there were many rumours whispered about his fate. Tamlyn, who spent as many hours as he could roaming the surrounding countryside and moorland, thought he'd seen

Willan working in a field, digging turnips, but he hadn't mentioned it. What they'd all learned from this episode had not been anything about the ubiquitous subject of enchantments, but the strong advisability of never questioning Master Garrid. Tamlyn had come to extend this to keeping most of his thoughts hidden inside his own head.

Now he dragged out his enchantment file and searched through for his five previous efforts on the subject. The first, written when he had only recently been promoted from Lower school, reminded him of how proud and excited he'd been to be allowed into Citadel Academy. Only those who were considered as being possible material for future Masters or even Lords came here, and he'd written pages of all he'd found in books or gleaned from listening to conversations. He winced at some of the rubbish he'd produced, even though he'd got a good mark. In later years he'd gradually adopted a different approach. He gave as many reported incidents and theories as he could find, carefully quoting authors or sources, but equally carefully giving no indication of his own thoughts on the subject. The fact that he wondered whether 'enchantment' was possibly blamed for many quite normal things which simply happened to annoy a Master or Lord was kept strictly to himself. Of course, he had to assume that it must exist somewhere. So many older and more experienced men including the High Lord couldn't all be wrong could they? Could they? He kept his eyes and ears open but his mouth firmly shut on this topic.

He was sitting there, drearily trying to think of something new that would satisfy Master Garrid, when he heard voices outside his window. Those boys like him who had made it through to the sixth year were rewarded by being allocated their own rooms in the outer reaches of the Citadel, and he was still excited by having a window looking out onto the world. He ran across and peered down onto the steeply sloping path leading to the stables in the base cavities of the Citadel.

The rules stated that this route was for riders only, or carts to bring hay or food for the horses to the stables. What he saw now, though, was a woman struggling along, weighted down with a bulging sack. She had a shawl tied close around her head so it was hard to tell her age, but she was obviously having some difficulty holding the sack over her shoulder with one hand while the other clung onto a small girl who was doing her best to escape. Probably one of the Donkeys bringing vegetables to the kitchens Tamlyn thought, though she must know this road was forbidden to her. He'd try and send her on a safer way. Opening the casement further in order to lean out and do so, he heard the clatter of hooves coming at speed. A horseman rounded the corner to the right at the top of the slope and Tamlyn recognized the plumed hat of Lord Zaroth. At the same moment the small girl managed to escape the woman's hold and, laughing with delight, danced away from her into the middle of the road.

Tamlyn's shout of warning was as useless as the woman's cry. Obviously startled by the yells and the sudden appearance of a small moving thing near its hoofs the horse reared and skittered sideways on its back legs. Its rider somehow managed to keep control, but slashed down furiously at the child with his crop before urging the animal on again and vanishing towards the stables. The small body of the child was lying still and silent on the ground and the woman dropped her sack as she ran to gather her into her arms. Was she dead? She hung limp as the woman dabbed at blood on her forehead with the corner of her shawl. Then she started to move and whimper.

"Take her to the kitchens," Tamlyn yelled down at her. "Someone will help you there." He hoped he was right. The workers there were mostly Donkeys so it would certainly be safer for her than out here on the road. The woman looked round for the source of his voice and finally saw him. She stared up at him, and a look of surprise flashed across her face.

"Go *on!*" Tamlyn urged. "D'you know the way? Down there on the left – a green door. There's a passage inside. It's a long way, but… no, no – leave the sack," he added as she struggled to pick it up while still cradling the whimpering child.

"I must take it… sir." Tam heard the pause before 'sir' as though the word came hard to her tongue.

"Leave it. I'll come down and bring it for you. Go on." Anger and disgust at Lord Zaroth's unnecessary savagery filled his mind and sent him hurtling down the stairs, out onto the side road and round to the stable path. When he reached the sack he realised that he could be landing himself in all sorts of trouble now – no one interfered with a Lord's actions without a stiff penalty, and Lord Zaroth might very well return to deal with the woman. Also if any of his classmates saw him shifting vegetables he'd never hear the end of it. He supposed he could say he saw the bundle lying in the road and thought it might endanger traffic… No, much better to get himself and the sack out of sight as quickly as possible. After all, he had said he'd take it for the woman. He gripped the neck and tried to swing it onto his back, nearly falling flat in the process. The thing felt like a ton weight – how had the woman actually carried it? As fast as he could, he dragged it down to the kitchen entrance, hauled it inside and slammed the green door. Whew! That was better.

The floor of the passage was uneven but the dark rock had been worn smooth by years of hurrying feet, so the sack slid along more easily here. Students made it their business to know all the ways in and out of the Citadel and though there were only glimmers of light from wall torches set at long intervals, Tamlyn followed the twists and turns of the passage easily. He hoped the woman had not found it too difficult with her burden. She'd obviously got through; no sign of her as he turned the last bend and saw the heavy sacking curtain across the kitchen entrance.

He paused, wondering how to deal with this now. Simply say, 'I've brought your sack', to whoever was there, leave it and walk across to the main door? He had no wish to return the way he'd come and risk walking up the stable path again. He was, after all, one of the Citadel people and needn't feel awkward – those in the kitchen would not question him or try to talk to him. The Donkeys didn't. As long as there was nobody there from the upper levels he should be all right. He shouldered the curtain to one side and walked in.

There was a frozen moment as he looked across to the wide fireplace where large pots sat on grids above the banked flames. The woman he'd seen sat on a stool in front of this with the child on her lap. At least he assumed it was the woman, but she'd removed her shawl and now dark red hair tumbled around her pale face and onto her shoulders. At her side knelt a much younger, fair-haired woman who Tamlyn was sure he'd seen quite often serving in the refectory. She held a small bowl and a piece of cloth with which she seemed to be bathing the little girl's head. Both the women stared at Tamlyn, then the younger one leapt to her feet, moving as if to prevent him seeing what was happening. She dropped the bowl and spilled the liquid in her haste.

"It's all right, Lyddy," the older woman said calmly. "I don't think this young man means us harm. Come forward, sir, I have much to thank you for."

Somewhere at the back of his mind Tamlyn noticed that the 'sir' had changed subtly to a more welcome tone, but mostly he realised that he was obeying her summons with no thought of being insulted by a command from a Donkey, a servant. He walked to within a couple of feet of her, bowed his head briefly and looked into her face. His eyes met hers – deep amethyst pools that somehow made him feel she could see right into his thoughts, far beyond anything in his outside appearance. The feeling was brief: she nodded her head and smiled.

"Goodness lies in your heart. Believe in yourself," she said in a low voice. Tamlyn didn't know what this meant, but the words felt warm in him.

"I brought the sack," he said, gesturing to where he'd left it near the curtain. "Is the child badly hurt?"

"Nothing that won't heal, I think. Lyddy's bathing her head."

"And I've spilt the water. I'll get some more," the girl said. With an irritated click of her tongue she retrieved the wooden bowl from the floor and reached for a ladle in a gently steaming pot. Tamlyn looked down at the little girl, noticing that the cut across her brow was not deep but a large bump had risen around the wound, already turning dark with bruising.

"Have you got arnica? It's good for relieving bruises," he asked, his mind jumping at once to his favourite subject.

Lyddy looked startled. "Not here," she said, and turned to the older woman. "Merla?"

"It would certainly help. Yes, we have some at home."

Tamlyn fumbled for the package which he always kept in the leather pouch at his waist. He unrolled a short length of linen and extracted one from among a number of folded papers inside. "Here," he said, untwisting it to drop a handful of dried flowers into Lyddy's hand. "Crush them lightly and soak them in the water. It really does help."

Lyddy closed her hand but simply stood staring at him.

"Get on with it, Lyd. He's absolutely right. I give you my thanks, sir, and I'm sure young Fliss here would too had she not been struck unusually dumb." The woman smiled at Tamlyn with a twinkle in her dark eyes. "You'll have her mother's gratitude as well – and now I'm reminded that I should return this imp of a child to her family very soon. Fliss wanted to know where the stable path went, and as it seemed quiet I was foolish enough to show her. I should have known better. I hope I have not caused trouble for you."

Forgetful of where he was and to whom he was talking Tamlyn watched as Lyddy followed his instructions. Merla was dipping the cloth into the infusion when they heard a loud and angry voice outside the main kitchen entrance.

"Out of the way, fool. Shift yourself and those boxes." There was a scuffle and a clatter, followed by a yelp of pain. "Donkey!" the voice snarled as the door was flung open.

Tamlyn froze where he stood, and stared open-mouthed as Lord Zaroth stormed in. "Where are those fools who nearly unhorsed me?"

Tamlyn looked round in a panic, and found that Merla, the child, and even the bowl and cloth had vanished, while Lyddy was seated at a table some distance away, calmly sewing some white material. Without a glance at Tamlyn she set her work down and stood to curtsey to Lord Zaroth.

"My Lord?" she said questioningly, keeping he head demurely bowed.

"Stupid Donkeys – woman and child. Wandering where they're forbidden and could have killed me. They must be punished. Where are they?"

Tamlyn was sure he noticed Lyddy stiffen, but she answered meekly enough. "I have seen no such Donkeys in the kitchens my Lord. Apart from this Scholar I am alone at this time. Others will come soon to prepare the evening meal."

Apparently unsatisfied, Lord Zaroth stormed around the kitchens, looking in cupboards and storerooms, kicking stools aside in order to peer under tables until he came up against Tamlyn.

"You, boy! Scholar are you? Seen an old crone and a scrawny child here?"

14

"I've seen none such, my Lord." He managed to make his reply sound nonchalant, though his hands were clenched behind him to control their trembling.

"Huh!" Lord Zaroth snorted, seeming to abandon his quest for vengeance at least for the moment, and looked more closely at Tamlyn.

"No place for Scholars.. What are you doing here?" He stood scowling down at Tamlyn, legs straddled and with his back to Lyddy,.

Tamlyn's mind went blank. Then he saw behind Zaroth that Lyddy had re-seated herself with her sewing and with a small gesture she held up the white garment towards him, nodding slightly.

"I... I tore my shirt, my Lord. Brought it down to be mended as I wanted it this evening."

"Name?" he barked,

"Tamlyn, my Lord. Year six."

Lord Zaroth stared at Tamlyn in silence for a moment then turned on his heel and stalked towards the door. He looked back over his shoulder briefly as if about to say something else but thought better of it, stared at Tamlyn again then marched out. They heard his heavy footsteps thudding away.

Tamlyn felt weak with relief. He started towards Lyddy but she stopped him with a gesture, holding up one hand and putting a finger to her lips. He heard the sound of voices in the next room. Must be other servants returning. Lyddy folded her sewing and walked to Tamlyn with it, speaking in a clear voice.

"Here, sir. I hope this will suit you for now. It should look better when it is washed." She put the garment into Tamlyn's hands and whispered, "Some big ears also have long tongues. I'll collect this from your room when I clean. I know where it is – Merla told me."

Tamlyn nodded. So many bewildering thoughts were flying round in his head, but he knew enough of how things went on in the Citadel. He mustn't put her, or indeed himself, in danger by demanding explanations now.

"Thank you," he said stiffly in the same loud tones, but hoped his smile and the touch of his hand on hers would show her what he would have said.

Chapter 2

Tamlyn opted out of lunch in the refectory, helping himself instead to bread and cheese from the side table, and picking up a hard green apple lying in the grass as he walked through the orchard. He enjoyed eating these sour little fruits. Most boys preferred the sweeter red ones, but so too did most of the inhabitants of the Citadel, so there was trouble if too many were taken without permission. Only the pigs seemed to share his taste, and they weren't likely to complain if he took a few. He strode on, scarcely noticing where he was, his feet taking him to his favourite thinking place without conscious direction.

The midday sun was hot and there was little shade at the top of Herder's Hill, but Tamlyn settled himself into a hollow where a clump of gorse bushes provided some shelter, as long as he was careful where he sat. The bread and cheese vanished, crumbs scattered for the insects in the sparse grass, and Tamlyn crunched into his apple. The sourness brought a burst of saliva into his mouth, making thirst less pressing. Eventually he hurled the core away and stared moodily down at the Citadel.

It had been his home forever as far as he knew. When he'd been very young, he'd believed that the High Lord had provided it for them. He'd learnt now that the massive outcrop of dark rock had been part of the making of The Land when the world was young, and many of the chambers and twisting corridors, particularly the inner ones, had been split open, tunnelled, cleared and smoothed within it by other people long before the Lords arrived. The Lords had built onto and around the central mass in all directions to make the strange yet wonderful place that was his home, and where he belonged.

For almost seventeen years he'd accepted and had no doubts about how things were. The succession through crèche and nursery to Lower school and now the Citadel Academy had seemed a good way to go, and he'd looked forward to becoming at least a Master. Even, in his secret dreams, he'd seen himself as a Lord, one of the elite surrounding the High Lord. Miserably, he remembered how he and the other boys who'd come into the Academy as eleven-year-olds had idolised these god-like creatures. Tall, strong and superbly dressed, they had seemed completely confident. Indifferent to all but their peers, they expected and received agreement with anything they saw fit to do or say. Tamlyn's friends had all had their favourites and – Tamlyn screwed up his face in a grimace now – his hero had been Lord Zaroth.

As he'd grown, he'd never doubted that the people who lived in the Citadel were the best because anyone who wasn't went somewhere else. Where, he'd never really considered. Probably they went to be a Donkey. Everyone used that word for the people who did the work in the Citadel or managed the fields, farms and animals – 'Donkeys' because they were slow and stupid, but strong like animals to do all the laborious stuff not fitting for Citadel folk. Citadel folk were clever. Lords were the very best, and whatever they said was right. They protected everyone from evil enchantments, and at the very top was the High Lord, who knew everything and ruled everyone. Forever, Tamlyn had assumed. He'd felt proud when he'd repeated the Words of Belief daily in training – 'The High Lord is all-knowing, I will give him honour and obedience at all times'.

But vague doubts had begun springing up in Tamlyn's mind, particularly questions about evil enchantments for one thing. They were told that study of them was an essential part of their education, but if the High Lord was all-powerful, it was not to be imagined that he would allow anything like that to thrive in this place, the centre of his power. And who cast these enchantments? Surely not anyone who'd been chosen to live in the Citadel. He fretted as his mind went round and round on this problem. He was sure that if he voiced his worries to anyone he would be diagnosed as the victim of an evil spell and treated as a pariah until he had been cleansed – an extremely unpleasant and sometimes fatal event he knew, though nobody but the Lords controlled the details. Yet nothing was ever said or done about the maker of the magic who, common sense told him, must be more of a danger than its unwitting victim. Words that Merla had whispered to him yesterday came into his mind – something about believing in himself. If he believed what was in his mind now, he would reject a large part of what he had thought was the truth all his life so far. Still, he sensed that this was the path he must take or deny what his mind told him.

Thinking of yesterday more problems surfaced. Why were there no women Masters or Lords? He knew there were Ladies, glimpsed very occasionally, though they lived in rich seclusion in the highest part of the Citadel, part of the Lords' quarters. Maids, cleaners and cooks were mostly women, but invariably they were Donkeys, so… It felt as though another wall crashed down in his brain. Donkeys! Stupid, slow, animals only fit to work for their masters. But in those brief moments in the kitchens he'd seen and heard enough to be utterly certain that Merla and Lyddy were neither stupid nor slow. Merla must have assessed the situation and acted with lightning speed to escape, and Lyddy had provided his way out of the panic that swamped him when faced by the angry Lord. He had, he realised, felt comfortable with them, and his lifetime teaching to regard himself as superior and them as beneath him felt ridiculous. Calling them Donkeys was an insult; the nearest to an animal on that occasion, raging and storming round in a temper, had been Lord Zaroth!

"Tamlyn! Ta-am!" Someone was yelling for him and he stood up to see Hallam climbing at speed up the hill. His friend stopped when he saw Tamlyn. "Thought you might be up here. Come on, get a move on. It's unarmed combat in ten minutes."

Tamlyn loped down. "What's the rush?" he demanded. "Master Vilaton can hardly see whether we're there or not."

"Old Vil's retired, or been retired. Guess who's taking us."

Tamlyn's mind was still full of his thoughts of the last half hour. He couldn't be bothered with new conundrums. "Haven't a clue. Who?"

"Sharkley!"

"*No!*" Tamlyn stopped dead in his tracks. "We *had* better hurry then," he added, starting down the hill again at speed.

"Exactly. But I've got your kit, so we can go straight to the combat hall. Slow down, don't want to arrive red-faced and panting."

"Thanks, that's great. But *Sharkley.*"

"Yeah. And in case you've forgotten, there are only six of us this year. No hiding behind the bulk of Batley and Briggs. They got excused for health reasons. If you've had Briggs land on you, you'd think it should be our health they were worried about, but I'm not so sure."

They managed to reach the hall seconds before Master Sharkley, but he eyed them with disfavour as he waited while Tamlyn and Hallam stripped and changed into their kit and soft boots. The boys gathered on the matting in front of the small dais where the master stood.

"The session starts on the hour," he said coldly. "Please make sure you're ready next time. Now, we'll do a brief warm up run, then I'm going to put you in pairs and watch each pair in action separately to get an idea of what level you're at. Four circuits round the hall first then, the third one sideways and the last one backwards."

That wasn't so bad. Hours of walking the fields and moorland had made Tamlyn strong in the leg, but he was dreading who he might be paired with. He hated fighting in any form. With Master Vilaton he and Hallam had usually got together, and with a few yells and ouches had got by. Master Sharkley looked as though he'd miss nothing – and who would he have to fight?

"Not too bad. Scholar Downham, you'd do well to skip puddings and lose a bit of weight. Shouldn't be out of breath with that short run." Downham, who was already scarlet, went an even deeper crimson. "Now we'll see what Scholars Crossley and Bolton can do. Start when you're ready and stop immediately when one of you is grounded."

After a self-conscious start the two did quite well. Master Vilaton, though elderly and short-sighted now, must have been an excellent combatant in his day and had taught them reasonably well. After some five minutes Crossley landed flat on his back, and Master Sharkley nodded with what might just be construed as approval.

"Fair, fair. Now let's see. Yes, we'll have Scholar Tamlyn and…" He paused to study the other three. "Scholar Bartoly I think."

Tamlyn felt his heartbeat constricting his throat. Bartoly was heavy and ungainly, and was one of the minority of scholars who knew their parentage. His father was Lord Mansor, and Tamlyn had never got on with this classmate. They stood facing each other and bowed as they had learned. When their heads were close Bartoly muttered, "Going to be a kitchen Donkey then, orphan boy?" Lord Zaroth must have told the story of yesterday.

He managed to control the anger that rose in him and they moved towards the centre of the hall, making tentative jabs and grabs at each other.

"Fancy the little blonde kitchen Donkey do you?" sneered Bartoly. "Shouldn't bother if I were you; couple of the Lords have her lined up." Somehow he managed to jam his heel down on Tamlyn's instep. It was painful, but hardly aware of this Tamlyn felt rage erupt in him like the flames of an inferno and he went at Bartoly with everything he had. His fists flew like pistons at that sneering face, and when Bartoly desperately flung his arms across his face, Tamlyn kicked like a fury at his body. He felt the glory of controlling the object of this all-consuming anger. Hatred fuelled him as he'd never experienced it before. He could go on all day, feeding his disgust into every slamming fist. As Bartoly cringed away from him in amazed fear Tamlyn managed a vicious kick into his crotch. The bigger boy curled over towards him, howling in agony, and Tamlyn hurled his fist again with all his power into his face. He heard the bone crack, saw blood spurt. Bartoly fell.

Tamlyn stopped, all that emotion draining away as suddenly as it had risen, leaving him empty of everything but a sudden revulsion at what he had done. What had happened?

"I'm sorry," he muttered, reaching a hand to help Bartoly up, but his opponent shuffled away from him on his bottom, clasping one hand over his nose. Tamlyn became aware that Master Sharkley was standing looking down at them. Now he'd be for it.

"He started before I was ready," Bartoly howled thickly through gushing blood.

"Scholar Bartoly, this class is preparing you to fight for your lives. Do you really think an enemy would kindly wait until you were *ready*? Is someone who wants to kill you likely to respond politely to you saying 'Hold on a moment will you while I pull my trousers up'?"

Tamlyn heard a slight titter from someone but it was soon quelled.

"This is not a joke. My exact words were 'start when you are ready'. It's up to you to see that you're ready first, or at least not after your adversary. Scholar Tamlyn, that was an excellent example of what can be done unarmed. Perhaps the technique could be polished a little," (was that really a smile flickering round the Master's lips?) "but I confess I shouldn't like to let you loose here armed with anything more lethal than a feather duster. Scholar Bartoly, get yourself off to the doctor, and let me hear no whining about fairness from you. Scholar Tamlyn, your opponent seems to have been very generous with his blood. I suggest you go down and bathe. I will now see Scholars Hallam and Downham."

A bemused Tamlyn grabbed his clothes and went down the steep flights of steps to the deepest part of the citadel. The low ceilinged place – more cave than room – had little in it but benches hewn from the rock, and in the middle the pool where warm water bubbled up, the same pleasant temperature at all times and in all seasons. In one corner another stream flowed from a fissure high in the wall and there the water was cooler. Tamlyn stripped off his stained boots, vest and shorts and showered Bartoly's blood from himself. Then he lay in the warm pool and tried to think.

He felt a deep disgust that he had allowed his anger to take control of him so completely, and that for a few minutes he'd actually enjoyed the feeling. He could find excuses for himself – Bartoly's taunting words and sneering manner were enough to make any decent person angry – but he did not want, ever, to hurt anyone like that.

"Hey, Tam!" Hallam came running in, stripping his clothes of as he came. "That was something else! Where did that come from?" He splashed in to lie beside his friend.

"Dunno. You tell me. I'm not exactly proud of myself."

"Well you prigging well ought to be. Bartoly's been due a thrashing for years, but I never thought it'd be you who did it."

"How did you and Downham get on?" Tamlyn asked, wanting to avoid any more of Hallam's enthusiasm.

"Oh. Not bad. Bit of an anticlimax after your effort you might say. Think you put Sharkley in a good mood. He was positively grinning when you got Bartoly down like that."

"He made me angry. Stamped on my foot and said… some nasty things."

"Must have been pretty foul then. I can't remember you ever being more than mildly annoyed at anything."

"Yeah? Look at my hands. I want to get something on them before next lesson." Tamlyn held up his fists and considered them. They were red and his knuckles were grazed, but the warm water was soothing them.

"Bet Bartoly looks ten times worse, all over. That last kick you gave him! Ouch! I even felt a bit sorry for him then. Well, almost! And his nose. Lord Mansor's little boy's never going to look the same again."

Tamlyn thought this Lord was probably not someone he wanted for an enemy, but he kept it to himself.

"Come on. Let's get dry and ready for maths."

They climbed out and grabbed towels from the store shelves. The workers would clear up after them but Tamlyn put all their dirty things tidily into the baskets. No need to increase their work, and he would not even *think* 'Donkey'. He was determined that word wouldn't mean anything but a mild, four-legged animal to him from now on.

Chapter 3

The news had obviously travelled through the Academy with its usual speed, for when Tamlyn came into the refectory after maths there was a sudden silence which turned into a buzz of excited chatter. A few students punched the air, many grinned at him, and he felt someone thump him on the back as he passed. Bartoly was not popular and it was obvious that there was considerable rejoicing at his beating. He was, however, a Lord's son and it didn't pay to show too much pleasure.

Tamlyn walked up to where Bartoly stood with a couple of friends, his back to most of the room.

"Bartoly, I'd like to apologise to you. I lost my temper and I wish I hadn't. I'm sorry."

Bartoly turned slowly towards him. His face was a mess, with some sort of ointment spread thickly on his swollen nose. A small trickle of blood still oozed from his right nostril. Tamlyn held out his hand. Bartoly stared at him; his eyes tracked down to the hand, then back up to Tamlyn's face. He made no move to accept the offered handshake.

"Not half as sorry as you'll be, Donkey," he spat, his voice low and tight. "Just watch out, you hear?" Deliberately he turned his back.

Tamlyn stood for a moment, then shrugged and went back to his usual seat with Hallam. In one way he felt glad that his apology had been rejected for now he knew where he stood with Bartoly; with his father, too, he supposed. He could expect some form of retaliation he was sure. Still, he couldn't keep looking over his shoulder for trouble – he'd just hope he could deal with it when it arrived.

"That's one complete and utter louse," his friend said. "If he ever makes Lord it'll be on his dad's shoulders."

"Oh, let's forget him. I'm hungry." Tamlyn was surprised to realise this was true. Preparing his apology in his head as he'd walked in, he'd had a hard knot in his stomach which felt as though it might stop him eating at all. If Bartoly had accepted what he'd said it would somehow have made him feel subservient and inferior to the boy he so disliked. Now he felt released. He could go on thinking that Lords didn't necessarily get everything right, especially in their offspring. Another sudden thought cheered him still more. He could also believe if he liked that his own unknown parents, whatever their status, had been much nicer people than the Mansors,.

By the weekend Tamlyn was getting tired of congratulations. It wasn't that he didn't think Bartoly was a nasty character who needed taking down a bit, but he still had a loathing for the way he'd felt when his anger had controlled him rather than rational thought. The fine weather continued into the weekend, so he decided he'd go a long walk and let the air and sunshine clear his head of the emotions hanging around in there.

"Fancy a bit of a stroll up to the moors?" he asked Hallam as they finished breakfast. "Master Greenwell reckoned there's probably some harewort coming through up beyond Forley's Smithy, and the new shoots are always best. We could make some lunch with what's left here."

Hallam snorted. "I know exactly what 'a bit of a stroll' means when you say it, Tam – a ten mile slog over rocks and brambles with the odd mud patch thrown in. Thanks, but not this time. Actually, Kenley and I are going to work on Greenwell's essay. He wants it on Monday. Suppose your one's already done."

"Only last week – and all I've managed so far on Garrid's is half a page."

Hallam groaned. "I'd pushed that so far to the back of my mind it was out of sight. Can we work on it tomorrow?"

"Good idea. See you this evening then." Tamlyn set to work salvaging slices of bread and butter and rolling uneaten bacon rashers into them. They were a bit greasy, but he found a page of fairly clean paper someone must have dropped, wrapped them in it and shoved them in his pouch. They'd taste good later, and once eaten it would leave room in his pouch for harewort and anything else useful that he found.

It really was a beautiful day, not too warm and with a breeze blowing from the mountains in the east that was just enough to keep him comfortable when he really got going up towards the moorland. The hint of colours changing made it clear that autumn was on the way. Many fields were already cleared, some to lie fallow for a season but others were being worked on as he passed. Tamlyn knew that the workers would usually studiously avoid looking up at anyone from the Citadel, but he'd wandered across this countryside for so long that some would at least nod now; a couple even raised a hand to him. It cheered him, made him feel part of The Land.

He passed by two small hamlets then came to Forley's Smithy which had a dozen or more dwellings as well as the smithy. He'd been told that the Forley family had lived there for generations and were reckoned to be the very best smiths, for most Lords used them to shoe their horses. They'd tried to force the family to come nearer the Citadel but the Forleys refused. They must have known the Lords wouldn't punish anyone who was irreplaceably useful to them. There were usually one or two horses outside the smithy, brought there by squires who got the job to save their masters the journey. These were boys who'd completed schooling and been chosen by a Lord who would train them and, if the High Lord approved, they'd become Lords themselves eventually. Tamlyn knew Ewan, one of the two who were there today, who was standing at the head of a fine chestnut mare. He'd been a year ahead of him at school but had shared Tamlyn's enthusiasm for plants.

"Hi there, Ewan," he called.

"Oh, hello, Tam."

"Greenwell reckons there might be some harewort sprouting up there. I'm going to have a look."

"Lucky you!" Ewan ambled closer and glanced round to see that the other squire was out of earshot. "I heard you beat up Mansor's son pretty thoroughly. Took some doing didn't it?"

Tamlyn groaned. "Is there anyone who doesn't know about that? Yeah. Sharkley's taken over combat classes and he paired me to fight with Bartoly. I sort of thought I'd get in first before I was flattened. I was lucky I suppose." This was the explanation he'd come up with for his uncharacteristic behaviour.

Ewan looked again to see where the other squire and horse were. He was a man, much older than Ewan, and was leading his animal into the smithy at that moment. Ewan stepped even closer to Tamlyn.

"A warning, Tam. Lord Mansor's really furious about it, and he's not a nice man to get on the wrong side of," he muttered. He stepped away again as the other squire reappeared.

"Thanks, Ewan," Tamlyn murmured. Starting to walk on, he called back more loudly, "I'll let you know if I find that harewort."

The encounter cast a small shadow on the pleasures of the day; he really hated the way everyone felt they had to take such care with what they said, who they said it to, and who might overhear them. He supposed it was necessary but wished it wasn't. He hurried on for another twenty minutes and then forgot his grumbles in delight at spotting the very thing for which he'd been looking. The soft, greyish and slightly furry leaves grew in pairs, and really did look like a hare's ears pushing up out of the earth. Kneeling down he got out his knife and cut three. On closer inspection he thought they'd probably be better in another week, so he stopped there and carefully wrapped the ones he'd cut in his linen strip. He'd come again next weekend if he could.

This seemed like a good place to have his lunch and he felt more than ready for it after his mainly uphill trek. Though he wiped his hands on a patch of moss, as he started to eat there was a faint smell of soil on his fingers, mixed with a light hint of bay. That came from the harewort, he knew, though he was pretty sure the plants weren't related. It was like adding a sauce to his rather squashed bread and bacon. He sat on when he'd finished, watching some small heath butterflies with their pinky orange wings edged with soft brown, their colours blending in with the autumn shades of the bracken and coarse grass.

The sun was dropping below its midday height and he didn't want to miss the evening meal. The bread and bacon had left plenty of room for more before bedtime. Suddenly needing real movement, he started off, half running, half jumping down the rough and steeply sloping hillside. Not altogether sensible, he knew, but he'd been this way so often he felt confident – and Hallam knew where he was if the worst came to the worst. Almost unrecognised, the thought lurked somewhere at the very back of his consciousness that one day it would be pleasant if he could stay forever in this place he loved; have his body sink in and change to become part of the land itself, as small wild animals did.

He could see ahead a stony ridge which he knew had a flat grassy area on its downward side. He could jump up on top of the stones and down straight ahead, or circle round to one side. He opted for the jump and leapt to the highest and flattest rock. As his momentum carried him forward he realised there was someone below him. A woman, and – oh no, she seemed to be squatting. Had she stopped to relieve herself? Instantly flooded with horror and embarrassment, Tamlyn somehow managed to swivel on the foot still in contact with the stone, jump outwards and sideways to land in a disorganised heap beyond whoever it was. He kept his back to her as he scrambled to his feet.

"I'm so sorry… I didn't realise… not usually anyone… you must…" he stammered as he finally turned, and stopped dead, staring. It was Merla. She sat with her skirt drawn up to her knees and grasping her left ankle with both hands. Her face was white, and he saw a grimace of pain on her lips. "What's happened?" he managed to say at last.

She looked up at him, staring in amazement when she saw who it was. "I was wishing, not very hopefully, that someone would come by. Hardly expected help to almost land on top of me. You're making a habit of coming to my rescue, aren't you?"

Tamlyn managed a grin. "Sorry if I frightened you. I love running down the hill, and there's not usually anyone around. Have you hurt your leg?" How was it that he felt so at ease talking to this woman he'd only known so far for about ten minutes?

"It's a lovely place," she agreed. "Unfortunately I'm not as nimble as I once was. Turned my ankle. No real damage, I think, but painful."

Tamlyn knelt by her feet. "May I?" he asked, and when Merla nodded he gently felt round the bones of the already swelling ankle. "I can't feel a break, but there are little bones deep inside. I'll bind it for you and go for help." He pulled the linen roll from his pouch, and with the help of his knife tore a wide strip from one edge. The harewort leaves fell to the ground.

"I can guess where you got those," Merla said, retrieving them. "Up above Forleys Smithy."

"Mmm," he nodded, busy binding the strip firmly round her ankle. "Too early really. I'll come again." He'd slashed the end of the material in half so he could tie the bandage firmly. Does that feel more comfortable?"

"You're really good at this, aren't you?"

"It's what I'd like to learn to do properly." Merla started to struggle to her feet. "No, stay still. Who can I fetch to help you?"

"Tamlyn, it might not be wise to be seen running around for me. Vitsell lives very close. If you can help me there he will care for me."

Tamlyn flushed. He hated the fact that what she said was true, but he knew she was right. He supported her with his arm firmly round her waist and they moved slowly down the hill. Before long he saw a chimney poking up from a dip. He'd never noticed a house there, but as they approached it he wasn't so surprised; most of it must be buried in the bank. All he could see were a doorway and two windows.

Merla paused as they neared the place. "Don't be alarmed now. I'll have to speak to Vitsell in a way that will sound strange to you. He's an obstinate old man. Insists on speaking the Old Tongue even though few know it now, and he can talk perfectly well like us when he pleases. His name means Long-and-Thin in the Old Tongue; you'll see why."

Tamlyn helped her hobble forward and she tapped on the door. After a wait during which Tamlyn thought he saw a window curtain twitch, the door was opened and a man seemed to uncoil himself from inside. Very much long and thin, he thought, not daring to stare or let a grin appear on his face. He wondered how such a man could live in so small a place. Maybe it went downwards inside the bank.

Merla spoke incomprehensibly, and the old man looked Tamlyn up and down. Emotions seemed to be fighting on his face, particularly when he saw Tamlyn's arm still firmly round Merla. At last he turned back to her and bowed.

"Lady, I obey," he said.

"Thank you, Vitsell." She looked up at Tamlyn for a long, silent minute and then squeezed his hand. "Thank you too. I rather hope we might meet again. Now you must get back or you'll miss your supper. Vitsell will care for me, I know." She transferred her hold to the old man who led her through the door with great care and shut the door firmly.

The detour from the route he had intended to take meant Tamlyn was approaching the Citadel further to the north, which would take him past the area where the kitchens lay. Easier to continue this way now and go in one of the side entrances. He walked along with his head full of what had happened. He'd like to meet Merla again too, he thought. Was this evil enchantment? Every part of him rejected the idea, and though he knew his feelings would undoubtedly be a sign to some others that he *was* enchanted, he was absolutely certain that there was nothing evil in this woman.

A small sound, a tiny movement, stopped him in his tracks. In the grass at the side of the path lay a small fox cub. Its dark eyes looked at him with fear and it struggled to move away, but it was either too weak or wounded, and Tamlyn knelt slowly beside it. He crooned soft words of comfort and reached to stroke its head with one finger. The little animal stopped struggling, and Tamlyn could see that one front leg was bleeding from a gash near the top.

"Poor little one," he whispered, and lifted it carefully into the crook of his arm. What should he do now? If the creature had been here long it must need food and water as well as treatment for its leg. The treatment he could do, but food? He could hardly take it in to supper with him. He realised how close he was to the kitchens, and remembered the rubbish bins outside – there might be food scraps there that he could take, and one of the kitchen staff would surely let him have a saucer. The cub seemed to have accepted him, and he walked down to the bins.

Tamlyn had never had cause to examine the rubbish. Why should he, not his business at all. But now he realised that everything there was organised. Some containers obviously held stuff that would rot down to make a compost to be spread on the land, some looked like burnable material, and there was a bin full of food scraps. He guessed this might go to the pigs. The sensible arrangement pleased his orderly mind, and he started poking in the pigs' bin for something that might tempt this small animal. Foxes ate meat, didn't they?

"Can I help you, sir... Oh!" It was Lyddy, carrying a bowl of rubbish. She looked startled to see him, and he was briefly speechless. He managed to focus on what he needed.

"I've just found this young fox cub. It's wounded, and I was looking for some scraps to feed it."

She came forward to peer at the small creature. He wondered how she'd react; not everyone shared his enthusiasm for wildlife he knew.

"Oh, poor little thing," she said, using one finger as he had done to stroke it gently. "I think a bit of raw meat would be more suitable than that cooked stuff. Wait here."

She emptied her bowl of vegetable parings into what Tamlyn had decided was for compost and vanished inside. After meeting Merla in such an unexpected way it seemed almost beyond belief that here he was, talking to Lyddy.

In a short while she reappeared with two small bowls and a cloth. "He's probably needing water if he's been lying out in the sun," she said, dipping part of the cloth in the water that was in one of the bowls. "Hold him steady." As Tamlyn did so she squeezed water from the cloth so that it dripped onto the fox's mouth. His tongue shot out and he licked with enthusiasm. "There you are. He doesn't look as though he's been long weaned, but I think he may lap from a bowl when he feels better."

"I don't know how to thank you," said Tamlyn.

"No need to, I love animals. Even rats, though not in my kitchen. They're really clever beasts, did you know that?"

"I suppose they must be to survive and flourish even when most of us are trying to kill them. You know a lot about animals don't you?"

"That's Merla, she's wonderful. I live with her. I'm off home when the supper's served and I'll ask her about this little one."

"Oh!" Tamlyn exclaimed. "She may not be there." He told Lyddy what had happened.

"Thank you for helping her. She might have been there till I went in search of her. She loves getting out on her hillsides so much, but forgets she's not as young as she was." Lyddy grinned then. "I doubt she'll still be at Vitsell's. Two in that place would be a bit of a squash. She'll have got him to help her home. I know he looks like a yard of string, but he's amazingly strong. Now," she went on, pointing to the second bowl on the ground, "I've chopped up some pork which should suit him. Don't let him gobble it all at once or he'll be sick on you."

"Is it all right for you to give me that?" Tamlyn didn't want her in trouble for him.

"I'm more or less the kitchen chief here, in fact if not in name. If you're worried some scholar might go short you can always eat only vegetables for a meal or two."

Thoughts flickered through Tamlyn's head like a pack of cards with a thumb running at speed across the edges. She was telling him what to do. Could a Donkey do that? She was not, not, not a Donkey. She was teasing him. And he liked it.

He grinned at her. "I'm a vegetable eater from now on for at least a week," he laughed

"Good." She smiled back. "Now you'd better not come in through the kitchens. Take the stairs up from the second door that way. If you come down in five minutes or so I'll put some more things for this little one at that door."

Tamlyn did as she said, smiling to himself. He'd got far more pleasant things to think of now than his problems with Lord Mansor and Bartoly.

Chapter 4

Tamlyn put an old towel on his desk and laid the fox cub on it. He thought it might immediately try to escape from such very strange surroundings, but it seemed quite relaxed. He drizzled a little more water into its mouth, and followed that with a few pieces of the chopped meat. The animal looked round hopefully for more, but he remembered Lyddy's warning.

"Let's have a look at your leg first, then you can have some more," he said. He took a bunch of thyme leaves from the jar on his window sill and crushed some in a little of the water, using an old pestle and mortar which Master Greenwell had passed on to him when it was going to be thrown away. He looked at what was left of the linen strip in his pouch and decided it wasn't much good for its original purpose now, so tore off a small square and used it to bathe the wound on the fox's leg with the thyme water. It wasn't deep but was obviously painful, as the animal winced and jerked a bit, but didn't try to escape. When the cut was clean, Tamlyn bruised more thyme and bound it over the cut with the last of the linen.

"There, that should stop it turning nasty. Once it's healing I'll take the bandage off and you can lick it." He started to go down and see what Lyddy had left by the door downstairs, but turned back, thinking he should put the animal on the floor in case it jumped down while he was out and gave itself more injuries. The cub stuck its nose into what was left of the water, lapping it greedily. Thankfully it looked as though it was quite capable of feeding itself.

Tamlyn was delighted with what he found tucked into a niche at the side of the door. There was a large shallow basket, the sort used for bread in the refectory, which had a good layer of straw in it. There was, too, another bowl with more raw meat, a stoppered bottle of water and a couple of uncooked rib bones, lamb he guessed; too small for pig and he hadn't heard of any hunts recently which might have meant a young deer. The last thing was a small collar and lead. Where on earth had Lyddy found that? It looked well worn: he could see teeth marks in the lead so it had perhaps been thrown away by a Lord after training a new deerhound puppy. If he himself had to work clearing other people's rubbish he'd certainly keep back anything that might be useful! Usually it wouldn't be possible to put a wild animal on a leash, but this one seemed amazingly docile.

This one? He must have a name. Tamlyn looked at the little beast with its beautiful dark red coat and thought Rufus sounded good.

"Come on then Rufus, let's sort you out," he said. He put the basket down beside his bed, and refilled the water bowl, setting that under his desk. He added another bowl of meat and a bone, storing the other one and the rest of the meat under a book on his shelf. When Rufus had finished the meat, he sat looking up with his dark, shining eyes, almost as though he was saying 'What next?' Tamlyn picked him up and put him in the basket where he turned round awkwardly several times but then settled down.

A knock came at the door; it was Hallam.

"Oh, you *are* back. Wondered if you'd got lost. Coming for supper? It's nearly… What on earth have you got there? Not that starving are you?"

Tamlyn realised he was holding a bone in his hand. He laughed. "I've got a guest," he said. "Come and meet Rufus. Softly though, I don't want him to get frightened."

Hallam walked round the bed and stared. "You're crazy, Tam. Where on earth did that thing come from?"

"Found it wounded, bottom of the hill by the kitchens. And it's a 'he'. I've called him Rufus. He's quite amazingly relaxed for a wild animal. I've never seen anything like it before. Here, give him this bone. Gently."

Hallam did so, and Rufus took it from him then pushed it down in the straw. "It, sorry, he's more like a tame dog isn't he?" He considered Rufus for several seconds. "You don't suppose he's, like, an evil enchantment do you? You know, sent to trap you."

"No, I don't. What could he do, do you think?"

"We-ell, he could keep you sitting up here with him till you starved to death. Or worse still, stop you helping me with Garrid's essay."

Tamlyn laughed. "Idiot. Ever known me to miss a meal? I reckon he'll be all right while we eat, then you can bring your books in here and we'll try and get something that makes sense on the everlastingly boring topic."

"Seriously though, you can't keep a fox up here as a pet. Some of the hounds would get scent of him, and that's not a pleasant thought."

"Don't intend to. He's a wild animal. Couple of days and his leg should be healed enough for him to get around again. Then I'll take him up the hill and let him go."

"Right," Hallam nodded, satisfied. "By the way, where did that basket and stuff come from?"

"Oh, I just asked in the kitchen," Tamlyn replied as nonchalantly as possible. "Come on, I have a feeling it might be pork for supper, and I'm really ready for it."

They took Rufus out onto some grass before they went in to supper, and he satisfied them (and presumably himself) by wetting at length. When the supper was served Tamlyn remembered he was supposed to be eating vegetables, but there did seem to be plenty of the pork stew so he thought Lyddy might allow him some after his day on the moors. He grinned to himself. Life at the moment might perhaps be a bit dangerous, but it certainly seemed interesting and definitely unusual. Master Garrid's essay was neither interesting nor unusual, but he and Hallam managed to cobble together enough for both of them to produce several pages which hopefully wouldn't look too similar.

"We'll have to make sure they're not together in the pile," said Hallam. "Do you realise though that those might be nearly the last enchantment essay we ever have to do? Old Garrid usually only sets two in a year, and this is our last year. Seems weird doesn't it? Wonder what we'll be doing in a year's time. Suppose you'll try and get something with Greenwell."

"That's what I'd like, or work in the doctor's department."

Before they went to bed they carried Rufus down for another successful visit to the grass, and Tamlyn noticed that the cub was already beginning to use his damaged leg more normally. Another two days he reckoned, three at the most and he'd have to let him run on the hills. Already he knew he'd miss Rufus, but no way was he going to try and make a pet of him. Firmly he put him in the straw-filled basket before he got into bed himself.

In the middle of a very pleasant dream in which he'd discovered an unknown herb with amazing properties, something unseen appeared to be pouring water on his face. He roused to discover that this 'unseen' was in fact Rufus. He was standing on his hind legs in his basket, front paws on Tamlyn's bed and industriously licking him. As Tamlyn realised what was happening the cub managed to push himself upwards and land with a satisfied grunt across his stomach. It looked as though his patient's recovery was progressing extremely well, and he wasn't going to do battle with a determined fox cub in the middle of the night. Rufus stayed curled up beside him until morning.

Tamlyn was right about the speedy healing of Rufus's leg. Two more nights, during which the obstinate cub discovered he could leap onto his bed with ease decided him that he must be returned to his proper place. Lyddy had continued to supply food, but he told her he would take Rufus back into the hills on Wednesday afternoon when he had a gap in lessons.

The afternoon was cool and overcast but not wet. He tried to attach the dog lead to the cub, but it was objected to in no uncertain way: Rufus shook, writhed and pulled, giving sharp little high pitched yips.

"All right," Tamlyn said, stuffing the collar and lead back in his pocket, "but you've really got to go." Maybe the lead smelt uncomfortably of hound, he thought. He picked up the little animal to tuck him inside his jacket, then walked with him for half an hour over the lower reaches of grassland and into the hills. He found an area of bumpy ground which had clumps of brambles and gorse alongside a couple of stumpy mountain ash trees. He'd got some tasty scraps of meat in his pouch, and his plan was to scatter food behind these plants, and vanish at speed while Rufus was rooting around for the treats. He stretched out on the grass after he'd distributed the food, pretending to sleep but keeping an eye half open. At first Rufus sat by him, but as he caught the food scents he started off exploring, and when he was behind a large gorse bush Tamlyn slithered away and ran back the way he'd come at a speed which brought him to the kitchen yards a great deal quicker than the journey out.

Hands on his knees, he bent over to regain his breath. Lyddy came out with kitchen rubbish, the easiest way they'd found of 'accidentally' meeting. After emptying her bowl she stood and stared, but not directly at Tamlyn.

"I thought you were taking Rufus back," she said quietly.

Tamlyn turned. Down the pathway trotted the little animal, head alert and ears pricked! A mixture of disbelief and annoyance but mostly huge amusement took hold of Tamlyn, and he shook with laughter. Lyddy laughed too.

"Never try to out-fox a fox," Tamlyn gasped. "I can't go again today, I've got classes," he added. "Have to think of something else. Any ideas?"

Chapter 5

After two more abortive efforts to return Rufus to his own terrain, including a search for an area which showed signs of foxes, Tamlyn and Lyddy decided the best thing was to ignore the little animal, stop giving him food, and hope he'd eventually get the message and take himself off.

"I think he got imprinted on you before he'd learnt to keep clear of humans," Lyddy said, "so you'd better keep away from this area." Tamlyn knew the sense of this, but he still couldn't resist wandering in the kitchen direction most evenings before or after supper. It was a busy time for Lyddy but he always half hoped she'd be around. They seemed to have similar ideas on lots of subjects, but he knew he mustn't make her life difficult by being too obvious around her. Almost always Rufus would appear and stop to be patted, but at least he'd then trot away. Lyddy thought he'd made a den under one of the tool sheds, but the 'no feeding' idea was proving hard to stick to since Rufus's presence had been noticed by other kitchen staff. Some of them, intrigued by the friendly fox cub, threw him scraps, so no wonder he could see no reason to move elsewhere. Maybe if a young vixen appeared he'd find that sufficiently enticing.

As October came, the sixth year Scholars had a new problem to think about. They were told to produce answers to a list of questions on all areas of their education and lives in the Citadel. When this had been completed they would be interviewed individually by the Masters of each subject they studied. This was all new. Usually Scholars in their final year talked informally with Masters in the subject they liked or were best at to see what they might be able to do when their schooling ended. If they'd made it through six years, it was assumed they were suitable for work somewhere.

"What on earth's this all about?" Hallam grumbled, copying the list of questions from the page stuck up in the corridor between the classrooms. "If I answered all these honestly I'd be chucked off the pinnacle."

"Don't! Don't *say* that," begged Kenley with a shudder. "That's my worst nightmare." It was known as one of the ways of executing anyone found guilty of evil enchantments or some other major crime, though none of them had seen it performed.

"Sorry," Hallam said, "but I mean to say, look at this. 'In not less than a hundred words give your opinion of the organisation of your timetable'. Huh! And here, look. 'Does the course cover the fight against evil enchantment in sufficient detail?' They should have added 'Which Master is most likely to be down on you like a cartload of boulders after reading your answers to these questions?'

Everyone laughed, but this was going to take some thinking about. There was silence for a bit as they scribbled.

"I reckon we'll just have to do what we all do in essays; write what we know the Master wants to hear," suggested Tamlyn. "That's as long as you remember what you put, of course."

"Sounds good, except we don't know who's going to read this. No signature or anything," Hallam grumbled.

The question pages took a painfully long time to complete and involved a lot of consultation among eleven of the twelve year six Scholars. Bartoly announced he'd completed his the day after the questions went up and the rest suspected he might know what it was all about. They'd really like to know, but would bite their tongues off sooner than ask him. They met together in the maths room on the day assigned for handing in their answers expecting to see Master Jessal, the mathematics teacher, but to their surprise Master Sharkley walked in.

"Ask him what it's about, Tam" Hallam whispered.

"No, you."

"You're his favourite since Bartoly."

"Not true!" But Tamlyn did know that the Master, renowned for his hard manner, did seem a fraction less acerbic with him. Oh well, he could only try.

"Master Sharkley," he said as the Master was checking that all the papers were fastened and had names on the first page as ordered.

The Master paused and looked up. "Yes?"

"Can you... I mean is it possible for you to tell us what this is for? It's a bit unusual." Tamlyn felt his heart thud and his face redden as the Master stared at him in silence for what seemed an age.

At last he spoke. "This is an order from the highest authority. The High Lord wants them."

"Whatever for?" Tamlyn was so shaken by the answer that the words were blurted out before he could stop them.

The Scholars turned as one to stare at Tamlyn, but his eyes were fixed on Master Sharkley.

"Scholar Tamlyn, perhaps you would like to accompany me to the High Lord's apartments and ask *him* his reasons for requiring this? I'm sure he'd be delighted to tell you." The Master leaned back with arms folded. Again there was the faintest of smiles on his lips

"N-no, Master. I'm sorry. It took me by surprise, is all."

"Very well." He gathered their papers and walked to the door, then paused. "Don't forget that classes start on the hour." They all stared at him until the door shut behind him, then turned and stared at each other. Even Bartoly seemed taken aback. Two thoughts filled Tamlyn's head: 'the High Lord's going to read what I've written' came first, closely followed by 'what on earth did I actually write?' It looked as though his classmates had much the same going on in their minds too.

The stunned silence was broken by a confusion of voices, and throughout the following days there was only one topic of conversation. Not that anyone came to any conclusions about anything, but talking seemed to help keep the horrible possibilities that were seething in their imaginations from driving them crazy. Someone suggested it was a way of testing the Masters, which would have been enthusiastically received if someone else hadn't immediately wondered if the Masters hadn't asked the High Lord to do it as a way to demote one or more of the Scholars.

When Tamlyn eventually managed to think quietly by himself about it all he decided that he would probably have written much the same as he had done if he'd known who might read his words. As had become his regular method, he'd tried to express generalities rather than personal opinions, '*Usually it is considered that...*' rather than '*I think that...*' for instance. It might be more difficult to keep this up in individual interviews. He'd just have to keep calm and think before he opened his mouth.

One surprising occurrence helped to take his mind in other directions for a while when he returned to his room one lunch time and saw a small package on his pillow. He opened it carefully. Experience had taught him that his classmates, knowing his interest in wildlife, sometimes donated objects like large spiders or squashed slugs in anonymous packages to his room or even into his pockets. Nothing so distasteful now: inside was a long linen strip, very similar to the one he'd ripped up for Merla and Rufus. It was neatly hemmed, and in one corner Tamlyn saw with amazement that a tiny T had been embroidered in blue thread. Lyddy, he thought. Well it must have been her who had put it in his room. Then as he unrolled the strip fully a small note fluttered onto his bed. 'Thank you Tamlyn. Merla.' She'd noticed! It made him warm with pleasure. He folded the strip carefully and stowed it in his pouch. Instinct bred of life in the Citadel made him shove the note well down in a pocket, and he would throw it in a fire at the first opportunity, but the message was stored in his mind.

The interviews with Masters turned out to be more what they'd originally expected, discussion about possibilities and blunt statements on what was definitely not. Tamlyn usually achieved good marks in all his school work except maths, so most Masters concentrated on saying that he should aim high, except that they supposed he'd be working in Master Greenwell's area. His interest in plants and herbs was well known. Garrid started by commenting on Tamlyn's last essay.

"Would I be right in thinking that this was written in rather a hurry, Scholar Tamlyn?" he said, looking at him over the top of his spectacles.

"Sorry, Master, yes," Tamlyn answered honestly.

"Well, it was a lovely summer. Lots of more interesting things to do, I don't doubt."

Tamlyn gaped. This was Master Garrid who accepted no excuses. "Yes, Master. I realise I should have…"

Master Garrid raised a hand to stop him. "Student Tamlyn, your work for me over the years has shown me that you have a very good brain. It's also shown me, I've come to realise, that you rarely let me see much about what goes on in it. That, I acknowledge, is an ability of great use in a society such as ours. I have presented you, along with all the boys I teach, with the material which I am given to disseminate. It will, in the near future, be up to you how you use it. I imagine... I believe and sincerely hope... that you could do well. If circumstances permit. Perhaps I say too much. You will remember that these interviews are confidential, will you not. Good day to you, Scholar Tamlyn."

"Thank you, Master Garrid," Tamlyn said. 'I think,' he added to himself. He hadn't time to begin to decide what most of this meant before he was entering Master Sharkley's study.

"Ah, Scholar Tamlyn. Come in, sit down. Now what are you thinking of doing when you finish this year?"

"I've always hoped, Master, that I could work with Master Greenwell. There's so much more to find out, about the interaction of people and plants, especially..."

"Yes, yes," Master Sharkley interrupted. "I do know about your liking for herbs, not to mention your taste for taking extremely long walks in pursuit of them."

"I hope that isn't looked on as in any way a fault," Tamlyn replied, rather too sharply. 'Keep cool, you idiot,' he told himself. 'Remember; think before you speak.'

"Apart from a somewhat large expenditure on footwear, I don't think it's a problem," the teacher informed him, "but if you can disentangle your thoughts from herbs for a moment, have you thought of anything else if for some reason that was not, um, possible? I have first-hand knowledge that you are an excellent combatant, you know."

"I don't... I should say that fighting is... I don't like it. At all."

"Really? You seemed very completely absorbed in it when you fought Lord Mansor's son."

"I... was provoked and lost my temper, Master. I prefer to be in control of it."

Master Sharkley regarded him thoughtfully. "Yes. I see. A praiseworthy attitude in normal circumstances, but what if circumstances were not normal?"

"I think I should need to know in what way they were abnormal before I could answer that, Master," Tamlyn said carefully.

There was a stillness and silence which dragged on rather too long, then Master Sharkley seemed to shake himself. "Scholar Tamlyn, I have a high opinion of your abilities which I know is shared by other staff members. I'm sure there is a good place for you and I hope we can help you find it. Off you go now."

"Thank you, Master." Tamlyn had reached the door when Sharkley spoke again and he turned.

"Scholar Tamlyn I have very acute hearing. In our first combat lesson this term I happened to hear the words which provoked you, so may I give you this advice? For a young man you are unusually adept at keeping your thoughts to yourself both in conversation and in your written work. Don't forget though that some people may read and possibly use against you what they glean from any unguarded actions and reactions. That could be, shall we say, unpleasant. Take care."

Tamlyn stared until Master Sharkley's, "Shut the door after you," sent him through it. That was two of them who seemed to be dropping hints about possible problems ahead, though for the life of him he didn't know why or what about. He'd simply have to take care what he did and said he supposed, but then he always did, or tried to. At least his last interview with Master Greenwell should be straightforward. He was as near to being a friend as was possible with a Master.

"Come in, Tamlyn. We'll sit by the fire I think, shall we?"

Tamlyn sat opposite his favourite teacher and smiled at him. "I expect you'll know what I'm going to ask you about work after school, Master Greenwell," he said.

The Master smiled back, but Tamlyn suddenly became aware that the man looked older. Much older. His face had more lines and there were dark shadows beneath his eyes. The hands in his lap were clenched together. Was this something to do with the veiled hints that Master Garrid and Master Sharkley had dropped?

"Are you unwell, Master Greenwell?" Maybe he was ill, dying even. At this thought Tamlyn felt a cold shudder as if ice had been dropped down his back.

"I'm – what is the phrase? – as well as can be expected. If things continue smoothly I shall be more than delighted to have you working with me next year." It felt as though he was going to say more and Tamlyn waited, but Master Greenwell gazed silently into the fire.

"That's really great," Tamlyn said at last. "It's what I've wanted for a long time."

The teacher looked up at him then, and it almost seemed as though there were tears in his eyes. "Sorry, I seem to have a cold coming," he said, and pulling out a handkerchief he blew into it vigorously. Again there was silence, but at last Master Greenwell sighed deeply and leant forward, his hands now loosely clasped as he rested his elbows on his knees.. "Tamlyn, I've something I must say and I know you'll obey me when I tell you that you must never repeat this to anyone. Life is, ah, a little difficult here at the moment. Nothing that need affect you students I sincerely hope, but it does mean that there is a possibility that I may not be able to work with you as I too have hoped for a long time. No, let me finish," he said as Tamlyn made to speak. "You know that I have managed to collect a number of books on the subject that interests us both. If the circumstances arise – and you will certainly know if they do – I want you to have them."

Tamlyn stared in horror. "Master Greenwell, that sounds as if…" He couldn't say the words 'you're going to die'.

His teacher stood up. "It sounds like nothing," he said. "It may be nothing. I just wanted to be sure… But I've said enough. Probably too much, but it can't be unsaid. I'm really looking forward to working with you for many years, just hold onto that." He opened the door for Tamlyn, but as he got there Master Greenwell put his hand on Tamlyn's shoulder and stopped him.

"If you can find a way to do it without drawing attention to yourself, there's one thing I think you might find of use and interest, if not now, then in the future. Read all there is in the library about the early years of the Citadel and its rules and laws. Not before the High Lord – there's little enough on that for whatever reason – but what has been written as our history. I know you have a good analytical mind, so use it as you read. Do you understand?"

Tamlyn really didn't, but he nodded. As he went on past Master Greenwell, he felt his teacher press something into his hand. "Spare keys for my room, just in case," he said, and shut the door.

Now Tamlyn's mind really was in turmoil. He had an hour or more before supper, for normal lessons for the sixth year Scholars had been cancelled while the interviews were held. He went into his room but could not settle. He needed to walk – he always thought more clearly when in the open air – so he slipped down the side stairs and out into the late afternoon. The sun must already be low though it wasn't visible behind the heavy clouds. He was just coming to the corner of the kitchen buildings when he heard sounds that made his blood freeze. A dog, a large one by the sound of it, was barking frantically, but over that were the shrill screaming yips of...

"Rufus!" he yelled, and pelted round the corner.

And stood transfixed by horror.

Chapter 6

Lord Zaroth stood on the path ahead, gripping Rufus by his bushy tail in his gloved left fist and holding him high in the air. He was tormenting his hound by lowering the cub almost within reach of the dog's jaws then jerking it up again and grinning as the frantic dog leapt and barked and Rufus shrieked in terror.

"Stop!" yelled Tamlyn, rushing forward. Lord Zaroth paused and turned slowly towards him, eyeing Tamlyn coldly.

"Stop?" he repeated, as though he couldn't believe what he'd heard.

"That animal. It hasn't hurt you. Let it go."

"So. One of our Scholars is a lover of vermin," sneered Lord Zaroth.

"Please," begged Tamlyn. They stood staring at each other, not moving until Tamlyn saw a change come over Zaroth's face and his right hand started to move. Suddenly he knew what was going to happen.

"Noooooooo," he screamed, but before the word had finished the man had unsheathed a vicious hunting knife and slashed at Rufus. The cub's head dropped to the ground and blood dripped from the body still held in the air.

"You. Are. Evil." Tamlyn spat the words, barely able to form them through the fury that possessed him. Lord Zaroth flung the body at Tamlyn, then kicked the head along the ground after it.

"Come," he ordered the dog, and strode away.

Tamlyn moved to the body and dropped to his knees. He was at the frozen centre of a swirling red storm of pain and rage. Only his hands seemed to work of their own volition, moving the cub's body and head together and stroking the bloody fur continuously as though somehow they would heal him. Tears streamed down his face unheeded. He had no idea of time passing; he would stay here forever.

"Tam." Lyddy's voice, and her hand on his shoulder. He still could not move. He was aware of her crouching beside him, spreading a cloth on the ground, and gently moving Rufus onto it. Robbed of their occupation his blood-soaked hands went up to cover his wet face. "Come with me," Lyddy said, folding the cub in the cloth and standing. Tamlyn obeyed; what else was there to do? He followed her without question, his brain functioning only enough to make his feet take one step after another.

They walked for some time, and gradually a small sign of awareness beyond his anguish began to surface. He realised they were going away from the Citadel and stopped.

"Where we going?" he mumbled.

"I'm taking you home. You can't go into the Citadel in that state."

"Home?" Where was home?

"To Merla's. Where I live."

A few more remnants of reality surfaced. "You can't. Not good for you."

"Not good for you in the Citadel looking like a blood-soaked phantom. We'll clean you up. Merla will help."

They walked on until reaching the village. It was the largest collection of living places outside the Citadel and the nearest to it, probably nearly two miles to the south east and near the river. Many of its houses were built round a village green where Lyddy took him up the short flagged pathway that led to one of them and pushed open the door.

"In you go," she said gently, then "Merla," she called in a louder voice.

"You're early, Lyddy." Merla was wiping her hands on her apron as she came through from the back of the house. For a moment she stood stock still, staring, then rushed forward to grab Tamlyn who had begun to sway and guided him to a wooden settle near the fire. "What's happened? Is he wounded?"

"I think it's shock," said Lyddy, who had placed the bloodstained bundle on the stone floor near the door. "It's not his blood." She told Merla what she could. Hearing the animal noises and then Tamlyn's yell she'd run out from the kitchen, seen Lord Zaroth storming away and realised Tamlyn needed help. She'd fetched a cloth and told the kitchen staff she was going to help someone who'd been hurt. "They're all right. Supper was almost ready and most of them know when not to ask questions."

Together they eased Tamlyn's shirt off over his head and washed the blood from his face and hands.

"I'll get him something to help," said Merla. "Wash his shirt, Lyddy. Should be able to get it dry enough for him to wear." She poked up the fire, put some more logs on it, and tucked a soft quilt round Tamlyn's shoulders. Then she walked across the room to a tall cupboard where she searched through the jars and phials and mixed liquids in a small beaker from three of them, bringing this back to Tamlyn.

"Drink this," she ordered, gently but firmly. At first Tamlyn didn't move. "Tamlyn, you mustn't hide. You may lose yourself for ever. This won't take the pain away, but it will help you cope with it."

From within the featureless grey confusion in which he'd rolled his thoughts to stop them hurting so much Tamlyn heard her. He didn't want to do it, but he opened his eyes and looked at Merla.

"Thank you," he said thickly, taking the liquid from her. He stared at it as though trying to work out what it was for, but eventually drank it. It tasted sharp and soothing at the same time and a tiny part of his mind said 'chamomile'.

Merla fetched a stool and sat in front of him. "Tell me," she said.

"Tell what?"

"Whatever needs to be said."

Slowly, in jumbled words, he told her. It was so hard to speak about those few terrible minutes. As he reached the moment of Rufus's slaughter he had to clench his hands to stop them shaking, but this was the end. Only it wasn't. Really he'd known there was something even worse and there it was. He flung back his head, eyes closed.

"And it was my fault," he howled.

Lyddy turned from where she was draping the shirt over a bar above the fire. "What..." she started, but Merla held up her hand to stop her.

"Will you explain that to me?" she asked in her quiet voice.

Tamlyn looked frantically round him, opened his mouth soundlessly, banged his clenched fists together and at last managed to find the words he had to say.

"I'm not stupid. I mean I know animals die, kill each other... eat each other. It's what they do. It's nature. Rufus would have killed; might have been killed himself by another animal, and that wouldn't have been so awful because that's how they're made. But this... oh, how can I explain? His death was horrible because that... that wicked man did it for *fun*. He laughed and enjoyed tormenting a living creature. Rufus would have died sometime, but not in that way. And it was all my fault. He was there because I interfered with the way he should have been. He should have run from a man, but I made him think people were his friends. I knew he should go back quickly to the wild, but when he wouldn't I sort of enjoyed it. I didn't think properly." Tamlyn's last words ended as a wail, and he buried his head in his hands.

"Why did you help me that day, Tamlyn?"

Startled by this change of subject, his head jerked up again. "You were hurt," he said at last.

"Why did you pick up Rufus, that same day?"

"Because *he* was hurt. Oh, but that was different," he exclaimed.

"Was it? Two living creatures, two living, breathing members of the natural world, needed help and you gave it. Not thinking of consequences, but because you saw that need and did what you could. Look at me now, Tamlyn."

For the second time he looked into her eyes, losing himself in those pools of wonderful deep amethyst until she leant forward smiling, and laid her palm gently on his cheek. "Never regret loving or giving, Tamlyn, nor stop doing what your heart tells you for fear of unknown consequences. If we tried to work out all the possible outcomes of something before we did it we'd never do anything at all. What do you imagine would have happened to Rufus if you had left him there that day?"

"I... I suppose he would have died."

"Yes. That's likely. Of hunger and thirst. Or of the infection in his wound. Or been pecked to death by the crows. Or he might just have survived and got away. And tonight he might not have been where he was, or Lord Zaroth might have exercised his dog somewhere else. I rather suspect that his dog was sniffing at this and that, the way dogs do, and lingered well behind its master, for if he'd been to heel Rufus would surely have run. I've yet to hear of a fox that would stay near a dog. Those are just a few of the might-have-beens. What actually happened was that you helped and healed a fellow creature, and for a fortnight or so he had a wonderful life. He experienced love and kindness. Tonight he came across Lord Zaroth. I don't think the man came that way looking for an animal to torment and kill. It was chance that he found Rufus, and what he did was disgusting and inhuman, but it was not *your* fault. Do you understand?"

Tamlyn's lips almost managed a smile and the tears that still wanted to fall were no longer those of anguish for his own imagined faults but more gentle sadness for the death of his small friend.

"Thank you," he said. He did understand, and it took away much of the terrible pain of guilt that he'd felt might kill him.

"Good. Now your shirt should soon be dry. You'll have missed your supper, but I've broth on the stove and there's some of Lyddy's morning-baked bread. Lyddy will go back with you when you've had that."

Reality was rapidly retaking its place in Tamlyn's head. "I think it must be past the curfew and the guards will be patrolling. I'd better go alone and risk telling them I walked further than I realised or something."

"There are more ways into the Citadel than the guards know of," Merla said with a smile, and went into the back room. Tamlyn had thought he might not be able to eat, but when the food arrived his stomach decided otherwise. He finished everything, and realised that the food was also helping in the process of dragging him back from the unbearable place into which he'd fallen so disastrously when he saw Rufus killed.

"Merla, Lyddy, you've been so good to me. I don't know how to thank you, me being from the Citadel and you... not." He could think of no other way to acknowledge the problems this might mean for them.

"Nonsense. It's not where you live but who you are. Now, into this shirt. Did you not have a jacket, lad?"

"I only went out for a breath of air," Tamlyn answered. The ridiculousness of this made him snort. "Some breath!"

"Walk swiftly then, there's a chill in the air now."

As they hurried along Tamlyn said, "Merla's wonderful isn't she?"

"Oh yes. She seems to see inside people and know what they need."

"How do you know another way into the Citadel?"

"Merla showed me."

"Well how does Merla know?" Tamlyn persisted.

Lyddy was silent for a dozen steps, but at last she said, "Merla obviously trusts you or she wouldn't have asked me to come with you and show you." Another long pause. "And of course lots of our people know, the older ones anyway."

"And?" he pressed her.

"Merla lived in the building you call the Citadel when she was young. Before the High Lord and all your… lot arrived."

Tamlyn wanted more – it was such an amazing statement – but Lyddy pressed a finger to her lips and pulled him off the pathway.

"Sssh. We're getting close now, and sometimes the guards come wandering outside. The night watch gets pretty boring, I suppose. Follow me as quietly as possible," she whispered. They skirted widely round the chicken runs and pig sties that lay to the north of the kitchens, then crept back close to the Citadel walls. At a point just before the door that Tamlyn often used the ancient rock bulged out over what looked like a small archway that had never been cut right through.

Lyddy stretched out to take Tamlyn's hand and guided his fingers to a rough hollow in the rock. "You press there and lean in," she said, so quietly he had to move really close to her to hear. She did as she'd described, and as she leant part of the rock swung silently inwards. The next moment she had vanished and the rock had closed. Tamlyn followed her instructions. At first nothing happened, but he wriggled his finger so that it was fully in the hollow, leant, and almost fell into a narrow space. There was a scraping noise and Lyddy lit a small candle from a shelf-like projection in the rock.

"That's amaz…"

"Quietly. Sound carries in these old spaces. I won't come all the way with you but listen carefully. Go forward about ten steps and the corridor splits. Left goes to the kitchen: the door looks like a cupboard on the kitchen side. It's where Merla and Fliss went that day. You must go right till you get to what looks like a chimney going up. It's got hand and foot holds and it's not very difficult to climb. You'll come out near the stairs you often use, but the top has a flat slab of stone covering it. There's just enough space to wiggle out on your stomach.. Merla can't get through there now," Lyddy said with a grin. "Good thing she was going out here that day. Oh yes, if you ever need to go out this way there's a latch here, on the inside of the door see? Always make sure it's shut when you use it."

Tamlyn took Lyddy's hand and kissed it. "You saved me tonight. I'm sorry. I must have seemed so silly. Seeing that… that murder… it was like a hammer smashing my head."

"Not silly. It showed you aren't hard and cruel like… like so many. I've got a place in the garden where I buried my pets when they died. Shall I put Rufus there?"

"Thank you, yes, if Merla doesn't mind."

"She won't. Take the candle and off you go. Be careful. Leave the candle at the top of the climb, under that slab. I'll put another here in case."

Lyddy opened the door and vanished as it closed silently. Tamlyn made his way along the passages and up the chimney without problems apart from a bruised knee as he climbed and a scraped elbow as he wriggled out at the top. Back in his room he lay in his bed and tried to think, but exhaustion overcame him. He slept.

Chapter 7

Tamlyn woke heavy-headed and, for a moment, unable to think clearly. A jumble of incomplete pictures swirled in his head: Master Greenwell's face… climbing somewhere… walking in the dark then…

Rufus. He sat bolt upright, the fragmentary memories crashing together as it all came back. He felt as though he'd been punched in the stomach, and a black, despairing tide threatened to rise in him. Then Merla's words echoed in his mind – 'it is not *your* fault' – and he felt again the comfort he had found in the cool purple depths of her eyes.

"Hey, Tam, don't you want breakfast?" Hallam stuck his head round the door. "Not even up? What's the matter? You missed supper, too."

"Sorry. I didn't feel too good and went to bed. Now I've overslept. I'm all right though. Hang on; I'll be with you in a moment." Tamlyn leapt out of bed, poured water from the jug and splashed his face vigorously then started to dress at speed. Just in time he noticed that his shirt from last night had dirty smudges and cobwebs all over it. Must have come from under the slab; it was unlikely that space got swept. Edging it under the bed with his toe he grabbed a clean one; he certainly didn't want questions on that particular subject. As he brushed his tousled hair, he stowed the memories of yesterday, particularly the night, into a 'think about later' section of his mind.

"How did you get on with your interviews yesterday?" he asked his friend as they clattered down the twisting stairs and passages to the refectory.

"All right, I suppose. Don't really know what I want to do, but Sharkley seems to reckon I could make the Citadel Guard. Not the Elites, I wouldn't touch that lot. I thought Greenwell looked a bit weird. I reckon because you help me get decent marks in my essays for him he was suddenly struck by the horrible possibility that I might be foisted on him and I'd trample all over his pet plants. Honestly, I'd sooner sweep floors all day. Guess he'll welcome you with open arms, won't he?"

"Well that's what I'd like to do, and he seems happy enough with the idea. It's still a long way off though, isn't it? Things might change, I suppose."

"Like how?"

"Oh, I don't know. We might all be enchanted into thinking we're meant to be pig keepers or something." Or I might not even be here, thought Tamlyn. He'd screamed at Lord Zaroth that he was evil. The memory sent a shudder through him. Not that he didn't still think that was true, but it just wasn't possible he'd get away with it. Some sort of punishment must surely be in the offing. He joined in the breakfast time conversations half-heartedly.

Through the day, Tamlyn had the nagging certainty that something bad was going to happen, and he couldn't concentrate properly on lessons or even food.

"What's up, Tam?" Hallam asked at last as they were leaving the supper table. "You've got a face like Master Garrid finding pig shit in his desk."

Tamlyn wished he could tell his friend about Rufus and the rest of yesterday, but he couldn't risk it. Hallam was kind and good humoured, but he chattered carelessly about anything and everything. It was amazing he'd not got into trouble at some point, but most people just thought he was a bit of a clown.

"Sorry. Still feel a bit under the weather. I'll have some ginger and peppermint and another early night I think."

"Yeah, right. You know what though, I reckon it's love, that pretty blonde Donkey in the kitchen."

"*What?*" Tamlyn yelled, causing several Scholars to bump into them by standing stock still in the middle of the corridor. Moving on he grabbed Hallam's arm and pulled him to the side. "What on earth made you say that?" He could feel his face reddening.

"Just joking." Hallam looked taken aback by Tamlyn's reaction. "You're not insulted are you? Saying you might fancy a Donkey."

"Course not. No. She is pretty, isn't she?" Tamlyn tried to smooth it over.

"And she did help you with feeding Rufus. You got more out of her for a fox than I can ever get for myself. Not so much as an extra carrot at meal times, even when I'm fainting with hunger. By the way, I haven't seen Rufus for days. I thought he was quite a fixture. You seen him?"

Tamlyn was ready for this. He and Lyddy had decided to say that the little animal had most likely taken off on its own for more fox-friendly territory. "No," he said as lightly as he could, though his heart had started to thud. "I reckon he's wandered away. It's what I tried to persuade him to do if you remember, much the best thing for him."

"Mmm. Probably gone to a place that slims foxes, to lose all the weight he put on with people feeding him so much."

"Yeah, he was getting quite overweight wasn't he?" Change the subject, change the subject, Tamlyn was screaming inside his head. "How do you fancy a walk with me tomorrow if I swear not to go far? Something I spotted a few weeks back you'd be interested in, I reckon."

"So long as you promise to carry me when my feet are worn away up to my ankles."

"Ha ha! You've put on a bit of weight yourself lately. Exercise'll do you good. See you."

Tamlyn took himself off to his room determined to make some sense of the thoughts he'd got swimming around so worryingly. He leant with his forearms on the windowsill and stared out at the countryside. It was less hilly in this direction than the view he loved so much to the east of the Citadel, where on clear days he could see the dark line of the mountains in the distance. Here there were gentle hills which he knew stretched westwards into much flatter areas and eventually, of course, to the City. They'd learnt so much about that place, the home of the evil King, the enchanter who could twist your brain as easily as you could twist a thread, and make you see, do and say things you never would in your right mind. While he longed to walk east to the mountains which seemed to call him, he had no wish at all to go to the City. Why would you go there and risk such danger without needing to? Tonight, though, he gazed out at beauty. The sun was just sinking out of sight and the whole western sky was flooded with colour. A brilliant gold rim still edged the horizon, but above it yellow and orange became rose and crimson threaded with palest green and grey. All the colours seemed translucent, as though you could dive through them and find a wonderful, magical place beyond. Gradually the colours faded and darkened to lavender and deep purple, which reminded him of Merla's eyes. The sky slowly put on the shades of night.

Tamlyn felt more relaxed. He moved at last and lit a candle, then sat propped up against a pillow on his bed with a book on his lap. He could pretend to be reading if someone came to see if he was all right. He had a method for dealing with unmanageable thoughts and set about using that now. First of all he had to separate the unruly mass into separate parts, try to make sense of each part and, if possible, see if there was any solution. He ran through yesterday in his head.

The unusual words and behaviour of two of the three Masters who'd interviewed him had left him puzzled and uneasy. Master Sharkley and Master Garrid had both praised his work, and commented on his habit of keeping his thoughts to himself with what seemed to be approval. That was fine, but then both, quite outside usual teacherish behaviour, had cautioned him about his behaviour in a very personal way. It made him feel they were hinting at problems ahead. He wasn't sure he'd heard Master Garrid correctly, but the old man, so rigid in his teaching of the evils of enchantment, had seemed to suggest that belief in the subject might be a question of choice. Could that really be so? It seemed so unlikely.

It was Master Greenwell who'd upset him most though. It really sounded as though he knew something unpleasant was brewing which might mean he would not be around to continue their work together. Considering the subject he taught, his suggestion that Tamlyn should study the history of the Citadel in the time of the High Lord was most unusual, and made even stranger by his gift of the keys, and the wish for him to have his books.

He thought about all this for a while, and came to the conclusion that there was little he could do but wait and see. He could, perhaps, ask Master Greenwell to be clearer in his meaning, but the man had been visibly upset yesterday and he didn't want to make that worse. Right, then, no action really possible there, except to keep eyes and ears open and watch his behaviour. All of which, with a few exceptions, he considered was his usual habit. So clear that problem off the table. There really was no use worrying about something he didn't understand and was unlikely to be able to change if he did.

Next was Rufus. It would be hard, but he knew he couldn't alter what had happened so he must concentrate on memories before his last moments and horrifying death. Grieving was inevitable, but Tamlyn pulled into his mind a picture of the little animal as he'd been in life. He saw the thick brush and the deep red-brown of his fur. He saw the dark eyes, knowing yet guileless, and the curve of his mouth when it was closed, ending on each side with an upward flick that made him look as though he was smiling. He must try to – no, he *would* – remember all that. He still felt sadness that he had not somehow been able to make the little creature move away, but Merla had helped him drop an unbearable burden of guilt about that. That was another thing dealt with, and the action he'd decided on should grow easier with the days. It was, after all, only twenty-four hours since all that had happened.

Lord Zaroth's reaction to being called evil by a Scholar was something he had absolutely no way of foreseeing or fending off. It would be a miracle if there wasn't some harsh retribution, but no use spoiling his life by continually wondering what it would be and when it would come. Much harder to stick to this resolve, but he'd do his best.

Tamlyn felt himself becoming less muddled and depressed. Merla and Lyddy were *not* a problem, thank goodness. By a series of, well, literally accidents, or at least unusual happenings, they had come into his life and he was glad of it. His only regret was that for his and their sakes it was best that it should not be open, but that was the way life was in the Citadel. Hallam had really shocked him when he'd talked about the pretty little blonde Donkey in the kitchen. Part of his reaction had been to 'Donkey', which he'd come to think was distasteful when used for any person, but particularly so for Lyddy. He really liked her, and would be distraught if she were to meet any trouble because of him.

Now one more minor problem which he'd brought on himself. What was he going to show Hallam on their walk tomorrow? He'd said it in a hurried attempt to get away from talking about Rufus, and without any real thought. He considered possibilities for a few minutes then smiled. Yes that would do. Tamlyn blew out the candle and, with his mind much easier, he fell asleep.

The next day was bright and clear, though autumn was now being firmly nudged aside by winter and it felt cold. Hallam met him with enough extra clothes on to see him through a blizzard.

Tamlyn laughed. "You don't need that lot on. You'll soon warm up as we walk and all those layers'll make you die of heat stroke," he said.

But Hallam was not to be dissuaded. "You promised a short walk, remember, and I don't go at your rate anyway," he insisted.

They set off facing into the bright sunshine, leaving by the northern door and going east round the kitchens and yards. Tamlyn cast a quick glance at the secret doorway and felt a tingle of pleasure at knowing it was there. He also wondered if he'd see Lyddy, but remembered she started work a bit later as she worked on through supper. Leading Hallam past the place where he'd first found Rufus and on up the hill he had to concentrate as it wasn't his usual route and he'd only walked this way coming down. As he'd expected Hallam was soon sweating, so they stopped to rest and Tamlyn produced two slightly wrinkled apples from his pouch.

"Whew!" Hallam lay back on the turf and fanned himself with his hat.

"Told you," said Tamlyn. "Take a layer off and we'll leave things behind that stone. Pick them up on the way back."

Hallam conceded defeat and agreed. "Is it much further? Must have come miles already."

"About half a mile I'd guess. Not so far now if I haven't missed the path."

"You'd better not have done," growled Hallam. "Come on. Let's see this thing I'll be so interested in."

They climbed a bit further till Tamlyn spotted the chimney. "Quietly now," he muttered as they came over a small rise and looked down on Vitsell's house on the other side of the shallow dip. "Better be sure nobody's at home."

"Is that real? I mean does something live there? Weird." Hallam was about to jump down and go across for a closer look, but Tamlyn held him back.

"Yes it's real, and someone does live there. I don't want to disturb him if he's at home."

"Oh come on, Tam, it can't be anybody big to live in there."

"You'd be surprised."

Then they were both surprised. Hallam was moving to get a closer look with Tamlyn following when a voice roared out a string of incomprehensible words. Vitsell appeared on top of the bank near his chimney. He looked even thinner and taller than Tamlyn remembered and it was clear he wasn't saying 'How nice to see you'. He stopped shouting and jumped down by his front door.

"What's… that?" Hallam stammered, backing away.

Tamlyn suddenly realised exactly how crazy he'd been to bring Hallam here. He must do something, and do it quickly, so he walked across to Vitsell and bowed to him.

"I am so sorry to have disturbed you Vitsell," he said. "My friend and I are out walking across the hills and we've stupidly got ourselves a bit lost." He spoke loudly and slowly so that Vitsell would understand him, and hoping too that Hallam would hear him and not say anything to disprove him. "We came upon your house and I wondered if you might be able to set us on the right path."

Vitsell looked slightly less fierce, and bent forward to examine Tamlyn. A look of recognition appeared on his face. "You help my Lady," he announced.

Tamlyn nodded.

"You lost?" The man sounded disbelieving, as well he might, since the top of the Citadel must be clearly visible from any slightly higher ground nearby.

Tamlyn looked up into Vitsell's face, held his two hands out in a pleading gesture and whispered, "Please help me, Vitsell." Don't let Hallam hear that, he thought desperately.

The long, thin man studied Tamlyn some more, then a small smile appeared on his wrinkled old face. Unbelievably, he gave a wink.

"Stupid little boys," he growled loudly. "I show you. Come with me."

Hallam had been standing with his mouth half open, but he understood and followed with Tamlyn as Vitsell led them on a winding route that might well have got them lost, in fact, but eventually brought them out where the Citadel was again clear.

"There. Go back to where youse belong. Don't disturb me agen or I let you to stay lost." The long, thin man turned and strode off down another path.

"'Interested' was maybe not quite the right word," Hallam said dryly. "Did you say he lives in that house? Bit of a tight squeeze, I'd think."

"I... sort of reckon it might be bigger inside. Floor lowered and ceiling lifted, you know."

"Well I'm not about to investigate. Let's get back."

Remembering Hallam's clothes, Tamlyn led them back towards the rock, both of them unusually silent. He wondered what was going on in Hallam's mind, but what to tell his friend was of more concern to him. From childhood onwards they'd all been taught that their happiness depended on them conforming to the right forms of behaviour and thought. These, of course, came directly from the High Lord, and were disseminated by the other Lords and the Masters in the school. Anyone who disobeyed or argued with this ruling was wrong. They might be the subject of evil enchantment but still they must be punished. This inevitably made everyone extremely cautious in how they spoke and acted in company; you never knew who might report you to authority.

Tamlyn had believed all this without thought for many years; it was the way things were. But lately his innately logical mind had begun to ask questions. Why was it so wrong to look at alternatives? How could you discover anything new if what was already known was the only acceptable knowledge?

They came to the rock and picked up Hallam's things. Tamlyn made to go on, but his friend stopped him.

"I think we've got to talk," he said quietly. "Shall we sit here for a bit?"

"Yeah," Tamlyn nodded. Better to see how his friend was thinking out here with no one else around. He waited quietly for Hallam to start.

"That man, you've met him before haven't you? You knew his name."

"Yes. Once."

"He's a Donkey isn't he?"

"He's one of the people of the land."

"Same thing."

Tamlyn wasn't going to argue that point at this moment. He waited quietly.

"All that gibberish he shouted, I thought he was casting a spell on us."

"He was just cross we were there near his house. He's old and he likes to talk the language that they spoke here once."

"How do you know this, Tam? He said something about you helping a lady didn't he?"

The moment had come when he'd got to decide. Should he tell the truth, which showed he'd become friendly with Donkeys, something very high on the forbidden list, or try and wriggle out with lies? He stared unseeing across grass for some moments then turned to his friend.

"A few weeks ago I walked by myself, up the on hills there. I was looking for harewort, perhaps you remember. It was just after I fought Bartoly. I took some food with me, and after I'd had that I started running back down. It's a great feeling, running downhill. A bit like flying, as long as you don't fall. I jumped over some stones and nearly landed on a woman the other side. She'd hurt her ankle, so I bound it up. I never gave it a thought that I shouldn't get involved with her; she needed help. I was going to try and get someone from their village, but she obviously knew I shouldn't. She said someone lived nearby, so I helped her walk there, to Vitsell's house. It was her that told me about him. I left her with him." This was exactly true as far as it went, but Tamlyn had not named Merla or that he'd met her before. He didn't think it was right or even necessary to complicate things with that information. Still, he'd told the truth.

Now what? Hallam was looking at him with a strange expression on his face which he couldn't read. It didn't look like anger or outrage, more like intense concentration.

"Hal you've been my best friend as long as I can remember," Tamlyn went on as his friend didn't seem inclined to speak. "I've told you the truth straight, as it happened, because I didn't want to lie to you. I made a big mistake in taking you up there and I'm really sorry. I didn't think it through properly when I asked you. I'm not going to ask you to do or not do anything about my behaviour now – you must decide that – but if you could manage not to let on about Vitsell's house, that would be really good. Whatever else he is, he's an old man who's lived there for more years than the Citadel people have been here, and if his home became known about, the least that would happen would be crowds of people going up to see it and upsetting him. He might be turned out, even killed if it was decided he was an enchanter or something."

He'd run out of words and stared at Hallam mutely. Suddenly his friend leaned over and grabbed his hand.

"Tam, I've always thought you were something special, but now I know it. The only thing I'm mad with you about is that you'd even think I'd turn you in to those, those pompous, overdressed idiots who rule us. There, I've incriminated myself now too. I'm so glad you've told me. It's about the first time I've really known what was going on in your head. Well we don't talk, do we? Nobody does. We all keep most of ourselves shut up in a tight little box for safety, in case something might not be correct." He almost spat the last word.

"Hallam, I don't know what to say," Tamlyn managed at last.

"Well I'll say one more thing then, while you get your voice back. I know I come over as a bit of a stupid joker who says the first thing that comes to mind, but there's another me, a Hallam who can watch his tongue like an eagle. You needn't worry about that. Here." He pulled Tamlyn to him and gave him a hug. "Now, let's run down hill and get some lunch. This emotion business makes me hungry."

Chapter 8

Hallam's revelation of his feelings about the rules and retributions in the Citadel had been surprising to say the least, but they made Tamlyn's spirits rise. To know that he was not the only one questioning authority, even if only in his head or by covert actions, made him feel that the future might hold something different. It also made him wonder how many others were thinking in the same way, though he'd no intention of trying to find out. He and Hallam did not talk a lot about things after that day, but he felt closer to his friend than ever before.

The year drew on towards the shortest day and they woke one morning to find the Citadel covered in deep snow. The younger Scholars and many of the even younger school children were out in it as soon as they'd finished breakfast, and as the Masters seemed content to postpone classes, it wasn't long before the fifth and sixth years joined in, too.

"Let's make a slide down that slope there," Kenley suggested, and a group of them smoothed and tamped down the snow for around a hundred yards, turning it into an ice path with a steep gradient down which they attempted to descend on their feet but usually ended on their behinds. Some even tackled it headfirst and on their stomachs. A good many bumps and bruises resulted but who was grumbling?

The kitchen staff good humouredly brought out hot drinks and buttery scones. Tamlyn spotted Lyddy and wondered how she'd got there through the snow until he heard her say that someone in the village who was rarely wrong about weather had said a snowstorm was coming, so she'd stayed in the Citadel overnight. He'd wanted to talk to her about his meeting with Vitsell since he had a strong suspicion the old man would have passed on his version of the occasion, but no possibility of privacy occurred.

Lunchtime took everybody indoors with double sized appetites, and soon every fireplace had clothes and footwear steaming around it. It had been such unexpected enjoyment that many were enthusiastically ready to rush outside again, but the snow was going as quickly as it had come, and the crisp whiteness of the morning was rapidly turning into slush. The magic had disappeared into drips and icy puddles, with sudden falls of semi-frozen wetness sliding from Citadel slopes and roofs onto anyone venturing unwarily outside.

The Masters allowed their relaxation of lessons to extend to the whole day, so the sixth-years stoked up the fire in their year room and lounged comfortably round it. Even Bartoly hadn't vanished into the Lords' apartments. Tamlyn, who found it very easy now to think the worst of him, wondered if he was snooping for his father, but the conversation remained idly and totally normal about food, a new fashion for lacing high-legged boots and the possibility of more snow. Suddenly the door opened and Master Sharkley came in.

"Ah, how pleasant to see our senior Scholars so keen to use their time profitably," he said dryly, and they all jerked into less relaxed attitudes. Hallam, who'd been lying on his back and toasting his toes, narrowly avoided dropping his feet into the fire.

"I see you are all here so I will read this notice out and then nobody will be able to plead ignorance. It will be put up in the corridor for the benefit of those of you who need a double application to retain the meaning of the written word. In fact, this is very much about the written word." He unfolded a paper and started to read. "Scholars who are now in their sixth and last year of education have been granted the privilege of studying in the Citadel library at times to be announced. They will be supervised by a Master at all times. The first of these times is ten o'clock on Thursday morning, and you will be waiting by the library entrance at five to ten with writing materials. The usual timetable will be reorganised to fit in with these visits." Master Sharkley refolded the paper and looked at the Scholars, who all appeared to have been stricken dumb. At last Downham found his voice.

"Shall we be studying the subject taught by the Master who is with us each time, sir?"

"I imagine that will vary. Some subjects are less well covered in the library, so be prepared for anything. Master Greenwell will supervise and lead your work for this first visit." Master Sharkley turned on his heel and left.

"Well that's a bit of a surprise," Hallam said. "I've not heard about this happening in previous years."

"Maybe it's because of that question paper we did. Must have all written that we wanted extra work. By the way, we've never heard any more about it, have we?

"Probably the High Lord's held up by the difficulty of deciphering your writing, Briggs," Hallam suggested and they all laughed, including Briggs, who was much better natured than his huge frame and rather surly looking face suggested. "Come on, better stir ourselves and check we've got the necessary for tomorrow."

Reluctantly they left the fireside to go to their rooms and make good on anything they lacked. "Could be quite interesting, don't you think?" suggested Hallam as he and Tamlyn climbed the last stairway together.

"Yeah, I like books. If I ever get the chance – and the money – I'll try to build up a really good collection," said Tamlyn as they stopped outside his door. "I'll come round your way when it's supper time, shall I? See you."

The talk of books had reminded him of Master Greenwell's words at their interview session. Tamlyn was to take his books 'if the situation arose, and he would know if it did'. But nothing seemed to have happened and Master Greenwell was taking classes as usual, though he still looked rather preoccupied at times. Tamlyn really hoped that whatever might have happened had now passed. He sorted out pens and paper, and made sure his ink bottle lid didn't leak.

The next morning saw the whole group clustered outside the library in good time, and just before ten Master Greenwell arrived. Masters and Lords, they knew, were able to use the library when they wished, and Bartoly was heard bragging that he'd been in there with his father.

"Didn't do his brain much good, did it?" Hallam muttered in Tamlyn's ear. Lord Mansor's son was not noted for getting good marks on his work, and most of them reckoned he'd have fared far worse without his connections.

Master Greenwell led them in and settled them at a long table with Tamlyn by his side at one end. No one was likely to think this odd, as his love of Greenwell's subject was well known.

"It's very good of the High Lord to give you the opportunity to use this place and perhaps explore topics in greater depth than we Masters can provide," Master Greenwell started. "The other Masters and I have worked out a system whereby in each session you will be given several books on a specific area that we think would interest you or where we feel you need extra work. You may not, of course, wander round or take books from the shelves yourselves, but if you feel the need of further information at any time you may ask me or the Master in charge and we will do our best to find it for you. Please be extremely careful with the books, and mind you don't spill any ink."

They'd all been eyeing the shelves around them, some with trepidation and some, like Tamlyn, with a degree of envy. There must be hundreds of books; how did you start looking for what you wanted?

"Today I have given everyone an essay subject along with one or more books connected to that. As you read please make notes. You will take these notes away with you and produce an essay within the following five days. Is that clear?"

A chorus of assent followed and Master Greenwell walked round the table placing books and a handwritten sheet by each Scholar. Tamlyn was last, and the Master sat down by him before sliding a large book and paper over to him. Tamlyn looked at them and felt disappointment well up at what he saw. He'd been looking forward to learning something new, but the book was one he had borrowed several times from Master Greenwell, and his essay topic was so easy he could practically write it in his sleep. He wasn't going to make a fuss, but he did turn his face towards his teacher. Master Greenwell was looking at him, and gave him the smallest of nods. Oh well, better get on with it.

He opened the book, and as he began to turn the pages he froze in surprise. Between pages two and three was a smaller, thin book which looked much older. Not only older but it appeared to be hand written, and the title was nothing to do with *Culinary Herbs and Their Usage*. He stared at it and read, *The First Glorious Years in the Citadel*.

Again he glanced sideways, but more cautiously. He remembered Master Greenwell's words, 'if you can, read all there is in the library about the early years of the Citadel and its rules and laws. What has been written as our history.' Was he being given a chance to do just that? The man beside him appeared to be reading from a heavy book, but Tamlyn saw him give another small nod.

Heart thumping, Tamlyn started reading, tilting the large herbal book to keep the smaller one from coming into view.

It is now three years since the wonderful day when the High Lord led us into this land. Three hundred of us rode in, followed by our carts, servants, and the carriages bearing our women folk. The sun shone as if to show that it welcomed us, and how glad we felt to have left behind the mean and sometimes cruel lives that had been ours in the City. Here we could show our deep allegiance to the High Lord – the handsome, smiling young man who rode at our head.

The people who live in this land are a poor sort – almost sub-human one might say, though able enough to grow the crops and tend the farm animals. Of late we have found them capable of doing household work quite adequately too. The High Lord feels that with training they may become useful to us in many ways. These people offered no objection to our arrival apart from one very small occurrence, which was dealt with easily. They seem to appreciate the excellence of our higher form of living, and are quite anxious to serve us by taking on the more menial tasks.

Tamlyn stared at these opening words and thought of Lyddy and Merla. He supposed this was how the incomers from the city looked at the people of The Land. Indeed, he realised, going hot with shame, it was how he had unthinkingly viewed them until recently. Donkeys. But his time was limited. He must read as much as possible. He hurried through several pages and slowed down when the word 'enchantment' caught his eye.

Behaviour not suited to this higher life that we lead is dealt with by the High Lord. As I have become as close to him as is proper, and keep a record of his days, I am often privileged to hear his views on subjects that others might feel he is above considering as important. In fact he keeps a watchful eye on everything. As an example, we were talking of two of the local men who were stirring up trouble in the villages. It is uncommon, as most there are perfectly happy with their lives. The High Lord makes sure they keep enough of the crops and animals they tend to

supply their needs, after the Citadel has been stocked as we require, of
course.

"Why are these donkeys so stupid?" the High Lord said with a sigh.

"It's almost as if the King in the City is sending evil enchantments
to disturb you, my Lord. Doubtless he would be glad to do anything to
spoil the great happiness which you supply for your happy citizens," I
said.

The High Lord seemed very taken with my words. "Evil
enchantment," he repeated thoughtfully. "An excellent suggestion,
Lessinger. I believe you have hit upon something very important."

Was that where the use of 'evil enchantment' had started? It sounded
as though it might be. Tamlyn read on as fast as he could while still taking
in the sense, until Master Greenwell quietly reached across and took the
little book from him to tuck it among his own papers. Tamlyn had not
taken notes, but felt he would remember the contents clearly. So many
small details there had become a normal part of the life he lived. He
wanted to know more though; would he be shown other old books?
Questions were now bubbling in his head. For the moment, though, he
wrote some hasty notes on culinary herbs in order to have something to
show on his so far blank sheets.

There were varying views on this latest enterprise. Some grumbled
that they couldn't read swiftly enough and write at the same time, while
others found it all very interesting. Tamlyn enthused with this last group,
though not as the others presumed because he'd acquired more herbal
knowledge. He couldn't wait to see what would happen next time. He
was sadly disappointed, though, when Master Jessal arrived to supervise
the next library class and he had to spend ninety minutes struggling with
instructions on proving theorems. Of all subjects, maths was the one that
gave him most trouble and least enjoyment. Nor was he alone; of the
twelve sixth-year Scholars, Hallam was the only one who actually
enjoyed tussling with figures, equations, the innate qualities of shapes
and other operations, happily writing QED at the end of a series of
complex mathematical statements.

"I just can't see the use of it," Tamlyn grumbled.

"It's like seeing where you're aiming for and building stepping
stones to get there. It's so satisfying when you can see all the individual

pieces sliding together to make a perfect pathway," Hallam tried to explain. "Maybe it's like when you find that by mixing three different plant oils together the result is more useful than any of them separately."

Tamlyn allowed that possibility, but preferred to reckon maths was a non-starter for him.

"Anyway, think positive," his friend laughed. "It's Scholar Disc morning tomorrow."

Tamlyn cheered. "I'd forgotten that. Haven't spent much since the last one, so I'm feeling quite wealthy."

Scholars at the Citadel were supplied with clothes, food, and basic needs for personal cleanliness and schoolwork, but they were issued wooden discs of different colours which could be spent as they wished at the regular Scholar Disc mornings. The discs, distributed monthly, increased gradually in number as Scholars progressed up the years, so Tamlyn and Hallam were now at the top of this ladder.

The Disc mornings were enjoyable occasions. Tables were set out in the refectory with various goods displayed. Beside the papers, pens, coloured inks and other small necessities for schoolwork, there were items of clothing, games and toys, second hand stuff of all descriptions, objects for gifts or personal pleasure, along with combs, brushes and lotions, what Hallam called 'the smellies'. Very popular too was the table where the kitchens supplied cakes, biscuits and drinks which were free. Masters often attended to buy, and even Lords would come in now and then.

Each table was supervised by one of the Citadel servants. As Tamlyn and Hallam joined the crowds milling round the tables or chatting with friends, Tamlyn remembered the words he'd read in that small book from the past. 'The people of this land are a poor sort, almost sub-human.' Yet here they were, as capable as any Master of watching their table, sorting out arguments, working out the number of discs owed and helping with decision-making among the younger customers; all at the same time too. Disc morning was in fact the one occasion when Citadel inhabitants and Donkeys met on what were almost equal terms, and it would be hard to tell from their behaviour which group was which.

The business of buying and selling was going on busily, and the two friends were enjoying looking round the tables when Tamlyn noticed a new arrival coming in a door at the other end of the hall. Lord Zaroth!

"Oh no," he whispered, ducking behind Hallam. It was so many weeks since Rufus's death that he'd almost stopped wondering when this Lord would find some punishment suited to his crime. Was it possible that the event had been forgotten? If so, he didn't want to remind him of his existence now.

"What's up?" asked Hallam, and Tamlyn realised his friend had no idea why he should be particularly worried about Lord Zaroth, other than the usual care which needed to be taken in any meetings with that group. But this was neither the time nor the place to launch into explanations, even if he decided it was the right thing to do. He'd have to hope for the best.

"Sorry. I thought for a moment it was Lord Mansor," he said. "He's not forgiven me for breaking Bartoly's nose."

Hallam glanced up the hall. "Mansor?" he hooted. "Are you going blind, Tam? He's half the height and twice the width of Zaroth."

Tamlyn knew it would certainly be very difficult to muddle the two Lords, with Mansor plump and dumpy and Zaroth tall and undeniably handsome, but it was the best he could come up with in a hurry. "Sorry," he said. "Got Mansor on the brain I guess. I've just remembered I need some red ink. I'll go and get it before I forget again." He hurried over to the school goods table on the opposite side from Lord Zaroth and studiously kept his back turned, but at last he couldn't find any more reasons to stand poring over boring school necessities. He turned and glanced across the room, and his heart stood still. Lord Zaroth was looking directly at him and for a split second their eyes met. This is it, thought Tamlyn. He must remember. But unbelievably the man turned away and became absorbed in the gift table. Moments later he strode out of the hall tucking a small object into his pocket.

Tamlyn's legs felt quite wobbly. He could scarcely believe that had happened.

"Let's go and get a drink and some of that almond cake before it all goes," suggested Hallam, and Tamlyn was only too glad to agree. Lyddy was serving hot chocolate and smiled at both the boys as they strolled away to the gift table themselves and idly looked at the things there while they ate and drank.

"She really is pretty, that blonde D... kitchen girl," Hallam said. He'd picked up that Tamlyn never used 'Donkey' now and was following his lead, but it was hard to break the habit of a lifetime. Tamlyn noticed the correction and grinned at his friend appreciatively.

Suddenly Hallam gave a yelp. "Hey Tam, look at this. It's just like Rufus." He held out his hand and Tamlyn saw a tiny wooden carving of a fox cub in his palm. His heart went out to it as he took it up to look more closely. For such a small object it was beautifully made, and the wood gave it the reddish shade that was just right. Heartwood acer he thought, and smiled even as he squeezed back tears, for the carver had shown perfectly the turned-up corners to the mouth.

"You found it," he said, holding it towards Hallam.

"Don't be an idiot. That might have been made for you."

Tamlyn couldn't speak for a moment, but stared down at the little thing. Then he held it towards the stall keeper. "How many Discs for this?" he asked. "Do you know where it came from?"

The man, who Tamlyn thought he'd seen refilling the lamps that were in constant use in the darker internal corridors of the Citadel, took the model and looked puzzled. He consulted a price sheet and shook his head.

"I'm sorry, Scholar, I don't seem to have it on my list, nor do I remember setting it out."

"I'd really like to buy it. Can you put a price on it for me, please?"

The man went to consult with another, older, man then returned. "Chemill says it's very small but well made. Would you consider eight Discs reasonable? If we hear that anyone has left it by accident we will let them know you bought it and you can arrange things with them."

Tamlyn gladly handed over the two red discs which were threes, and two singleton blacks. He would have tipped out all his remaining discs to obtain the little fox. He and Hallam admired it again and several other Scholars who'd known about 'Tamlyn's fox' joined in. He didn't let it from his hand for the rest of the morning.

Things were being cleared away and the tables set for lunch as Tamlyn and Hallam started on the long trek up to put their purchases in their rooms. Just as they got to the door Lyddy came running up. She curtseyed to Tamlyn, so he realised this was 'official'.

"Scholar, you dropped this among the beakers earlier. I saw something fall, but could find nothing till we were clearing just now." She handed him one of the large green Discs, pressing it onto his palm.

"Thank you. I hadn't noticed," he said coolly, placing it in his pouch then turning back to Hallam. His fingers had felt something stuck on the bottom of the Disc, and back in his room he stood by the window to inspect it. A scrap of paper had been folded still smaller and stuck on the Disc. Very carefully, he prised it away and unfolded it.

'Merla wants to see you. Watch your Trees and Shrubs *book to know when and how. L.'*

Chapter 9

Tamlyn was miserable. For more than three weeks he'd been checking his *Trees and Shrubs* book, but nothing appeared. He could never catch Lyddy's eye in the refectory, and if he hadn't saved the scrap of paper with her message he might have thought he'd imagined it all. He hadn't, thank goodness, imagined the discovery of the carved fox cub, and Rufus II sat by his bedside, but neither had he been able to get any information about where he'd come from. Tamlyn usually liked puzzles, but not ones he'd no way of solving.

The weather at the end of February and the beginning of March was unremittingly horrible. No more snow, which would have been fun; that one happy morning seemed to have been their ration of that. Instead, icy winds from the north east, with continual outbursts of slashing rain and hail were relentless. Not once did the sun show through the cover of dense, soot-black clouds. Everyone was irritable, even Hallam, who rarely lost his temper.

"For pity's sake, stop moping around like a wet hen," he growled at Tamlyn, who was drifting from window to window in the small school hall with hands in pockets and shoulders hunched, as if he thought there might be something better outside the next one.

"I just want to go out."

"You and the entire population of the Citadel. You're no worse off than anyone else. Oh, come on, let's have a game of sevens."

"Nah. Think I'll go and look at that maths problem. Thanks though," Tamlyn added grudgingly.

"Please yourself," Hallam shrugged. "I'm sure that'll cheer you up no end."

Tamlyn slouched up the stairs towards his room. He ached to go for a long walk, which always made him feel life was worth living, but only a complete fool would try that at the moment. It wasn't only the lack of news from Merla that was depressing him, but everything around this business of learning the history of the earlier years in the Citadel. At first it had seemed exciting to be involved in such a secret activity, but now he was beginning to wonder. Questions kept arriving in his head with no visible possibility of answers, and he began to wish he'd never got involved in any of the unusual happenings in which he now seemed to be embroiled. When and how he could have stopped the process he wasn't at all sure.

Until now, he had unthinkingly accepted that the High Lord was all-powerful, always right, and to be given unswerving allegiance because it was what he had been taught all his life. It was part of him, as were all the rules of behaviour and thought. True, in the past months he had started to wonder more about things, and had shared a little of this with Hallam, but mainly it was just him. He could think in his own time with no danger of discovery. Now he was being pushed into seeing records of happenings which, if true, would overturn everything he believed in, and he had no real idea who was doing this. Or why? Specifically, and most worrying, why him?

One horrible idea kept nudging at him: someone might be leading him into this so that it looked as though he was plotting against the High Lord. If that was so, he was unlikely to stay alive much longer. Or could it be that the whole thing was not the work of another person but an evil enchantment? When he confronted himself with this possibility he was completely sure he was in charge of his own mind and even more definite that strange external forces had not taken him over. Unfortunately he knew he could still be charged with being enchanted, and to prove he was not would take a great deal more than simply denying it.

Merla had said 'believe in yourself'. With all his heart he wanted to do that, but beyond himself how could he be sure of what to believe in, when nothing seemed to make sense? Desperately he wished there was someone he could talk to. He knew he mustn't burden Hallam any more for that might put his friend in danger, and there was no one else in the Citadel he dare approach with something so dangerous, even the three Masters who seemed to be involved. It was during the supervision periods of Masters Greenwell, Garrid and Sharkley that alternative reading appeared for him in the library, but he could see no way of discovering what their objective was.

Tamlyn was so deep in thought he'd taken several wrong turnings in the maze of winding passages and crooked stairs on his way up to his room, but he knew the place so well that his feet simply took him another way of their own accord. Now he reached his door, shut it behind himself with an irritable slam and flung himself on the bed. If he'd been six instead of sixteen he might have cried at the mess he felt he was in, but now he turned onto his face and screamed his frustration into the bed clothes, thumping the pillow with both fists. Eventually exhausted, he drifted into a doze for a few minutes, then decided he might as well really tackle that maths. It couldn't possibly make the day worse.

It was tough. His overburdened brain couldn't seem to focus, and after several abortive attempts he flung his pen down, leaned back and stared unseeingly up at his shelf. But something was... not quite right. That book was... it was in the wrong way round... and it was... With a whoop, he stood so quickly that his chair toppled backwards, and grabbed *Trees and Shrubs*. Kicking the fallen chair out of the way he sat on the bed with the book on his lap and opened it. His hands shook. He took up the folded sheet he found between agapanthus and arbutus, slid the book to the floor and opened his letter.

Dear Tamlyn, sorry this has been so long, but Merla said she had to wait for the right time. Will you come home with me to Merla's tomorrow evening when I've finished in the kitchen? If you allow an hour from the end of supper and wait at the empty henhouse then you can shelter if it's still raining. It doesn't smell much! To save messages I'll think you're coming, but if you can't, just shake your head at supper. Better burn this. Lyddy.

Tamlyn read this again and again, a broad smile on his face. The rain was still pelting against the window where he'd come to stand in order to get enough light to see Lyddy's writing, but he felt as though the sun was shining on him again at last. He knew with an inner certainty that he could trust these two women as he trusted no one else, and he was going to get out in the air. It could rain all it liked; he was going to be free of the stultifying atmosphere of the Citadel and his problems for a few hours.

Amazingly the rain stopped during the night and a pale, watery sun blinked through wispy streamers of cloud as though it had only just remembered that this was what it was supposed to be doing. Everyone cheered up so Tamlyn's high spirits didn't seem unusual, though when he walked into the classroom whistling, Hallam stared.

"If this is suddenly the result of doing maths, I'll suggest it more often when you've got the grumps," he said.

Tamlyn laughed. "Sorry to disappoint you, I gave up on that when my rubbish bin was full. You'll help me with it, won't you?" he wheedled. "It's such a lovely day I can't help feeling happy."

He wished the time away with a ferocity that exhausted him, but at last he could slip from his room and make his way out through the side exit. He'd have to come back through the secret door, he thought, and it added an extra thrill to the evening. Lyddy had already arrived by the henhouse, and they made their way silently onto the pathway to the village. It felt like walking on squidgy sponges, the land was so full of water from weeks of downpours, and they kept silent until they were a safe distance from the Citadel. It was quite likely the night guards would also be relishing the outside air after weeks of patrolling indoors.

"A good thing the rain's stopped," Tamlyn murmured at last.

"It's what Merla was waiting for. She said she didn't want to drown us."

"But you wrote before it was dry."

"Merla's pretty good at knowing what the weather's doing. Remember the snow? She knew that was coming."

"But how? Sounds like she's a magician. A good magician," Tamlyn added hastily.

"Merla says magicians are just people who notice more, and think more about what they notice. Centuries ago there was a very great magician who lived in these parts. Merla's descended from him. She says she watches the clouds and the winds and how heavy the air feels. It works, anyway."

They'd arrived at the edge of the village, and Lyddy signalled for them to be quiet until they'd entered Merla's home.

"Almost all the people here would never dream of telling they'd seen you, but there's always one who might be tempted to sell information," she explained once she'd closed the front door.

Merla came through from the kitchen, beaming a welcome.

"Come closer to the fire, it's still none too warm. Supper's nearly ready."

Tamlyn was glad to hear this. He'd been too excited to eat much of the evening meal in the refectory, and with the walk here he was really hungry. They ate around the fire: spicy crisp vegetable pancakes with a cheesy sauce which he loved. There was always a queue for second helpings when they were served at school, but here he was pressed to eat as many as he could manage. There was some sort of fruity mousse afterwards, very light and fluffy which was just as well because he really hadn't much room left.

Lyddy took the plates out and Merla leaned towards Tamlyn.

"Will you do something for me, Tamlyn?"

He started to say 'of course' but she held her hand up

"Wait till you hear what I want. You may not feel you can to do it. Do you know the ravine where our river falls from the high crags and starts its way across this land through a cave?"

"Merla!" Lyddy was standing by the kitchen door, and she almost hissed the word. Merla turned; the two of them stared at each other. Finally, Lyddy moved away as though something had been decided between them. "I'll go and wash up then," she said quietly, and vanished back into the kitchen.

"I know where it is but I've never been there," Tamlyn said after a moment's pause. "It's a bit far for one day. I usually go more northerly, anyway. You can see so far from up there as the land rises."

"I need someone to go there next weekend. Could you walk there overnight on Friday do you think? It will be a full moon, and I think the sky will be clear. Then you could come back on Saturday."

The idea of an overnight trek was exciting. "I'm sure I could do that, yes," he replied.

"Listen then. I need you to be there as the sun rises over the top of the falls, which it will do on that day. There are heaps of boulders at the bottom of the falls and beyond them the water has hollowed out a deep pool. It is from that pool that the water flows out as our river. At the eastern end, where the boulders stop and the pool begins, there is a huge slab of stone which makes a bridge that you can cross. Do you understand what I am saying?"

"Uh-huh," Tamlyn nodded. He really felt as though he could already see the place.

"Good. Now when you've crossed, look on the southern side of the pool for a very special water plant that grows there. It came somehow from a mountainous land across the sea. I don't know how it got here but somehow it did. It's called *tache-de-sang* in the language of that land which means drop of blood. The leaves are tiny red globes, so you can see why. I know you are interested in plants and herbs, and it is some of this one that I need."

Tamlyn felt excitement rising; the idea of a new plant he'd never seen or even read about was wonderful.

"I'd love to go for you," he said.

"The plant is best harvested at dawn on the day of the spring equinox, which is next Saturday. I have been going for many years, but my ankle still pains me and I don't think I could be sure of getting there this year. Are you certain, Tamlyn? I don't want you in trouble."

"People are used to me going off early and wandering at the week's end," he assured Merla. "Is this plant very useful?"

"It is in two ways. In very small quantities it is an excellent pain relief. A larger dose, especially if blended with the essence of the foxglove or nightshade, will kill painlessly and certainly in a few minutes."

"I wouldn't like... I couldn't do that," Tamlyn whispered, almost cringing away bodily from the very idea.

"I'm glad you feel that, but you are young. Sometimes, you know, the worst things can look different. If you were caring for someone who was suffering from terrible pain for which there was no cure, someone who begged you to help them gently into the death they longed for, you might think again. Do you want to change your mind now about doing this?"

"No. Of course I'll go."

"I have a small box with a wide-mouthed jar and lid inside as the plant is best kept in water. Collect only a small amount, enough to go easily in the jar, so that it will renew itself. Come next Friday as you have tonight, and I'll have food ready for you and see you on your way. I know you have a good sharp knife, so bring that with you to cut the plant rather than tear it. Now I think it's time you got back. You know how to get in now, don't you?" Merla finished with a grin.

Lyddy insisted in walking part of the way with Tamlyn. She would say nothing about his task the next week so he returned to the subject of Merla's weather skills.

"You said she might have inherited abilities from that long-ago magician," he said. "Have you got them too?"

"I'm not related to Merla," she said, sounding surprised.

"Oh. I thought you were her granddaughter or something."

"I'd love to be, but no, I'm a foundling."

"A foundling?" It was Tamlyn's turn to be surprised.

"Literally. I was found wandering out in the countryside, way down in the western part of the land. I could walk, and talk a little bit, but not enough to say where I came from. It was Vitsell who found me, early one morning near his camp. He wanders round with his cart and tools, doing odd jobs you know. He brought me back here to Merla and, well, there you are."

Tamlyn was amazed. "And you've no memories at all?"

"Nothing. I sometimes have dreams that I'm in a place I know, but it all slips away when I wake up. I belong here now, and I couldn't wish for a better mother than Merla."

"In a way we're alike, then. I don't know who my parents were, but many of the Scholars are like that. Here, you must go back. You've got to get up earlier than me. I shall be all right you know. Next week I mean. I'm used to wandering over the land on my own."

"Yes, I know."

"I thought you sounded cross when Merla first asked me."

"Oh, that was because... I thought it might be... you know, you might get caught or something."

Tamlyn sensed that she had been going to say something different at first, but he let it rest. "Goodnight," he said. He thought it would be nice to give her a hug, but the moment passed as she waved and ran back home

Chapter 10

Although the weather seemed to be making amends for its recent bad behaviour the next day and the sun was tempting him out, Tamlyn spent some time writing down what Merla had said. He then read it all through three times and burnt the papers, knowing he would be able to recall it when he needed to. His brain worked like that; he could visualise the writing as though it was in front of him, a very useful thing when it came to examinations. He'd been surprised to find others couldn't do the same.

That was really all the preparation he could do for the coming Friday. His small knife he always kept honed, and the weeks imprisoned indoors by the weather meant his shoes were far less worn than usual at this time of year, and were quite fit for a long tramp. Now the days ahead stretched before him and he tried not to waste the time in wishing them away. He concentrated on school work, and managed to enjoy his usual life with his friends.

One event had almost slipped his memory, his birthday. When he was born someone must have noted it somewhere, and on March the seventeenth he would be seventeen. When he came down to breakfast on that day he was greeted by applause from his classmates, and others joined in as they saw who was being hailed. He still retained kudos for his fight with Bartoly, and it was an opportunity to show support openly to him, even if for a different reason. Round his place at table were wrapped gifts, and it was tradition that you had first choice of food on your birthday.

He could see his friends were all eager for him to open their presents to him, so he began: a small mirror on a stand, soap, a soft brush, a little phial of perfumed oil and, from Hallam... a razor. Tamlyn looked at them all grinning at him, picked up the mirror and looked at himself.

"Oh," he said.

"Seen it at last have you?" Hallam asked. "We thought you were aiming at being the Hairy Horror or something."

Tamlyn turned his face from side to side and ran a hand over his mouth and cheeks. With no mirror in his room and none in the cave-like bathroom below, he so rarely looked at his reflection he hadn't noticed the soft, auburn shadow that had appeared.

"Thanks. Thanks a lot." He was half delighted and half embarrassed, especially as Lyddy was clearing a table nearby. She had a huge smile on her face, but luckily wasn't looking directly at him. He thought he might have crawled under the table if she had. "I'll have to find out how this lot works," he said.

"Come on, let's give him a lesson," suggested Kenley, and the six of them carted him bodily down to the bathroom where, for an hilarious half hour, they gave him so many instructions, hints and actual assistance that he thought he'd never get the hang of it. He was the youngest of the group, and he simply hadn't noticed that two of them already had the beginnings of goatee beards and moustaches. Even Hallam had shaped his blonde fuzz to a line that followed his jaw.

"Honestly, Tam, for someone who notices plants in such detail it's incredible you didn't notice your own growth. There, that looks better. Just a dab of oil I think."

They all gathered round to give their approval, and Tamlyn, who'd been almost helpless with laughter, recovered enough to thank them all again as they made their way to the first class. It was with Master Sharkley, who walked in, sniffed the air and stalked across to open a window.

"Hmm. Smells as though you've set up as perfume dealers," he remarked, but he had a most uncharacteristic smile on his face. "Happy birthday, Scholar Tamlyn."

The day also included another library session with Master Garrid, where he found an information sheet about employment of men and women. While the men's list went onto a second page and ranged from quite humble occupations to becoming a Lord, the women's only mentioned house cleaning, cooking and care of younger children. Here there were handwritten notes in a flamboyant scrawl and signed with an elaborate Z – the High Lord himself, Zerac. *Females need only basic education, being by nature incapable of further learning. The youngest male children may be cared for by women, but as soon as they start schooling they must be taught by Masters. Boys who prove unmanly or lacking in ability in any way will be removed from school and dealt with elsewhere.*

'Dealt with elsewhere'. Tamlyn considered what this might mean, and remembered Willan. He hoped he'd been right in thinking he saw him working in the fields after his 'removal from school'. He thought it was something he would not have disliked too much himself, had he been judged 'unmanly or lacking in ability', but 'dealt with' sounded ominous, as though it could mean many things. The notes about women didn't surprise him, for they had been absent from his life except as servants from the day he started the first school. That was the life all Scholars lived, and it was only since he'd begun to question the organisation of his world that he'd become aware that women were reckoned as second class beings, even those who worked in the Citadel. He almost snorted at this, but luckily remembered where he was. He was supposed to be studying the everlasting topic of evil enchantment, not something at which he should be heard to express derision.

His thoughts drifted to Merla and Lyddy who had so surprisingly come into his life. Nothing second class there, he thought. But they would be seen as such because they were women and because the High Lord said it was so. Perhaps it was to their benefit in some ways; they could hide their abilities behind other people's blind assumptions of stupidity. Though he'd come to see that Merla had knowledge and powers far greater than most of the Masters, and Lyddy, who was probably about his own age, ran the kitchen world with ease and efficiency, they were both female and Donkey, therefore practically worthless. At this thought he actually did snort, but managed to turn it into a sneeze.

Thursday passed, and Friday had to be got through somehow. Tamlyn crept down to the bathing room to try shaving with nobody in attendance. Not bad, he thought, looking in his little mirror. He'd managed to avoid cutting himself and even risked a dab of the oil. Perhaps not a good idea, as Hallam and Kenley noticed it immediately at supper and wanted to know why he was smelling so beautiful.

"You lot can't give me all that fancy stuff and not expect me to use it," he protested. "Tomorrow I plan to walk right up to that high point where you can see for miles, so I'll be competing with the spring flowers. Want to come?" he finished nonchalantly. He was almost sure they'd refuse, but had his fingers crossed until they both launched into a list of things which meant that, sorry, they couldn't possibly make enough time for a long walk. He'd also purposely suggested he was going in a very different direction to his actual destination.

As on the previous week he met up with Lyddy and they walked, silently at first, towards the village. Merla had, of course, been right, and a brilliant, full-bellied moon made the countryside clear for yards around them. Suddenly Lyddy grabbed Tamlyn's arm and sidestepped round to stand facing him, forcing him to stop. She reached out a hand and stroked his cheek.

"Mmm, very nice," she said. Then she leant forward and put her face close to his and sniffed. "But that's not," she added. "Not your perfume at all. I must get Merla to make something for you; lavender with a touch of sandalwood I think."

Tamlyn knew his face must be scarlet, and was glad that moonlight turned all colours into shades of grey. He lifted his hands to take hold of her, but she skipped away before he could touch her.

"Come on," she said. "Merla will be anxious to get you started."

He wanted to say something but seemed struck dumb. Finally he managed, "I don't think I'll use that stuff actually. I might want to hide or something and it would give me away. Probably hang around every place I've been in too."

"It would depend who you were hiding from. If it was an animal they'd go for your body scent, and that stuff might put them off in fact, it's strong enough. Who knows?"

Lyddy took them on a long arc behind the village and brought them in through Merla's back door.

"Moonlight like this, someone was almost sure to see us if we'd gone along the main street, you particularly," she explained, as Merla stopped the food preparation with which she was busy at the table.

"I'm packing something for you to eat," she said. "Nothing like a long walk for working up an appetite." She looked him up and down, nodding approval at his clothing, particularly the fact that he'd chosen to wear full length breeches. "Good. Easy at night to walk into a gorse bush or something else thorny. Now do you remember my instructions?"

Tamlyn closed his eyes for a moment, pulled from his memory the notes he'd made and repeated them to her. Merla gave a little laugh. "You're a good listener, that's for sure. And you remember clearly. Now the best way is to follow the river this side. There is an old bridge some way along, but don't cross there. Where the river flows from the cavern on that other side it washes right against the cliff. There's no pathway and the water is turbulent and dangerous. Cross at the foot of the falls, remember."

"I will." Now the moment was here he was becoming nervous, but anxious to get going. Strangely he felt that Merla was uneasy too. Maybe she wasn't sure he could do this. He swung the hessian satchel from his back and she put in the packages of food she'd prepared, and the stoppered jar in its protective box for the *tache-de-sang*.

"I'll take you to the river path by the back way. Lyddy's right; it's not a good idea for you to be seen around here."

Lyddy whispered, "Good luck," and waved from the back door, then Tamlyn and Merla made their way first southwards until they neared the river, then turning eastwards towards its source in the mountains.

"You'll be fine from here." Merla stopped as she spoke. "When you return I'll meet you and you need not come into the village at all." Standing there, side by side, Tamlyn realised she was as tall as he was. She reached for his shoulders and turned him to her. Very gently, she placed a kiss on his forehead. "Thank you, Tamlyn," she whispered, then walked briskly away.

He set off at the easy pace he knew to be the most efficient way of covering the ground. For a great deal of the distance the river bank was well-trodden: animals coming to drink, people fishing, a farmer on the lookout for a straying sheep; it was a natural thoroughfare. Twice an outcrop of rock interrupted the level and he had to scramble up and over. More than an hour by his guess after he passed the stone bridge Merla had told him of he realised he was nearing the cliff face from which the river flowed and the whole area became rocky, with sparse and stunted bushes and little grass. He had to pick his way carefully, for the moon was sinking, and though the sky was still bright with stars their light was not enough to make his way easy.

At last he reached the cleft from which the water flowed. Had he not been told he could, he would have doubted the possibility of getting in, but with great care he pressed forward. It was so dark. The moon had vanished completely behind the cliffs, and the rocks themselves were almost black. He stopped for a few minutes, leaning his back against the sheer, towering rock-face that was the true beginning of the mountains at this point. First he felt in his bag for something to eat. No light to choose by, but he bit into something that felt like a pasty and found it was filled with apple and cinnamon. He closed his eyes tightly as he munched, and when he'd licked his fingers he opened them again. Doing this tricked his eyes into making better use of what light there was, and he realised too that the stars in the sky over the lower lands he'd crossed were fading a little in the pre-dawn promise of a new day. He must get on.

Although it had seemed impossible, there was, in fact, a rocky way wide enough for four or five people that rounded the sharp vertical cliff edge, but Tamlyn kept as far from the black, swirling water as he could. Inside he could make out that he was in what felt like a huge cave which had a small part of its top sliced off like an egg so that he could see a faint, starry circle high above him. In the centre of the cave was the pool. Its waters were dark and appeared still, though he knew they must be flowing all the time to the gap he had just come through. He could see the glinting movement of the waterfall at the far end and the noise of it, trapped inside this huge rocky bowl, was overpowering. There was a flat area all round the pool, and he made his way towards the fall where he found the slab of rock which bridged the water. It was the scariest place he'd ever been in; he was glad the bridge was wide, for the dark water rushing beneath it seemed to reach out for him.

Merla has been here many times, he told himself, and he screwed up his determination to go on. It was definitely getting lighter now, so he turned right as he left the bridge and moved as fast as he dared, watching the water's edge for the plant he was after. There it was. Masses of tight-packed foliage moving gently with the flow of the water, and in the nearly-dawn light he could see it was dark red like clotted drops of blood.

He crept to the edge, found a safe position from which to bend over, and with his knife in his hand, he waited for that first glint of the sun.

Head tilted towards the top of the falls, he stayed motionless, almost not breathing. The glow grew brighter, and then came the first flash of brilliance. He turned again to the plants in the water and carefully eased a handful onto the rock, severing the stems at what he felt was the best place. He pushed the rest back into the water and repeated it in a different area. That looked enough. He dipped Merla's jar into the pool to fill it, and lowered his harvested stems inside. Pressing the stopper into place he replaced it all in the box and tucked the box into his satchel. Phew! He had done what he came for and could make his way home again. Although he could now see round the chasm more easily, the light had not made it feel any more welcoming. He hurried back to the bridge and started to re-cross it.

In the middle, cold struck; a cold so sudden and cruel that Tamlyn dropped to his knees and curled up, his arms tight round his chest as if he'd been punched. At the same time a mist enveloped him so that all but the bridge beneath him and the dark water to his left were invisible. But there were sounds: footsteps at first, and soft voices, then shouts of fear erupted, which rapidly turned to screams. There were running feet going in all directions; a terrified voice yelling "No... no... no," and further away, "Run. This way." Tamlyn could hear, above all this panic, men's voices shouting, raucous and triumphant, and the clash of steel. Suddenly a small child ran from behind him... ran *through* him though he felt nothing. She skidded, fell and rolled to stare up in horror at something above her, above him. She was screaming, mouth agape. A blade slashed down across her body and scarlet blood spurted. She could not live with a wound like that, but still she screamed. The blade, dripping blood, rose and fell again and the screaming stopped. It had come down through him, Tamlyn knew, but he heard only the swish through the cold air, and the horrific sound of living flesh being butchered. A manic cackle of glee burst out above him and a man's foot in a leather boot came forward and kicked the bloody corpse towards the edge of the bridge. Although there was nothing he could do for the child Tamlyn reached to stop this last indignity but his hands passed through her and...

… And there was nothing. Only the dark rock, the thundering water behind, the black pool before, and him. Tamlyn still knelt in the centre of the stone bridge, shaking and overwhelmed by the horror of what he had witnessed. He would never be able to forget it, but the picture that was seared into his mind most deeply was that foot in its fine leather boot, beautifully decorated on the outer side with golden studs making the shape of a Z. Zerac! Kicking the child he had just murdered into the water and laughing.

Without warning Tamlyn was sick. Leaning over the water he retched again and again till he felt his heart might come up too. At last he lay still, exhausted, till he knew he had to move. Slowly he scooped up handfuls of water to clean his mouth and stood. He wasn't sure how he moved to get out of that place, but gradually the world outside began to make its way into the forefront of his mind and he walked down by the riverside in a soft, spring morning. He thought he ought to eat, but couldn't. At last he scrambled over some rocks and saw Merla standing some way ahead. She was staring over the river and her lips were moving.

Tamlyn suddenly felt anger rising in him. Not at what he had seen – that was beyond anger – but that she must have known, yet had sent him there with no warning He had no idea what it was he'd experienced in the cave, but of one thing he was certain: it had been real. Not this morning, but at some point it had happened, just as he'd seen.

He strode towards her, ready to shout his fury, then she turned towards him and he saw tears running down her pale face and unbearable pain in her eyes. He stopped and she came to him.

"You saw," she said quietly. "Oh Tamlyn, I'm so sorry." She took his hand and led him away from the river to a grassy bank where she'd spread a blanket. Tamlyn sat as she directed and Merla knelt in front of him. She took a small phial from a pocket and held it to him. "Drink that, it will help."

It was, he realised, the mixture she had given him the night when Rufus had been killed, but for the moment he held it in his hand.

"What was it?" he croaked. "Why didn't you tell me?"

"It was what happened fifty three years ago today, and I couldn't tell you because it might have made you imagine you saw something. The chances were you wouldn't see it anyway."

"I couldn't imagine that. Who could imagine something so... so terrible? And what do you mean, I might not have seen it?"

"Drink that, Tamlyn. I will tell you everything, don't worry."

Tamlyn drank and felt the acid anger lessen and the horror begin to fall away to something more manageable. He realised he was curious about Merla's tears and wondered what she'd been saying when he saw her just now. Well, she'd promised she would tell everything. He would wait.

Chapter 11

Merla made Tamlyn eat some of the food from his satchel and though he felt he might never enjoy eating again it did make him feel better. He ate in silence and waited for her to begin.

"I did not lie to you, Tamlyn," she said at last, sitting beside him and looking out towards the river. "I do need the herb – there may be a need for it only too soon I fear – and though my ankle is healing well I didn't think I could make that journey with certainty. What I didn't do was warn you of what you might see. I wish I could have done, but I couldn't. I will tell you the story from the start and I believe you'll understand then.

"Fifty-five years ago Zerac and all his company came here. It was an evil day, though we didn't know just how bad at first. I think you will never have been told it, but this land has for centuries been led by a woman; The Lady is her title. At the time of Zerac's coming my mother was The Lady and my father stood at her side in everything. I was ten, and we lived in the Citadel. It didn't have all the extra buildings that Zerac has added since then, but it was still huge, all the rocky central part, and it was used by everyone, more a working place than just our home. We are not, and never have been, a fighting people, so we moved from the Citadel at his command because he threatened terrible things if we did not."

Tamlyn listened avidly, fearing but still wanting to know. Without really being aware of what he was doing he reached into his satchel, pulled out a sausage and bit into it.

"For a while we tried to live with his rulings in peace, but we soon realised that he would never be satisfied. There was no way we could all leave, but we planned that a large group of the children and the older people would leave secretly, hoping they would be safe until things changed and they could come back. I don't think my parents really saw that happening, but it gave us hope, and without hope you cannot live. There was a rough way out of the waterfall cave to the right of the falls which led into the mountains and to a country which we knew would welcome them when they arrived."

"I saw no way up there," said Tamlyn, puzzled. He'd called up the scene in his mind and both sides of the fall were formed of piles of huge boulders, almost certainly unclimbable, especially by children.

"You are right, now. Then it was different. Our plan was to go to the cave at the day of the spring equinox because my mother felt the weather would be fine for them, and we walked up there during the night, as you have just done. Those who were leaving went in a long line into the cave, led by a man who had travelled that path before. Some who had come to say goodbye stayed outside. I was there; I went with my parents. My mother and father along with two other men were the only ones of all that number to carry weapons, and once the travellers were in the cave they meant to stand guard at the narrow entrance and stop any of Zerac's men getting in, for they feared that so large a group might not have gone unnoticed, and they wanted to give the travellers as long as possible to escape. We didn't know that the plan had been betrayed some days before by a poor young man. He had the body of a giant but the mind of a child, and the Citadel guards had got him drunk and teased the secret from him. Zerac, with many armed men, had already hidden in the cave after blocking the route past the falls by causing a landslide. You know what happened; you saw it, Tamlyn. Some at the back of the line managed to turn and run out when they realised what was happening, but thirty-seven children and fourteen adults, all unarmed, were killed by the sword or hurled into the water to drown. The four of our people who were armed stood at the entrance and fought to stop Zerac coming out to hunt for those who'd escaped. As you know it is very narrow there and they managed to hold them back just long enough for those who'd run to get to safety, but in the end they were killed too. My mother, my father, Vitsell's older brother, Vansell, and Barent, a farmer. Though my parents had told me to run, I'd stayed and hidden myself. I saw them die."

Merla's voice had been steady as she spoke, but at these last words Tamlyn heard it waver. He turned to her and saw the tears once more on her cheeks. He had no words; nothing he could say that would show he longed to comfort her but didn't know how, so he simply reached his hand and took one of hers to hold.

She wiped her tears with the back of her other hand, though they still fell as she turned fully to him with the smallest of smiles.

"Fifty-three years. You might think the pain had lessened by now. And so it has. Most of the time I can wrap it safely in my heart and get on with living, but each year on this day I mourn for all those lost lives. Each year on this day I return and speak each name in that place of death so that it won't be forgotten. But today I spoke them to the river which washed their bodies and the blood they shed."

"That was what you were doing when I came," whispered Tamlyn, and she nodded.

"Today was different. Today *you* went, and I think that is very important. I think hope is creeping back into our land at last."

"I don't understand. What difference can I make now to what happened all that time ago?"

"Because you are who you are. I felt the first time we met that you were special, and all I've learnt of you since has only strengthened that feeling."

"But I'm not special at all," he almost wailed.

"Listen to me, Tamlyn," she said fiercely. "Just as I can feel the changes in the weather I can feel that change in our lives is coming now. I don't know how, or what it will be, but it is good, of that I'm certain. I'm equally sure it involves you. Events that seem like coincidences are happening in their proper places if we could only see the whole. Why did you, of all the people in the Citadel, come to a window and see what happened to Fliss that day? Not only see, but feel its wrongness and do something about it, though you might have brought trouble on your own head? Why was it you of all others who found me injured? Not only found, but helped me, though all your life you had been taught that I was a nothing, a Donkey, to be ignored. Why are your mind and heart now taking information from the past, and feeling that what you read is giving the lie to all that has been poured into your head to the contrary for seventeen years? Oh yes, I know about that."

"I don't know why. I just don't feel special." Instead he was beginning to fear that his whole world was falling to pieces and him with it.

"Why, most of all, was it you I felt I could ask to visit the cave for me today?" Her voice had grown quiet and gentle again, but still determined. "Tamlyn, I not only knew I could trust you, but I sensed that it must be you I sent. You want to know why I didn't warn you. I had to be sure that you were the one I thought you were, and to do that it was vital that I didn't put ideas into your head. If I had told you that you might see something you could, without realising, have imagined that you did. That place can make anyone think strange thoughts, but it would have been just that, imagination, and I would have known it for that. You said yourself that you couldn't possibly have dreamed up anything so terrible and you're right. We have found through all the years that the only people who see that true and terrible vision are those who have a direct blood link to a man or woman who was killed that day. I had to know for sure that what I have only felt since I met you is true. The most powerful force in you is your love of this land."

Merla stopped talking, and Tamlyn stared and stared at her, not able at first to take in what she said.

"You mean I'm related to... but I don't know who I'm related to. I've no idea. Lots of the Scholars are the same."

Merla sighed. "I know recently you've read about some of the things Zerac has done over the years, but perhaps not yet this. His whole desire has always been to be supreme, to have everything and everybody totally in his power and to punish anyone who tries to evade his control. After that day at the cave the people of this land knew we could never beat him by force, but we decided we would resist passively. We obey with our bodies but our minds are not his, and he knows it. He does everything he can think of to demean us, but we still know who we are.

"Some thirty years ago he decided he would really crush us by making children in his ordained pattern who would eventually take over the land completely. His men – the Lords, Masters, even some Guards – were ordered to force our women to bear their children. I don't know if any have ever been brave enough to rebel. Possibly some have, and been punished. I imagine some enjoy having the power, for it still goes on, and they may tell themselves they are doing the High Lord's will. These children are removed from all contact with their parents and brought up by the Citadel to Zerac's rules. He believes, because in his mind only the people of the breed who came with him are of value and all women are inferior to all men, that in these children the Citadel's blood will be supreme. He will build a race as far as possible in his own image. That's why so many of you are so-called orphans."

"But that's horrible. It's like breeding cattle. It makes me feel… dirty."

"No, Tamlyn," Merla said sharply. "There is no fault in any of you, but I believe that Zerac may have sown the seeds of his downfall by the blind, arrogant stupidity of his thinking. Children inherit from both their parents, regardless of their sex, and in some the mother's blood will be predominant. We cannot know who your mother was, but I believe she was strong, thoughtful, loving and kind, just as you are. Not that all the women of the land are like that, of course," she added with a laugh, "but probably enough to make many of their children ready to disagree with what they come to see is wrong and to fight against it. I think you are special, but I doubt you're unique."

Tamlyn tried to take in this information. "I may know someone," he said slowly, thinking of Hallam. "He's my best friend."

"There, then, you are not on your own, even with the barriers that have made trust so difficult in your life. If your heart says you can trust him now, then do. As much as you feel is safe and right."

Tamlyn's mind went off on another path. "I am secretly being shown writing in the library. I suppose much of it was meant to record the High Lord's glory, but it makes me think quite differently. You know about this, don't you? How is that?"

"It is through Master Greenwell. He was one of the first babies in Zerac's scheme, and he was the first to make me think that the plan was not working as that cruel fool believed it would. What do you know of him?"

"I like him a lot. We both enjoy walking across the land, and he knows such a lot about plants. He seems to be rather worried though, lately."

"He's very like you then, isn't he? The people respect him out in the countryside, and I've got to know him over the years. In a small way he's tried not to brainwash his Scholars, and it was he who first told me about you. He's anxious that you should be aware of how things really are, but I fear he has put himself in danger."

Tamlyn thought a moment. "Ah," he said, "but why…"

Merla stood up quickly. "There will be time for more questions, I hope, but now I think you should be getting back. Lyddy's making one of your favourites for supper at the Citadel, those crispy fritters!"

He glanced at the sky, saw that the sun was well past midday and got up too. "Yes, you're right. I guess you're right quite a lot, aren't you? Can I have one more question, please?"

"A short one, then."

"I heard Vitsell call you Lady. You are The Lady now, aren't you?"

"I am. Since that day when my mother was killed. Not as it should have been, but I try."

Tamlyn bowed to her. "Thank you, my Lady. I am honoured to be one of your people."

Once again tears came to her eyes, but she smiled round them. "I can see what Lyddy means," she said cryptically. "Come on now. We can't have you missing supper."

Merla left him in the trees behind her house, taking the box carrying the *tache-de-sang* with her. Tamlyn made his way back to the Citadel, his head buzzing with new knowledge and thoughts, and amazed at how he felt now. In the cave he'd been frightened, angry and desperate, and so horrified at the slaughter that he could not imagine that he would ever feel differently. He'd been furious with Merla, and then dully unable to think at all about what could come next. Her explanations had brought him back to something nearer normality, for knowing the reality of the images and, to an extent, who he was made things easier to understand and stopped everything overwhelming him. He was still angry, but not at her; his fury was now firmly directed at the High Lord, Zerac, for he would never forget that manic laugh and the booted foot kicking the little corpse away. What to do would have to be worked out later, but now he needed more food and then sleep. I've missed a whole night, he thought, and quickened his step so as not to fall asleep before he'd eaten.

He made his way up to his room, changed his shirt which only then did he realise was sprayed with his sick, and got himself down to the refectory.

Hallam glared at him. "You look disgusting and you stink," he said, and turned back to talk to Kenley on his other side.

"Sorry. I'm ravenous and worn out. I've been a lot further than I thought today." Which was true in more than one sense.

Chapter 12

A really early night, and sleep that was deep and thankfully dream-free had Tamlyn waking refreshed well before breakfast, so he used the time to soak himself, including his hair, in the warm subterranean bath. As he wallowed comfortably in the water he wondered if this place had existed when Merla and her parents lived here. He reckoned it probably had, for the warm spring must have been here for ever, and the shaping of the benches and the pool edges were smooth and simple. Places the High Lord created were always elaborately decorative.

Hallam still seemed surly at breakfast, but Tamlyn scarcely noticed; his head continued to be full of yesterday. Making a determined effort to stop going over and over it all, he considered what he should be doing today and, as so often, the subject most in need of attention was maths. He groaned inwardly.

"Hal, do you think you could give me a hand with Master Jessal's work? Sorry, but I'm really stuck," he pleaded.

Hallam turned. "As always," he said, without any hint of a smile. "All right, but I'm not doing it all for you. It's time you got to grips with it. I'll come up in a minute."

Tamlyn registered his friend's unusual attitude. "Only if you don't mind," he said, placatingly.

"I said I'd come, didn't I?" Hallam snarled, and turned away again.

Puzzled, Tamlyn went to his room after borrowing an extra chair from an empty room so that he and Hallam could both sit at his desk. He got out his maths work and had another go at puzzling out where he was going wrong, but without success.

"Right, what don't you understand?" Hallam asked when he arrived, and seated himself grumpily in a chair.

"It's this bit. I thought you had to find the difference, but it doesn't seem to work like that. I end up with less than I started with and it's supposed to be a gain."

"But we did all this weeks ago,"

"I know, but I didn't really understand it then."

Hallam snorted disgust and launched into another explanation, at the end of which Tamlyn felt even more muddled. Why couldn't he get his head round something his friend seemed to think was child's play?

"But why that?" he wailed, "I just can't…"

Hallam threw his pen down, shoved his chair back and glared. "I'm not priggin' well wasting any more of my time on you when you seem to have plenty to spare for… for other activities," he spat, and stalked across the room to the window.

Tamlyn stared. "What on earth are you talking about?"

"You. I thought we were friends. That day when we met that weird man up the hill and we talked, I thought we would go on. You know, talk, share things. I thought you trusted me."

"I do, Hal, honestly."

"So how come you can sneak out for hours and hours and not a word."

Tamlyn saw his friend was really upset, but suddenly he was apprehensive about exactly why. Hallam had never been worried by his long excursions before.

"Just tell me what you're really mad about. I often go on long treks, you know that."

"Not all night, you don't."

Tamlyn stared, speechless, and suddenly Hallam exploded.

"I came up here Friday night. Ran out of paper and I wanted to write something for Jessal before I forgot it. Numbers, you know, or rather you don't! You weren't here, but I knew you weren't far 'cos I could smell that shaving stuff and I followed the stink and realised you must have gone out. Right out. After Guard time. So I put a wedge in the door and came looking. It was bright moonlight, as you might remember, if you hadn't got your mind on other things, and I spotted you after a bit, walking away from here with your satchel over your shoulder, cocky as a crow." He paused for breath.

"So?" Tamlyn said, as evenly as he could manage, though his heart was thumping.

"So where were you off to that you didn't get back till supper next day, looking and smelling like a pigsty and sooo tired and hungry you could hardly walk? I've heard some activities are *very* tiring. How long did you spend, rolling in the moonlight daisies with the little blonde Donkey from the kitchen? I saw…"

He got no further. Tamlyn leapt from his chair, crossed the room in two strides and smashed his fist into Hallam's face.

"Shut up, shut up, shut up," he yelled.

They stood glaring at each other. Tamlyn saw blood trickle from a cut above Hallam's eyebrow, and as quickly as it had risen his fury left him.

"Oh Hal, I'm sorry. I didn't mean… I shouldn't have… Come over here and I'll bathe that."

Hallam eyed him warily for a moment, then did as he was told. "So are you going to tell me what it's all about?"

"If you only knew how much I've been longing to do just that," Tamlyn said. "There, your head's not too bad. I'll put some lotion on. It'll sting a bit."

Hallam fingered his forehead, where a bump was already rising. "Lords above, Tam, I'm amazed Bartoly had any face left if you can throw just one punch like that." He dropped down onto Tamlyn's bed and swung his legs up, leaning back on the pillows. "I'm sorry too. That wasn't what you say to a friend, but I was so mad at you, seeing you going off up the road with her and not so much as a hint."

"It had nothing to do with moonlight or daisies believe me. I really want to tell you, but before I do I've got to ask you something."

"If it's whether I can keep my mouth shut you already asked. Answer's the same."

"And I believe you on that, but this is different. What I'll tell you now is more serious than saying rude things about the Lords or criticising the High Lord. If it ever gets known you've been paying attention to and agreeing with me you could be facing death, a very unpleasant death at that. Once you've heard me, you can't un-hear it can you? I just want you to know that. Do you still want me to go on?"

Hallam sat silent, more serious than Tamlyn had ever seen him. At last he sat forward and looked soberly into his friend's eyes.

"Yes. I understand what you're saying, but I'm absolutely sure that if you're into something, I want to be there too. For, I dunno, couple of years I guess, I've had this feeling growing that things here just aren't right, though I don't know enough about anything to see what or why. We've nothing to compare ourselves with have we, not in this place? But like you said, we've been friends for years and I'd believe you over anyone here because I've never known you to lie. Fibs about why you haven't done school work don't count," he added with a grin. "Oh yes, and where you were walking to yesterday, but that's going to be explained, I'm hoping."

"I promise. Do you feel up to a walk now?" Tamlyn asked. "A short one. Short as you like, but I'll feel happier out in the air where I can be sure nobody's listening outside the door."

As they strolled up the hill Tamlyn thought through all the happenings of the past months to be sure what he could tell his friend. He didn't think he should give all the details of his visit to the cave, if only because Hallam thought, as he had, that he was an orphan, but was quite likely to be part of Zerac's plan for continuing domination. He didn't want to overload him with everything at once. It had been hard enough to come to terms with all the new ideas himself, a bit at a time.

They settled themselves into a comfortable dip, already warmed by the sun, and Tamlyn began. He'd decided a straightforward story would work best.

"Last September, just before school restarted, I was trying to catch up on our holiday work in my room. I heard some voices in the road below my room. You know, the one that goes down to the stables..."

He went on to tell Hallam about his first meeting with Merla and Lyddy and of Lord Zaroth's behaviour. "Honestly Hal, I suppose I thought like all of us that the people of this land were stupid Donkeys because that was what we were taught, but I had my eyes opened that day. The amazing way Merla and Fliss vanished – oh, I'll tell you more about that in a minute – and the way Lyddy was suddenly sitting there calmly doing her sewing and being polite to that man! She even saw my difficulty and got me out of it. Like you, I'd had some thoughts, but that day made me really start asking questions."

"I always reckoned Lord Zaroth was pretty top notch, but I think I've changed my mind," said Hallam.

"You wait," said Tamlyn grimly. "You remember I told you about finding the woman who had hurt herself up in the hills? That was Merla again. She wouldn't let me get help from the village because she knew it might get me into trouble, so that's how I met Vitsell too. It was also the day I found Rufus." He went on to tell how Lyddy had helped to care for the little animal, and then of the evening the cub died.

Hallam leapt to his feet. "He did *that*?" he yelled in disgust, and Tamlyn nodded. He still found it hard to take his mind back to it all. The pictures that came to him were too harsh and painful.

"Sit down and don't yell." He patted the grass beside him and his friend flopped down again. "Lyddy heard all the fuss and saw what happened. I was in a real state. Couldn't move, or think; I was right out of it. She came and wrapped Rufus in a cloth then took me to Merla's home. She lives there too actually. They were… amazing. I somehow felt I was to blame because Rufus had become so tame he didn't run away from Zaroth, but Merla helped me see it differently. She gave me a potion to calm me and Lyddy washed my shirt because I'd got Rufus's blood all over it. Then she took me back to the Citadel. You'll like this bit, Hal."

And when Tamlyn told him about the secret entrance, he did. "A secret passage! Fantastic. And one exit is in the kitchen. Could be useful if you get hungry around midnight. Only joking, Tam, but do you think you might be able to show me? Sometime. When it's safe, I mean."

Tamlyn nodded. "Yeah, sometime."

"How come Lyddy knew about it? I bet no one else in the Citadel does."

"Merla. She lived in the Citadel when she was a child, before the High Lord came."

Hallam gaped. "She's quite something isn't she?"

Tamlyn toyed with the idea of telling him Merla's real identity, but decided it wasn't his secret, so he just nodded again. He did tell briefly of Lyddy's being found as a toddler, which amazed his friend further.

"Well now we come to yesterday. Actually to a bit further back first." He related the details of the message on the Scholar disc, of his long wait, and then of going again to Merla's home and being asked to visit the cave from which the river flowed and to fetch the water plant.

"It was a long way I can tell you, and the plant had to be gathered at sunrise so I went overnight. Really rough going the last stretch of it was; I guess that's partly what made me mucky and smelly, though I didn't take my mirror with me to check."

"So where's all this leading?" asked Hallam. "I mean, it's really exciting, but is it going somewhere?

"There's a bit I haven't told you yet. Merla's not only brilliant with herbs but she can sense things ahead, like the weather. She says it's not magic, just being more aware at a deeper level of what's going on around her. She is absolutely sure that change is coming to The Land. Good change, although she can't define it clearly. She believes that far more people in the Citadel are feeling as you and I do and a few are already trying to make things change. Trouble is, you can't go round discussing that sort of thing because you'd pretty soon be accused of evil enchantment and the High Lord's got some nasty ways of dealing with that."

"Some people trying to make what change?"

"Making it possible for others to see beyond what the High Lord says and ask questions. Particularly us Scholars I think."

"Haven't noticed it."

"No, but I have. That's the other bit I've got to tell you. In the library sessions we've been having, some of the Masters have been secretly showing me books and papers from the past which look very different from the 'glorious High Lord' stuff we've been taught as the wonderful truth. Evil enchantment, for instance. I've seen something which makes me think that it all started with a chance remark to the High Lord by one of the early Lords. He's found it very useful, because it's almost impossible to prove you're not enchanted if he's there to twist anything you say and make it prove you are."

"Master Garrid would damn you to hell and back if he heard you say that."

Tamlyn hesitated; then he came to the conclusion that if he'd decided to trust Hallam he should do it properly. "I haven't got any proof, but I think he's one of the Masters feeding me this other stuff. Greenwell, too; he's sort of hinted things to me, and he knows Merla. The other one might be... don't shout... Sharkley."

It was just as well he'd warned Hallam in advance, for he nearly choked over these names. "Greenwell, yes, I can believe that, but Garrid and Sharkley?"

"Well, they've been the supervisors when there's been other reading tucked inside the book I'm given. Of course, I can't tell if they're all in it or if one of them's a spy for the High Lord."

"Hmm. Difficult. But listen, Tam, how come you're in on all this yourself anyway? And what's it all leading up to?"

"I simply don't know why me. I've asked myself that over and over. Merla says she knows I'm important in some way but not how, except that I love this land. As to where we're going, I get the feeling that we're meant to change the whole system."

Hallam snorted. "And for our next trick? How do we go about that? Any ideas?"

"It's wait and see, I think. Merla seems to say that things will happen and we'll know what to do when the time comes."

They sat in silence until Hallam said soberly, "Thank you Tam. I should have known you better, and I'm really sorry about what I said. I'm with you all the way, whatever."

"It's been great to tell you. We'll hang together and see what comes up. One thing though, if you ever use that D word again I might just whack you even harder!"

"Certainly shan't risk that," Hallam laughed, tenderly feeling his forehead.

They wandered back down the hill together, Tamlyn feeling more relaxed than for weeks now that it was two of them. Part of him longed for some peace and quiet for a bit, but he also hoped something would happen fairly soon so that he could prove to Hallam that he really was included. Not that he could do much about it either way, whatever 'it' was.

Chapter 13

Three days dragged by. Hallam relented and sorted out Tamlyn's maths, with a threat to take him right back to 'one-plus-one-equals-two' before long.

"I suppose I have to believe you've got a brain, so the only reason you act like a frightened rabbit at the sight of a row of figures must be because you've got a gap somewhere. Sort of like having a wonderful bow and top class arrows but no bowstring."

"Thanks very much, I don't think," snorted Tamlyn. "How much do you charge for your advice, Master Mathman? Next time you can't tell a root from a rhizome I'll remember your methods."

They were on the way down for the next library session. Tamlyn thought Hallam was probably more excited than he was, though he always wondered what he'd discover. They were a bit late, so surprised to see the rest of the sixth year still outside the library doors.

"What's the hold up?" Hallam demanded. There was a general shrugging of shoulders and mutters of "Dunno" . The time ticked by until Master Sharkley came round the corner. Tamlyn was surprised, for the Master was a rigid time-keeper but then he saw the teacher's face, pale, tense, and looking as though he might explode at any moment. He carried a large pile of books.

"I'm sorry, sixth years," he said in a voice that was nearly but not quite his usual sharp tone. "I imagine it will not cause inconsolable grief on your part, but this session has had to be cancelled. You may dismiss and count this as a free period until your next lesson. You will be informed of further library sessions. Off you go. Oh, Scholar Tamlyn, a moment, if you please."

"See you," Tamlyn muttered as he and Hallam exchanged glances. Master Sharkley waited until the corridor was empty and the sound of voices and footsteps had died away, then he slumped slightly from his usual alert stance.

"Scholar Tamlyn, a one word answer will suffice. Do you keep notes from these sessions?"

"No sir."

"Good. It is better to train your memory than to rely on pen and paper which can be... mislaid."

"I understand, sir." And he did. Master Sharkley was warning him, and he felt a shiver at what the reason for this might be. The teacher opened the library doors and looked around inside, then he turned back to Tamlyn.

"I know you find Master Greenwell's classes suit your own pursuits very well. He has, I believe, a number of books and if you were careful with them you might perhaps continue your studies using them. Now I must return these to the library. Good day to you."

Tamlyn stood staring at the closed library doors. What had all that meant? How had Master Greenwell come into it? Did Sharkley know what Master Greenwell had said at his interview? More worrying was the suggestion of carrying on by studying with books, which seemed to imply a long absence. Where was Master Greenwell? He moved slowly away while he was in this public part of the Citadel, then raced up to his room. As he expected Hallam was there.

"Did he say anything?"

Tamlyn repeated what had passed between him and Master Sharkley. "He looked very upset. If anything's happened to Master Greenwell and they really were doing something together, it might be bad for him as well," he reasoned. "I wish we could be sure what's going on."

"I reckon we'll hear before long. Not many things stay completely secret in this place," said Hallam, and he was right. Long before supper time it was common knowledge that Master Greenwell had been taken by the Citadel Guard in the early hours of the morning. Though there were varying theories about why, no one liked to suggest exactly where he'd been taken. It wasn't really hard to guess, but never wise openly to mention the High Lord in such a connection.

Tamlyn was deeply upset by the news. He felt sick at the idea of the gentle and friendly man in the hands of the inner circle of the Guard. Those Guards who did general duties like night watch were generally quite amiable, but the members of the elite band were feared with good reason. He and Hallam talked round in circles, getting nowhere, until Tamlyn suddenly thumped his head with both fists.

"Stupid, stupid, stupid," he berated himself.

"Having stated the obvious, why exactly?"

Tamlyn told Hallam in more detail what had happened during his earlier interview with Master Greenwell. "He must have guessed this might happen. He said I was to get his books, and I would know when. Oh why didn't I think of this before. We could have gone straight away this morning when we suspected something. That's probably what Sharkley was hinting at, not help with my work but get the books. He could hardly walk in himself could he? Especially if he might be a suspect as well?"

"Might have looked a bit odd if you'd gone marching in, too. Greenwell could just have been in bed with a bad head cold."

"Oh I could have thought up a reason for that. Can we go now, do you think?"

"Nope. Too many people about and anyway how many books has he got, d'you know? Carrying them might be a problem. Also we'll have to hide them. I don't know what the Guard are accusing Greenwell of but I guess they'll go through all his things and be suspicious if there aren't any books. That means you can't just shove 'em on your shelf, because who do you think they might decide to look at next? Teacher's favourite."

Tamlyn stared at his friend, and shuddered. "You're right. I'd have gone barging in without thinking all that through. I still want to do something quickly though. And we should somehow let Merla know; she's his friend."

Though tricky, they decided they could try to tackle this last problem at once while they considered ways to get the books. They hoped it would be possible at supper time to tell Lyddy they wanted to see her, so Tamlyn wrote a note on a small scrap of paper – 'See you? Henhouse. Usual time. T & H.' – then folded it still smaller. They peered into the refectory to make sure Lyddy was behind the serving counter, waited till the long queue of students were all at the tables eating, then strolled up last to be served themselves. Hallam managed to have difficulty with keeping his knife and fork on his tray and stood masking Tamlyn as he quickly passed the note and Lyddy scooped it into her apron pocket in an instant. By the time they sat down Tamlyn's hands were shaking, but as they scraped up the last of their prune pastry later their table was empty and Lyddy was able to nod to them as she cleared plates.

They went to their own rooms having decided to act as normally as possible, and Tamlyn tried, without success, to tackle some homework. It was for the history Master, and he couldn't bring his mind to concentrate properly on what he now thought were quite possibly lies. Thank goodness his school days would be coming to a close in a few months, and whatever he might be doing after that, he hoped that particular charade would be unnecessary. He shifted himself onto his bed and considered another puzzle; why was he feeling more nervous working with Hallam than he did on his own? It wasn't that he didn't trust his friend; it just seemed strange to have to add an extra layer to his thoughts. Up to now he'd had to think, decide, and act in swift succession without consulting anyone, but now plans would be discussed. Being one of a pair somehow meant that things, right or wrong, weren't completely in his hands. Even so he decided he was glad he'd brought Hallam in, especially with the possibility of tangling with the Guards.

Hallam joined him, and when they judged enough time had passed they carefully let themselves out through the northern door and crept round to the hen houses. Lyddy hadn't arrived so they stood quietly in a sheltered corner, listening to the subdued clucking of the hens as they settled down on their roosts for the night.

"Phew! A bit smelly," Hallam whispered, poking around at the bottom of the fencing.

"Prefer the pigs? They'd probably think we'd brought an extra feed and disturb the whole neighbourhood with grunts and squeals."

At that moment Lyddy appeared and Tamlyn hastily introduced Hallam, explaining he'd taken Merla's advice in trusting his friend.

"Ah, the ever hungry Scholar." Lyddy bobbed Hallam a curtsey and smiled sweetly at him. He looked momentarily astonished, but recovered sufficiently to bow in return.

"Well now, what do you want? The evenings are getting lighter so it's not the best of times and places to have a meeting."

"Sorry, Lyddy, but we wanted to tell Merla that Master Greenwell has been taken by the Citadel Guard, the Elites," Tamlyn told her. "I know she's his friend and that she was afraid he was putting himself in danger."

Lyddy looked sad. "I was taking that news to Merla now anyway, though it's possible she's heard already."

"And you knew," Hallam exclaimed. "How?"

"Oh, we know most of what goes on in the Citadel, us Donkeys. We go everywhere – cleaning, mending, tidying, feeding – and we're so commonplace we're like part of the furniture. Usually no one gives a thought to the fact that we do have ears and may be using them."

Tamlyn had just had an idea. "There is another thing. Master Greenwell asked me to take his books if something happened to him, and we're going to try to do that. Problem is, we can't think of a safe place to put them. Can you help at all?"

Lyddy looked thoughtful. "I don't... oh, maybe you could... yes. You know where you come up the last bit of the secret passageway Tam? Where you have to slither out on your stomach? That cavity goes further in, behind the top of the chimney, and makes a sort of shelf. That should be safe."

"Great, thanks, Lyddy, that's perfect. Now it's just a case of getting the books out of Master Greenwell's room."

"Be careful, Tam," Lyddy said softly, touching his hand. "And you, Hallam. Not too many second helpings either now if you're going to use that passageway or you'll get stuck." She gave him a dig in his midriff. "I must go. If you want to contact me now, make an excuse to come to the kitchen in the afternoon before the others come back to prepare the evening meal. I'm usually there on my own, sewing and mending. If it's not safe I'll talk Donkey, so be prepared to act accordingly." She gathered up the basket she'd set down and started away, then turned and hurried back. "If I want you, I'll do something unusual when I'm serving you. Haven't thought what but you'll know," she said, and was off again.

"Does she go all the way to the village at night on her own?" asked Hallam. "Bit dangerous for a girl."

Amused at his friend's sudden burst of protective gentlemanly behaviour, Tamlyn shook his head. "I don't think anyone out there would touch her. She lives with Merla," he said.

Later they sat in Tamlyn's room, both of them dishevelled and dusty. Hallam had managed to scrape his nose on the way back, but was highly delighted at coming through the secret passage. He also declared he'd had an idea.

"Tell then," demanded Tamlyn who'd been unable to think of anything himself.

"It'll be best if you go in to Master Greenwell's room because you know it better than I do, and where things are. I'll hang around in the corridor. If anyone comes I'll whistle to warn you and try to cause a diversion. You can sneak out while I do that. Or hide I suppose. Have to play that last bit by ear."

"Good," agreed Tamlyn, though he couldn't imagine what sort of diversion Hallam could produce at this time of night. "I've been trying to remember; I reckon Master Greenwell's books will fit in two satchels, so if you let me use yours, that should do it."

Tamlyn got the keys he'd been given, slung the satchels across his chest and they were off. It was very quiet as they crept down to Master Greenwell's room on the ground floor, although Tamlyn could hear his heart beating so loudly that he felt it must be heard. The key turned, the door opened and he was in. He closed it silently – an open door, especially this one, would look suspicious if anyone should pass – and got his bearings. As Hallam had said, he knew the room well, and by the small amount of light from the window he made his way across to the Master's desk and shelf. Rapidly he took the books down. More than he'd thought, but he managed to divide them between the two satchels and stuffed in an envelope which had been flat against the wall behind the books. It was the only other thing left there. Almost done, he thought, drawing a deep breath. He'd just got back to the door and had his hand on the latch when he heard Hallam whistling shrilly, as though he was calling a dog. He moved close to the door so that if it was opened he'd be behind it, and stood with his ear pressed to the wood, listening

"Oy! What are you up to down here, this time of night?"

"Sorry, Sergeant, I know I shouldn't be, but you'll never guess what I've just seen. See, I suddenly remembered I'd left my cap down in the refectory, and I didn't want anyone to walk off with it in the morning so I came and got it."

"Yeah? You're a long way off the refectory here."

"I know, but this is the amazing bit. I was going back when I suddenly spotted a fox in the corridor with a hen in its jaws. Trotting along as calm as you please. I started to follow it, and it ended up going this way. I whistled it, like you would a dog. You probably heard me. Daft, I suppose, but I wondered if it would respond. All it did was turn and look at me, then run off down here a bit faster. Look, you can see the hen's feathers on the floor. It might be hiding round the corner if it hasn't found a way out. Let's have a look."

"Right." The Guard's tone had changed to interest. "Priggin' animals get everywhere. Bet those fools left a door open in the kitchen. Come on then. Might even get a bird for my dinner tomorrow."

Tamlyn heard the footsteps and voices fading. He eased the door open, checked the corridor was clear and bolted, remembering just in time to re-lock the door. The satchels were heavy and banged against him as he ran, but he didn't stop till he reached his room. He was beginning to worry about Hallam when his friend walked in too and flung himself on the bed with a broad grin on his face.

"Hal, that was brilliant."

"Yeah. Worked a treat, didn't it? Amazing how being frightened half to death gets the brain working. You got the books out, didn't you? Couldn't work that one again."

Tamlyn pointed to the two bags. "But what on earth was that about feathers?"

Hallam felt in his pocket and held up a few hens' feathers. "Picked up several handfuls down by the hen house when we were waiting. Lots of 'em, blown up against the fence. I like feathers, really clever, their design; so mathematically organised. You can pull them apart, then stroke them and they hook together again. I was going to have a proper look at them in the daylight, but most have gone to a better cause. I scattered 'em before the Guard turned up."

"I nearly wet myself when I heard you whistle!" Tamlyn admitted. "If I'd been on my own and the Guard had tried the door I'd have been found 'cos it was unlocked."

"Think we'd better stow the books now, while we're on the job?"

"Sooner the better," Tamlyn agreed. "Let's have a look first though, to see if there's anything odd."

Nothing strange was apparent, but when Tamlyn checked the envelope he gasped. It was full of very thin sheets of paper, closely covered in Master Greenwell's writing, and the first one he looked at was something he'd read in one of the library sessions. He slid the pages back and put the keys there too, for safety. Then he added the envelope to the books.

"This goes too. Looks like he was making copies of the sort of stuff I've been reading from the library. "

They managed to hide everything with no more scares. They'd not used the passageway in reverse before, but Tamlyn crawled backwards under the slab and lowered his legs down the chimney so he could stand with feet wedged on the holds in it. Like this he had his head and arms above the top, and Hallam passed the books and envelope to him a few at a time. There was plenty of room for all of them.

"Better get some sleep now," Hallam said. "Soon be breakfast time. See you." He crept away towards his room and Tamlyn did the same. It felt very satisfying to get Master Greenwell's books to safety.

They were tired the next day, both admitting they'd lain awake going over what had happened. Luckily it was a fairly light day, but in the mid-afternoon Tamlyn realised he hadn't brought his work with him to give in at the next class with Master Jessal.

"Pity if I missed that, after all my hard work." He grinned at Hallam who aimed an easily dodged thump in reply. "I'll go up and get it. Apologise for me if I'm late, shan't be long though." He really hadn't got the energy to run, but as he climbed the last stairs he heard a noise from the direction of his room and quickened his pace. He swung open his door, and stared in complete shock.

"What are you doing?" Tamlyn's voice came out flat and expressionless. His eyes took in first the man with the silver Z-shaped badge on his grey uniform, then his wrecked room.

"What d'you think I'm doing, sonny? Searching your room o' course."

Fury rose in him in an explosion of hate for this... this *thing* that had invaded and ruined his home, his territory. His muscles tensed to spring, his hands bunched to hit and hit again until he'd killed it... A voice from deep below this turmoil said, 'No'. Somehow the strength came to obey.

"And what for, can you tell me?" His voice was still level, and barely above a whisper.

"Evil enchantments. What else? You dim or something?"

"Evil enchantments can be found in a plant pot, can they?"

The man looked down at the pot whose contents he'd been tipping onto the chaos of smashed and ripped things scattered over the room.

"Yeah, find 'em anywhere if you look hard enough," the man sniggered

"Oh well, keep looking. Do let me know if you find any. As far as I know there's been no evil in this room. Until this moment."

The Guard stared at Tamlyn and Tamlyn stared back. The Guard's eyes dropped first.

Tamlyn turned and walked away, and the Guard stood looking puzzled for a minute, as though trying to work out Tamlyn's words. Then he shrugged, tossed the pot down and left the room, sheathing his knife.

Tamlyn didn't remember getting back to the classrooms. The next thing he was aware of was opening the maths room door. It all went silent, everyone staring at him.

"I'm sorry, Master Jessal, my homework has been destroyed." He sat next to Hallam and stared into nothing.

"Scholar Tamlyn, you look, um, rather unwell. Would you like to take a little time off and have a rest?"

Tamlyn simply got up and walked out again. With no recognisable thought behind it, his feet took him to the privy room they'd used in the first and second years. He sat on one of the closed lids, back stiffly upright, fists clenched on his knees. A moment later the door opened again and Hallam entered.

"Saw you come in here, Tam. Jessal sent me after you. What the hell happened?" He laid a hand on Tamlyn's shoulder and squeezed gently.

"I wanted to kill him. It felt like... I was... nothing but hate and anger. Never thought I could feel like that. Worse than when I went for Bartoly. Every bit of me wanted to kill him."

"Kill who?"

Suddenly the tension that had been holding Tamlyn rigid snapped. He dropped forward, his head in his hands. "My plants, my books, my room," he wailed.

Hallam squatted in front of him. "Tell me, Tam," he said softly.

"Guard in my room, one of the Elites," he managed at last. "Searching for evil enchantments, he said, but smashing up's more like it. Everything. Books, clothes, bedding, and all my plants. Hallam, I've never believed I could actually want to kill someone, but I did him. I wanted to tear him into a million pieces." Tamlyn subsided into another wail.

"Tam, by the sound of it any one would have felt like that; I know I would. The thing is, you didn't do it, did you? So it strikes me you should be proud of yourself, because that would have been a particularly daft thing to do to with an Elite Guard. Now listen, the little 'uns'll be coming out of class soon, so unless you want to be surrounded by pint-sized nippers needing a pee, we'd better move. Let's go up to my room for privacy, come on."

Rather more aware of himself and his surroundings, Tamlyn got up. "Sorry, Hal. You're missing your favourite lesson," he said, but was glad to flop down on Hallam's bed when they got there.

"I've got something to do. Back soon," Hallam said briefly. Tamlyn sat against the pillows and made himself think about the last half hour. He'd over-reacted again hadn't he? Like he had with Bartoly and when Rufus was killed. Both times he'd felt such anger, such a furious desire to retaliate. That was what made it all so unbearable; he realised: not so much the cause of his anger but the fear that he might not control it, the fear of being responsible for another person's death.

But Hallam – kind, funny, and above all level-headed Hallam – had looked beyond that thought. 'Any one would feel like that... The thing is, you didn't let yourself do it,' he'd said. And that was the important part: not that he'd wanted to kill in a moment of rage, but that he'd not done it. He must hang on to that – keeping control – and not let the fear of killing overwhelm him, or else everything else might be lost in stupid panic. Tamlyn went to stand at Hallam's window and promised himself he *would* do this, somehow.

"All sorted." Hallam bounced in looking pleased with himself. "Good. You look human again, Tam. Really got to you didn't it?"

"Silly really, wasn't it? We knew they might… what d'you mean, sorted?"

"Well, I had a look at your room. I totally agree it's enough to make anyone want to commit murder. Then I trotted downstairs to visit the little lady."

"Lyddy?" Tamlyn was startled.

"Yeah. Lucky thing, she was alone. I told her the story and she's organising a clean-up for you."

Tamlyn didn't know whether to laugh or cry. Who but Hallam would have managed that in what felt like ten minutes?

"You're fantastic," he said, giving his friend a hug.

"We-ell – I didn't really fancy sharing a single bed with you, did I? Let's go down and show people you're alive and in your right mind. Might as well let them know about your room because they'll find out sooner or later anyway. They'll assume it was because you and Greenwell got on well, I bet. Also I'm remarkably hungry."

Tamlyn thought Hallam would deserve any second helpings he could get this evening. "Isn't it…" he began, as Hallam started, "Lucky we…" They laughed and Tamlyn finished, "…a good thing the books weren't in my room."

"Exactly what I was going to say," said Hallam.

Chapter 14

Tamlyn lay on his back, dreamily watching small puffs of cloud scurrying like anxious sheep across the sky. What could they see below them that they were in such a hurry to get away? Would they find new blue fields to browse in, or would they merge and re-form into rainclouds and fall to earth? It would be wonderful to travel so quickly and smoothly, he thought, although you'd have to choose the right wind. These clouds were scudding towards the west and he'd like to sail the other way, above the mountains, to see what lay beyond.

He was lying in a grassy hollow halfway up Herder's Hill, waiting for Hallam. He still found it difficult to understand how his friend could choose to stay indoors with Master Jessal on such a wonderful morning, but he had to accept that solving the problems in pages of complicated numbers and symbols had the same attraction for Hallam as he found in discovering a plant he hadn't seen, or working out different uses for those he already knew.

Tamlyn patted the pouch at his waist. This morning he'd already found a patch of thyme, which he hadn't expected to see in this well-trodden area. His thoughts turned back to his room as they had so many times this week since the day it had been searched. He'd dreaded going back to it that evening, and was glad when Hallam walked up with him. He'd opened the door slowly to delay the moment, then they'd both let out a gasp. No sign of the chaos they had both seen earlier; at first glance it looked almost untouched.

"That is… unbelievable," said Hallam.

"How on earth did they do it?" Tamlyn wandered round, shaking his head. There were some ink stains on his desk and more, paler but just visible, on the wall behind it. Torn pages from his treasured books had been smoothed and neatly stacked, and he could stick most of them back together. He appeared to have new bedding, and a few of his clothes were missing, but most amazing of all, some of his plants had been re-potted and sat on the window sill as if they'd never been moved. He'd not yet managed to thank Lyddy, and several others as well he guessed. A quick thumbs-up gesture really didn't do it. During the week most of his clothes had returned too, mended and laundered. Such efficient care and kindness soothed the ragged edges left in his mind by the original attack.

"Having a snooze?" He hadn't heard Hallam coming.

"Nearly." In fact he *had* almost fallen asleep; it was so warm and comfortable up here on the hillside. "Did you manage to get a bit of lunch for me?"

Hallam felt in his pockets and produced a somewhat squashed ham pie, a chunk of crusty bread and a handful of early carrots, scrubbed but with their leaves still attached.

"Looks like the gardeners have been thinning these," he said. "Some idiots were complaining but I love them, all sweet and crunchy like this."

"Leave me a few then, I like 'em too. Thanks, Hal."

"I didn't see Lyddy. Heard one of the other servers say she'd had to go home. Hope she's all right."

"Guess we'll see her at supper. She probably thought she'd like a stroll in the sunshine," Tamlyn said easily, though Hal's news had started a small worry in his mind too. "This is just the sort of day to really enjoy the outdoors. Funny to think we were sliding on ice down there not that many weeks ago."

The boys idled the rest of the afternoon away, joking, laughing, and simply enjoying the day, but as they got up and started back towards the Citadel, Hal suddenly said, "It's almost too peaceful isn't it? Makes you wonder when... well when something else might happen."

"Yeah. It's not that I want bad stuff, but if change is coming as Merla says, and we're involved, I wish it would get on with it. It makes me imagine all sorts of impossible things. Mostly I'd like to know about Master Greenwell."

Hallam looked serious. "I've heard before of people being vanished, but when it's someone you really know... much worse then, isn't it?"

They were just reaching the place where their track crossed the village road when they saw Lyddy approaching. They were in full view of the kitchens and some upper rooms in the Citadel so they didn't greet her as they'd have liked, and nor did she pause. She simply glanced round as she came level with them and muttered, "Pig sties, ten minutes," and went on without losing a step.

"Shouldn't have mentioned getting on with it," Hallam said lightly, but Tamlyn could tell his friend was feeling the same tingle of apprehension and excitement as he was. They went in the main door near the kitchen area and ran up the stairs towards the refectory. Hallam collected his satchel from a cloakroom.

"Just time to dump this," he said.

"I'll take my thyme up. See you by the north door." They raced away up two different stairways.

The area round the pigsties seemed deserted, apart from the smell.

"Good place to meet, no one's going to come here from choice," Tamlyn said.

Lyddy came scurrying round the corner, looking less cool and collected than usual.

"I'm so glad I saw you; I was wondering how I'd be able to find you without letting half the Citadel know. Listen, I shall have to be quick. Merla got word from one of the village men who clean in the Guards' quarters. It's Master Greenwell, and it's bad."

Tamlyn felt his stomach lurch. "He's not… dead?"

"Perhaps better if he was, poor man. He's going to die anyway because the High Lord has declared he's 'incurably enchanted', and we think they're planning that horrible thing, where they throw him from the highest roof. Supposed to be a warning to others. Oh, it's so cruel." Lyddy's face crumpled briefly, and Tamlyn and Hal stared in horror.

"But what can we do? We don't even know where he is," Hallam said.

"We do. And there is a way to help, but it needs three of us. Are you willing?"

"Of course. How? Can we rescue him somehow?"

"No. We've heard he's badly hurt and couldn't move himself enough. They'd soon find him. Merla thinks the most we can do is to offer him a quiet, gentle death before they drag him out as an example. She gave me this, Tam." Lyddy pulled a glass phial from her pocket. It was full of a blood red liquid, and Tamlyn guessed at once what is was.

"Tache-de-sang," he whispered.

Lyddy nodded. "And nightshade," she added. "Two minutes, and he'll be at peace. Will you take it and offer it to him if he wants it?"

Tamlyn gulped. In some ways this was worse than asking him to kill, but the alternative was so appalling. He nodded, unable to speak.

"That's poison," Hallam stated bluntly. "Better than the other though." His face was pale and set. "What's the plan?"

"He's in the cell in the lowest level. Do you know it? Tamlyn and Hallam both shook their heads.

"The entrance is pretty well hidden. There's a Guard on duty by a locked gate, then a passage down to this cell, also locked. The Guards obviously think it's completely safe, but what they don't know is that there is a way out beyond the cell into the bathing area. Merla says in her childhood the place was used for drunks who were causing trouble, to let them sleep it off. In the morning they'd take them out through this other door and clean them up before they went home."

"Another secret passage," Hallam suggested.

"Not really, just a door. The only problem is that it can only be opened from the bathing side; that's why we need three of us. I can distract the guard at the top entrance, while Tamlyn goes in through the other. We have to have you in the bathing room, Hallam, because that door must be kept shut. It would be too obvious if it was propped open. Once Tam has gone in you must open the door at intervals when the bathroom is empty to let him out again. Can you do this?" They both agreed at once, and Lyddy told them to meet her in the bathing area after the Night Guards came on duty.

Neither of them felt like eating much at supper time, though Hallam said they should try.

"If I'm going to be sick with fear I prefer to have something to throw up," he said with an effort at jokiness, but thoughts of what might happen in the night weighed heavily on both of them. The evening dragged by, but eventually it was time to go down to the bathing room with towels slung over their shoulders as cover. Tamlyn had the phial wrapped in a cloth and tucked in his pocket. Lyddy was there already, sorting dirty clothes and towels into piles.

"Over here," she murmured, pointing to a corner of the cave-like room behind them. There was no sign of the latch, but when she guided

Hallam's hand to the right place it worked in much the same way they'd learned to get out of the passage upstairs. A vertical crack appeared and it was possible to open the door more fully by putting finger tips into this space and pulling. Lyddy made Hallam do it several times to be sure.

"Count up to three hundred slowly before you go in. I need time to deal with the Guard," Lyddy whispered. "Good luck." She gathered a pile of used towels and went. They took off some of their clothes in order to look as though they were simply there to bathe should anyone come, but nobody did. Three hundred seemed a long time, but also far too short. Hallam put his fingers into the door catch, and Tamlyn closed his eyes and took a deep breath.

"I'm ready," he whispered.

"I *shall* open the door Tam, but I might have to wait if anyone comes," Hallam reminded his friend, and squeezed his arm. He pulled the door open and Tamlyn went in. At first it seemed completely dark once the door closed, but he screwed his eyes shut for a few seconds and when he reopened them he could make out the glimmer of a tiny torch flickering in a bracket on the wall to the left ahead. As he edged forward he found bars on the right, and beyond the bars... He dropped to his knees, forcing himself not to cry out. Master Greenwell lay on a tattered, stained cloth on the rocky floor, near to the bars. Even in this dim light Tamlyn could see bruises and slashes all over his body. A hand hung at his side, all the fingertips bloody, and a foot was twisted into an unnatural position. Tamlyn thought he must be dead already, until he heard a harsh breath and a low moan.

He could hear voices ahead – a man's and Lyddy's – laughing together, so he dared to whisper, "Master Greenwell."

The man's head turned slowly and one eye looked at him. The other was swollen shut.

"Tamlyn?"

It was barely audible, but something lit in that battered face as Tamlyn said, "Yes." Slowly and painfully Greenwell rolled still nearer to the bars. Tamlyn put a finger to his lips, and gestured towards the door to stop him from making too much noise.

"Was careless... they found a page. Not good at secrets. Haven't talked though. All I wanted... to let others know... perhaps we could change… but he's evil… sat and watched them hurt me, waiting for me to speak. I didn't." The words tumbled out in gasps, as though he must say them while he could.

Tamlyn reached through the bars and gently took one of Greenwell's bloody hands in his. "We'll let others know for you, Master. There are others now who see and know. Merla believes change is coming, and it will, I'm sure."

"Merla's good… listen to her."

"I do, sir. We've tried to think how to help you, but there's not much… I'm so sorry, this is all wrong."

"You're a good boy, Tamlyn. Don't worry." There was a moment as pain seemed to shake him, but he went on, his voice a little firmer as though Tamlyn's presence had strengthened him. "I'm just so frightened of tomorrow. It's silly, but I'm terrified of heights. Not worried about death… I'll welcome it. Lying here wishing myself dead… didn't work as you see." Greenwell's mouth twisted in a tiny smile, and Tamlyn could only give his hand a gentle squeeze; there was nothing he could say.

The Master went on. "Always have feared going up even a little way. Room's ground floor. I'm so scared that I'll crack and tell them something when they drag me up there. If only I *could* die now."

The moment had come. Tamlyn pulled the phial out, pushed the stopper from it and showed his teacher. "Merla sent this. She said… if you wanted… oh, it's so horrible."

Again he couldn't go on, but he saw Master Greenwell's face change. In spite of all the damage he suddenly looked happy.

"That is… the best thing… thank you… thank her. Please…" He tried to reach out, but his strength failed. Tamlyn stretched an arm through the bars and slipped it under the Master's shoulders to raise him slightly. With his other hand he held the glass to his lips and tilted it gradually. Greenwell drank it all, greedily, and sank back with a little sigh.

"*Tache-de-sang?*" he said, almost conversationally.

Tamlyn nodded. "And nightshade. She said it would be… quick."

"I can feel it already. It is an ending I couldn't have hoped for just now. Then you came… will you stay a moment?"

Tamlyn took the shattered hand in his again. "I'll stay. I've got your books safe like you said. I don't know what's going to happen next, but we will go on. You were so brave. I'm sure others have seen, but you did something…" He heard a tiny sigh, and the hand in his went limp. He laid his own hand on Greenwell's chest; there was no heart beating there. With one finger he closed the eye that was visible, returned the bottle and stopper to his pocket and stood up.

"Goodbye," he whispered, and backed away to find the door.

It seemed an eternity, waiting there. If the guard looked in he would see no change in his prisoner, but would he be able to see the figure crouched beyond? Tamlyn hoped the brighter light in that outer corridor would blind him to anything back where he was, but he kept motionless, hardly breathing, until he felt the crack opening and almost rolled out.

Hallam helped him up. He had obviously been in the water and was dripping.

"Quick, get your things off and into the water," he said urgently. "One of the office men came to check if the pool was free. I said my friend was just relieving himself, but we'd be gone soon. Didn't want to leave you stuck in there while they bathed. He's gone to get some others."

Tamlyn moved quickly, and the two of them were climbing out of the water when the man returned with three more.

"Just off," Hallam said cheerily, as they quickly rubbed themselves, and struggled to pull shirts and trousers on over their half-dried bodies.

"Scholars aren't you? Bit late for this," one of the men remarked.

"Got stuck into some maths work. Thought we'd freshen up before we went to bed. Sunday tomorrow, remember, we can sleep in. Good night." Hallam took Tamlyn's arm and marched him away. "Come up to my room, you can tell me then," he said when they were far enough away.

Tamlyn did. He felt unbearably sad, but realised he wasn't upset about what he had done.

"It was so peaceful, Hal. He really wanted to die and welcomed it. He just went, between one moment and the next, and he had a smile on his face."

"He was really brave. Not sure how I'd cope in his situation," said Hal. "Funny really, he never struck me as having that in him. Not that I imagined this, but you know what I mean."

"Suppose you never know until you have to find out," said Tamlyn.

Hallam found some biscuits he'd secreted from the refectory, and they nibbled them with water from his jug. "Better try and sleep I suppose. Wonder where Lyddy is. She must have done a good job on that Guard, don't you think? No panics tonight. Strange, isn't it? Merla said to me on the day I got the *tache-de-sang* for her, that it can be right to help people die. I didn't really believe her, but it's true. Master Greenwell welcomed it with... well, almost with joy." He paused for a moment. "But I also feel that if I got the chance, I'd slaughter the men who did that to him, without turning a hair, including the High Lord! Not tonight though."

"Count me in," said Hallam grimly. "But as you say, another time."

Chapter 15

'All Masters and Scholars will attend in the great hall before classes this morning.' The notice was displayed in every classroom on Monday morning, and there was a great deal of discussion as to the reason for this unusual assembly. Masters hustled the youngest Scholars into orderly lines and led them up the wide stairs to the hall, while the fifth and sixth years followed behind. A few suggestions were made, most of them ridiculously optimistic on the lines of longer holidays or cancelled homework, but mainly there was complete puzzlement. Only Tamlyn and Hallam exchanged wary glances, fearing they knew all too well what it might be about.

The Scholars sat in the central body of the hall, while the Masters gathered in seats at each side. Gazing round as they waited, Tamlyn saw that Master Sharkley was looking in his direction. For the briefest of moments their eyes met, and he had the weird feeling that the Master was trying to say something without words, but then he turned and spoke to Master Garrid who was sitting behind him. A number of Lords entered and took places in the ranks of seats that curved upwards behind the platform.

"What's going to happen?" Hallam muttered at his side, but Tamlyn couldn't have given an answer even if he'd had one, for at that moment a man in dark green robes came through a door at the right and announced, "All rise for the High Lord,"

Everyone did so, though a few of the youngest Scholars at the front had to be poked. Either they were too overawed to move, or they were busy playing flicksticks on the polished wood of the bench seats. Tamlyn rather hoped it was the latter.

Zerac, the High Lord, came onto the stage from the side entrance. He was dressed sombrely in dark red trimmed with silver grey, and a black velvet cloak draped across his shoulders billowed out behind him as he moved. Tamlyn had to admit he was a striking figure. His black hair was still thick, with only an elegant streak of white at either temple. The same showed in his trimmed moustache and pointed beard, but there was little sign of age in his face; the skin was still taut over high cheekbones and an aquiline nose. If there was any drooping beneath his chin it was concealed by the starched and pleated collar of his white shirt. Tall and upright, he walked slowly to the centre of the stage where he turned to face the Scholars and Masters.

"I have called you here on a very sad occasion," Zerac said slowly. His voice was not deep, but had a lilting, musical quality to it. Suddenly Tamlyn knew what was going to happen, and an icy chill ran through him.

"One of your Masters, a man who lived all his life in the community of the Citadel, is dead. Master Greenwell taught most of you I am sure, and his work as a teacher was well regarded by all who knew him. Sadly, in spite of the fact that I and my fellow Lords work without ceasing to prevent it, an evil enchantment crept in and attacked Master Greenwell, and we were unable to cure him of it. He died on Saturday night, and we must all hope he is at peace now. He will be buried tomorrow after the noon meal, and all those of you who knew Master Greenwell before he was so sadly struck down will, I am sure, want to be there to say goodbye. I am instructing the Masters to cancel any lessons planned at that time and for the rest of the afternoon."

The High Lord turned back and left the stage. As he walked Tamlyn noticed the silver studded Z on the side of his boot, and his whole body clenched as he remembered where he had seen that before. The Masters and Scholars stood, uncertain of what they should do next, but the Lords walked slowly after Zerac. When they'd all disappeared, the younger Scholars started to shuffle and whisper so the Masters led them out and back to the classrooms. The sixth years were timetabled with Master Jessal, and when they were settled in his room he stood at the front, white and visibly shaken. For several minutes he seemed unable to find any words.

Tamlyn, and he guessed Hallam too, though they hadn't dared even look at each other, was rigid with fury. That the man who had ordered and watched Master Greenwell's torture could put on this show of sadness and regret was so disgusting it made him feel sick. He must hide his feelings, he knew. The fact that his room had been searched by the Guards meant he must be suspected of sharing Master Greenwell's thoughts if only because people knew they had been friendly. Well, he did share them, but that must stay hidden until… Until what? Until the changes seen by Merla arrived. He just prayed it wouldn't be too long.

Master Jessal stammered out a few words of sadness for Master Greenwell's death. That he was truly shocked was obvious – surprised too, Tamlyn thought – and he was relieved that the Master said nothing about evil enchantments. He thought he might very well actually throw up if that happened. They had seen nothing of Lyddy since Saturday night and he started trying to think how he could let Merla and her know what the High Lord had said and done this morning. Well, they might actually know of course. Their lines of communication seemed very well organised.

Hallam nudged him, and he realised the maths lesson was now on-going. Luckily Master Jessal didn't pressure him, probably assuming that he was taking Master Greenwell's death particularly hard. He did his best for Hallam's sake. It must be infuriating to sit next to someone so painfully inept in a subject you found completely engrossing. He remembered being unable to comprehend how anyone could dislike botany.

They had free time before lunch and Tamlyn and Hallam joined the rest of the sixth year in their common room. They'd talked endlessly yesterday and didn't want to appear too exclusive. Tamlyn in particular was worried that he might be putting his friend in danger by too close an association with him, since he was probably under close scrutiny himself. He hadn't voiced this thought – he could guess how explosive Hallam's reaction might be if he did – but he determined to do everything he could to prevent anyone becoming suspicious.

Of course the talk was all of Master Greenwell. It was an exercise in imagination to keep up a show of bewilderment and surprise when he knew exactly what had happened, and he envied Hallam's ability to come up with easy sounding conversation when he must be feeling the same. Tamlyn remembered his friend's fluent and believable comments in the bathing area on Saturday night, and the fox and chicken tale with which he'd lured the Guard away and let him escape from Master Greenwell's room. Luckily, he'd never been as chatty as Hallam, and he could rely for a little while now on the other sixth year members assuming he would be the most upset.

He was very glad to hear the others, apart from Bartoly, all expressing varying degrees of amazement. They could not, of course, even hint at outright disbelief. That would be implying that the High Lord was telling lies – particularly dangerous with Bartoly there – but Tamlyn sensed a lot of sympathy for their teacher, and no one mentioned evil enchantment. Perhaps there really were others thinking as he and Hallam did, but he knew that things would have to change a great deal before anyone would speak those thoughts aloud.

The day went on, seemingly normally, although Tamlyn and Hallam felt they were living a double life. Openly they were the amazed and puzzled Scholars who had heard the news about Master Greenwell's death that morning, while underneath they were the only two who were full of fury, having seen what had been done to the man and who had helped him to die.

In the mid-afternoon, Tamlyn chased up to his room to fetch his green ink to lend to Kenley. He flung open the door and rushed in, to find himself hanging on to Lyddy who had been on the way out.

"Oops, sorry," he panted, letting go reluctantly. "Are you all right? I didn't expect…"

"I'm fine," she smiled. "Just brought your last shirt back." She pointed to it on the bed.

"I've wanted to thank you for all you did in here. It was amazing. And Saturday." Tamlyn's answering smile faltered. "It was all so horrible, but hearing your voice outside helped me know it was reality and not a nightmare. We wouldn't have known, couldn't have done anything if it hadn't been for you and Merla. I'm so glad we saved him from that last horror. You've heard what Zerac said?"

Lyddy nodded mutely, and Tamlyn saw there were tears in her eyes. "We must go," she said at last. "Can't have you consorting with a Donkey!"

"Don't say that. Please. It's horrible."

"It really doesn't bother me, Tam. And very often it's useful to be thought stupid. We call the men here Bulls you know – stupidly proud, fierce and angry – good for nothing but making babies."

Tamlyn had to laugh, though the reality behind this was not at all funny. "You go first, I'll come in a minute and use the eastern stairs. Thanks again, Lyddy." He checked the corridor was clear and she went. "Perhaps you'll bump into me again," she whispered as she passed him, and the day suddenly seemed a little less desperate.

The funeral was an ordeal. Tamlyn kept seeing Master Greenwell's broken and bloody body in the ornate coffin, carried to its place in the burial ground by elite Guardsmen in their dress uniforms. Were their everyday clothes still spattered with the Master's blood; did their downturned faces hide looks of cruel glee at what they had done? Tamlyn refused to even move his lips when they were asked to say goodbye. He'd said his goodbye at the moment of death. His only grim satisfaction was that they'd denied the tormenters their final orgy. When he went back to the grave that evening, he found a small posy of wild flowers lying on the freshly turned, bare earth. Was it from Lyddy and Merla, or had someone else done this as the only way in which they dared show their real feelings? It was so appropriate for the man who had loved the wildlife of The Land all his life. Standing there as the light faded he remembered his words as Master Greenwell died. 'We will go on'. He whispered them again, folding his sadness away as Merla had said, to fill himself with determination.

He found Hallam waiting for him as he walked back. "Thought I'd find you here," he said. "Now we've got to make sure he didn't die for nothing, haven't we?"

"I'll do anything," Tamlyn answered fiercely. "I believe Merla; we'll know the way when we see it."

Next morning a way appeared, though Tamlyn could see no chance that it could possibly help. As they were preparing for unarmed combat under Master Sharkley's stern eye, a man from the offices walked in.

"The High Lord wishes to see Scholar Tamlyn," he announced, and stood waiting while Tamlyn scrambled into his usual clothes. He could scarcely breathe, his heart was thudding so hard, and his suddenly numb fingers fumbled with his fastenings. Master Sharkley stood beside him, and bent to retrieve Tamlyn's satchel for him.

"Remember, take time to think before you speak," he murmured, his voice low enough that only Tamlyn heard. Tamlyn nodded, and left with the man. As he went out he caught Hallam's eye. His friend looked as panicky as he felt himself, but he gave him a wink. At least he'd know where Tamlyn had gone.

"Do you know what the High Lord wants?" he asked as they climbed through the levels of the Citadel, but the man made no reply. Finally they came to the High Lord's door. Tamlyn left his satchel against the wall and obeyed a 'come in' when he knocked.

He was aware of only one despairing thought as he entered. Sitting with Zerac were Lord Mansor and Lord Zaroth, the two men most likely to wish him ill. There'd be no going on now. This must surely be the end.

Chapter 16

Nothing had ever been as difficult as walking forward to face the three men. Tamlyn stopped in front of the High Lord and bowed.

"My Lord?" he said, and was pleased that his voice didn't quiver. Zerac was leaning back in his massive chair, his hands curved lightly on the wooden arms and his right foot balanced across his left knee. Tamlyn was aware that the other two men sat at ease on either side, but he kept his eyes on the High Lord. After a silence that seemed to last forever Zerac dropped his foot to the floor and leant forward, elbows on his knees and hands linked. He smiled.

"You will be wondering why I have summoned you, Scholar Tamlyn."

"Yes, my Lord."

"Feeling, perhaps, just a little afraid?"

'Think before you speak.' The words echoed in his mind. He took a breath and looked right back into Zerac's dark eyes. "To be summoned alone before the High Lord is an honour I have never had before so I am nervous, yes. I can find no reason for fear though," he said calmly.

"Well spoken, Scholar. I hear that you were one of Master Greenwell's best pupils. What did you think of him?"

In spite of guessing this would come up in some way, Tamlyn stiffened; he must choose his words so carefully here. "Master Greenwell taught me for almost six years, and he was an excellent teacher. I have always loved the wildlife of this land, and he encouraged me to explore and experiment. He was ready with help when I needed it. Except as a teacher I didn't really know him, but he was always pleasant with everyone in the classes I attended."

"You did not notice any change in him recently?"

"He seemed a little worn and worried sometimes, but I could say the same of all the Masters. It must be difficult not only to control us but to try and teach us too."

"So when you heard what had happened?"

Careful, careful. "It is hard to find the words, my Lord. I was horrified, and very sad that any man should come to that. I have to think that death was the only thing for him in the circumstances. Before this happened I don't think he would ever have hurt anyone, so the evil that took hold of him must have been very powerful indeed." There, he'd managed to tell the truth while seeming to do otherwise. He must hope that they wouldn't pick his sentences to pieces and see the mirror image within them.

"And can you suggest where this powerful evil came from?"

"Our studies don't cover that question in any depth. I can only suggest, my Lord, that you are far better equipped to answer it than I am."

Zerac leant back in his chair and considered Tamlyn thoughtfully, stroking his bearded chin with one forefinger. Then he sat upright quickly and tapped a sheaf of papers lying on a small table by his side.

"I have here all the question papers your school year filled in many weeks ago. You and your fellow Scholars may have thought it a useless exercise or that I had forgotten them, but I have been studying them carefully to find what I wanted. Some I dismissed at once: they showed little maturity for sixth years. Some so obviously gave the answers they thought were expected that I had no trust in their ability to think. In the end I came down to three, and of those I realised you were the one I wanted. Does that please you?"

"To be singled out by you is an honour in itself my Lord. To decide about pleasure I would need to know for what purpose that choice had been made."

Had he gone too far? Zerac gave a sharp, barking laugh and looked in turn at the two men beside him, tapping the papers again.

"You see, my lords, it is what I found here, and what some of the Masters detected also. A born diplomat who can answer convincingly yet keep much of himself hidden." The High Lord turned again to Tamlyn. "I asked you just now where you thought the evil enchantments came from, and you realised that my knowledge of the matter is deep. I am convinced that the King in the City is at the root of it all, and wishes to destroy us. Are you willing to undertake a mission to the City?"

Many possible reasons for having been summoned had passed through Tamlyn's mind before he entered this room, but this was not one of them. He stared blankly at Zerac.

"Take your time, Scholar. It would be a dangerous mission, but a great deed if you were successful."

"I've always thought that nothing would take me to a place which we have been taught is so deeply evil, but if you really consider me to be capable of what you require, then I am willing to do all I can to lessen that threat, my Lord."

"Well spoken again. Time will be needed for you to prepare for this. We'll send you a week from now, I think. During that time I will arrange various details – clothes, money, instructions and so on – so be ready whenever you are summoned. Obviously you have to give some account of what is happening, but you must simply say you are preparing to go on a journey on my behalf, no more. Do you understand?"

"I do, my Lord."

"Very well. Return to your classes now. I shall see you before you go."

Another bow, then Tamlyn managed to turn and walk out through the door, pulling it to behind him. He was reaching for his satchel, pausing as he did so to steady himself by leaning his head against the cool stone of the wall, when he realised he had not latched the door properly for it swung open slightly. He heard the harsh cackle of Zerac's laugh.

"I have him. I can still turn on the charm you see. He'll be no more trouble. Pity though, a nice looking lad, but too clever by far. I'd wager he's already asking awkward questions in his head, especially if Greenwell got to him. He could certainly be a danger later, so better out of the way now."

There were footsteps, and the door opened more fully. Tamlyn's heart nearly stopped but whoever it was paused there.

"You still plan to do it before he gets to the City?" Zaroth's voice.

"Oh yes. We can't rely on the good citizens to finish him off for us. Set up some of the guards in that copse by the bridge, no uniforms of course. They can have whatever money he has on him. So sad. Set on by robbers. Such a brave lad. Zaroth, you'll organise that."

"Certainly, my Lord."

"Mansor, you can instruct the boy on the use of real money, and give him a suitable amount that will satisfy the men."

Tamlyn had frozen, certain that Lord Zaroth would now come out and find him. His death would certainly be instant then, not in a week's time. He could scarcely believe it when he heard Zaroth speak again.

"Bother, I've left my gloves over there. I'm off to take Star out; he's not had a good gallop for days.

The door was pushed shut again. Tamlyn grabbed his satchel and bolted at top speed, only pausing to catch his breath when he was near the school area. At first as he ran he felt like a small animal escaping a predator, but by the time he reached the gymnasium he was consumed by anger. He was not going to walk meekly into this trap, not if he could help it. And he most certainly intended to help it. It felt as though hours had passed since he'd left the class, but incredibly it was still in session. He walked in calmly and, with a small bow to Master Sharkley, resumed his combat clothes. Twenty minutes of vigorous exercise into which he put every ounce of his energy calmed him down considerably, and he was able to start thinking more coherently about what he might be able to do.

Master Sharkley asked him to stay as the others walked out, and Tamlyn wondered, not for the first time, exactly where the teacher stood in what he was beginning to see as a much more divided and dangerous world than he had ever imagined. He would be a good ally, but very hard to deal with as an enemy.

"I'm not going to ask you anything, Scholar Tamlyn, but I'm quite good at identifying repressed rage when I see it. If there is any way in which I can help you deal with – well, shall we say a situation – I would be happy to do so. Off you go."

"Thank you, sir. I will think what... Thank you," he finished abruptly, and ran off to find Hallam outside the door.

"Well?"

"Not here, Hal. I've got to sort my head out, and there's such a lot to tell. Can we take a walk later?"

"Fine. I'm actually getting to like walking at long last. Want to skip chemistry this afternoon? Old Pargette will only be making loud bangs again. Think it's all he knows."

"Um… might be better not to break too many rules right now, especially the two of us together. After supper. The evenings are quite light now."

When they'd eaten they wandered up to what had become their talking place, and Tamlyn told Hallam all that had gone on in the High Lord's room. He was completely amazed.

"Trying to work out who could be sent to risk his life! Wonder who the other two were. If they knew they'd be delighted not to be picked I should think. D'you reckon you'll manage whatever it is he wants done in the City?

"Not a chance. I haven't told you the rest of it," Tamlyn replied, and let his friend know what he'd overheard through the open door.

Hallam exploded. "The evil, lousy, filthy, stinking pigs."

"I don't like them much either," Tamlyn said with a laugh.

"Lords above, I knew Zerac was foul because of Greenwell, but the others too! What are you going to do Tam? Get out while the going's good? Problem is, where to? We know the City's not a good place to be."

"Do we? We've been taught that, but I've been thinking. The High Lord dictates what we're taught, and how inclined are you now to believe him when he says someone else is evil?"

Hallam stared. "Oh," he said slowly, "Oh yeah. Hundred per cent against, I'd say. So what now? Are you going to try and get there then?"

"Well it sounds as though I'm going to be fitted out and given money, so I might as well make use of that. Yes, I think I'll go, see what it's really like."

"What about that welcome party they're planning for you?"

"Come on, Hal, when did you ever know me to stick to the beaten path?"

"You'll go another way. Of course. Do you know the land to the west?"

"Not much. That's something I'll have to try and find out. I'd really like to talk to Merla about it and everything else as well. I can't see how my going the City will do much good for what's going on here, but maybe it's all part of the coming changes she feels."

"Let's wander back down. We might spot Lyddy going home if we're lucky."

"Hello, Scholars, did I hear my name?" As though they'd somehow summoned her, Lyddy appeared and sat down beside them. "I heard you were called to the Big Bull's pen this morning Tam, then I saw you two coming up here. Is everything all right?"

"Is there anything you don't hear?" asked Hallam.

"Very little. But come on, Tam, what's happening? Are you in trouble?"

Tamlyn repeated the morning's events for her, and Lyddy looked horrified.

"I was hoping I might see Merla somehow. Get her advice," he added.

"Come tomorrow night, both of you" she said without hesitation. "Leave it till it's nearly dark, and come the back way. You know it, Tam. I'll tell Merla what you've told me so she'll have time to think. I'd better go now, or I might be seen." She started climbing briskly up the hill, but paused to call back softly, "Don't have too much supper tomorrow. We'll cook."

"Where's she going up there?" Hallam wondered.

"I'd guess she knows a hundred and one different ways home," Tamlyn said. "Useful if you might have anyone too interested in what you're doing. Come on, we can make it in before the Guards come on duty. We'll have to use the passage tomorrow evening so let's avoid getting covered in dust tonight. I think I'd like a word with Master Sharkley too."

They ran at top speed down the hill and arrived by the refectory out of breath.

"Phew. Think I'd better do some running practice," Hallam panted, bending over and holding his side as he got his breath back. "D'you want company to see Sharkley?"

"I think this had better be on my own. He offered me help if I wanted it with... how did he put it? With a situation. I can't quite make up my mind about him, Hal. What do you make of him?"

"Know what you mean, but I *feel* he's all right. He's a bit like you, actually, hard to tell what he's thinking, but he comes over as straightforward. You didn't look at anything but your toes at Greenwell's funeral, but I watched him and Garrid and I'd swear Sharkley was nearly in tears."

"Being afraid to trust anyone is horrible, isn't it? I think I've got to risk it. I'm going to see if he can give me some quick lessons in how to get someone down if they attack you, without ruining your own knuckles punching them to bits. More like just throwing them over your shoulder. He did mention that once. Would you be willing to join in a bit of extra combat training if he'll do it? Promise I wouldn't kill you!"

"Huh! You and how many others? I'm heavier than you."

"Scared are you?"

"Idiot. Of course I'll help. Just say when. Not tomorrow evening perhaps. Don't want to turn up at Merla's with an array of bruises do we?"

"Thanks. I'll let you know if he can help."

Master Sharkley answered Tamlyn's knock. "Scholar Tamlyn," he said as though he'd been expecting him. He opened the door fully and stood to the side. "D'you want to come in?"

The Master seemed different somehow. He was usually very formally dressed for classes, even when in combat clothes. Now he was in a loose, open-necked shirt with baggy trousers, and his feet were bare. He looked a lot younger, Tamlyn thought, and much less firmly official.

"Thank you, sir," he said, and walked into the room.

"Sit down. How can I help you?"

"This morning you offered me help, and I really would like some," Tamlyn started. "I've been told to say I'm preparing to go on a journey for the High Lord. It's not been mentioned but I think some of that preparation could usefully include a bit more knowledge of self defence. You once mentioned some skill where you use your opponent's movements to your own advantage rather than just trying to batter them to a pulp. That sounds more my sort of fighting, you know."

"Yes, I do know. How long have we got for this?"

"I leave in a week, sir,"

133

Master Sharkley threw his head back with a shout of laughter. "Tamlyn, I'm a teacher, not a magician. It takes months, even years to learn that sort of thing." He obviously saw the disappointment in Tamlyn's face for he went on. "However, if you're prepared to put in a few hours of really hard work, I could most likely teach you some basic moves which you'd find very useful, especially as the skill isn't known around here."

"How…" Tamlyn shut his mouth on the question. "Thank you, sir. I promise I'll work."

"I think you were going to ask how I know about it." Sharkley sat looking at Tamlyn in silence. After a long pause he seemed to make up his mind. "This is not something that many people here remember, or even know about, Tamlyn. I believe you are one of the very few students who could and would keep your word if you promised silence. Am I right?"

"Yes, sir, in nearly all circumstances."

"And what are your exceptions?"

"Torture, sir. I'm not sure how long I could last."

"I think we would all say that."

"And the other thing is that my friend and I are… working together. I must share what I know with him, but I'm sure he's safe too."

"I'm guessing you mean the ebullient Scholar Hallam. Well I've long thought he masks an extremely good brain behind his chatter and nonsense. That's a useful ability, so very well. Now I'm not telling you this simply to answer your unspoken question, though it was justified and shows you can think quickly. I also hope it may answer doubts which I'm sure you will have about me, for trust is in short supply here isn't it? You would be very stupid if you did not wonder, and I know you are far from stupid. I have not lived in this land all my life as almost everyone else has, but came to it years ago. I learned this skill we're speaking of before I arrived, in a land beyond the mountains in the east. I was young and wanted to see the world, and when I eventually came here I liked the place. I applied to the High Lord and managed to impress him with my abilities when I floored three of his guards who all came at me at once."

Tamlyn's mouth and eyes opened wide. "He'd certainly be impressed by that, but forgive me sir, I would have thought it might make him fear you too, and that can be dangerous."

You're right, but remember this was years ago. I made it clear that all I was interested in was teaching my skills and having reasonable pay and living conditions, which I've certainly had." The teacher paused for a moment, looking at Tamlyn in silence before he went on.

"If you are not the person I believe you to be I'm probably signing my death warrant with what I'm going to say next. However, I do feel I can trust you, as much as anyone can be trusted in this secretive and fearful society. Before I came here I visited several other countries, and learned that they all have their own ways, their own rules and government. When I arrived in The Land I thought it was a peaceful, rural and rather backward society which I enjoyed. I went on thinking that for a long while, and even when I began to see that things were not quite as picturesque as they seemed I didn't see any reason that I should be bothered about it. Then I learned several things which were truly nasty and I had to make my mind up what to do. At first I thought I might simply go elsewhere, but I've come to feel this is my home and that I should do something about the evil that has grown here. I'm sure you know that discussion of anything concerning the rulers of this land is highly dangerous, as poor Master Greenwell discovered. He was a very brave man, but not aware enough of the extreme care that must be taken when men like Zerac are concerned. I… miss him greatly." Sharkley bit his lips together and stared into nothing for a moment.

"Master Sharkley, as you said I did have doubts, but I believe what you say. Is there anything that can be done, do you think?"

"Not immediately. I feel the beginnings of change, but until people here believe they can be open safely there'll be little that's obvious. We must wait and be prepared when a chance comes."

"You sound like Merla. She thinks change is coming. Do you know her? She was Master Greenwell's friend."

"The Lady. I have not met her, but from what I heard from Greenwell and have seen of the efficient organisation of her people, she must be special, I think. Now about these lessons. How about a short session now? Would your friend Hallam be willing to join us? It's often a good thing if I can observe as well as demonstrating."

"That would be wonderful, and yes, I'll go and get Hallam. Thank you, sir. You make me feel there is hope."

"In the gymnasium then. I'll go and get the mats out to reduce the bruising!"

Chapter 17

"Ouch, I ache all over." Hallam grimaced as he bent to put on his shoes.

"All to benefit someone else, in other words, me. At least you've not got black eyes and a bloody nose," laughed Tamlyn. In fact he was feeling pretty battered himself, but he knew Hal had had to endure rather more thumping landings on his back while Sharkley demonstrated exactly how to do a throw and Tamlyn tried to copy him.

"I might get a bit more sympathy if the damage was visible, and I'm not sure I'll get up that funnel tonight, the state I'm in."

"I really do appreciate what you're doing," Tamlyn said, oozing mock sympathy. "Would you rather not come to Merla's then?"

"Are you joking? It's the thought of a really good meal that's keeping me going."

Sharkley had insisted that because time was so short they must have a practice before they went to their 'very important meeting'. The grin on his face as he said this suggested that he might have a good idea about what the meeting was. In three days the sharp tongued Master had changed amazingly when he was directing just the two of them. To start with he'd suggested that as Tamlyn and Hallam had all but finished their schooling they might as well all drop the use of 'Master' and 'Scholar' except when in regular classes. He was just as demanding when teaching them, but joined in their chat easily at other times.

It was a moonless night and they decided it was dark enough to set out for the village, so as soon as Hallam had finished getting into his shoes they crept upstairs then down again and out of the north door at the bottom of the stairs from Tamlyn's corridor. It was safer this way than going out near the gymnasium. They held it open until they'd checked nobody was around, then set off behind the hen coops and pigsties and up the hill to take the track that led them to the small copse behind Merla's house. Tamlyn gave a light tap on the door and Lyddy opened it at once.

"Come on in," she said quietly. "Food's just about ready. Hope you've got room for it."

"I'm starving." Hallam announced, sniffing the air appreciatively. "This extra exercise really gives me an appetite."

"Extra exercise?" Lyddy looked curious.

"Don't tell me there's something you don't know?" he asked in exaggerated amazement.

Merla came through to the kitchen and they were able to tell the two women about the combat lessons they were having.

"Greenwell had a very high opinion of Master Sharkley. That sounds like an excellent idea," said Merla. "I hope you're not relying on it to tackle the men who are planning to trap you though."

"I don't imagine I'll be up to that by next Wednesday," Tamlyn agreed. "It's one of the things I want to ask you about."

"Let's eat first. Everything's ready." Lyddy sat them down at the kitchen table and served out the delicious venison stew with mountains of fluffy mashed potatoes and chunks of warm bread. Hallam mopped his plate clean with his last piece of bread and sat back with a sigh.

"That was amazing," he said, "I'm full right up." Tamlyn agreed wholeheartedly, but they still managed their share of a creamy junket. Then Merla led them into the front room where they sat round the low fire. The nights still had a chill to them in spite of the warmer days.

"I'm glad Tam's asked you to join us, Hallam," she said. "A friend is so welcome when times are difficult, and if Tamlyn gets away to the City it will be good to know you are still here while he's gone."

"You think I'll be back then? I'm glad of that."

"You belong here, Tam," Lyddy said, and it gave him a tingle of pleasure to agree with those words.

"You wanted to ask about getting to the City safely, and that's something I can help you with, or rather Vitsell can. He knows every inch of The Land, from the mountains to the borders of the City's domain, and beyond. He'll lead you well north of the road and to within sight of the City walls."

"That's *so* good," said Tamlyn, feeling relief flood through him. "I intended to go by a different way, but I rarely walk far west of the Citadel so I didn't know which direction would be best. The only problem now is that I think I may have to set out on the road in case I'm watched."

"I've sent to contact Vitsell and we'll arrange a meeting place. There's a dip in the road a mile or so from the Citadel, that might be suitable. I'll let you know. Now so far you've no idea what Zerac's pretending you've got to do in the City have you?"

"I don't suppose it'll be serious since he's planning to have me killed before I get there," Tamlyn answered sourly.

"It will have to sound serious. He doesn't know that you're aware of his plans."

"Well I can't make any plans of my own because I've no idea of what I'll meet. I'll have to take it as it comes won't I? But I'd love to know what the City's really like. Have you ever been Merla?"

"I'm sorry, Tam, I may have gone as a baby, I don't know. I was only ten when Zerac came, and if I'd left The Land after that I doubt I'd have got back again. He keeps close watch on me, at least as much as I let him. He's scornful of all women, but he knows the people look to me."

Hallam had been leaning against the cushioned back of the settle, looking half asleep, but he now sat forward. "Tam and I talked about this. We've been taught since we could talk that the King is a wicked magician and that the City is a dark place full of his enchantments. It's been built into our brains, like knowing water is wet and ice is cold. But as Tam said, that's what the High Lord demands we should believe. Do we believe him now we're learning what he is?"

"That's well thought. I don't believe in magic, so I'm sure the King isn't a magician. He's probably no worse than any ruler, and may be better than some. You'll have to find out. We're not much help for you, Tam, but I have got one piece of very sketchy information. It's an old map."

"I'll get it." Lyddy jumped up and lifted a thick book down from the top of Merla's large cupboard. She laid it on the floor, opened the front cover and took out a folded, yellowing sheet. "Here it is," she said, handing it to Merla who unfolded it carefully and spread it out. Hallam and Tamlyn had little experience of maps; they knew The Land as far as they'd walked but had never needed more than their own eyes or spoken instructions to find their way about.

"It's a kind of picture of what a large bird would see from high in the sky," Merla explained. "There's not a lot on it, and some things may have changed; not the rivers and mountains though." She pointed to the right of the sheet. "These lumpy shapes are supposed to be the mountains, and here's our river, winding across to the west. This big spot is the Citadel, and the tiny speck nearer the river must be the village. Now can you see this other river coming down from the mountains in the north-east? It's not as wide as our river, but it runs swiftly because the slope of the land is steeper. It's harder to cross, but Vitsell knows where it's safe. This line is the road west from the Citadel, and where it crosses that other river is the bridge where they're planning to attack you."

Tamlyn and Hallam studied the page. Hallam was particularly fascinated. "It's like reality squashed onto a page," he said. "Look down there, Tam, right near the bottom. The two rivers join up, and where they make a sort of corner there are little houses. Is that the City? It looks like there might be a wall round it."

"That's it," said Merla. "The City once had a wall all round it, but Vitsell says there's only the bit left of it towards the east now. It's got so big that it's spread out in all directions except over the rivers."

"It's quite hard to think that into reality, but I have a feel of it now. When I see it in fact I think it will help me sort out where I am. Thanks Merla."

They talked on for a while until Merla said they needed their sleep, and shooed them on their way back to the Citadel.

"She's a bit like the crèche women used to be," Hallam said thoughtfully. "Nice."

"Or like having a real mother. That must be really good," Tamlyn said.

They crept in without any alarms, and Hallam managed the chimney climb, saying he thought the venison must have oiled his joints.

"See you in the morning," he whispered as they parted. "Shan't be able to say that soon. I'll miss you, Tam."

Not nearly as much as I'll miss Hal and everything here, Tamlyn thought as he tumbled into bed. He knew he was scared by what might

140

be waiting for him ahead, but if he could help to make his home, his land, a better place, then he'd do whatever was needed.

The next days were full of frantic activity for him. He tried to stick to his usual classes but was called out time and time again. He was measured for new clothes and shoes, and then had to attend for fittings. Lord Mansor, very unenthusiastically Tamlyn thought, threw a selection of coins onto the table and told him their names. He then ordered Tamlyn to give him varying amounts, or to work out how much must be returned after buying something of a lesser value, snorting derisively when he got it wrong.

"I was under the impression you were supposed to be clever, Scholar, but it seems to me you're little better than a Donkey," he snarled. Tamlyn gritted his teeth and kept his temper.

"If I might take these coins and practice on my own I think I might be able to manage better," he suggested meekly. Mansor seemed to weigh up the benefits of continuing to berate this boy who'd beaten his son, or shortening the task that he'd been ordered to do.

"Very well, I'll test you on it again tomorrow, so I'd better see an improvement. And I know exactly how much there is in that purse, even if you can't count it, so no slipping any coins into your pocket. I'll send for you tomorrow and don't keep me waiting."

Hallam examined the coins with interest, and once he realised that Tamlyn thought value went with size regardless of the metal used, he soon had him sorted out and using them as easily as Scholar discs.

"They've all got a number on them," he explained. "I know you can add and subtract, so just do it. Look, the smallest coin here has the largest number, a hundred, and I guess it's gold. The biggest coin is only five, probably brass. If I were you I'd keep the hundreds separate for safety."

Sharkley kept their gruelling combat work going, and by the Sunday Tamlyn knew he was getting the feel of it. He even managed to throw Sharkley a couple of times, which pleased him mightily.

"Well done," the Master said, "If you can do that when I'm expecting it you should have little trouble with someone who hasn't any idea how to fight you except by hitting you on the head."

The hardest thing was dealing with the growing curiosity of the rest of his class members who were not completely satisfied by being told

Tamlyn was going on a journey for the High Lord. Several of them cornered him in the common room and demanded more.

"Forget it," he said wearily. "If the High Lord told you to keep your mouth shut, what would you do? If I ever can, I'll tell you everything. Until then, it's no good to keep asking me."

Finally Tuesday evening came. He had been ordered to attend the High Lord's room after breakfast the next day, dressed in the more commonplace of his two new sets of clothes. He'd packed everything else in a sensible back pack. By Lyddy's dextrous hand, he'd received a message to explain exactly where Vitsell would meet him, and he'd stowed his small knife and his carved fox cub in his belt pouch which he refused to leave behind. At the last minute Hallam gave him a miniature abacus, the sort the babies in the crèche used as rattling toys.

"Thought it might come in useful," he said with a grin.

Even with his head aching and his stomach in turmoil Tamlyn had to laugh. "You will water my plants, won't you?" he said for something to say, then grabbed Hallam and hugged him. "Whatever happens I'm coming back if I've got two legs to walk on," he promised, and turned to his empty desk to hide tears that simply would come.

The dishes at supper were his favourites though he could scarcely eat, and Sharkley said he thought they'd done as much as possible. He shook Tamlyn's hand very formally as there were people around, but the whispered 'Good luck, Tamlyn' was quiet enough for him alone. Finally he and Hallam walked up Herder's Hill and looked at the setting sun away in the west.

"Funny to think I might be over there tomorrow night," Tamlyn said. "Take care, Hal. I may be the one going adventuring, but you're in a very dangerous place too, don't forget."

They were wandering back by the kitchens when Lyddy ran out and pressed a small package into Tamlyn's hand.

"To remind you of home and me. Good luck." she said softly, and vanished inside again. Tamlyn stared after her and then at the parcel. He didn't think he'd need anything to keep either of those memories in good order.

"Interesting," Hallam said, with an enigmatic smile. "What is it, Tam?"

He tore the paper off as they went indoors and found a small bottle. When he opened and smelt it he realised it was the shaving lotion she'd once said he should have; what he thought of as a green smell, like early Spring, but with the slightest hint of a more floral scent he couldn't quite identify. It was also a masculine version of the perfume she wore herself.

"Wow," said Hallam when he sniffed at it. "If there are girls around where you're going you'll have to watch out. They'll be after you."

Chapter 18

Tamlyn woke at first light and knew there was no chance of going back to sleep, so he collected his toilet things and towel and crept downstairs, deciding he'd use the time before breakfast to have a luxurious soak. He had no idea if the City would supply anything like the warm spring below the Citadel, or even, he thought, if he'd be able to use it if it did. This place was so familiar to him that usually he scarcely noticed it, but now he lay in the warm water and gazed round, fixing the details in his memory.

Eventually he decided it probably wasn't a good idea to stay there till he looked like a wrinkled prune so he dried, re-dressed in yesterday's clothes and returned to his room. He felt unwilling to put on the new clothes he'd hung over the back of his chair the night before. They were smart of course, and fitted him exactly, but they weren't his choice and he didn't feel right in them. He doubted if he would ever bring himself to wear the other new clothes, carefully folded and packed into his back pack. The ruffles at wrist and neck of the shirt and the cut of the trousers which made him feel as though he'd been poured into two tubes had horrified him when he was pushed in front a mirror the size of his door and expected to admire his reflection. On an impulse he took yesterday's clothes, smoothed them and rolled them as tightly as possible, then tucked them into the pack too. Then he dressed in the prescribed wear and hoped his long walk over open country would mess them up a bit so that he could feel more normal. The shoes he regarded with more approval; they'd be fine once he'd walked a few miles in them.

There was a tap at the door. Hallam usually charged straight in, so Tamlyn was puzzled.

"Come in," he called. It *was* Hallam, but Tamlyn could see a crowd of other Scholars jostling behind him. "What on earth…"

"Guard of honour, reporting for breakfast duty." Assorted muffled laughs sounded outside, and Hallam was grinning all over his face. He grabbed his friend by the arm and pulled him into the corridor where the entire sixth year (less Bartoly), greeted him with a cheer. They hoisted him up and proceeded to carry him down the flights of stairs. Only minutes before he'd been feeling nervous and depressed, but that mood couldn't survive this treatment. His laughing protests were ignored and he was carted, shoulder high, into the refectory. Gusts of laughter, followed by rhythmic hand claps sounded as his supporters did a circuit of the room and finally dumped him in his usual chair.

"Couldn't let you sneak off without a bit of ceremony," Kenley explained, as they plied him with assorted breakfast items. Tamlyn had thought he wouldn't be able to eat anything this morning, but they insisted that it was essential to fill up before a journey.

"Oy! Don't drip egg down my new clothes," he spluttered. He was really touched by this show of friendship, finding it hard keep his face fairly cheerful. Whatever happened from now on he'd have this time to remind him of how good life could be with people you liked and who cared about you.

At last the moment arrived. He put on his jacket, slung the straps of his pack onto one shoulder and climbed through the levels to the High Lord's apartment, his mood descending as he went up. At the door he stayed for a moment to breathe deeply and steel himself. Now he'd find out what task the High Lord would pretend he should tackle. He dropped the pack on the floor and knocked.

"Come in." The High Lord was seated as before in his huge chair, but he rose as Tamlyn entered and walked towards him, hands outstretched and a gentle smile on his face. "You are ready then, Tamlyn? I know you've been prepared for your journey, but now I must tell you why you are being sent". He took Tamlyn's hand and walked with him across to the window where he could see the track that led away to the west.

"There you see the road to the City where that evil man, the King, rules. He has caused so much sadness in my land with his wicked enchantments that I feel it is now the time that he must die. Would that I could perform that duty myself, but alas I am too easily recognised. It is in you I must trust. You are young and nobody will know you, so I charge you to do my work for me. Are you ready for it Tamlyn?"

"I am, my Lord."

"I know you to be intelligent and resourceful, so I will not instruct you, but have you any questions?"

"I will do everything in my power to do all that is necessary, but it occurs to me that a King will be closely guarded, as you are, my Lord. Can you suggest how to overcome this, for I fear I am not equipped to tackle many grown men?"

"You think clearly, Tamlyn, but here the King's arrogance plays into your hands. He is said to be so sure of himself that he rarely has a guard, either in his palace or when he goes out. So use those wits of yours. I have a small gift which you may well find useful in this endeavour."

From beneath the short robe he wore this morning Zerac drew a small dagger in a belted sheath. He pulled out the blade and showed that Tamlyn's name was engraved on it, then he bent towards Tamlyn, fastened the belt round his waist and replaced the blade.

"It is time for you to be going. I shall watch you, my brave warrior, as you start on your quest." He leant down and placed a kiss on Tamlyn's forehead. Tamlyn squirmed inwardly as Zerac's lips pressed against his flesh, then he stepped back and bowed.

"My Lord, I cannot but be safer on my way with such a blessing." He bowed again and left the room. Indeed, anywhere would be safer than in that room, he thought. He tried to imagine how he would be feeling now if he really believed he'd been sent out to commit murder. Furious and sickened as he was at this moment, he was at least comfortable with his decision to totally disregard Zerac's orders. Since the High Lord was not expecting him to be in a position to obey them he couldn't logically grumble, but he doubted the man thought logically.

For the first mile or more as he set off he could almost feel Zerac's eyes on his back. Then he topped a ridge and from the small valley beyond he could no longer see any but the highest point of the Citadel, and a sensation of freedom filled him. The day was fair but not too hot and a light breeze blew into his face. He began to enjoy walking as he always did, swinging along with a steady rhythm, and as he went he could hear skylarks high above him, and an occasional vole or a rabbit scampered across his path. He almost felt happy; only the thought of why he was making this journey kept a corner of his mind dark and anxious, both for himself and for those at home.

When he judged the sun to be near its zenith he sat at the side of the road for a while to munch a cold sausage, and drink from his water bottle. A package of food had been presented to him at breakfast time by a small first year who blushed crimson and ran away when he was asked who it was from. He guessed that it was Lyddy's doing and he sent a mental 'thank you' to her for it.

From his instructions he knew he must be nearing his meeting place with Vitsell. He was to look for him where the road crossed a sudden and very steep valley, and the road had to zigzag down and up the valley sides to make the gradient less problematic for travellers. That would certainly be necessary for wheeled vehicles, elderly horses or less able walkers. Tamlyn would have loved to take off straight down, but he didn't want to risk a fall today. He cast his eyes around him as he went but could see no sign of the man he sought until a bush quite close to him spoke and Vitsell rose from the middle of it.

"Youse looks like a fair strider, boy. Was a bit worried, way we gotter go, but reckon youse'll do."

"I do like walking," Tamlyn acknowledged. "Thank you for being my guide. Which way is it?"

"Up along there." The man jerked his thumb over his shoulder signalling that they must follow the bottom of the dip which Tamlyn thought would send them north or north-east. "Ready?"

They started at once, Vitsell setting a pace that was manageable though a bit fast for Tamlyn as the way sloped up nearly as steeply as the sides and was very rocky in places.

"This looks like a stream bed," he ventured, trying not to sound puffed.

"Ah, 'tis in winter; early spring too when t' snows in mountains melts. Right fast 'tis, couldn't walk here then."

On and on they went, Vitsell's long legs covering the ground in great strides that Tamlyn had no way of matching. He was almost at the point of begging for a rest when Vitsell clambered from the gully which had become much shallower and sat on a grassy knoll, looking back the way they had come. Tamlyn flopped down beside him and pulled his water from his backpack. He offered it to Vitsell.

"Youse keep un lad, thankee. We get to t' little river soon; right good taste that un is. Youse done well comin' up here though. Look over there, long way. See t' smoke? 'At's them priggin' ijits is waitin' on you. S'posed ter be hidin' is they? An' lights a fire us can see miles off."

Tamlyn shuddered. He didn't think the Guards would bother with hiding, and he might not have taken pains to avoid them on this strange journey had he been travelling without overhearing the High Lord's plan. The men would surely have someone on the lookout for him.

"How's tha fer jumpin', lad?" Vitsell said suddenly.

"I... I don't really know. Not bad, I suppose. Jumping what?"

"T' river. Only way, hoppin' t' stones." Tamlyn must have looked worried for Vitsell suddenly grinned. "Don't youse fret, lad, I'll get youse over. T' Lady sez youse a goodun an I reckons she'm right. Blood line she sez, an' she don't get 'at wrong."

As though embarrassed at so much talking he jumped up. "Come 'long now. Good ways 'fore us gets down yet."

They set off, going westerly across land that deceptively looked smooth but was riddled with deep ruts and stony outcrops. To Tamlyn's relief Vitsell went at a more moderate pace. Perhaps he'd been trying him out on that first stretch; if so he seemed to have passed the test. The sound of running water became gradually louder and eventually they stood on the banks of what Vitsell had called the little river. True, it was far narrower than the one that ran through The Land past the village and Citadel, and with which Tamlyn was familiar, but the flow was so fast that the whole surface looked as though it was boiling. There was a ragged line of uneven boulders across it just below where they stood, and he eyed these warily. Was this where jumping was needed?

"Only place t' cross, them stones," Vitsell announced, confirming Tamlyn's fears. "See that big un with a flat top, four out? Can youse git there?"

Tamlyn studied the first stones. Three jumps from the bank using three small ones and leading with his left foot, then he'd need to leap up as well as forward to get to the big one. On land it'd be no problem, he thought, but with the river rushing between them… At least the big one had an area large enough to hold him if he sprawled forward on landing.

"Yes," he said firmly, as much to convince himself as Vitsell.

"Gi' us yer pack then. When youse gits there, stand up over to t' right. Shut yer eyes if youse giddy, an' don' wriggle whatever."

Tamlyn handed over his pack, found a firm place on the bank to launch from and took a deep breath as his brain rehearsed what he must do. One, two, three, then he heaved himself up and out towards the big boulder. He got one foot on it, wobbled, and flung himself onto his stomach.

"'A's right. Stand up," he heard. He did so, edging as far right as he dared. The swirl and dazzle of the water made him sway, so he shut his eyes. The next second he felt a strong arm grab him round his waist and he was lifted on a series of jumps and dropped on the far bank. He turned to say thank you, but Vitsell was already hopping back across the river as nonchalantly as if he was strolling on a flat field. He picked up Tamlyn's pack and fetched it back just as easily and quickly.

"Phew. Didn't think I could do that. Thanks, Vitsell," said Tamlyn.

"Ah, but youse did. Makes it easy-like for me, if'n you does t' start, 'cos them three stones is little uns; not much foot space if'n I'se loaded. Lot a' folks bigger'n youse daresn't do it."

"Other people come up here?" Tamlyn asked in surprise.

"Oh ah. City folks. Thinks them's that brave, out in t' wild. I tecks 'em round about an' sleeps 'em agin t' gorse. Some thinks them's better'n me, so I lets 'em slip in t' little river." Vitsell gave a huge grin, and Tamlyn laughed.

"But how do you get these people? Not from the Citadel I'm sure or I'd have heard. Do you go to the City?"

"Not me. My brother's fam'ly live agin t' border. 'E were kilted, long time back, an us feared as 'at priggin' murd'rer in t' Citadel might come a-knockin one night, so us moved 'em down west'ards. Got an 'ome like to mine, but bigger. City uns likes to stay in a funny 'ouse see, an' t' fam'ly tells 'em 'bout my a'venter walks. I gives me nephew money as I earns an' 'e gets things I needs."

Tamlyn was amazed at this going on almost under the High Lord's nose. "That's fantastic. You're really clever," he said in admiration.

"Good fer Donkeys, eh? Come 'long, us'll get down nearer City an sleep. Better youse go in early termorrer, I reckons."

They went on steadily, the land dropping lower and becoming ever easier walking. The sun sank in front of them. As the light faded and Tamlyn began to see pinpoint stars in the darkening sky Vitsell suddenly turned aside into a clump of trees.

"Us'll sleep 'ere," he announced. "No gorses," he added with a grin. He rummaged around under a pile of dead branches and produced two thick sheepskins and a basket. "Tellt me nephew us was comin' an' to leave us a bite."

The bite proved to be delicious pasties and a couple of bottles of what Tamlyn thought smelled like a fruity sort of beer. Whatever it was, as soon as they'd eaten he rolled himself in a sheepskin and fell into the deepest sleep he'd had since that first meeting in the High Lord's room.

Chapter 19

When he woke to birds singing above him and an uncomfortable lump under his right shoulder blade Tamlyn had no idea where he was. It took some time to fit the jumble of odd memories into yesterday's reality. The journey with Vitsell had so much the quality of a dream that it wasn't till he sat up and saw the gangly man himself rolling up a sheepskin that he got everything straight. Today he was going into the City; the place that all his life he'd been taught was evil.

"Thought youse was sleepin' till noontime," Vitsell grumbled. "I's got things t' do."

Tamlyn jumped up. "Sorry, Vitsell. You should have woken me."

"'S'aright, 't i'nt much over sunup. Stream that ways, if'n youse want t' wash."

Tamlyn followed the direction of Vitsell's pointing finger and splashed himself fully awake in the small stream just beyond the trees. He also refilled his water bottle, and when he returned Vitsell had set out the last of the food.

"Youse teck that; me nephew'll feed me. I's callin' there now so youse got t' go alone. I s'll point the way."

"Vitsell, how do you say 'thank you' in the old tongue?"

The smile on Vitsell's face nearly reached his ears. "'T'is 'dants amarler'."

Tamlyn walked over to him, and held out his hand. "Dants amarler, Vitsell. One day if – no, *when* I come back to The Land – you can teach me some more, yes?"

"Youse'll come back. I knows." He took Tamlyn's hand and squeezed it between both of his. "This road now." He picked up the sheepskins and the basket and stood while Tamlyn settled his back pack. They left the trees and went up a rise high enough to take them above the tree tops..

"'At's t' City," Vitsell announced. "I 's goin' t' other way. If'n youse wants a message tooken, go 'long t' path I'se goin'. Can't miss it, like my house. Tell 'em and theys'll tell me. Not lots a words or I s'll fergit."

He clapped Tamlyn's shoulder with his big hand and strode off. Tamlyn watched him go, then turned to look out to the west, suddenly feeling very lonely. Yesterday had been a strange sort of holiday from all the troubles and problems that had been building up around him, but now they'd returned; now he had things to do. The trouble was he didn't know what, and there was nobody to ask or to discuss ideas with. He studied the view ahead in wonder. The Citadel had always seemed huge to him, but here was the City, and it appeared to stretch away forever. The rise on which he stood ran down into a strip of farmland, then a bridge over a small stream, probably the one he'd washed in, he guessed. Beyond that, flat grass led up to a stone-built wall with a huge arched gateway in it. He couldn't see immediately behind the wall, but because his view was from a good height he could see that buildings lay beyond for further than he could guess.

'Well, got to get moving,' he told himself, and started down the slope. Nothing was likely to happen until he entered the City so that was what he must do. Walking briskly, he approached the gateway. Close to he could see that the wall looked ancient and must be very deep, for a huge wooden gate hung open against the inner thickness of the archway to the left. It didn't look as though it was shut often because he could see grass sprouting up along its lower edge, and in the right hand side of the arch a small alcove had been scooped out with a bench outside. An elderly man sat there sipping from a mug, and talking to a woman carrying a basket. If this was a guard he didn't look as though he'd be hard to overpower.

"Morning, young sir." The two stopped talking and the man called to Tamlyn as he approached.

"Good day to you," Tamlyn replied. "That's a huge door isn't it? Do you ever shut it?"

"Not often," the man laughed. "Quite a weight it is. Difficult to shift."

"I remember once," the woman put in. "The year we had those awful snow storms blowing in from the east. They shut it then to keep the snow out."

"That's right, I do remember. When they opened it again 'twas like a white wall up to the top of the arch. Couldn't get out this way for a week."

"You'll be a visitor, sir. Come far, have you?"

"A fair way. But I slept over there last night." Tamlyn gestured vaguely behind him. Questions weren't always as innocent as this one sounded. "I thought I'd have a look round as I've not been here before."

"There's a lot to see. Great place this is, though that does sound a bit boastful. Yes, a real good lot to see. There's a fair on over in Gallopers Square this week, isn't there, Margie?"

"That's right," she said.

"Sounds like a horse fair," said Tamlyn, and they both laughed.

"It does that," the man laughed, "but it's an old name for the place where they used to hold the annual horse sales, and then had races. Nowadays there's all sorts – stalls and food and music. Heard there're some good jugglers doing shows this year."

"But if you're a stranger you must see the palace. Like a city inside a city that is, and the gardens are lovely," Margie urged. "I'm going in that direction myself now, so I can set you on the right road if you want. Easy to get lost if you've not been here before."

Tamlyn decided that as he'd no idea what to do or where to walk he might as well go along with this. "Thank you, you're very kind," he said, and followed the woman as she set off. It was a walk full of amazement for him. Streets went off in all directions, criss-crossing each other, some straight and some curving this way and that, and they were all bordered by houses and other buildings of all shapes and sizes. Some had gardens in front of them full of summer flowers; others, built right up to the edge of the paving, still had flower baskets hanging from hooks in the walls. He realised that his mind was imprinted with a city of his imagining, drawn from listening to endless descriptions of a grey and dreary place filled with miserable people enchanted into slavery. The citizens in these streets seemed perfectly normal. Some were intent on whatever business they were hurrying to, some chatted as they walked, some stopped to admire flowers, but two things had Tamlyn completely dumfounded. The first was that in some streets many buildings were open-fronted to the street and had differing foods and other goods displayed invitingly. People were going in and out, choosing items and giving money for them. It was like Scholars Disc days but extended beyond all he could ever have imagined. Margie beside him, who kept up a non-stop chat pointing out things for his benefit, seemed to call them shops. The second was that there were as many women about as men, all mixed together, walking and talking together and quite often holding children's hands or pushing them in little wheeled carts. Seeing them, something inside Tamlyn longed to be part of such a group.

The woman came to a halt. "This is where I'll have to leave you. It's still a bit of a walk, but if you take that street over there on the left and just stay on it, you'll come right out to the front of the palace. Best view, that is. Enjoy your stay, young man."

"Thank you for your help." Tamlyn gave a little bow and crossed to go along the road she'd pointed to. He was quite glad to be alone and without her constant talk; he really wanted time to go slowly and take in all the things that were so different from home. The buildings seemed to be mainly of stone in this street, but not as in the Citadel, hewn into and through the gigantic piles of rocks. These were of shaped squares fixed together in straight vertical walls. He was walking more slowly with his head tilted up to try and see how the roofs were made, when he collided sharply with someone else who'd rushed out from a small entry, and he toppled backwards onto the paving.

Tamlyn looked up into the concerned eyes of a young man who held out his hands to help him up. He proceeded to brush Tamlyn down, apologising all the while.

"I'm terribly sorry. So careless of me. Are you all right? Are you hurt at all?"

"No, no. I'm fine. Honestly. I was looking up at the roofs instead of where I was going, so I should apologise."

"The roofs?" The young man glanced up and back again as if he'd expected to see something unusual but not found it.

"I've not seen... we don't have buildings like that..." His voice tailed away in embarrassment at what must sound rather stupid here.

"Of course! I can see now you're a visitor to the City. Oh dear, that makes me feel even worse for knocking you flying. Were you on your way to see the palace? It's well worth a visit; we're very proud of it. I work there, actually. Shall we walk along together? Perhaps I can buy you a drink when we get there?"

Tamlyn, nearly overwhelmed by the torrent of words, managed to agree to walk on with the cheerful stranger. He wondered if it was common for visitors here to find themselves accosted by chatty citizens. Three in the first half hour! Perhaps they were encouraged to sing the praises of their City to obvious strangers. Thankfully, the woman, Margie, hadn't asked him questions and this young man seemed equally incurious. He should have thought up some suitable facts about himself, he realised. Hallam would have had them on the tip of his tongue.

They turned round a corner and Tamlyn stopped dead, open mouthed.

"It really is something, isn't it?" said the young man, obviously pleased with this reaction.

The building ahead gleamed, white and beautiful in the morning sunlight. Buildings really, thought Tamlyn, for there were at least five, but they had been designed to complement each other so that they looked both separate and yet an integral part of the whole. There was an elegant, pillared entrance in the centre building, and as he watched, men and women were entering and leaving in a constant flow.

"Who are all those people?" he asked at last.

"Um... well all sorts really. There are lots of offices and government departments in there, so some of them will be staff. Then cleaners, repair workers, gardeners. Cooks of course and visitors; you can get pretty good meals in there. And locals wanting to have a moan about something – plenty of them."

"I thought the King would live in the palace."

"He's got a bit of it, yes."

"And there's no guard on the entrance?" Tamlyn asked.

"Whatever for?"

"In case of, I don't know, trouble of some sort."

"Oh that," the young man said dismissively. "There are some security men. They've got a nice room just inside, off the entrance hall.

Mostly they tell people the way to wherever they want to get. It's a bit of a maze in there until you get used to it. Or they'll answer questions about the building. If anyone got awkward they'd soon chuck them out, or shut them in one of the court rooms till they cooled down. Come on, let's go and get that drink. Or I could show you round a bit first if you like. Anything you'd especially like to see?"

Tamlyn was still thinking about guards, or lack of them. Yesterday morning – only a day ago, although it felt so much longer – the High Lord had spoken of the King's arrogance in not having guards. He really didn't want to believe anything Zerac said, but it looked as though he'd been right on this. Then suddenly it came to him. The fact wasn't wrong, but Zerac's conclusion that it must show an arrogant disregard of necessity could well be. The King had ruled here for over fifty years and presumably had not been harmed, so why should he feel he needed armed men round him all the time? Perhaps it should be asked why the High Lord did. He thought he might know.

"Gone to sleep?" The man nudged him.

"Oh, sorry. It's so much to take in." Tamlyn thought it might be interesting to test the guard-free situation a little further. "I don't suppose it's permitted, but I'd love to see where the King lives. We don't have a King," he offered as reason for his request. He waited for excuses or denials, but his companion simply raised a surprised eyebrow.

"Really?" he said. "It's not half as nice there as some of the staterooms where foreign visitors stay, but if that's what you want. This way." He led Tamlyn across the paved courtyard, dotted with small trees and flower beds, and in through the front door. The hallway was busy, and several people obviously knew his guide, offering him a bow, a wave or word of greeting, but he didn't stop. Up wide stairs and along spacious and well-lit corridors they went, then another flight of stairs. "Almost there," he announced. Round the next corner he stopped. "Here we are. The royal apartment. Well, the front door at least."

Tamlyn stared. The door was the same as a dozen or more they'd passed. The only thing to differentiate it was a cut out paper crown that looked as though it had been coloured by a child from the crèche. It had been stuck on crookedly at about his waist height.

"One of Lala's brood did that." The man must have spotted where he was staring. "Let's see who's home."

This must be a huge joke, Tamlyn thought, but before he could work out what was really happening he'd been taken by the elbow and led in through the oddly crowned door.

"We're here, Grandad," the man called across a large and comfortable looking room. An older man put his head round a door on the far side. He was tall and edging towards plump, though certainly not fat. He was clean shaven but had a mop of tousled grey hair, and seemed to be wearing some sort of apron.

"Hello, Mardell. Ah, you've brought a guest. Just a moment, I've left some water heating. He vanished, and Mardell followed him. Tamlyn felt bewildered. Something very odd here, and it made him uneasy. Was the old man a caretaker? Did Mardell make a habit of doing this to strangers? He had rejected the reality of evil enchantment so recently that the thought of it still crawled out of the shadows and into the forefront of his mind. Maybe he could walk out... but at that moment the old man, who had removed his apron, came back with Mardell.

"May I introduce my grandfather, His Majesty King Almaran the Third," the younger man said, sweeping an extravagant bow, but with a huge grin on his face.

"Stop it Mardell. Our visitor will think we're all as crazy as you," the older man said, though he too smiled. "How are you, my friend?" He held out his hand.

Tamlyn's head spun. What was this? Had he been trapped somehow, and for what purpose? What would happen to him? All that would come out of his mouth was "K-k-k-k-King?"

"I am, yes."

"But you've... no robes... crown... guards." That all sounded particularly stupid, and he found, staring at the man, that he hadn't any doubt about him. There was a feeling of certainty there, a comfortable acknowledgement of himself and who he was.

"Shall we sit down, and I'll try and sort that out for you. Mardell, fetch us some of the apple juice in the jug out there."

Tamlyn almost fell into a chair. "I just don't know what's happening. It all seemed accidental but it feels like a plan now."

"Let's start with your criteria for recognising a King. Thanks, Mardell." Almaran took up the jug Mardell had brought in and poured some of the golden liquid from it into three glasses. He put one onto a small table by Tamlyn, handed one to Mardell and held up the third. "Here's to understanding," he said, and drank. Mardell followed suit and finally Tamlyn did too. It tasted good.

"I *am* the King, as I said, have been for over fifty years. I do have robes, a crown too, somewhere. I wear them for ceremonial occasions, but they're not really ideal garments for doing ordinary, everyday things, like washing the breakfast dishes as I was when you arrived. As to guards, if you mean fierce armed men glaring at everyone and making them feel uncomfortable and afraid then no, we don't have them. You didn't recognise our City guards because they're ordinary people who care, and keep their eyes open. Old Gerack at the east gate; Margie who directed you the long way round and then ran to let us know you were coming; Mardell here, into whom you bumped not quite accidentally. We all stand to guard each other here, Tamlyn."

He knew he hadn't told anyone his name. He did not believe in enchantment, he really didn't, but the thought of it, so long embedded in him, drifted like coils of smoke into his mind... how else... He slammed his mind shut against it. "You know me?" he managed to say in an even voice.

As if the King had read his mind he said, "Oh yes. No magic or anything like that either. Look!" He reached carefully into a pocket and pulled out Tamlyn's knife. "I found your name on this."

Automatically Tamlyn's hand flew to his side and discovered the empty sheath, then with a small laugh he sat back. "How?"

"Among his many attributes my grandson here has learnt to be a very able pickpocket! Officially I don't approve, but it does come in handy. You probably remember him brushing you down quite vigorously when you collided. Tamlyn nodded, with a sideways look at Mardell.

"We wanted to get you here," Mardell said, almost apologetically. "Didn't want to drag you in by force or anything."

"But how did you know? How could you be looking for me?"

Almaran sat on a chair near Tamlyn and held out his knife, handle towards him. "Before we go on, take this back. Just to show we mean you no harm."

Tamlyn shuddered. "I don't want the thing; I hate it. I intended throwing it away when I could find somewhere safe." He wrenched the sheath off and dropped it on the ground.

Almaran's eyebrow shot up as Mardell's had done earlier, and Tamlyn realised he could see a resemblance between them. That was probably why he'd had a slight feeling of familiarity with the King when he first saw him.

"Now that *is* interesting." said the King. "I thought maybe it had been given you as a special gift when you were sent here with a mission to kill me. And no, that's still not magic. It happens every five or six years."

Tamlyn gulped and stared. So others had been sent here? But he knew of none; certainly none had returned. "You are right about the mission and the gift, but I haven't the slightest intention of trying to kill you, your majesty."

Almaran smiled amiably. "Glad to hear it. Surprised too. By the way, 'sir' will do. 'Your majesty' rather holds up the conversation, don't you think?"

"Thank you, sir."

"I have a feeling this isn't going to be quite what I expected," the King said. "Mardell, go down to the morning room and say I may be a little late, will you?"

Mardell swept another fancy bow. "Your every wish," he laughed, and vanished.

"My grandson likes to play the fool, but he's far from foolish," Almaran commented.

Like Hallam, thought Tamlyn, and a pang of longing for his friend and his home swept through him. "Will you tell me, sir, how you could have been expecting me?" he asked.

"We were expecting… someone. As I said, we have a visitor every few years, sent by your High Lord supposedly to kill me, and I had been thinking we were about due another such. They come here, full of courage and grand ideas that they are doing the High Lord's work, intent on ridding the world of what they've been taught is evil enchantment of which I am the source."

Tamlyn listened, surprised by the accuracy of Almaran's assessment.

"This time things appear to be different. For one thing, the would-be killers of the past have been younger than you and deeply fearful beneath their show of courage. They believed fully in the High Lord's account of things, including the power of evil enchantment. On this occasion I find a young man who is quite naturally nervous, but not terrified. Unless I'm mistaken, he also has a much better view of reality. Am I right?"

"I don't believe in evil enchantment, sir, though it has been so much part of the years of my teaching that sometimes the thought of it jumps into my mind against my will. As to reality, I'm not sure that I know what that is at the moment."

"There is something else that makes me think change is in the air. This time we were actually given knowledge of your coming, with no mention of when, but with the suggestion that we might find it in our interests to welcome you."

"What? Who from?"

"I have no idea, but it came through a source that I trust. I thought you might know, but I see you don't."

"Indeed I don't. I really can't think..." Tamlyn shook his head.

Almaran sat back in his chair and laced his fingers together. "So here we are, and the question is what to do with you. I feel that you are someone I should like to know better, but you'll understand that I can't immediately trust that you are not a very clever trickster, out to get the better of me. You, on the other hand, have been told by me that I am not the cruel and evil man you have been taught about. You would be very stupid if you did not have doubts still lurking in your mind, and I don't really think you're stupid. Would you agree?"

"That seems... very fair, sir."

"What I would suggest then is that we will both agree that you will not murder me, and I will not entrap you with evil magic for at least a week. It will give us time to find reality on both sides." Almaran stood and held out his hand, and Tamlyn jumped up to take it, still bewildered but much happier. He knew he'd keep his side of this odd bargain and he felt reasonably sure the King had no means to break his.

"First things first, have you had breakfast?"

"I… had a pasty around sun-up." Tamlyn had to think hard to remember when that was.

"You'd better have something else now. That was hours ago," the King laughed. "Come through here." He took Tamlyn into what must be the kitchen and put bread, butter and cheese in front of him with a tall glass of milk, before sitting down opposite him. "You can read and write, I presume."

Startled and a bit indignant Tamlyn said, "Of course."

"This is what I suggest then. I'd like to keep you by me, at least for a day or two, so would you accompany me and make notes of all that happens? My son is abroad on a state visit, and he's borrowed my secretary because he speaks the language, so you could fill in. Suenne has been doing it but – I won't say unfortunately because she's delighted – she's left to have a baby."

"I'd do my best," answered Tamlyn. He had a sudden thought. "I'm not very good with numbers though."

"Don't worry, neither am I. We've got plenty of experts if we need them. I'll go and change. You can wash and tidy up through there. Leave your pack, it'll be safe till the evening."

Tamlyn discovered a room that had an elegant basin and a large bath; not like the citadel, but big enough to lie down in. There was also a privy in a small separate room. He tidied as well as possible and stared at himself in a mirror over the basin. He was washing himself in a King's bathroom! He could never have imagined anything like that, but it seemed he was surely going to learn a lot about the King and the City.

Chapter 20

Almaran and Tamlyn walked along corridors and up and down stairs until Tamlyn had no idea in which direction they were actually going. He clasped the writing materials he'd been given, and the King, rather more smartly dressed, was explaining his task to him.

"I want you to write down what you see and hear, and make a note of any questions that occur to you or any comments that you think might be relevant. I can usually recall the basic details of the day, but I like to have someone else's record. It often reminds me of things I've forgotten. Think you can do that?"

"I'll do my best, sir."

"Our first meeting is what we call problem time. We've got a large staff here who are very efficient at almost everything. Sometimes, though, a difficulty does crop up; the staff may see the answer but the people involved can't agree. That's when I listen and try to settle things. To be honest, I think some people involved often agree to disagree because they want to get me on the job. Top dog you know. Here we are, the morning room."

They walked in to find six people waiting on chairs set in a semi-circle. They all stood as the King came in, reseating themselves as he waved his hand and took his place facing them. Tamlyn noticed that his seat was the same as the others; no huge, ornate throne-like chair for him. Almaran introduced Tamlyn as his temporary scribe, and asked if anyone wanted to discuss their problem in private, but it seemed these particular citizens were quite happy for everyone to share in the retelling of their grievances.

Tamlyn listened hard, scribbling at top speed and putting a mark in the margin where he wanted to question something. Occasionally he had to ask for a name or other detail to be repeated. He didn't believe that the High Lord had ever interested himself in anyone else's problems, nor could he imagine Citadel dwellers even contemplating the possibility of asking his advice. Here the King listened, asked for things to be explained further, made suggestions, and treated everyone courteously. At the end of the meeting, four citizens went out with smiles of satisfaction, and the other two, who were arguing over a piece of land, seemed happy when the King promised he'd look further into the matter.

"No need to take detailed notes here," Almaran said as they walked to another room. "I'm meeting with two Chief District Councillors, and their scribes will be with them. I just like to know what's going on. Write anything that interests you." The man and woman already in the room welcomed Tamlyn kindly and he discovered for the first time that the King also ruled over much more extensive lands outside the City. The discussion here was wide ranging: schools, harvest forecasts, drainage, and the future building of a small hospital. Tamlyn realised that though Almaran had brought papers with him, he seemed to know already in some detail what was going on all over his kingdom. The two other scribes often joined in the talk, especially to make sure of facts from past meetings.

They all shared a meal of cold meats, fresh bread and fruits, which were brought in at the end of the meeting, and Tamlyn realised that the King carefully steered the talk in another direction when he was asked where he came from and how long he was staying in the City. He was beginning to hope 'quite a long while' in answer to that last question; he thought he'd like to enjoy this very different style of living for some time.

Almaran announced that he was going to sit in the garden for a while. "Now I'm getting old, I've decided I deserve a bit of spoiling. Dallis – that's my son, and Mardell's father – takes a lot on when he's here, of course. Come and have a look round. The main gardens are open all day, but this little bit is mine." He led Tamlyn through an archway in a wall made of soft red blocks.

"What's this stuff?" he asked, patting the wall to feel it.

"That? That's brick. Oh, of course, you wouldn't know. Made from clay dug from the river valley, then shaped and baked. Not as tough as stone, but better for climbing plants. Look round here where the wisteria's blooming."

Through the arch was a garden full of flowers and scents. Green turf, neatly trimmed, was surrounded by beds blazing with colour. Tamlyn found it overwhelmingly lush. The blooms of The Land were mostly dainty and delicate; you had to get close to catch their perfume. These blossoms fairly hurled it in your face.

"I'm going to sit in the shade over there. Have a look round for a while, Tamlyn." Was the King testing him, to see if he'd run off? Well, he didn't intend to, but he did think he might find somewhere that didn't make him feel as though he was drowning in a perfume bottle. Almaran had spoken of 'this little bit' but it seemed to him to be pretty extensive, with areas planned differently but all blending into each other, rather like the palace itself. Tamlyn wandered here and there, wishing he had a book so that he could identify plants he'd never seen, until he came to a sheltered, sunny place which, to his delight, was planted with herbs. Even here some were strange to him, but in the far corner a beautiful bay tree grew, its wide-spreading branches casting flickering speckled shade over a green bank. The green was chamomile, Tamlyn was sure. He'd seen pictures and read about it, but never seen it in reality, though he knew Merla had some. He lay down on it to catch the light perfume as it was crushed , then closed his eyes, imagining this was growing in a sunny dip above on Herder's Hill… it was so peaceful here… he could hear bees… maybe Lyddy would come up if she'd seen him… or…

"Tamlyn. Tamlyn, are you all right?" It wasn't Lyddy's voice… not even Hallam… a man! He sat up with a jerk to find the King bending over him.

"Oh! I'm sorry, sir. I must have fallen asleep." He tried to scramble to his feet, but Almaran pushed him back down and sat beside him.

"I realise I've been a bit thoughtless here. You told me you were up at sunrise and, if I'm guessing correctly from the look of your clothes, you probably had quite an energetic day yesterday. Add to that the experience of being hijacked from the City streets and then set to work by me. I ought to be surprised you haven't collapsed before. You chose a good place didn't you? Chamomile. Often used in sleeping draughts."

"I recognised it, but I've never seen it before. Probably too cool or the soil's too poor at home. Sorry again, sir; I do go on about plants, especially herbs. Did you think I'd tried to escape?"

"No... no I didn't." Almaran said slowly. "My first thought when I couldn't see you was that perhaps you might not have been as alone as you thought when you came to the City."

Tamlyn stared at him uncomprehendingly, and then simply said, "Oh." After another silence he added, "But that would have been hard, wouldn't it?"

"Hard, but not impossible. As you discovered, we don't do guards in your sort of way here, but thank goodness it was a baseless fear. Now how do you feel about another short session of note taking? I plan to visit the two squabbling gentlemen you met this morning, which might be interesting. After that we'll find you food and a bed, and you can sleep a long as you like."

Tamlyn jumped up. Almaran rose more slowly. "Ah, the lost spring of youth," he sighed, but with a smile.

"I'll have to get my writing things, sir. They're in the room where we saw the Councillors, and I'm not sure I can find my way back."

"Soon solved." The King led them through the buildings to the entrance hall, where a messenger was dispatched who quickly returned with Tamlyn's things. "It's only about half a mile, down by the river. Ready?"

They walked out into the City and Tamlyn saw that the people in the streets weren't alarmed or surprised by their King strolling among them. A few, intent on business of their own, rushed past without even noticing him; others bobbed a brief curtsey or bow, while children waved or simply stared. The street they were on started to slope gently down, and a broad river came into view. Remembering Merla's map Tamlyn thought 'that's my river', but by now it had been joined by the rushing torrent of Vitsell's little river. Apparently calm here, the water moved smoothly and slowly across the plain towards the sea.

The houses of the two men stood side by side, and both had spacious gardens. One claimed that the other had given him a strip of his land, which he had cultivated and grown good crops on. The other insisted it had only been a loan and now wanted his land back. Almaran walked round the plot, discussing what was growing there.

"What would you suggest?" suddenly he asked Tamlyn.

"I don't really know," he said, very surprised. "Your Majesty could, I suppose, take the land for yourself and there'd be nothing to argue about."

The two old men looked aghast, and Tamlyn saw the King's lips twitch.

"Hmm. That's certainly an idea," he said slowly. "However, I think we could try something else first. Jed, you may keep and rent the land," he nodded to the man who had been using the strip, "but you will pay Tanti rent with some of the produce from it. I'll send a lawman to say what is fair. How does that sound?" Both men agreed enthusiastically.

"Did you see their faces? Your suggestion certainly frightened them," Almaran laughed as they walked away. "What did you really think?"

"Well I couldn't see why the man who owned the strip really wanted it back. He's not much of a gardener by the look of the rest of his plot."

"Exactly. Jed loves gardening and Tanti hates it, but I guess when he saw fine crops growing he fancied having it back. Now they'll both have what they really want: Jed a bigger garden and Tanti some crops without working for them. Did you make a note for me to send a lawyer?" Tamlyn nodded. "If it's all written out with a nice red seal on it'll be properly settled in their eyes."

They returned to the King's apartment in the palace to be greeted by a delicious smell. Tamlyn found he wasn't at all surprised to discover that the pleasant woman cooking in the kitchen was in fact Queen Veranne. How soon the extraordinary had become almost normal. He handed his day's notes to the King who sat reading them as he ate, while Mardell chatted with his grandmother about a dance taking place the next week.

"Do you like dancing? Will you still be here?" he asked Tamlyn.

"He will be if I can persuade him," Almaran answered for him, patting the pile of papers he'd been reading. "These are some of the best records I've seen. Detailed, concise and perceptive. We'll have to have a talk, but I'd like to employ you as a scribe."

"That's praise for you," Mardell said. "He wouldn't let me do it."

"You're family, that wouldn't do. Besides, you never stop talking long enough to listen."

166

"Well if you stay, will you come to the dance? It'll be great fun."

"I don't know how," Tamlyn replied, smothering a yawn.

"Really? We'll get some of the girls to give you lessons then."

"Leave the poor man alone, Mardell. He's nearly asleep sitting there," Veranne chided him.

"Yes. I promised him food and a bed. Will you go down and ask them to get a room ready straight away in the lodging house while I have a quick word with him, Mardell?"

Mardell went to the door, then turned to grin at Tamlyn. "I'm still going to get you dancing though," he said.

"Come through to the sitting room," Almaran told Tamlyn. "I won't keep you from your bed very long, but there are things I'd like to get clear." They sat on two very comfortable chairs, but Tamlyn leaned forward, feeling sure he might go straight to sleep if he rested on the cushions.

"How do you feel about the City now you've spent a few hours here?" the King began.

Tamlyn struggled to find words for his thoughts. "Almost everything is so different that I find it hard to believe we're in the same world. You know what I was brought up to believe about you and the City, and you know that I'd rejected that before I came, but I hadn't imagined what you were really like. I'd no experience to shape a different image from. A day is a short time to settle a new picture in my head, but it seems to me that this is a good place to be. I suppose things go wrong here too, but the whole feel is open and kind, more than anything I've ever known. I don't mean I haven't known lots of kindness, but so much in The Land is hidden, fearful and secretive. I've not said that properly. I really would like to stay here for a while, but I know I shall have to go back."

"Have to?" Almaran queried.

"Yes. The Land is my home. I love it and its people; the friends I know, and others I'd like to know sometime. You said this morning, sir, that things were different with the way I've come here. Merla feels the same, and I believe her. She says that she thinks I'm part of the changes, so I must believe that too. I don't know how or when, but I suppose things will happen, like me coming here." The words came tumbling out.

Tamlyn hadn't meant to say as much, and maybe it was tiredness. but it felt good.

"Who is Merla?"

"She is The Lady." Suddenly cautious, he decided he mustn't say any more, but he did add, "I think you'd like her, sir."

Almaran sat looking at Tamlyn thoughtfully. Then he pushed himself up from the chair and smiled. "Things certainly are looking different now, but I am being thoughtless again in keeping you from your sleep. Can we talk more another time?"

"I'd like that, sir."

Mardell returned to say all was ready, so Tamlyn thankfully picked up his pack and followed him back through the corridors to find his bed. I woke up this morning on the ground in the open air and now I'm going to sleep in a palace, he thought dreamily. Sleep overwhelmed him before he could summon another thought.

Chapter 21

For the second morning in a row Tamlyn had to struggle out of sleep to sort out where he was. Even when he remembered, nothing looked familiar. Comfortable bed, large window with curtains, table, chair, water jug and basin; everything said 'bedroom', and he'd most certainly slept here so why couldn't he remember it? Mardell had brought him here but... He came to the conclusion that he must have been already more than half asleep when he walked in last night. He needed to find the privy so he pulled on shirt and trousers and put his head out of the door.

"Hallo. Awake at last?" Tamlyn turned to find a young man carrying a pile of books. "Privy's that way, last on the left, and bath's next door. D'you want a bath?"

"Um, yes, I really would like one."

"I'll tell Deelah and she'll see to it. Sorry I can't stop, I'm a bit late this morning. I'm Cotter, by the way." He held a hand out awkwardly from beneath the books.

"Tamlyn." He assumed he should take the offered hand, but then had to stop the pile of books from cascading to the floor.

"Thanks. Really must run. See you around I expect." He bustled off, pausing only to turn and say again, "I'll tell Dee you're awake."

Tamlyn came out of the privy to see another man taking two large buckets of steaming hot water through the next door.

"You're not, er, Deelah are you?" He felt pretty sure he'd heard Cotter say 'she'.

"Hope not," the man laughed and entered the bathroom. "She's doing your breakfast in the kitchen. Room straight opposite." He jerked his head back over his shoulder. "I'm Bart. Cotter said you'd like a bath so I'll put this in. It's very hot; there's cold over there, those buckets, see. When you're done, just lift this round bit in the bottom and the water runs out through a pipe into tanks outside. Clever, isn't it? Gardeners use it then."

"I'll get my things. Can I use one of those towels? I haven't got one with me."

"That's what they're there for. Leave it in that big basket; any clothes you want washed too. Someone'll see to them."

"Thank you very much."

"My job, sir. Oh, I suppose you know about baths?"

Tamlyn suppressed a smile. "Yes, I do thanks. Ours doesn't have a stopper thing like that though. Good idea."

"No offence meant, only they had a woman visiting over in the ladies' apartments, and she got in with all her clothes on." Bart shrugged and grinned. "I expect we'll meet up later if you're working here."

Tamlyn was pleased to feel properly clean again. He dressed in his own clothes, glad that he'd brought them, and put the others in the basket. All the while he was wondering what he ought to do when he'd breakfasted, for besides not knowing how to reach the King's apartment, he hadn't any idea if that was where he should go anyway, or what Almaran would want him to do. He vaguely remembered mention of employment as a scribe.

"Hallo." A cheerful young woman greeted him as he entered the kitchen. "I've done a bit of everything for you as I didn't know what you'd like."

"You must be Deelah."

"That's right. Dee, usually. Come and sit down, sir, and I'll bring you what you want."

'A bit of everything' proved to be the biggest breakfast Tamlyn could remember eating. As he ate Dee sat opposite him, gazing at him in silence; it was disconcerting. Eventually she said, "The others are going to be so cross they weren't on duty here this morning."

"Oh? Why?" It seemed an odd thing to say.

"We don't often get handsome young strangers like you staying. I've got first chance with you."

Tamlyn almost choked on a mouthful of bacon, and felt himself going red. It was clear that women were much freer here, and he really didn't know how to respond. What might Hallam say? Something a bit jokey maybe.

"Perhaps you should get some eye glasses," he offered solemnly, which caused Dee to dissolve in giggles. Tamlyn pushed his plate away. "I'm not sure what I'm supposed to be doing now, so could you guide me to someone who might help me?

"Oh that's all right. There was a message left that you were to go to the King's office when you'd finished breakfast. I can take you up there."

Tamlyn made a determined effort to start remembering the plan within the palace. The problem was that inside it was difficult to tell which section he was in. Dee took him past Almaran's apartment to a door further along the corridor which proved to be his office. The outer part had four desks where two women and a man were sitting. Perched on the fourth was Mardell who seemed to be amusing the rest, who were all laughing. He jumped up when he saw Tamlyn.

"Awake at last. Will you come..."

A door at the back opened and Almaran stood there. "Come on in, Tamlyn. Mardell, can you stop entertaining my staff and do some work yourself?"

"I just wanted to ask Tamlyn..."

"Later. Please." Mardell obviously knew when Almaran was being King and not Grandfather. He touched his hand to his head in brief salute and went out. Tamlyn followed the King into his office. "Shut the door, will you? Come and sit over here."

The room was definitely a working one, but comfortable. Besides cupboards, shelves laden with books and papers and a desk there were two easy chairs by the window and it was here that they settled. A tray with glasses and a jug of water stood on a table between them. Almaran, elbows on his chair arms, linked his hands and tapped his chin with the two forefingers as he looked at Tamlyn.

"I've been thinking a lot about you since yesterday. You are – and I have no doubts about this – completely different from the former youngsters that your High Lord sent to annoy me. I'm convinced that he did not expect them to succeed in what he asked them to do. You, on the other hand, could probably make a viable plan for my assassination, with a strong possibility of success."

"No," Tamlyn almost shouted.

"I didn't say would; I said could. You are older, far more mature, and from the little I've seen of you, thoughtful and intelligent. However, though I've no actual proof, I do believe you when you say you wouldn't kill me. Maybe I'm wrong in saying 'no proof'; your rejection of that expensive and really quite beautifully crafted knife was obviously heartfelt, and most interesting."

"I hate the idea of killing anyone. If I believed, as I was taught, that you really were a wicked magician causing evil enchantments in The Land, then I might consider the possibility of killing you, but I don't believe that, and neither do I believe that evil enchantments exist." Tamlyn's voice was quiet but intense.

"Hmm. So now I have a dilemma. If what you say is true, why are you here? You didn't deny that your High lord sent you here, as he did the others, to try and kill me and I find it difficult to think that he, being what he is, would not have made sure of you first."

Tamlyn looked down at his hands, tightly clenched in his lap. He wanted to trust this man, but trust did not come easily to inhabitants of the Citadel. He seemed to hear Merla's voice: 'believe in yourself'. Deep down, he did believe that this man was the generous, kindly and honest person he seemed. He decided. He *would* believe in Almaran and tell him the truth.

"When the High Lord told me what he wanted me to do, he was lying. He didn't expect me to reach your City because he'd planned to have me killed on my journey here; a group of his guards were supposed to waylay me and make it seem that I'd been set on by robbers. I discovered this by accident and travelled another way. I have no proof of this except the large amount of money in the purse I was given, which was meant to pay those men, but it is the truth, sir, I swear."

The King suddenly looked much older. He sat totally still with his eyes closed. When he opened them Tamlyn could see a glint of tears in them. "I do believe you," he said. "Can you tell me why he wanted you dead?"

"I think he believed that I was working against him, or would do in the future."

"And were you?"

172

"That's difficult to answer. There are others now who have become aware that things in the Citadel are not good and need changing. I had been having thoughts like that, and these others showed me proof that seemed to confirm those thoughts. I've actually done nothing against the High Lord, but one of my teachers was killed very brutally because he was suspected of treachery, and I was close to him. I think that was why I was suspect."

"What did you think you would do here, Tamlyn?"

"I really didn't know; I still don't. I had to leave or I would have been suspected even more, wouldn't I? Find the truth, perhaps, and I've already discovered that what we've been taught about the City is totally wrong. Merla believes that change is coming, and many things that seem like chance are actually part of that change. I want be part of whatever is happening, and see The Land as it should be."

"You said yesterday that you would have to go back sometime, but didn't know when. To me now it seems you'd be going back into a very dangerous place."

"It is my home. Others are in danger too."

"I understand."

"Can I ask you two things, sir?"

Almaran nodded. "I'll answer if I can. You'll understand that I too must always put the safety of my kingdom first."

"Can you tell me what happened to the others who came before me?"

"Ah, let me see. There have been five, I believe. Yes, that's right. Two live and work here in the City; one went to work for a farmer in the south and has married the farmer's daughter; another went down to the coast and became a sailor. The fifth I don't know. Though we tried to dissuade him he wanted to go home and tell everyone we weren't so wicked. I rather think he would not have been welcome."

Suddenly Tamlyn remembered. It was in his first year at the Academy when they'd been called together and shown the beaten and bloody body of a boy not much older than they were. They'd been told he'd been killed by the evil King because he had wandered into the City, a stark warning against such stupidity. Tamlyn had pushed the memory from his mind because it was so terrible: now he knew that it was far worse than he had feared as an eleven year old.

"He died," he said starkly, "but it makes me think of yet another difference between those early would-be killers and myself. In the past, we never knew that anyone had been sent to the City, and if people vanished, well... we didn't ask. But everyone knew I was going on a special mission for the High Lord. That's odd, isn't it?"

Almaran nodded. "It is," he said. "Now you said two questions. What is the second?"

"I've noticed that you seem to understand the High Lord very well, although obviously you don't come to the Citadel. In fact I've never heard of any visitors from here. How is that, sir?"

The King made a small sound, half laugh, half sigh, and a wry smile touched his lips.

"Zerac, your High Lord, is my brother, my twin brother. Though we have not met in more than fifty years, I know him and his ways all too well."

Tamlyn could only gape in amazement. "Your... twin brother?" he gasped at last.

"It's a long story. Shall we go and sit in the garden while I tell it? We shan't be disturbed out there. I think something tastier than water would be welcome too. What would you like?"

"Water is what I usually drink, but the juice you gave me when I arrived was good."

Almaran stood and went to the door. "We're going into the garden, Larris. Would you be kind and get someone to bring apple juice and glasses to us, probably in the herb garden," he added with a smile at Tamlyn. Larris held the door for them to go out, then ran off in another direction.

"The ladies will now discuss you thoroughly, no doubt. We don't often have handsome strangers in the office," laughed the King.

"Oh help, the woman who gave me breakfast, Dee, said something like that. I'm really not used to chatting with ladies."

"Lady Deelah! According to my grandson she's a bit of a tease."

"Lady? But she was cooking my breakfast."

"Oh yes. It's my theory that even if you're never likely to have to work for your living, you should at least have hands-on experience of how your floor is kept clean, the wood is chopped for your fire and the food gets on your table. All those sorts of things. As I'm King I'm allowed my little fancies. Some find they quite enjoy it; my wife, for instance, really loves cooking. It drives the Head Cook to distraction. I have to stop her going in the kitchens when we're having a banquet."

Tamlyn suspected that the King was chattering like this to stop having to talk before he was ready about the fact that he and Zerac were twins. It was something he had still not quite taken in himself. They came out into the garden and Almaran led them to the chamomile bank under the bay tree, where he sat down and patted the ground beside him.

"I'll get a seat put here; it's very pleasant. Ah, here's our apple juice."

A very young man set the tray on the ground and scuttled away after bowing deeply.

"A new recruit by the look of it. Now, Tamlyn, where to begin? At the beginning I suppose." Almaran poured juice into the glasses and sat staring into his as though it contained the words he needed.

"Seventy-three years ago the Queen of this country gave birth to twin boys. She and her husband, the King, who had been childless for many years, were delighted, and named them Almaran and Zerac. That's me and your High Lord, of course. I was born first, so by the law of the country I was heir to the throne. This didn't matter for years. Zerac and I were inseparable, sleeping, eating, playing and learning together with no difference in our treatment. I was, perhaps, a little better at our lessons, but he could beat me at anything physical, like riding, swimming and fencing. Then we reached the age of twelve and I had to begin learning what it was to be King. That was when Zerac realised he was excluded from all this as he was not the heir. We were both upset, and I tried to include him. After all, I argued, something might happen to me, and then Zerac would succeed me if I had no children. It was no use. The law was the law and must be obeyed. I tried to pass on what I was taught, but at this point he turned against me and refused. He railed continuously about the unfairness of it all; that I would have all and him nothing simply because of half an hour, as he saw it. He blamed our mother bitterly too, for not having him first. It made her desperately unhappy, but nobody in the family could calm him. Beyond the family, he was still the same handsome, witty, charismatic young man he had always been, and he gathered round him a large group of friends with whom he'd ride, hunt, joust, and feast in the large house our father gave him in an effort to make him see that he hadn't lost everything, only the crown. For him, though, the crown *was* everything. Gradually I believe he actually thought he was the victim of a plot rather than an accident of birth."

Almaran paused to sip his juice, and Tamlyn did the same, realising as he did so that he'd been gripping the glass so tightly in both hands that it had become warm.

"Our father died when we were eighteen and I became King. I went to Zerac and suggested that we shared the kingship, but he rejected the idea. He would either have all or nothing. He informed me that he and his friends were leaving the country to find a new home where he would be ruler, and I'm ashamed to say I didn't try to stop him. I badly missed the brother he had been, but not the man he had become. You know, of course, where he and his followers went."

Tamlyn nodded without speaking, remembering what Merla had told him of Zerac's arrival in The Land and its aftermath.

"At eighteen, I was young to take on all the duties of becoming King of the City and its lands. I was also in love, and planning to marry Veranne. My mind was too full of all this to worry very much about Zerac. Had he returned, unable to find his daydream kingdom, I would have welcomed him, but he didn't. I knew where he was, but he made sure that there was no real contact between our countries, and I acquiesced in that. I didn't try to find out what was happening in your land, and when he sent his little assassins I let myself believe he was just doing it to annoy me, because he knew me well enough to be sure I wouldn't harm them. My thinking was that perhaps these were boys who for some reason he wanted to be rid of. He never had much patience with anyone who didn't do exactly what he planned. I knew nothing of his fantasies about evil enchantments until the youngster before you who babbled about it, but even then I thought it was a story fed to an impressionable child. Now I have met you. The things you've said, and even more the things you've not said, have made me see that it would have been better if I had made an effort to know. I should have done something. I did not, and I am deeply saddened by that."

Almaran bowed his head and was silent, and Tamlyn tried to think what to say. He didn't want the King to blame himself for what was entirely his brother's fault.

"What could you have done if you had known?" he asked. "Would you have brought an army to turn your brother out? Where would he have gone then?"

"We don't have an army. I vowed when I became King that I would never take my country to war. Perhaps I was wrong."

"I don't think you were, sir. I've no experience of these things, but if you had come to fight the High Lord lots of people would have been killed, and you might not have won at the end of it. I believe he enjoys killing. I shouldn't say that to you about your brother, but I know it's true. I can't really explain it, but I feel something *is* growing in The Land which could be the end of him and we must wait and see. Your City and kingdom are good places. When the changes come to The Land, will you help us make it as open and happy as it is here?"

Almaran looked up at him. "Tamlyn, you show great understanding in spite of your youth. We can't change what is past, can we? But I'll help all I can from now on. We've talked enough on this for now, but we need to decide what's to be done with you while you stay with us."

"I should like to be of use here in some way, if you can employ me as you suggested. For now though, may I go out of the City for an hour or two? I would like to let my friends know I am safe, and I know how to send a message secretly if you'll allow it."

The King eyed Tamlyn with a twinkle in his eye. "Permission granted, and if it involves the family in the house in the bank, please give them my best wishes."

Once again Tamlyn was startled. "You know them?"

"Of course. They're some of my subjects, after all, and quite a few locally have experienced what I think are called 'wild walks' with their Uncle Vitsell. I've not met him personally but I suspect he has an unusual sense of humour."

Tamlyn laughed. "Very unusual."

They made their way back into the palace. "Speaking of humour," Almaran went on lightly, "and also of what you might do, I'll gladly use your observance skills sometimes, but I'd also like you to have some enjoyment while you're here. You are, what, eighteen?"

"Nearly, sir."

"Far too young to spend all your time working or worrying. I realise you have a great deal on your mind, and maybe it feels to you that you should be thinking of it constantly. However, can an old man advise you that if there is nothing to be done at the moment, some time spent in laughter and fun will refresh you and lighten the load."

Tamlyn remembered how Hallam and his classmates had made him feel so much better with their antics on the morning of his departure from the Citadel. He laughed now as he thought about it. "I'll be happy to take your advice, sir," he replied.

"I'll leave you in Mardell's hands for that then. I know he's anxious to get you dancing, but don't let him have it all his own way."

Chapter 22

It was, as Vitsell had said, easy to recognise the house belonging to his family, known locally as the Vansells. Tamlyn discovered this from the name board outside their home-in-the-hill, which was considerably bigger than Vitsell's. On the other hand, there were many more Vansells, but all of them much shorter and plumper than him, and they greeted Tamlyn kindly in accents very much like those he'd heard in the City streets.

"Of course we'll give Uncle your message," Vitsell's nephew assured Tamlyn. "He'll be here before long I reckon. Just 'all is well', is that it? He'll remember that all right."

"And the King sends his best wishes," Tamlyn added. "That's not for Vitsell, just for you."

The family received this with smiles and nods. "He's a real good 'un, he is," the father of the family declared. "Me and the wife remembers The Land just about, but this lot," he gestured to the widespread family clustered round them, "here's their home. Grandchildren were all born here. Don't reckon as we'd ever go back, but 'twould be nice to visit. Not while that High Lord's still around, though. Can we offer you a drink or a bite?"

"Thanks, but I need to get back. I'll come again if I may," and Tamlyn set off, glad to be stretching his legs in the open air. Remembering he'd been told that only a small part of the eastern city wall was still standing, he turned left outside it and walked towards where the river must be, to discover where the wall stopped. It must have been a really strong defence in the past, but quite soon as it curved towards the south west it began to peter out into ragged stumps and finally disappeared. It was easy to see that some of the missing stone had been used in the building of houses nearby.

The river soon came into sight, and in places houses had gardens that stretched down to the water's edge. Tamlyn followed the roadway that wound along between this sprawl of buildings stretching in front of him as far as he could see, and he was beginning to wonder how to get back to the palace when he recognised the two houses he'd visited with the King. He felt unexpectedly pleased that one small part of this widespread City was now familiar to him, and he turned up the street to return. He was crossing the gardens in front of the palace when he heard a voice.

"Hoy, Tam." Mardell came running across towards him, dressed in well-worn and somewhat grubby clothes. "Saw you come in. I've organised a few of us to start your dancing lessons," he announced with a grin. "After supper; and Grandmamma says you're to eat with us till you get settled in. I'm staying with them too, while my parents are off doing their royal duties. Must get back to my group now before they start to wreck the place. See you later." He was off before Tamlyn had time to say anything. Mardell rarely seemed to leave space for breaths, let alone answers.

Dancing! He had very little idea of what that meant. Did you need special clothes or shoes? Well, he'd try his best. For the moment, since it must be long past lunchtime but not nearly suppertime, he decided to wander and try to get at least some of the layouts of the buildings in his head. It was so much harder than out of doors where the shape of hills and the position of the sun were known points to guide you. Tamlyn found the King's garden and went indoors from there thinking things might look familiar, but before long he was wandering aimlessly. By peering through windows he reckoned he was in the central part of the building complex, and when he'd climbed a flight of stairs he came to the entrance of a grand hall which brought him to an amazed halt. The ceiling, higher than any he'd seen, was covered with brilliant paintings, and a huge candle holder, for at least a hundred candles he guessed, hung in the centre. There were smaller sconces on the walls between tall windows draped with rich gold and crimson curtains. The floor was of gleaming, smoothly polished wood. Tamlyn had thought the large hall in the Citadel was splendid but it would have been lost in this place. He wandered into the centre and stood with his head tilted up as he studied the ceiling.

"Can I help you?" A voice close behind him made him spin round, almost losing his balance. An elderly woman was standing there.

"I hope it's all right for me to come in. I've never seen anything like it," Tamlyn said.

"It is lovely, isn't it? Yes, of course; we like people to see it. The ceiling was painted for His Majesty's grandfather who employed someone from over the sea to come and do it. Can you see, the pictures are in circles and show the seasons, starting with spring on the outer edge. Then in the corners those figures are meant to be the spirits of the seasons. I've always suspected that the artist must have come from a very hot country to dress Winter as scantily as that." The woman gave a little laugh. "Are you a newcomer, sir?"

"Yes. I was trying to find my way round, but it's very muddling."

"I've worked here for years and I still take wrong turnings sometimes. I can help you a bit though. Come through to my office; we've got some plans that show what's in each section of the palace." Tamlyn followed her as she trotted off, explaining all the time that this was the great hall, used for the grandest occasions. "We only light the ceiling candles for extra special times because it smokes the paintings. They have to be cleaned very carefully every ten years or so, and the wall lights are fine for most things. A bit more romantic, I always think. Ah, here we are." She turned into a small room which seemed to have books and papers everywhere. Shuffling among the piles on a desk, she came up with a sheet and handed it to Tamlyn, who studied the diagrams and writing as the helpful woman explained.

"The five main areas have letters A to E, and at the side of each the floors are numbered from 1 upwards with a note of what's on each floor. See here. This is where we are on C2. Shalanna worked this out when she was still in school. So good with things like that, she is. Starting in the treasury this year, I hear."

"It's really kind of you. I think I'll go and look at this," said Tamlyn.

"Glad to help." The woman picked up a handful of small red books. "I must take these up to the housekeeping office. I was just going when I saw you. Come again and I'll show you round a bit more."

She walked away briskly and Tamlyn took the plan to a seating area in the entrance hall he found marked on C1. Once he realised how to look at it, he began to understand how to use it. Hallam would get on with Shalanna, he thought. As he noticed people beginning to leave the building, he worked out how to get from where he was to the King's apartment and managed it with only one wrong turning.

Tamlyn thought the prospect of dancing lessons was one of the most terrifying things he'd faced. As Mardell led him through the palace after supper he kept trying to tell himself that people actually thought it was fun, but his brain wasn't listening. The room they came to was about the size of the gymnasium in the Citadel, and a group of people were laughing and chatting at one end. He recognised Dee and the man who'd poured water into the bath, Bart, that was it. Larris from the King's office, and two girls he didn't know made up the group. Mardell introduced the girls as Stevy and Felissa.

"Where's Cotter?" Mardell asked.

"He'll be here, he's always late," Dee said, and Tamblyn remembered the man with the pile of books that morning. He ran in at that moment.

"We'll go slow and just do the steps for a start," ordered Mardell, "and you girls go in front so Tamlyn can see your feet." He pulled Tamlyn into a line between himself and Cotter, while the girls held hands in a row in front of them. Bart produced a small pipe. "All ready? Off we go then."

For the first half hour Tamlyn wished he could run away and hide as he stumbled and mis-footed, hands firmly gripped on either side by the two men. Then gradually the pattern of short and long steps, the dips and rises, the lift and fall of hands and arms made its way into his body, and the steady rhythm of the pipe music was like a ribbon, pulling and guiding him.

"That was really good," said Mardell, when at last Tamlyn managed the length of the room with no mistakes and without being pushed or pulled. "You've got a great sense of rhythm." The others all crowded round to clap him on the back. "Right, now we'll do the first part of Green Manikin. You all right, Bart?"

"Could do with a drink, I'm blown out,"

"Oops, sorry, I forgot." Mardell ran out and returned with large tumblers on a tray. "Put these here earlier. Help yourselves. Drink up, though, before Tam forgets what we've so arduously taught him."

By the time Mardell decided they'd done enough, Tamlyn had managed to get all the way through Green Manikin, including grasping Stevy by the waist and twirling her off her feet as they changed sides. A cheer went up, not only from his fellow dancers, but from others who had come in to see what was happening and were standing round the edge of the room. He felt so exhilarated that he didn't even feel embarrassed.

"Thank you. Thank you so much," he laughed. "You were all very patient, and that really was fun".

"Told you it was. Now you've got the idea with an easy dance you can soon learn the harder steps," Mardell told him.

Everyone, including the spectators, seemed happy with the evening's work, except one rather surly looking young man who appeared to be glaring at him. Perhaps that was just his normal look, decided Tamlyn, and happily went off to his room with Bart and Cotter.

Almaran had record-writing work for Tamlyn on the next two days, but in his spare time he wandered out into the City. How quickly he'd begun to feel at ease here! People were friendly and helpful, not only in the palace where they must know that he was working with the King, but out in the streets. A stranger was not someone to distrust or fear, but a person who might be interesting, or perhaps need help. This was how The Land should be. Would be; he had to believe that. Although he was really enjoying his time here, in his heart he still longed to be back in his real home.

In the palace he gradually discovered that Mardell was not simply the wealthy young joker he seemed, always looking for the next bit of fun. He worked regularly with groups of youngsters who, for one reason or another, had run into trouble with their lives. Tamlyn was quite relieved to find that all was not perfection in this place – his first impressions had suggested that everyone was happy and satisfied – but the methods of dealing with wrong-doers were as far from the High Lord's as it was possible to get. Mardell's easy-going cheerfulness apparently found acceptance with non-conforming, angry young men. He introduced them to more legal ways of making a living, and it was from some of his groups that he'd learned how to pick a pocket. He'd hinted to Tamlyn about learning other disreputable skills which as yet he'd not mentioned to his grandfather.

"You're invited to Dee's home for her birthday tomorrow evening," Mardell told Tamlyn early one morning when he'd been in the City two weeks. "Mostly in the gardens, but there may be some dancing. Have you got any more dressy clothes? Her parents are nice, but a bit old-fashioned. Can never make out how they managed to produce Dee."

"Um... I have got something made for me before I came, but I'm not sure..." The idea of wearing the clothes which still lay folded in his bag filled Tamlyn with horror. He'd seen no one in anything like them.

"Let's have a look." Mardell was already out of the door. When Tamlyn laid the things on his bed they were greeted with hoots of laughter. "I've never seen anything like this. Hmm. They're good material though. Tell you what, I'll take you round to Jecks, my tailor and see what he can do with these. He's brilliant at alterations. Come on. Sooner the better if you want them tomorrow."

The tailor, whose shop was close to the palace, managed to keep a straight face when presented with Tamlyn's clothes.

"Hmm. Well, ah... yes. I can do something I think," he said, after examining them.

"Can you do them really, really quickly, Jecks?"

"The day you come in here and don't want something done the day before yesterday I shall probably die of shock, sir. However, I will do my best."

"That means 'yes'," crowed Mardell. "Jecks, you're a miracle worker. When can my friend fetch them?"

"Tomorrow midday. That will give time for any last minute touches. Luckily they were made to measure, after a fashion, so that cuts down the time."

"They are awfully tight on my legs," Tamlyn put in

"I had noticed, sir," the tailor said, perfectly straight-faced.

"Come on, Tam, let's go so he can get started."

Later that day Tamlyn started wondering about payment. Perhaps Jecks thought Mardell was paying, but Tamlyn wasn't having that. He'd got very mixed feelings about the money in the purse from the High

Lord; mostly he felt sickened at the thought of touching it, but when he returned, pretending of course that he knew nothing of the plot to kill him, it would be logical for him to have spent something on necessities. He'd been told that he would receive a salary for his work at the palace and he'd use that most of the time, for however long he was here.

At midday next day Tamlyn walked round to see Jecks, and was delighted when he tried on the results of the tailor's skill. His clothes now felt comfortable and looked smart, better than he'd ever imagined.

"I'm really very grateful," he told the man. "I'm not used to the money here, so would you take the cost from this and tell me if you need more." He'd taken a handful of coins from the purse and now tumbled them onto the counter of the workshop, Hallam's instructions on values forgotten.

Jecks stared at them, and then eyed Tamlyn with a small smile. "It's a good thing I'm an honest man, sir. There is probably sufficient there for the entire cost of three new suits." He picked up four coins. "This is all I need for the work done. May I suggest that you don't try paying like that too often or you'll soon be rather poorer than you should be."

Tamlyn flushed, feeling very stupid, but Jecks patted him on the arm. "Never you mind, sir. I appreciate that you wanted to pay me. I hope you enjoy yourself in these clothes now."

Suitably dressed Tamlyn set off in the evening with Mardell and Bart. Dee's family lived in one of the houses near the river, and they walked up to see the grand front door open as they approached, held back by two uniformed footmen. There was already a crowd in the hallway, but Dee came dancing out onto the porch to meet them. Mardell and Bart produced wrapped gifts to give her, but Tamlyn had not thought of this.

"Happy birthday, Dee… I'm sorry I haven't…" he stammered.

"Of course you haven't. I only asked Mardell to invite you yesterday, but you can give me a birthday kiss." She leant towards him, lips puckered slightly and blue eyes sparkling with laughter. Tamlyn panicked! The only kisses he could remember were from Merla and the one the High Lord had pressed on his forehead. He didn't think he'd ever kissed anyone himself. What should he do?

"What's the matter? Haven't you ever kissed a girl before?"

Tamlyn shook his head. "No," he whispered.

"Ah, lovely. Then I shall teach you how." Dee stepped up to him, cupped his face in her hands and pressed her lips to his. He felt the softness of her fingers, smelt her perfume, and marvelled that such a gentle contact should make him tingle all over.

"Don't eat him, Dee," he heard Mardell choke out through his laughter. She stepped back, smiling.

For a moment Tamlyn stood frozen, then he grinned back. "Lesson number one, maybe I should practice!" he said, taking hold of Dee's shoulders and lightly returning her kiss.

Dee looked amazed, then she was smiling at him as Mardell and Bart applauded. "That was a lovely birthday gift," she said. "Come and meet Papa and Mama now."

Tamlyn enjoyed the evening, the food, the silly games, the music, just walking through the gardens, it was all so light-hearted, and everyone was sociable. As the sky darkened a full moon rose over the river and he stood alone for a moment on the grassy bank, thinking that this water had flowed past his home. He wondered how and when he would know it was time to return, and whether he would ever be able to come back to this friendly place.

"Come on, Tam, we're going to dance and they want to start with your one." Stevy and Felissa took his hands and ran with him back to the house. Wide doors had been opened that led them into a room with a polished dance floor and he was pushed, laughing, into his place between Mardell and Cotter. The music, played now by several musicians, gave them a starting chord and Tamlyn found himself dancing as the music called up the memory of what he should do. He stood and watched as other groups performed different dances, though he found he could see similar steps in each. Finally everyone joined in a circular caper in which it really didn't matter what you did as long as you kept moving round.

They all ran into the garden to cool off after this. Tamlyn was standing near Mardell and a few others when a voice shouted above the chatter.

"Oy. You. Tamlyn. I want you."

He turned to see a man who at first he didn't recognise. Then he realised it was the one he'd seen glaring at him on the evening of his dancing lesson, and his face now was even more furious as he advanced with clenched fists.

"It's that idiot, Durgan. Been drinking too," he heard Mardell mutter behind him. "We'll deal with him."

"No. It's all right." Tamlyn signalled to stop Mardell or anyone else taking over. "Can I help you my friend?" He stepped towards Durgan.

"You're not my friend, you prigging foreigner. You can just stop prancing around, cuddling up to Stevy. She's mine, and I'm going to give you a lesson to make sure you remember that."

By now a silence had fallen round them and suddenly Tamlyn was back in the Citadel with Hallam and Sharkley. Durgan in front of him was about Sharkley's build, but it was obvious his one thought was simply to smash his fists into Tamlyn's face.

"What lesson is that?" he asked calmly.

"This." The fist swung. The next moment Durgan was flat on his back on the grass, and Tamlyn was brushing his hands together as he smiled down at him. It really had been easy when the man didn't know what was coming.

"Was that the lesson you meant?"

There was a whoop from the watchers. Tamlyn held out a hand to pull Durgan to his feet, and the fall seemed to have sobered him a bit. "Listen, Durgan," Tamlyn said quietly, "Stevy is a very nice young lady who kindly joined in with others to teach me to dance because I'd never done it. I did nothing more than follow instructions. I don't believe she's yours because you can't own other people, but if you want her to stay being your friend then I suggest you stop being an idiot." He turned his back on the man and gradually the party continued.

"How in the name of Hecate did you do that?" Mardell muttered in his ear.

"I'll tell you if you teach me some of your tricks," promised Tamlyn. When he got the chance he'd have to learn more from Sharkley himself, he thought. He'd only succeeded this time by surprise.

Chapter 23

Tamlyn had explained to Mardell that he was really only a novice in the method of fighting he'd used on Durgan.

"I took him by surprise so it was easy," he said. "I can show you what I've learnt, but don't expect it to work so well if your opponent knows what you're up to. When I go home I'm going to get some more lessons from Master Sharkley. Maybe I'll be able to pass them on to you sometime."

"You're always on about going home," Mardell grumbled. "I'd have thought you'd be better off staying with us. Grandpa likes you, says you're the best scribe he's had."

"It's amazing here, and I do like it, but The Land is my home. I need it, and I think it needs me," Tamlyn said simply. "Come on. You said you'd show me how to pick locks." The two of them wandered off to the room where Mardell met his 'boys'' as he called the youngsters he worked with.

Tamlyn now ate breakfast regularly at the lodging house, and other meals with some of the friends he was making in the palace, trying out one or other of the eating places there. Veranne still insisted on his taking a meal now and then in the King's apartment, which was no hardship as she certainly was an excellent cook. Lyddy would enjoy knowing her, Tamlyn thought, though secretly he judged Lyddy's cooking as the best.

One morning Mardell rushed up to him as Tamlyn was making his way to the King's office.

"Great news. My parents and the rest of their party have landed and are on the way up from the harbour. They're stopping overnight at Marrambury and I'm going to ride down to meet them there and come back here with them tomorrow. Grandpa's ordering a banquet in the Great hall to welcome them: make sure your best clothes are ready."

Not only Mardell but most of the palace were excited by the news which had been brought by a fast messenger late the previous night.

Normal work was put aside and everyone was busy with preparations, when they weren't chatting excitedly. Tamlyn hadn't realised quite what a large party had gone with Almaran's son and his wife, Dallis and Joselle, but it seemed that some fifty others were with them as wardrobe keepers, hairdressers, advisors, general assistants, luggage organisers, and various others necessary to make sure the royal couple knew all they needed and looked as they should in representing Almaran in a foreign kingdom. Tamlyn felt a bit out of it at first, but soon found himself occupied when a spare pair of hands was needed in fixing festoons of greenery, or legs to take messages here, there and everywhere. By this time he was fairly secure in finding his way around the palace, although he did rush into the kitchens by mistake when looking for the Cellarer.

"Out, out, out," screamed a red-faced man. "No more messages from Her Majesty if you value your life." When Tamlyn reassured him on that point he was whisked off to give an opinion on two sauces, (which both tasted delicious), before he could manage to ask for the man he wanted.

Mardell and a groom rode off to Marrambury at midday and the whole party were expected in the City by the middle of the next day, which would give time for the travellers to rest and dress for the banquet in the evening. When there seemed nothing left for him to do, Tamlyn retired to his bedroom. Early on in his stay in the City he had discovered with incredulous delight the royal library with shelves full of books available to all the palace dwellers, and now he curled up with a book on sea plants. He'd had no idea anything could grow in salt water, but hoped he might actually see them one day.

The next day he woke to hear rain, but it was only a brief shower and soon the sun was shining. The travellers would cross the river by a bridge a mile or two away on the south-west of the city and ride in from that direction. Tamlyn went out well before they were due and found crowds in holiday mood waiting to cheer them on their way. He thought of the difference when the High Lord and his lords rode out. Then as many as could would keep out of sight, or simply stand, blank-faced and with heads bowed, until the riders had passed. He came back to the palace and stood among those waiting in the grounds there. As the sun reached its high point the sound of cheering came nearer and Almaran, Veranne and their daughter, Laletta, with her husband, Coraman, came out on the steps of the central entrance. Tamlyn had only met these two briefly. They lived a mile or so away and had two small children, the ones Mardell dubbed 'Lala's brood'. Tamlyn had seen him playing on the lawn with them once, and guessed he was actually delighted to be 'Uncle Marda'.

At last the clatter of hooves sounded just beyond the gates and the leading riders entered the palace grounds, a man and woman who must be Dallis and Joselle, with another man and woman riding at their sides but slightly behind. Mardell brought up the rear of this group, but after them came a troop of other riders. These reined in their mounts while the leading five dismounted and climbed the steps to be greeted with hugs and kisses. Then there was a general dispersal, with grooms running forward to lead the horses away to the stables, and small carriages and carts being driven off to be dealt with elsewhere.

The royal party on the steps turned to wave to the crowds before they went indoors, and suddenly Tamlyn's heart leapt and his breathing almost stopped.

"Lyddy," he whispered. Then common sense took over. The woman standing beside Joselle was far older than Lyddy, but her blonde hair and blue eyes had made her look remarkably similar at first glance. She was obviously close to Joselle; now that the formality of the royal arrival had passed the two of them were chatting, pointing out and waving to people in the crowd and generally behaving like friends. Tamlyn determined to ask Mardell who she was. He guessed that the man now standing by Dallis, and who seemed equally at home in the royal group, was probably the blonde woman's husband.

The evening banquet was both splendid and happily friendly. Tamlyn sat with Cotter, Larris, and the three girls from his dancing group, feeling amazingly at home as they enjoyed the wonderful food and joked together. When the last toast had been drunk and the tables cleared away they wandered round the great hall, the five city dwellers catching up with people they'd not seen for a while. Mardell joined Tamlyn and began to point out notables for him. Tamlyn had found his gaze returning to the blonde woman time and time again so he thought this was a good opportunity to satisfy his curiosity.

"Mardell, who's the blonde lady by your mother?"

"Who? Oh that's my Auntie Bel, Lady Belsanna actually. She's lovely, isn't she? She's my mamma's best friend and her husband's over there by my dad. Uncle Daven. They do the attendant thing when it's formal, but mostly they're just great friends. She's not a real aunt, of course, but she's my favourite. Lala's been looking after their two girls while they've been away. Bel and Daven were rather nervy about leaving them; guess I'd be too, if I was them."

"Why's that?" Tamlyn tried to sound normal, but his heart began to thump.

"They lost a little girl, years ago."

"Lost? You mean she died? That's so sad."

"No, she just vanished. Kidnapped probably, though there was never any demand for money. I was about seven I think. Yes, that's right. I can remember all the panic and searches, but Rosanne had disappeared totally. Really awful for Bel and Daven. The nursemaid was absolutely distraught too, of course. She'd been meeting this young man and he'd vanished at the same time so she thought the two things were connected, but no reason or clue was ever found."

Tamlyn could scarcely breathe. It all seemed to fit, except for why a kidnapper had just dumped the small child. Could have lost his nerve perhaps, or been seen and made a run for it. No, that last didn't work; the child would have been found and returned in that case. Maybe whoever disturbed the kidnapper had taken her until all the searches disturbed them. Too many ifs and buts, but he must be on the right trail. Somehow she'd been left near Vitsell. He was certain of one thing: the old man hadn't been part of any kidnapping.

"Mardell, don't get too excited, but I think it's just possible I know where she is."

"WHAT?" Mardell's yell made people turn and look in surprise.

"Shush. It's only a possibility. When all the celebration here is over I'll tell the King and we can decide how to make certain. A day or two isn't going to make any difference after all the years is it?"

"But what made you think that? You hadn't seen Bel till today had you? At least tell me that."

"There's a young woman of the right age who works in the kitchens of the Citadel where I live. She runs them actually, and she's so like your

191

aunt I actually thought it was her at first sight. She calls herself a foundling because she was found when she was a toddler. Merla took her in and has brought her up; they're really like mother and daughter."

Mardell stared at Tamlyn, for once bereft of speech. At last he managed, "You must tell Grandpa straight away. It's fantastic."

"I will, first thing tomorrow, I promise. Everyone's tired now, and it's too late to do anything anyway." Tamlyn tried to calm the young prince down. Probably he shouldn't have told him first, but he'd been so excited himself it had all burst out. He began to see huge problems that might arise which would take careful planning to overcome. "Go and get some sleep. I'll come straight up to the King's office in the morning."

Tamlyn left his curtains open to make sure he woke early, but he needn't have bothered for he was roused by loud thumps on the door when it was barely light. He found Larris there, looking as though he'd been recently roused himself, with rumpled hair and shirt fastenings askew.

"Quick. You're wanted in the King's office right away. Get your clothes on, Tam. Not sure what it's about, but the whole family seems frantic about something. Come on."

They raced up together and into the outer office. It was empty, but the door to the King's room was open and Tamlyn walked through, trying to get his breath back. Almaran, Veranne, Laletta, Coraman, Dallis and Joselle were all there and turned to him as he entered.

"You wanted me, sir," Tamlyn said with a bow to the King, but he'd scarcely got the words out when Joselle launched herself at him, grabbed his arms and shook him.

"Where is he? Where have you sent him?" she screamed in his face.

Dallis stepped to her and gently pulled her back. "Be easy, Josie. He doesn't know what you're talking about yet."

"Of course he does. He's sent my son off to get killed. Make him bring him back." She burst into tears and Dallis pulled her into his arms.

"I don't understand. What is it? What's happened?" Tamlyn looked round frantically, but a horrible fear was growing in his mind. Mardell was not there.

Almaran soon turned the fear into fact. He'd been standing by his desk, and now picked up a piece of paper from it and came across to give it to Tamlyn. "Mardell appears to have gone off in the night. He left this."

My Dear Mamma and Papa, I've gone east on a quest to rescue a lost maiden. Tamlyn will tell you. Mardell

Tamlyn's chin dropped on his chest as he screwed up his face in horror. "Oh no," he wailed. "Oh stupid, stupid." He looked up at the family and shook his head. "I am so, so sorry. I never dreamt… I must go after him, quickly."

"First you must tell us what this is all about," Almaran said firmly.

"Yes. What's this about a lost maiden?" Veranne added.

"I should never have said anything last night, but I was so excited," Tamlyn started. "It was when I saw Lady Belsanna, you see."

"No, we don't see. What's Auntie Bel got to do with it?" asked Laletta. So Tamlyn told them all about Lyddy and her story, and how he'd asked Mardell who the woman who looked so like Lyddy was and heard the story of her lost daughter.

"It all seemed to fit, and I could see Mardell was excited so I promised I'd come and tell you first thing in the morning, sir, and that one night wouldn't make any difference after so long. I never dreamt he'd go off on his own. Oh, I must go and stop him. He has no idea what the Citadel is like."

"I'm afraid my son doesn't know the meaning of the word 'wait'," Dallis said quietly.

Joselle looked up, calmer, but not entirely satisfied. "What do you mean about not knowing what the Citadel is like?"

Almaran interrupted before Tamlyn could think of an answer. "I know what he means Joselle, and we don't need to waste time on that. We must think what to do. Tamlyn, I don't imagine you could catch up with Mardell even if you had our fastest horse."

"I'm afraid I don't ride anyway, sir, but I can keep up a good walking pace. It's possible that one of the people who are… well, *aware*, sir, if you know what I mean, might see him and find a safe place for him. We must hope so."

Coraman, who'd not spoken so far said, "I could take the young man pillion for a safe distance. That would speed him on his way."

"Well thought. Is there anything else, Tamlyn? I don't believe the fault here is really yours, and I do realise what this means, you know," the King said.

"I think maybe this is one of the things that are meant to happen. I don't know if it's possible in a short time while I get ready, but is there something I could take… something that is not of great importance to you but which I could pretend was a secret I had stolen and give it to the High Lord. It might put him in a good mood."

Dallis had been speaking with Joselle in low voices, and he now said, "Father, would it be more suitable if I were to go and rescue our errant son?"

"Oh no," cried Tamlyn.

A small smile appeared on Almaran's face. "I believe that means Tamlyn thinks it would be doubling the trouble, not curing it," he said. "It was a good thought, but I'll tell you later why it's not a good idea. I've learnt a lot about the High Lord while you've been away. As to your idea, young man, there may be just what you need right here."

He patted the desk. "Come back when you are ready to travel and I'll explain. Coraman, can you be ready in half an hour?"

Everyone seemed to be concurring with the King. He had, as Tamlyn had noticed many times, a quiet authority which gained obedience without force or fury. He spoke again.

"Until we are sure of the real facts I think it would be kinder not to tell Bel and Daven. Although Tamlyn's news is very hopeful, we should wait until it is a certainty; do you all agree?" A chorus of assent came to this. "Very well, off you go. I'm sure Tamlyn will let us know as soon as he can."

"I will, sir. If by no other means I should be able to send a message with Vitsell to his family. I'll go and pack my things."

Chapter 24

Tamlyn returned to the King's office and found Almaran waiting with a bulky envelope. It looked well used, with the red seal chipped and broken.

"Not long ago someone found a small quantity of gold while digging over a new field east of the smaller river and just before it joins the main one. The frontier between The Land and the City lands is very indefinite, but it certainly runs somewhere there. We did some prospecting digs and there *is* gold, but not sufficient to make it worth mining. Here are all the papers about the work we did, but I've removed our decision and details of the quantity to make it seem as though we're contemplating going on. Zerac may well feel that land belongs to him. I've scattered my signature here and there; he'll probably recognise that. I think this should suit your purpose."

"That's really good of you, sir. Thank you," Tamlyn said as he tucked the envelope into his pack. "I may have to say some really nasty things about you," he added with a grin. Now that a plan was taking shape and he was actually on his way he felt more at ease, and 'I'm going home' circled like a song in his brain, producing a bubbling joy that even the prospect of many problems ahead could not squash entirely.

Almaran accompanied him to the door and took his hand. "I feel in my heart that I shall see you again before too long," he said. "Take care of yourself."

"Thank you, Your Majesty," Tamlyn said formally, then he bowed and left to go round to the stables. A stable boy helped him up behind Coraman into the saddle on a large bay horse. He'd never had much to do with the animals and felt nervous at this close encounter.

"Guido's not the fastest, but he's steady and strong. I thought that best for this journey. Our two boys like coming for a ride on him. I realise you're not a horseman, so just hang on to me," Laletta's husband told him.

Tamlyn was glad of this direction; he didn't feel at all safe with his feet so far off the ground. He did try to match his body to the horse's gallop as Coraman did but couldn't get the feel of it. Perhaps it was like dancing; he hoped he'd gradually get the rhythm, but as they rode out of the City and up the road that followed the course of the river between the Citadel and the City he was soon longing for the journey to end. They crossed the little river, then rode on for what seemed like miles, before Coraman reined in the horse to a halt, jumped off himself and helped Tamlyn down. His legs felt incredibly wobbly at first.

"I think this is as far as I'd better go. I can see some houses not far ahead so probably best I leave you here. Good luck to you, young man. Mardell was really stupid to go dashing off like that, but we all love him and would hate him to come to harm."

"I'll do my very best," promised Tamlyn. "Thank you for bringing me this far; I should be able to reach the Citadel by nightfall now." He watched as Coraman remounted, turned the horse, and with a wave galloped back down the way they had just travelled. Then he started walking on and soon fell into his usual easy stride. This was a part of the road he hadn't travelled on his way to the City, but he realised he wasn't that far from the place he'd met Vitsell that day. It seemed an age away, and he'd learnt so much about the City and its inhabitants, all completely contradictory to what he'd been taught for years in school. He'd been trying to work out why the High Lord should insist on these falsehoods; did he actually believe them himself? From what Almaran had told him about his twin brother, Zerac had become obsessed by the idea that he'd been wickedly deprived of what should have been his, though this was certainly untrue. From this, and from what Tamlyn had learnt in his secret readings and from Merla, it seemed more likely that Zerac was driven by a desire, a destructive all-consuming madness really, to be in total control of everything around him, and he had no compunction about using any means he wanted to achieve this.

As the setting sun behind him sent his shadow stretching ever longer on the road ahead Tamlyn switched his thoughts to the more immediate problems waiting for him. In his usual fashion he tried to separate individual items, put them in order, then attempt to deal with them one at a time. First was how to tackle his re-entry into the Citadel. If he'd been simply returning by himself he might have used a main entrance and hoped to bluff his way into seeing the High Lord with his important 'stolen' information, but Mardell's crazy journey here meant that it was more important to discover if he'd actually arrived and if so where he was. He would need to keep himself hidden for as long as he could in order to be free to act, and for this he decided to approach the Citadel from the less overlooked northern side where there were not only more hiding places around the kitchen areas, but quieter entrances, including, if absolutely necessary, the secret passage. It was vital that he tried to get the prince away towards the City as soon as possible, and hopefully before Zerac learned he was there.

Next came Lyddy. Tamlyn was convinced now that she must be the missing Rosanne, and she too would go to the City to be reunited with her real parents. He felt that Merla would agree with this, however hard it was to lose the child she'd cared for over so many years, because Merla believed families were important. His spirits drooped at the thought of Lyddy going, but he believed for her sake it was what should happen.

While these thoughts were going round in his head, Tamlyn hadn't realised how far he'd walked until he topped a small hill and was surprised to find that he could see the flag on the topmost point of the Citadel. The sun was setting in a blaze of colour behind him, and he struck out across the land to his left so that he could work his way north while there was still light to see his way across unfamiliar land. Then he could wait out of sight when he reached a point from which he could easily reach the kitchen area. Taking care over the rougher ground, he tried at the same time to continue planning. Merla would have to be consulted, and maybe Vitsell could be brought in again to help whisk both Lyddy and Mardell away. He suddenly remembered that Mardell must have ridden here, so there was a horse to think of, but there was very little possibility the two could just ride off without being discovered and caught. What would Zerac do if he found he had Almaran's grandson in his power? He shuddered at the thought, and decided to give up planning until he actually knew how things stood.

Tamlyn reached a place where he could see the pigsties and chicken runs outside the kitchens and tucked himself down in the bracken to wait. He was very hungry and thirsty. All he'd had to eat and drink since he woke up had been two sausages and an apple which he'd grabbed in the kitchen of the lodging house as he ran through to pack his things. Coraman had thoughtfully given him the flask of water which was kept lodged in his saddle, but that was now empty. When the light had faded enough to let him approach the buildings without being too obvious, he crept down and edged his way along the wall towards the kitchens. A delicious smell drifted into his nose and his mouth watered; it must be nearly supper time and he'd give a lot to be going down to the refectory with no more worries on his mind than a late essay or a maths problem. He came up to the north door he'd used so often and found it propped open with a bucket of grimy water. Someone must be mopping the stairs and corridors, and he thanked whoever it was for working so late. Stepping in, he listened for sounds of activity, and when he heard nothing raced to the top of the first stairs before stopping again to check. There were voices ahead, but quite distant. If he could just get a few yards along he'd be able to… yes, up here. His heart thudding he shot up another twisting flight, along a corridor, up a further ten steps and… there was Hallam's room. His hand reached towards the door just as it was flung open and Hallam himself charged out and cannoned into him.

"Tam!" Two arms wrapped themselves round him tightly enough to squeeze the remaining breath out of him, then he was lifted off his feet and whirled back into the room. Hallam kicked the door shut, released him, and stood staring at him in amazement.

"You are real, aren't you? I've been wishing so hard you were here, I thought for a minute I'd conjured up a spirit or something. You just don't know how glad I am to see you."

"Me too," said Tamlyn when he'd got his breath back.

"How did you get here? Are you after that hare-brained crazy idiot from the City? What on earth did he think he was doing? We've had such a time today. Oh, I suppose you do know what I'm talking about, do you?"

Suddenly weak with relief, Tamlyn sank onto Hallam's bed. It sounded as though Mardell had at least not yet got into the High Lord's hands. "Yes, I do know," he said. "And that hare-brained, crazy idiot is the King's grandson."

"Oh, I know that. He's still crazy though. Riding up like a Lord, saying he wants to find Lady Rosanne or something. All I can say is he had the devil's own luck choosing today to try that sort of caper."

"That sounds better than I dreaded. He's not in the High Lord's keeping then?"

"The High Lord and most of their lordships have gone off up to the Hunting Fields for five days fun and games killing things. Taken the Elite guards with them too."

Tamlyn stared, then suddenly he was laughing. After all the terrible possibilities that had filled his mind and driven him on during the day, the relief was so intense it was as though every part of him was overcome with hilarity at this respite from dread. Hallam looked as if he thought his friend had lost his senses.

"Not sure I see the joke at the moment," he said.

Tamlyn got up and fetched himself some water from Hallam's jug, drinking it in long, grateful gulps. "Sorry, I've not had much to eat or drink today and I've been imagining such awful things. It was sort of my fault Mardell came. He hasn't got the least idea of what it's like here. Where is he?"

"In Sharkley's rooms."

Tamlyn's jaw dropped. "Sharkley's?"

"It seemed like the best place. He can lock his door, and when he's in his Master mode he can make anyone shut up and listen you know. It was a difficult task with that nitwit."

"I can guess. He's not really stupid though, just never been in a dangerous situation like this. Look, Hallam, I really am starving but best if I don't show myself yet. Could you manage to get me some food and then we'll talk properly, and see what's to be done?"

"I was on my way down to supper just now. I'll go and eat mine and find something that I can bring back. Wedge the door with my chair just in case. I'll whistle a tune when I get back."

Tamlyn was so tired he thought he'd probably fall asleep if he stayed on Hallam's bed, so he leant his elbows on the sill and stood gazing out of the window, soaking up the familiar sights and sounds with the cool evening air. To prevent anyone recognising him if they looked up he shaded Hallam's candles by putting them on the floor beside his desk.

Twilight had almost given way to night, but lights from the Citadel windows cast a low glow on the immediate surroundings, while the moon, just curved in below half, was still bright enough to let him see the outlines of the land beyond. An owl must have been perched somewhere above him, for he heard its hoot, then glimpsed it as it floated silently out in search of its supper. It was all so different from last night's banquet in the great hall, but in spite of everything this was where he was truly glad to be.

A tuneful whistle sounded so he moved the chair from where it was wedged under the door handle and let Hallam in.

"Lyddy might have known you were coming, your favourite pancakes, look." Hallam unwrapped four of them he had in a cloth and handed them to Tamlyn. "I managed to tell her, and called by Sharkley's rooms to let him know you'd turned up. He wants us to go down there so we only have to say things once. Supper was nearly over so we should be able to make it fairly soon, after you've eaten those."

Tamlyn was intrigued by the increase of decisiveness in his friend's speech and actions. The jokey Hallam, always playing the fool, had vanished now that he had grim realities to deal with. He thought he'd changed himself with his weeks in the City, but in the other direction. Apart from Hallam, he'd always preferred his own company and solitude, but while working and living in the palace he'd begun learning to enjoy having fun with others in a place where you didn't have to watch every action and guard your every word. He filled the waiting minutes with some stories of the things he'd been doing, which had Hallam's eyes goggling.

"You set off thinking you might get killed, and end up dancing and going to parties. Some people get all the luck," Hallam laughed.

"I did work for my living too," Tamlyn protested, "and I'm going to be trying to persuade the High Lord I'm still his devoted servant as soon as he gets back. I just hope his hunting trip is going well so he's in a good mood." The thought of this made his insides squirm, even with Lyddy's pancakes gradually satisfying his hunger.

They made their way to Sharkley's rooms using the back stairs and with Hallam going ahead at corners. Hallam tapped a rhythmic knock on the door and Sharkley opened it to peer through a crack before flinging it wide.

"Come in the two of you. Tamlyn, it's good to see you. I gather from my talkative guest you had a better time than you anticipated in the City."

Before he could answer with more than a laugh Tamlyn was stopped in his tracks by the sight of Mardell and Lyddy face to face and obviously arguing.

"Look, your majesty or your highness or whatever you are, you may be able to order people around in the City but not here," hissed Lyddy, clearly only keeping her voice down with an effort.

"But you must come and see Aunt Bel. You are so like her it's unbelievable. You simply must be Rosanne, it all fits," Mardell pleaded.

"I'm Lyddy, and I live here. If I'm someone else as well, it's not your job to tell me what I must do about it."

"But I've come all this way and…"

"…And caused us a terrible lot of trouble," she interrupted. You don't seem to realise even now the danger you're in – that we're all in – if you're found here. Just stop talking and listen will you? I've seen Merla and I want to hear what Tamlyn says. They're the only two I'll listen to. Well you, Master Sharkley and Hallam as well, because I know I can trust you to think straight." Lyddy glared at Mardell, and Tamlyn was torn between amusement at Mardell's face and secret delight that he'd been included with Merla in Lyddy's list of people she'd listen to.

"Calm down. Tamlyn needs to know what we've done here. He can tell us his news later, but this is of more immediate importance." Sharkley took charge, as if dealing with an unruly class. "I'll run through what's happened and you can tell me if I've missed anything. Tamlyn, I expect Hallam's told you that the High Lord and a large number of the Lords and guards are up in the Hunting Fields for several days. It's an incredible stroke of luck. If he hadn't been I think it's highly likely we shouldn't all have been sitting here now, but we must take action quickly before he returns."

The Master went on to detail the day's happenings. Mardell had arrived in early afternoon, and remembering that Tamlyn had said Lyddy worked in the kitchens, he'd ridden round until he saw them. He'd gone in, and found Lyddy, alone as she often was at that time of day, another stroke of luck. She'd obviously been startled and bemused, especially at being called Lady Rosanne by a complete stranger, but when she began to grasp what was happening she realised the danger and knew she must act quickly. She'd fetched Master Sharkley from his class with the pretence of an urgent message; he'd asked Master Jessal to take over and they'd managed to get Mardell to Sharkley's rooms without being seen. Hallam had taken Mardell's horse to the stables, which were fairly empty at the moment, and a young stable boy ordered to deal with him and provide food as though Master Sharkley had decided to acquire a horse. Lyddy ran home to see Merla, ask her advice, and tell her the reason for Mardell's sudden appearance.

"Merla's getting Forley to collect the horse and take it up to the smithy. I think he'll be able to change his appearance a bit, tail and mane cut and some patches of dye," added Lyddy at this point. "He won't look such an interesting thoroughbred then. I think the stable boy will be all right, he lives near us."

Mardell yelped at these suggestions about his horse, but otherwise he'd kept unusually quiet till now. As Lyddy stopped he spoke quietly.

"I'm truly sorry I've caused all this worry, really I am. I should have listened to you, Tam; you said wait till you'd told Grandpa, but it was so exciting to think we might have found Aunt Bel's daughter, I wanted to get started at once. I couldn't believe your High Lord would object when he heard the story."

"You'd better believe it," growled Hallam. "Wouldn't surprise me if he had something to do with her being taken in the first place."

Tamlyn stared at his friend. This hadn't occurred to him, but it certainly wasn't impossible. Zerac could have planned it, but something had gone wrong somewhere and Vitsell had brought the child here anyway, without the High Lord's knowledge. Mardell looked amazed at the possibility.

"That's it so far, Tamlyn," said Sharkley. "Now we have to get you sir," he nodded at Mardell, "out of here as soon as possible."

"Merla thinks Vitsell's at home. She's going to ask him," said Lyddy. "He'll grumble, but he'll do it to please her."

"I want to take Lady Ro... Lyddy with me," said Mardell stubbornly.

"I've told you, it's not your business." Lyddy eyed him narrowly for a moment, then went up to Tamlyn. "Tam, I've talked with Merla, but I want to know what you think. Should I go to the City and see if there's any truth in this story?"

Tamlyn stared at her for a moment until he felt tears sting his eyes. He knew what he must say. He picked up her hands and looked down at them until he'd regained control and could look into her face again.

"I think you should go, Lyddy. When I first saw Lady Belsanna I really thought it was you, the two of you are so alike. You must be about the right age, and the time of your appearance here fits with what I've been told of her daughter's disappearance. To lose a child must be a terrible sorrow, so for her sake as well as your own it feels right that you go. It may be there are things that can prove the case one way or the other."

Lyddy stared back at him, and he saw the sparkle of tears in her eyes too. "You've said the same as Merla. She lost her own daughter, so she knows that sadness and speaks from her heart. Also she has the clothes I was wearing when Vitsell found me. I could take them with me." She took a deep breath and spun round to face Mardell. "Very well, I will go. But even if we find I was this Rosanne, I can't replace fifteen years of my life here with two of which I remember nothing. I belong to this place and I will always be Lyddy, remember that."

Chapter 25

"I would like to see the High Lord." Tamlyn stood in front of two scribes in Lord Zerac's outer office He held the envelope given him by King Almaran low in front of him so that it was below the desk level and out of sight of the two men. Neither of them stopped their writing.

"I expect you would. The High Lord is very busy," one of them drawled without looking up. "Try another day."

Tamlyn didn't move. "Off you go, Scholar," the other scribe ordered. "You've been told. The High Lord is busy and so are we."

"Of course. I do appreciate your problems," Tamlyn said meekly and started for the door. "Perhaps when you do have time you would let him know that Scholar Tamlyn is back from the City with some papers." Both pens abruptly stopped their scratching as he walked through the door and out into the long corridor which ended to the right in the High Lord's rooms. He grinned and kept walking to the left as the door he'd just closed was flung back and one set of footsteps raced towards Zerac's room.

"Er, wait a moment, Scholar". The voice of the other scribe called to him. "We, er, we didn't realise… so many calls on the High Lord's time… you understand. Please come back in."

Tamlyn returned and sat on a chair. Well that had been a moment of fun which had helped briefly to calm the fear that was making his stomach feel as though it was full of angry and overactive frogs. Now he was faced with producing an account of his time in the City that Zerac would believe. Over the last two days, since Mardell and Lyddy had been secreted away to travel east with Vitsell, he'd discussed this interview with Hallam and Sharkley several times but, as they all knew, it would really depend on how Zerac chose to deal with someone he'd previously planned to kill. What his mood and approach would be were completely unguessable.

"You mustn't let him know you were aware he wanted you dead," Hallam reminded him more than once.

"The best advice I can give you is to stick to the truth as nearly as possible," Sharkley said eventually. "If you start making up too many things you're bound to slip up on details sooner or later."

Now the moment was here and Tamlyn concentrated on stilling his ragged breathing and trying to look as though he hadn't any desire in the world except to be of service to the High Lord. He heard footsteps and stood to face the door. Zerac strode in, holding out a hand to Tamlyn. He dismissed the apologies of the two scribes with a brusque "Enough," and, as Tamlyn bowed, he reached to put the hand on his shoulder.

"My dear young man! Had I known you were in the Citadel I would have called you to me before. Perhaps you know, I have been on an expedition for a few days, and things are not as well organised as usual. Come with me to my room and we can talk. You," he snapped at the scribes, "a tray with refreshing drinks for two."

This answered the question of how the High Lord would choose to react, but Tamlyn remembered the kindly cheerfulness of his first interview, followed instantly by that cackling laugh and the plan to have him killed when he was presumed to be out of earshot. He wasn't going to trust Zerac for a moment. When the two of them reached the High Lord's room, Zerac walked to the chairs and table by the window and flung himself down in one chair where some half-eaten fruit lay on a plate nearby.

"My Lord, I am sorry if I've disturbed your meal," said Tamlyn.

"No, no, I had finished. Sit down, Tamlyn; you must have so much to tell me."

Tamlyn did not sit. Instead he knelt with bowed head. "First, my Lord, I have to confess that I did not achieve the initial object of my journey. Though I managed to get employment in the King's household, I was unable to harm him in any way. I am so sorry, but it was beyond my power. As you warned me, he does not have guards around him, but he seems to have protection that it is equally effective. Perhaps you are able to understand that more fully than my feebler learning allowed to me."

There was a quick intake of breath, almost a hiss, but Zerac's voice was still calm and friendly when he spoke. "To be honest, I did not think there was much possibility of your success, but to have told you that would have put doubt into your head before you'd even started out. Now get off the floor and sit there where I can see you. Put it there and clear this away." This last, in a much sharper tone, was to the scribe who'd come in with a tray on which were a jug of juice and two glasses. He obeyed and left speedily, with a bow and a murmured, "M'Lord".

Zerac poured the drink, and Tamlyn could not help being reminded of his first meeting with Almaran. He'd been amazed when he learnt that the two men were twins, but now, as he sat opposite Zerac and was able to study him, he could see the likeness: the same aquiline nose and high cheekbones; the same habit of raising an eyebrow which both Almaran and Mardell had. Zerac was leaner and also wore a beard, but Tamlyn suspected now that the grey streak in his hair was the natural colour and the rest was kept artfully tinted.

"You've had breakfast, I hope."

"In the refectory, m'Lord, but I heard then that you'd returned to the Citadel and came straight up."

"Good, good. Well now, let's hear your story. How was your journey to the City?"

Yes, he would be curious about that since he'd have learnt, as soon as the Guards realised and dared to tell him, that he hadn't been trapped and killed. "It was fairly straightforward. You will know that I have a great love of exploring this beautiful land, so I chose to travel by a more northerly route than the direct road so that I could discover some of the countryside I didn't know. I slept one night on the way, and entered the City the following morning." That should be sufficient, Tamlyn thought.

"A good ploy to avoid anyone trying to stop you. Well done. And what of the City?"

Had there been a hint there that Zerac suspected a different reason for his travelling by a different route? No way to tell. Tamlyn needed no warning to be careful, but the thought made him doubly determined to watch his every word. He told much of his first day in the City in a factually truthful way, but garnished the truth with detail of his awareness of all the differences he noticed between the City and its citizens and his

206

much loved Citadel and The Land. All these, he managed to show by implication, proved how much better the High Lord's domain appeared to him.

"I admit I was frightened when I was taken before the King, but I told him a tale of being tormented by bad things here, and begged him to let me stay in the City. I hope you will forgive me using lies to hide my real purpose."

"It was a clever ruse. And he believed you?"

"Partially, I think. He told me he would keep me by him and I could work for him as a diary scribe until he was sure of me. In fact I was delighted with that for it worked to my benefit. I was able to observe much that would otherwise have been hidden. After some days he allowed me greater freedom and I was even paid for my scribing work." Tamlyn managed a small laugh here, and pulled from his pocket the money bag he'd been given before he left for the City. "I had some expenses in those first days, but I can return most of your money, my Lord." He laid the bag on the table, and felt that he'd disposed of something distasteful.

"Hah! An honest spy!" Zerac sounded genuinely amused, and for a brief flash Tamlyn felt he glimpsed Almaran's brother, the man he might have been. "Well, continue. What brought you back here?"

"From talk I overheard I began to think that certain people, if not the King, were beginning to doubt me, though I was as careful as I could be. From being a diary scribe I was set to copying documents and it was while I was doing this that I chanced on some records – quite recent ones I think – that I realised could be of interest to you. I sensed my usefulness there was coming to an end so I removed the papers and left in the night. I arrived here three evenings ago, but when I realised you were absent I decided I would wait until I could give these directly to you." Tamlyn handed the envelope to Zerac. "I hope my work has been of use, my Lord. Although I failed at the start, I would be glad to feel I had eventually served you in some way."

The High Lord pulled the sheets from the envelope and flipped through them. Tamlyn saw that he looked at the last page first, and nodded. Then he went back and began to read more closely, pausing to study a page with a map on."

"This document is indeed interesting, and genuine I believe. How did you manage to get hold of it?"

This needed quick thought; he should have anticipated that question. "I was in the office when a message came from the King to send this envelope up to him and it was taken from a locked safe room. Later it was returned to the chief official just as he was hurrying out, and I saw him put it in a drawer, presumably not wanting to be detained at that moment by getting the keys for the safe room. I imagine he meant to lock it away on his return, but I noticed that he didn't do so and I was able to remove it because, as the most junior scribe, it was my duty to wait until everyone had left for the day and lock the office. I glanced at the contents and decided to leave with them at once as I was sure their loss would be apparent very soon."

"Well done, you have put some very interesting information into my hands which I shall have to consider carefully. Now we must think what reward I can give you. I'm pleased with your work – your perception and quick thinking are exemplary."

"My Lord, your praise is all the reward I want. I should like to return to my studies in the Academy with your permission."

"Back to school? No, no. I hardly think you need that. You have already shown greater initiative and ingenuity than any of the Masters' facts and figures could teach you. I think I will find a place for you here where I can help your further development myself. How does that sound Tamlyn?"

It sounded terrifying. Tamlyn had been so busy planning his approach to this interview that he'd given very little thought to what would come after. His heart thumped and his hands felt sweaty.

"The honour is too great, my Lord." He couldn't control the quaver in his voice and hoped it would be put down to excitement.

"Nonsense. Yours is the sort of ability that needs nurturing to produce the best results, and I shall enjoy watching you develop. I am busy for a few days and you deserve a holiday. Take yourself off walking or whatever it is you enjoy, but report to me here on Monday. You have had experience of being scribe for the King, so you shall do that work for me now."

Zerac waved a dismissive hand and returned to reading the papers from the City. Somehow Tamlyn's legs took him out through the door where he almost paused to listen, wondering if he'd hear the High Lord's hateful, triumphant laugh. He thought he might collapse in a heap on the floor if that happened, so instead he shut the door firmly and walked on. What he really wanted now was to get back to his own room and try to make sense of all that had happened.

Hallam, with Lyddy's help he guessed, had kept his room ready and tended his plants while he was away. He stood gazing out of the window as he'd done so many times before, but now everything had changed. When he'd looked towards the City then he'd believed it to be a grim and evil place; now it held memories of happiness and enjoyment, as well as many friendships which he would like to continue. Now too it held Lyddy. He saw her in the palace and imagined the joyful reunion with her family. He saw her meeting the people he knew and enjoying the occupations he'd tasted. Would Almaran have to keep her out of the way of the palace cook as he did Veranne? Would Dee tell her about his kissing lesson? He went hot at the thought, but wished he'd had the courage to kiss her before she and Mardell vanished into the night with Vitsell. Maybe she'd marry Mardell; she'd make a beautiful princess. She'd whispered, "I'll be back," into his ear just before she left, but at that point she hadn't known the sort of life she would be able to enjoy with her new family.

He shook himself and turned from the window. There were more immediate and problematic things he had to think about, greatest of which was what the High Lord was planning in inviting – no, ordering – him to do. On the surface Zerac had seemed to accept his story, but Tamlyn didn't trust him. Only a few weeks ago he'd wanted to kill him because of his friendship with Greenwell, so was he now planning to carry this out himself? If he made himself seem friendly and helpful to Tamlyn, who would openly suspect him if his new favourite fell dead from a poisoned drink or a dagger in the back? There would be plenty of others to blame while the High Lord made a show of grieving.

His mind was in a complete turmoil, and he was angry with himself that he couldn't seem to list and order his thoughts in his usual way. The High Lord had made one unambiguous suggestion, a walk. Perhaps that would actually help him sort out the tangle of 'what ifs' and 'maybes' that were beginning to drive him crazy, so he strode off, up and down Herders Hill, but returned as confused as when he'd started. He would dearly love to visit Merla; she had such a way of letting you see things from a different angle, but without Lyddy he was unsure how to arrange this. Hallam only had time for a brief 'hallo' at lunchtime so although he was obviously full of curiosity there was neither the time nor place to talk, and in the end Tamlyn became so frustrated with himself he went down to the gymnasium. Luckily it was empty, so he set half a dozen hard balls up on a bar and punched them off, one after the other, as hard as he could, and went on doing this until he was exhausted. Back in his room he flopped on the bed and in moments extinguished his torment in deep, dreamless sleep.

"Hi, Tam," Hallam greeted him as he sat beside him and they started on thick leek and potato soup with hot crusty rolls. The food was good still; obviously Lyddy had trained her kitchen staff well. A group of scholars in riotous mood were sitting at their table, which made any other communication impossible, but Tamlyn managed to whisper, "My room, later," into Hallam's ear as he leant across for the water jug at a moment of particularly raucous laughter. Then he slipped away to lie in the warm water of the bath and soak away the sweaty reminder of his afternoon's exertions. He should have done it before, but he'd only woken in time for supper.

It was still quite light when Hallam tapped on Tamlyn's door. "Thought I'd better get my school work done before I came up," he said. "Come on, tell! What was it like with the High Lord this morning?"

"He was so friendly it was scary. He seemed to believe what I said, and I was just beginning to think I'd got away with things when he said..." Tamlyn paused and gulped, "said he wants me to go and work for him. Starting Monday."

"Hell on a holiday!" Hallam exclaimed, staring at his friend. "That's more than scary, that's terrifying. You can't really be as calm about it as you're looking."

"I'm not. I've driven myself half mad thinking about it today."

"What does he want you to do; did he tell you?"

"Scribing, like I did for Almaran. I wondered if he said that because he still hates his brother having things he doesn't, or if it's just a way to keep a close eye on me. Have to wait and see I suppose. Look, Hallam, I seriously think we mustn't make it obvious that we're still friends. Could be dangerous for you."

Hallam snorted. "Don't be so priggin' stupid, Tam. You warned me before what the dangers were, and I accepted them. We're friends, and that's that. I'm not about to change my mind, especially with you being shoved right into the middle of the worst of it. I don't mean we should wander around arm in arm, discussing for all to hear how to bump off the High Lord, but I'm here for what you need, as much as I can be."

Tamlyn blinked hard to get rid of tears in his eyes. "Thanks, Hal, you're great," was all he could manage, but he punched his friend gently on the shoulder. He didn't entirely give up on his idea of distancing himself from friends he might put in danger, but Hallam's support was melting some of the icy knot of fear in his chest.

"That's settled then. What do you want to do tonight?"

"The thing I really want is to talk to Merla, but I'm not sure how to organise it. Any ideas?"

"Well, how about we just go and knock on her door. Now for instance, or when it's a bit darker? What's the use of a secret passage if you don't use it?"

Tamlyn laughed. Trust Hallam to think so directly. Why not indeed? "Yeah, fine," he said. Hallam related some school gossip as they waited for the dark to soak away the remains of the day.

They took the circuitous back route to the village to avoid any night guards who might be out enjoying the warm night.

"Hope Merla's not in bed," Tamlyn said.

"It's not that late. I know Sharkley visited her well after lock up time."

Tamlyn stopped dead in his tracks. "Sharkley did?"

"What's so surprising? Friends of Tamlyn getting together. He's all right, he is; I forgive him all those thumps on the mat."

Their knock on the back door was soon answered by Merla, fully clad, who invited them in with evident pleasure.

"Come on in, both of you. With no Lyddy keeping her eyes and ears open I'm not getting quite such speedy news of what's happening in the Citadel. Tam, I really want to hear properly about your time in the City too." Within minutes, she'd set a jug of milk and a plate of biscuits on the kitchen table and the three of them sat round to talk. Tamlyn told her as fully as he could about all he'd discovered in the City, particularly how warm and welcoming everyone had been.

"I got there in a suspicious sort of way and was working in the King's office, but everyone seemed to accept me and had me joining in." Merla laughed aloud when he told her of his dancing lessons, and about using Sharkley's instructions to toss the grumpy Durgan flat on his back. "It wasn't just the family and workers in the palace either," he went on. "The people out in the streets seemed to want to be friendly, to chat and help, especially when they realised I was a stranger. I don't mean there aren't problems and difficulties, like everywhere I suppose, but it felt a good place to be. You must miss Lyddy so much, Merla, but I'm sure she'll be happy in the City."

"I'll be glad for her mother and father if she really is their Rosanne," said Merla. "To lose a child must be even worse than having your child die, for you'd never stop wondering if they were alive somewhere. That young man seemed absolutely convinced she's the missing child you say, and it does seem likely, doesn't it? Vitsell came today to tell me that the two of them got there safely, but that's mostly thanks to Master Sharkley, you two, and me. Mardell – is that his name – hardly deserved the luck he had."

Tamlyn felt he must say something to show Mardell in a better light. "He really thought the High Lord would welcome him. He hadn't the least idea of how things are here because I didn't speak of it much to anyone except Almaran, and only a little to him. He understood. I suppose he knew his brother, and I think he felt he should have realised and done more to help in the past. I honestly don't see how he could have though."

"He sounds a good man," said Merla.

"I believe he is. I'm sure he'll help now, if he can."

"You've not told about today," Hallam put in. "Tell about your meeting with the High Lord, Tam. I'm afraid he's in for an even more difficult time now, Merla."

Merla listened attentively and looked grave. "I feel two ways at once," she said. "I'm worried because, like you, I don't believe in his friendly attitude, and it will be hard for you to live and work there all the time knowing that. But I also feel that he has made himself more vulnerable by taking you so closely into his immediate circle. Perhaps Mardell's escapade may have been for the best in that it brought you back so that it could happen. Oh Tam, it's going to be so difficult for you. You'll be alone with that man, having to watch your every word, but those who care for you will help all we can, you know."

"I want to ask you about that," Tamlyn said slowly. "I do have fear for myself, but what worries me most is that my friends may be in real danger simply because they are *known* to be my friends. Wouldn't it be better if I tell all of you to keep away from me?"

Hallam began to splutter, but Merla held up her hand to hush him. She looked at Tamlyn quietly for a moment, then asked, "What was it you told me King Almaran said to you about guards, Tam?"

He looked at her in surprise. "He said that guards in the City are ordinary people who care. He said they all stand to guard each other."

"And when you arrived at the city gate, did it stop the woman from guiding you through the streets that she must have known there was a possibility you might attack her? It sounds as though she and the man thought you were probably not the polite young stranger you seemed."

"No."

"So which is best, would you say? The King who knows and trusts his people enough to allow them freedom to choose their own way of behaving, or the High Lord who rules by force and fear, and who trusts nobody because he is full of fear himself that someone is plotting to take away his power?"

"There's only one thing to say to that," Hallam put in.

"Tam?"

He shook his head and smiled. "Of course there is. I knew you'd give me the answer, Merla. I'm just Tamlyn, not a King or High Lord, but I'm glad you've shown me that it won't be wrong to welcome the help of my friends."

Chapter 26

During the next two weeks Tamlyn was more than grateful that Hallam, Merla and Sharkley were around, although it was always evening before there was any chance for a normal conversation with them. He was rarely in a room alone while doing the High Lord's work, but few spoke to him except to make it clear they considered him an interloper. Gradge and Harmison, the scribes in Zerac's outer office, were particularly unpleasant, and Tamlyn guessed they resented him being given a desk with them as it limited the time they could spend doing nothing or enjoying a drink. He also suspected that they ran a profitable sideline in supplying overpriced stationery goods to lower-ranked office workers who didn't dare to query their charges. The two had probably decided it could be dangerous for them if Tamlyn knew about this scheme as he seemed to be so close to their overlord. In fact he would never tell the High Lord anything about anybody, however unpleasant they were, but the men weren't to know this. They grumbled continually about the loss of space in their room, and would manage to lurch against him whenever they passed. When he'd three times had to re-write pages, he learnt to hold his pen away from his writing whenever he sensed them near him. They also supplied him with faulty pens, put balls of fluff in his ink if he left it open when visiting the privy, and studiously avoided offering him even a drink of water. In three days he'd arranged to get his pens from the academy stores by way of Hallam, took his writing tools and papers with him when he left the room even for the shortest time, and kept Coraman's flask filled with fresh water in his pocket. If any of those who came into the office with queries, requests for stationery or to bring messages had any sympathy for him he had no idea; they certainly didn't show it.

He wasn't sure if he was glad or not that the High Lord seemed to have abandoned the idea of his being his personal diary scribe. That would have kept him in a greater state of tension, but at least he would have moved round more, seen different people and heard a variety of conversations, even if he couldn't join in. Instead of this he was set to copy tedious lists or notices, often in triplicate, and he began to wonder if Zerac was planning to kill him with boredom. His ability to copy accurately took up a very small part of his brain, so he managed to retain some feeling of reality by letting the rest of his mind wander elsewhere, taking a favourite walk, planning a good layout to display pressed leaves, or assembling dishes for a really tasty meal. At the end of the working day he'd deliver his completed work to the High Lord's apartment and race down the increasingly familiar stairs and passages to the refectory for supper and a ration of normal life. Food was delivered to his desk at midday, but although it looked good he didn't risk eating it, so he ate as much as possible at breakfast and supper.

But as the third Monday of this dreary life began, it changed dramatically. He was setting out paper, pen and ink to get started when the door was flung back and Zerac came in. Tamlyn had to admire the speed with which the usually snail-like Gradge and Harmison managed to get their feet from desk to floor and assume the stance of men who had that instant been hard at work on the High Lord's behalf but, of course, were pausing at his entrance to leap up and bow to him.

Zerac treated them to his usual cold glare, but then his look seemed to acquire a touch of warmth as though he thought of something pleasing.

"Gather your things, Tamlyn, and come to my rooms," he said. "You two, arrange to have the extra desk removed."

"Yes, my Lord," Gradge said, not quite smothering a grin. "Should I have it brought to your apartment?"

"To my *apartment*? Do you really imagine *I* might want it?"

"Sorry, my Lord... I didn't think."

"Perhaps it would be a good thing for you if you did try thinking occasionally." Zerac spun on his heel to walk out, and the two scribes watched as Tamlyn gathered his equipment and followed him. He doubted if the reprimand had filled Gradge with anything like the anxiety that was now screaming inside him.

"You probably wondered if I'd forgotten our talk, Tamlyn," Zerac said as they entered his rooms.

Tamlyn couldn't think of anything to say, so he stayed mute, clasping his things.

"It wasn't so; far from it. Of course I had to make sure your writing was of sufficient quality for the work I have in mind for you, and I'm happy to find that is so."

"Thank you, my Lord," Tamlyn managed to say, but Zerac waved his thanks aside.

"I expected no less. It is in keeping with what I see in you. Now come over here and see what I have prepared." He led Tamlyn to a shallow alcove near the window. "There! You see I intend to keep my word and supervise you personally. You will work in my apartment, and I have had this desk made to fit here for you. The chief carpenter has made an excellent piece to blend in with my furniture don't you think?"

If Tamlyn had been anxious before, he now felt as though a whole world of terror had fallen on his head and buried him. He stared, open-mouthed and unable to move or speak.

"I see you can appreciate beautiful objects, unlike some of the oafs in this place. Very good. We shall get on well, you and I. Come over to my desk and I'll show you what I want you to do."

It took the rest of the day for Tamlyn to begin thinking coherently beyond simply following instructions. He assumed he must have done this sufficiently well, for Zerac patted him on the shoulder with a, "Well done," when it was time for him to go down to supper, and the High Lord seemed determined to see only the best in him. This was perhaps the most frightening part of it all. The strangeness of the situation and worry about what it was leading to must have shown on his face, for when Hallam joined him at the table he stopped in mid-sentence and stared.

"You look like... um... not sure what you look like, but not good. Are you feeling ill or have you seen a ghost? All right, I know. Later. Let's get some food into you then."

Grateful for the understandin,g Tamlyn nodded, and though it was difficult to swallow the first mouthfuls down, the food eventually brought him back to a closer approach to normality. The evening was warm and the sun was gradually sinking to the western horizon down the bluest of skies, so the two of them wandered out and sat themselves by the river where it made a curve between the village and the Citadel.

217

Tamlyn told his friend about the latest strange – and very unwelcome – happenings of the day.

"I mean, if you describe the situation, it sounds fine. I'm away from those two in the office, my work's going to be far more interesting, and the High Lord's being pleasant and encouraging, but I just know it's not real. He's planning something else and from what we know of him, that's not good." Tamlyn shook his head in frustration.

"I reckon you're right," Hallam agreed. "He wanted you dead a few weeks ago, so what's happened to make him change so much? He could have stopped any plans you were making by completely isolating you there, but he lets you eat and sleep down here as usual. Doesn't make sense does it?"

"And the work he's given me, copying the earliest handwritten documents from his years of Lordship here. He says it's to preserve the originals by storing them safely and using the copies. That makes a sort of sense, but why let me of all people read them, if he still distrusts me?"

"Listen, Tam, I know what Merla says means a lot to you, and she thinks you're somehow important in changing things, but I'm absolutely sure she doesn't want you to put yourself in danger unnecessarily. She cares about you a lot. If you get the least hint of how Zerac's after you, get out. I'm serious. You can't do anything if you're dead, and you could make a run for it in the night. You'd be safe in the City, wouldn't you?"

The City! The City with Lyddy in it! Tamlyn looked at that vision longingly, then turned from it with the greatest difficulty. "Thanks, Hal. It might come to that, but at the moment I think I can learn more where I am. I'll stick it out for now."

They clambered down to the water's edge where the curving current had scooped out the bank on the far side and dropped an arc of fine, sandy earth where they were. Like five-year-olds, they took off their shoes and paddled for a while, kicking water at each other till they realised they needed to get back indoors.

"I feel much better about things now," Tamlyn said. "You're right. I must be able to get out if it really starts going bad up there. D'you think you could put one or two things in a pack in case I want them in a hurry?"

Hallam promised, obviously pleased that his friend had taken notice of his words, and they raced each other back to avoid being locked out.

Apart from the continuing sense of foreboding, the following weeks were far more interesting for Tamlyn. The thing that irritated him most was Zerac's habit, when they were alone, of leaning close against his back with his hands clasping both his shoulders as he inspected Tamlyn's work over his head. He wore some sort of perfume that, while not exactly unpleasant, was overpowering at such close quarters. But visitors came to the High Lord's rooms regularly, and although he guessed they didn't speak as freely as they might have done if he'd not been there, the talk was still more interesting than anything in Gradge and Harmison's room. From senior members of the household staff, he heard details of building work to extend the sun rooms on the south of the Citadel, and of a proposed new garden for the Ladies. The head stableman came with news of a horse seen at the Smithy.

"Smith reckons it just turned up out of nowhere, if you can believe that, m'Lord, and its coat's in a right state. It's a classy beast though; been well cared for, I'd say. Smith wants eighty, but reckon I can knock him down a bit."

"Do that. Never say no to quality in a horse," Zerac said.

Tamlyn smiled to himself at this point. Mardell's horse would be well looked after in the Citadel stables for many of the Lords spent more on their animals' accommodation than on anything else.

"I'll look him over when you've cleaned him up," offered Lord Zaroth. Of the Lords who came visiting, the most regular were Zaroth and Mansor, both of whom eyed Tamlyn with distaste but otherwise ignored him. What they thought of his continuing presence in the High Lord's rooms he never heard, but he guessed their opinions were anything but positive. The Lord he liked the best was Lord Destralion. He must have been one of the oldest Lords, but he was still active and upright, although he carried a walking stick. He would come across to Tamlyn's desk and ask if he could see what he was working on, pointing out with a laugh some misspelling or odd phrasing in the old pages and complimenting Tamlyn on his neat work. He obviously approved of the copying of the documents, so maybe he'd suggested it. Zerac seemed to speak to him with more deference than anyone else.

The copying itself took far more concentration than the lists and notices of previous weeks. Quite often the scrawled words took some time to decipher, a few of them had faded and others had been affected by damp. It was really interesting work, though, and sometimes Tamlyn wondered if the High Lord had actually read what he was copying. He remembered Almaran saying that Zerac was not as good as him at school work, and maybe as an eighteen-year-old when he took over The Land, he would have been happy to delegate the least interesting and most inactive work to others. In particular, much of the early law-making work was fascinating, and he memorised as much as he could.

He continued to be puzzled though by the fact that he was being allowed to see these papers at all, until one night as he was dropping off to sleep a thought came which had him sitting bolt upright in bed again. Of course, how stupid not to see it before. It was a logical thing to do really. For whatever reason, Zerac wanted these papers copied and probably did know what was in them. Whoever copied them would gain unprecedented knowledge of things, particularly legalities, which the High Lord would prefer the general population of the Citadel to be unaware of, so he would choose someone he wanted to be rid of to do the copying, keep him happy during the process and then kill him as soon as he'd finished. The thoughts kept coming: if Zerac would really prefer the old documents to vanish altogether he could destroy them, blame the scribe (who was already dead), and then declare that the copies he'd made had been falsely altered in many important details. He'd be rid of the scribe and the uncomfortable evidence in the documents with one clever plan. That sounded more like Zerac. In the strange way that the brain sometimes works, the fact that he'd solved the puzzle sent him straight off to sleep again!

He remembered his thoughts as soon as he woke, though with rather more emphasis on the part which meant that, with only a few more days' work remaining, his death sentence could be imminent. He scrambled to wash and dress and ran to catch Hallam before they went down to breakfast.

"It all fits so neatly," he said when he'd told Hal his theory.

"Mmm, well, it's one idea I can see, but there may be other possibilities; don't lose sight of that in your enthusiasm. Still, I think maybe you should leave before you finish those last pages, don't you?"

"Before I finish?"

Hal laughed. "You're not thinking you ought to complete the priggin' things are you? Tam, you amaze me. Of course before. If you're right, Zerac might be waiting behind you with his dagger drawn, watching until you complete the last full stop."

"Don't think he'd do it there, it might make a mess on his beautiful carpets and furniture. Come to think of it, he'll probably get the Elite guards on the job so he doesn't have to soil his hands. All right. Unless things change I'll plan to go when I'm on the last piece."

Unless things change! If he'd been capable of thinking of these words that afternoon he might have wished with all his heart that things had remained as they were. At least then he'd had a plan and some chance of escape. Lord Zaroth was in the room, extolling the qualities of the new horse, but the High Lord seemed restless, walking to and fro and rubbing his hands together in front of his chest. Suddenly he sat himself down on his throne-like chair.

"Tamlyn," he called, and Zaroth stopped talking.

Tamlyn put pen and ink safe and came to stand before him. "My Lord?"

Zerac seemed uncertain for a moment, then he leant forward and took Tamlyn's hands in his. "Tamlyn, I said when you first came to work in my care that we should get on well, and I spoke truer than I knew. Your work has been excellent, and your looks are befitting a man of high rank. As well as all this you are always attentive to my needs and wishes. I have come to feel very strongly towards you and I intend to make you a Lord of the Citadel. As well as that I wish you... I wish you to take up residence here with me. So we can be as father and son."

Tamlyn pulled his hands away and sprang back. "No!" he shouted.

Zarec looked surprised but still spoke softly. "I have sprung this upon you too suddenly I see. Think now of all this would mean for you; your life would be beyond all you have ever dreamed of. No more school, the best food and clothes, living here in the finest apartment, and we could share so much. You could show me the joys of walking, and I would take you riding, just us together in the distant hills. Maybe that horse..."

"No," interrupted Tamlyn again, not as loudly, but just as firmly. He'd never imagined it would happen this way, but now that the moment had come when he must stand against the High Lord he recognised it and felt quite calm, though he knew this was probably his ending.

"No, my Lord. I realise your great kindness to me in the last weeks and am grateful. I owe you allegiance, but this I cannot do."

"Cannot? Of course you can." Zerac sounded petulant and his face had darkened.

"Will not."

Now Zerac was glaring with fury. He strode from his chair and slapped Tamlyn's face so hard that he landed on the floor.

"Will not? You dare say that? You will obey me. I am the High Lord. I rule everything and everybody in my land. You will obey me and come to me… won't you?"

His words all through this tirade shook with his anger until the last two, which held almost a note of pleading in spite of his wrath.

Tamlyn had scrambled to his feet and stood, a red mark blazing on his cheek, still looking calmly into the ferocity of the High Lord's face.

"I cannot and will not," he repeated quietly.

Zerac's teeth were bared in a snarl, and his clenched fists were quivering. He stormed to fling open the door: "Guards!" he screamed down the corridor. Two men with the Elite flashes on their tunics came running.

"Take this to the cell," he spat. "We'll see what a day or two there will do to his obstinacy. Don't hurt him… yet. He may still see sense and I have a liking for his pretty face and body."

It felt like the worst of insults. Tamlyn kept silent as he was dragged away and down to the place where he had helped Master Greenwell die. He was thrown to the floor and the gates shut and locked. Then he was left with only the minimal flicker of the small wall torch to save him from total darkness.

Chapter 27

Tamlyn was trying to think. He sat with his back against the cell wall and with his eyes closed to block out his surroundings while quite calmly he followed the day through in his mind from early morning until now. He allowed himself to see that unless he'd run away last night there was nothing he could have done to alter anything. Could he have said yes to Zerac? On that he was quite positive. No! Mind and body revolted, almost to the point of throwing up, at the thought of such intimate closeness to a man he knew to be heartlessly cruel and selfish, a scheming murderer and liar.

Following that was the question of what was possible next, and the answer seemed to be nothing as far as he was concerned. He was completely in Zerac's hands, and as he would always refuse to change his mind even if given the chance, the future looked bleak, painful, and almost certainly short. Yet somehow he didn't feel as terrified as he should be. Perhaps his mind was refusing to really consider what that meant.

Tamlyn opened his eyes. He wasn't at all sure what time of day it was out there, but he assumed the hunk of stale bread and small jug of water that had been shoved into the cell not long ago was supposed to be his supper. Without thinking, his hand went towards his pouch, and he felt a small surge of pleasure when he found that he did still have it. They hadn't searched him and it didn't show beneath the hem of his loose shirt. There wouldn't be a great deal in it, but his searching fingers found his knife and he proceeded to cut the bread into small pieces which he ate slowly with sips of water from Coraman's flask. That was still in his jacket; the guards were really not very well trained in anything except being unpleasant, he thought. He licked his finger, pressed up every crumb from the wooden platter with it and ate them, then emptied the water from the jug into his flask so that hopefully they would refill it. Unless they had orders to starve him, was the grim thought his mind insisted on adding, but at least that didn't seem to have occurred to them yet.

Housekeeping done, he stowed his knife away, and in doing so his fingers touched something else. Two somethings in fact. First – he almost laughed aloud – was the set of lock-picks which Mardell had presented to him when he'd mastered the art of opening all the different practice locks the prince had given him to work on. "You'd make an excellent criminal," he'd laughed. "Don't show 'em to Grandfather though." The memory of the happy hours in the palace brought a lump to his throat. Somehow he must stay alive; there was too much he still wanted to see and do. This brought Lyddy vividly into his mind, and he remembered hearing her as she'd kept the guard outside amused when he'd crept into this very place and found Master Greenwell lying tortured and bloody against the bars. The bars which now held him.

He must not let these thoughts overcome him. The second item in his pouch was the strip of linen Merla had given him to replace the one he'd torn to bind her ankle. It was such a long time since he'd gone looking for plants and herbs that he'd almost forgotten it, but though he could think of no use for it in his present situation, touching the soft material made him warm with memories of comfort and kindness.

He decided he'd save the pleasure of trying his skill on the locks till later, when he wasn't likely to be visited again. He didn't fool himself with thinking he'd actually be able to escape, but it would be good to see the panic when he was found in an open prison. Something positive to keep up his spirits. Instead, he thought he'd try to sleep for a while, so he rolled his jacket to form a pillow and searched around for the smoothest bit of the floor. It felt warmer than you'd expect in an underground cell, so he guessed the springs from the bathing room so close to him must run underneath here. He relaxed as much as he could, thought of yesterday evening by the river, and slept.

"Tamlyn... Tam." His whispered name edged its way into his sleeping mind.

"Uh!" He sat up, still half asleep. "What..."

"Ssh. I'm here. Don't make a noise."

Someone was crouching beyond the bars as far from the door to the outer passage as possible.

"Sharkley!" Tamlyn gasped in amazement.

"I can't stay long. Hallam let me in and he's on watch in the bathroom. It would have looked odd for a Master to hang around there. I think your guard in the corridor is having a doze, but keep your voice down."

"How did you know?"

"The Lady got a message. One of the village people who work here, but he wasn't clear where it came from. We wondered if it was a trap, but when you didn't arrive for supper we decided to take the risk. Can you tell me briefly what's happened?"

Tamlyn gave him the bare bones of the story. When he'd finished he burst out with, "But what on earth set Zerac off on that track? With me, I mean."

Sharkley didn't answer for a moment, then, "Um… that probably needs quite a long answer. Not sure now's the time for it." He actually sounded uncertain; most unusual for him.

Tamlyn almost laughed when he realised why. "It's all right; I can make a pretty accurate guess at what he wants to do with me. You've lived here. You must know you can't spend your lives in a society that's nearly all male without catching on to that. A couple of boys? Well, that doesn't worry me if they're both happy about it. This is different, isn't it? I'd be anything but happy, and as I said, why me?"

"Well thank goodness I haven't got to give a lecture in the dark, on my knees in a prison cell about alternative sex! You're right, this is totally different and very wrong. I'd grown to have suspicions about the High Lord on that score, but… Well anyway, it makes it even more important we get you out. As to why you, it's probably mainly about gaining control over someone he's afraid of, but I have to say there's also the fact that you're quite a handsome young man."

Tamlyn snorted, but Sharkley hushed him and went on quickly. "We haven't had time to plan, but we wanted you to know we're working on it, fast as we can. I've brought some food, and we're with you, Tamlyn. There's also this hopeful hint that someone else in the Citadel seems to be with you too. Now I'd better go before the guard wakes or Hallam melts. Oh yes, Merla told me to let you know there's a flat stone somewhere over in that corner that covers a drain!" Sharkley pointed, then reached his hand through the bars and shook Tamlyn's hand. "Play along a little if you can, and try not to worry too much. Huh! That's stupid in these circumstances. Sorry!" He crept soundlessly away, and a few moments later Tamlyn saw the brief increase of light that meant Sharkley had gone.

Two chicken pasties and a handful of preserved cherries added to the hopefulness that Sharkley's visit had woken in Tamlyn, and he was grateful too for Merla's timely information. He felt a deep objection to being forced to relieve himself on the cell floor, so the small drain was a blessing. When he slid the flat covering stone aside he could hear running water below, and warm air drifted up.

He'd revised his thoughts about leaving his cell door and the door to the passageway open; he realised a charge of using magic would do little for his prospects. He did open them both though to keep in practice, then locked himself in again. He'd been tempted, too, to leave the cherry stones on his plate, but for the same reason dropped them into the drain hole. More optimistic than it seemed possible, he returned to sleep.

Must be morning, he thought, as voices in the passage roused him, but when a guard eventually came in with another supply of bread and water he was sitting against the wall again, feigning sleep

"Wake up there. Lovely day. Wonder if you'll get to see it." Chortling at what he obviously thought was humour he retreated again, and Tamlyn was left to wonder if in fact he *would* see it; if the High Lord would make him wait down here for more days or drag him up to have another go at him. 'Play along a little' Sharkley had suggested, but he didn't think he could. He'd sooner find out straight away what was in store for him.

What seemed like hours later, and just as he was starting to think that he was in for a long stay, two guards came and ordered him to go with them. Not the Elite squad, he was glad to see, and he toyed with the idea of making a run for it. He knew the Citadel so well it might just work, but that would only delay the inevitable. Without a plan and help from his friends he'd soon be caught. He was marched between them along the now familiar corridor and pushed through the High Lord's door so fiercely that he staggered and nearly fell.

Zerac sat in his chair, and said nothing. Lord Zaroth lounged by the window. Come to see the fun, thought Tamlyn. He made a brief bow to both men and waited, looking steadily into Zerac's face. He was good at stillness and silence, and he had no intention of making any move until he found out why he had been brought here again. Eventually Zerac stirred and leant forward.

"Hours in the cell haven't taught you anything, then?"

"I learned that it's a dreary place and that the floor makes a poor bed, my Lord. I find the food rather unpalatable too." He said this lightly, knowing it was not a sensible reply in this place, but he wasn't going to show fear.

Zerac's face darkened. "You have one last chance. Will you accept what I offered yesterday?"

"No. I will not."

Tamlyn saw the High Lord's body tense and quiver, while his face went white with rage. He leapt from his chair and strode across the room.

"Then you have chosen death," he hissed in Tamlyn's face. "You will be executed and they will all see it and know that I will not be disobeyed. This land and all in it are mine, and any who think they can deny it will soon find their mistake and go the way you're going."

Lord Zaroth lazily pushed himself upright and strolled across to stand beside Zerac.

"My Lord, may I make a suggestion?

Zerac turned to him, and nodded.

"I have information that this stupid fool is held in some regard among the lower classes. It might not be prudent to do as you suggest, much as he deserves it. Perhaps a death seen to be, shall we say, more accidental would be appropriate."

"Such as?"

"The Midnight Hounds comes to mind. My pack is ready for a good run, and with a day's starvation they will need no urging, especially if he's scented. From your east window, my Lord, you will be able to hear them, and his screams too, as they rip him apart. You can then be sorrowful he disobeyed a curfew and grieve for so young a death.

Zerac's face went blank as he considered this, then a malicious gleam came into his eyes.

"Clever. Yes… yesss. An excellent idea Zaroth. I'm sure I can rely on you to organise it to perfection."

"Certainly, my Lord. It will be a great pleasure."

"Is tomorrow night long enough for the dogs?"

"Ideal."

"And you, he sneered, turning back to Tamlyn. "See how kind and generous I am. You have a chance, just the tiniest chance, of living. About that big." He held thumb and forefinger up, almost touching, and laughed with the mad cackle that turned Tamlyn's stomach. "That's if you can run faster than Lord Zaroth's hungry dogs. Can you do that?" Now his teeth showed in a snarling grin.

It took every ounce of Tamlyn's determination to say anything at all, but he managed.

"I shall try."

"Guards!" yelled Zerac, and the door flew open. They must have been waiting outside and Tamlyn wondered if they'd heard anything. "Take this thing back to the cell," he ordered. "I'm sure you'll have delightful dreams tonight," he spat at Tamlyn.

Determined as he was to avoid wasting his last night alive considering the manner of his death, Tamlyn still could not quite stop his mind slipping towards it. He'd heard of the Midnight Hounds, though he didn't remember it ever happening. Zaroth's pack of hounds were large hunting dogs, usually used on smaller mammals but quite capable, when hungry and in a pack, of killing a man. The victim, taken some distance into the countryside, would be set free to run, and at a later time, presumably at the whim of the tormentor, the hounds would be released to hunt him down. In theory he might gain a sanctuary, but that was theory only. Tamlyn couldn't imagine being able to run nearly fast enough over rough ground in the dark to keep from them for very long.

Every time these images arose he tried to remember more pleasant things, but always the thought of those hungry teeth, gripping, tearing, biting, crept in and made him shudder. He woke once, remembering Lyddy's perfume from a dream, so he must have slept briefly, but not for long. In what he assumed was morning he was surprised when the guard called him over to the bars rather than shoving his food through in silence. Then he realised it was one of the village youths who had joined the Citadel staff. He beckoned for Tamlyn to come close, and while pushing bread and water onto the floor near his feet, he brought his lips to Tamlyn's ear.

"The Lady says eat this, but don't eat none of the other, in case they puts a drug in." He thrust a package into Tamlyn's hand and backed off quickly, vanishing before he'd time to say anything. The package contained ham, beef, hard boiled eggs, a small fresh loaf and fruit. There was even a bottle of clear water. He moved swiftly to stow these things under his jacket in the darkest corner of the cell. He hadn't thought of it, but it would be like the High Lord or Zaroth to drug him so that he couldn't run at full speed.

During the long hours he ate the food in a series of small portions, but determined to eat no more when it was all gone. Only the water he kept, hoping he could somehow carry it with him. The bottle was square and flat and would fit his pouch or a pocket; it would be like Merla to have noticed the size of his pouch. He stopped trying to guess the time. He almost managed to stop thinking at all until a man came down the passage, waited for the guard to unlock the two doors then entered the cell.

"Scholar Tamlyn you are to come with me," he said. Tamlyn picked up his jacket and followed him. The moment had come. He was about to leave the Citadel that had been his home since he was born, leave his friends, leave his memories... leave his life. Then surprise jerked him out of these thoughts for the man didn't lead him upwards, but down towards the bathroom. What was this? Actually, who was the man? He thought he'd seen him about, but couldn't quite remember where. They entered the bathroom and the man stopped. There was no one else in the place.

"When you go up to the starting place later you will ride behind Lord Zaroth so that you don't try to escape. Nobody can drag you away because you will be tied to him. He does not, however, wish to be so close to someone who has not been able to wash for more than two days, so you are to bathe. I will stand guard." The words were said quietly, almost emotionlessly, and suddenly Tamlyn knew him. He was something to do with Lord Zaroth. He'd seen them together more than once, but not really noticed him. Zaroth was the one who got noticed; tall and dark haired, handsome and strong. Zerac must have looked a bit like

229

that once when he was an eighteen-year-old prince, riding proudly at the head of his followers. Even in later years he'd taken great care with his appearance, and still looked great at a distance, but Tamlyn had been close to him in the past weeks and seen the old man behind the facade of fine clothes, artfully designed to hide the slackening skin and wrinkles. As Tamlyn stripped and entered the pool, thankful that Zaroth's delicate nose was allowing him this unexpected comfort, he thought of Almaran. He was exactly the same age as Zerac but made no pretence about his age, yet he seemed more alive, more real somehow, and much more pleasant to be with.

Bathed and dried, Tamlyn did feel better, though he had to put on the same clothes again. Now he was taken to a small room in the area above the stables and a plate of bread and cheese was put before him. When he refused it Zaroth's man smiled slightly.

"Probably wise," he said. "We will go down to the stables soon, but now we wait for Lord Zaroth. He is checking that the preparations are correct."

Tamlyn had barely been aware of the world around him since he left the cell, but now he sat staring through the small window, and realised how strange the light was. The sky had a weird coppery tinge to it and there was a feeling of breathless stillness. The treetops he could see were completely motionless, and though they were only just into summer, there was a hot heaviness in the air.

"It feels odd. Bit like a storm." He wasn't sure whether he was allowed to talk but the man made no objection.

"It could well be. The clouds are heavy over the mountains." He was looking down from the window and must have seen some signal. "Come now," he said, and led Tamlyn down narrow steps to the flagged yard outside the stables.

Lord Zaroth was waiting on his horse, with bulging saddlebags and a blanket belted across the beast's back behind him. He held a coil of rope and threw one end of it to the man.

"Get him up," he ordered, and Tamlyn was heaved astride the blanket. The man then circled the horse twice so that the rope bound Tamlyn to Zaroth's back and was knotted in front where there was no chance of him loosening it. Not that he would have tried. He had the odd feeling that he was a spectator of all that was happening rather than a prisoner going to his death.

"Thanks, Will," Zaroth said. "I'll see you later." It seemed to Tamlyn to be a strangely relaxed farewell in the situation, but then these two weren't going to be running for their lives were they? They rode off up the slope from the stables and turned left around the south of the Citadel, where the new sun rooms were visible. Nobody was working there now; indeed, they seemed to be the only people about. Curfew must have started, Tamlyn realised, and they didn't want him to be seen of course. Zaroth guided them towards the river, and then turned east towards the mountains along the river path.

They went at a very easy pace and, comparing it with his ride from the City with Coraman, Tamlyn felt more comfortable, although it was the only positive thing in this situation.

"Have you ridden before?" Zaroth asked suddenly in a curiously stilted voice.

"Once." Tamlyn was not offering any more information

"When we get to the steeper part you may hold on to me. I don't want you to slip sideways or something. We shall go steadily; the keepers with the dogs are on foot of course. They're well ahead."

Was he seriously trying to make conversation? Tamlyn wasn't giving him that satisfaction. "Thank you," he said shortly.

It was getting darker, though how much of that was true nightfall and how much the lowering black clouds tinged with indigo piling up ahead of them was hard to tell. They rode along the bank-side path and Tamlyn remembered walking it in the moonlight when he'd visited the river cave for Merla. How much he'd learned that day, and how much had happened since. They passed the stone bridge and got into the rougher rock-strewn area. Soon it was really dark, and Zaroth let the horse pick its own way. Though he'd had no intention of holding onto this man who disgusted him, Tamlyn found he had to in order to keep himself upright.

At last Zaroth reined in the horse and undid the rope. Quickly he swung himself to the ground, pulled Tamlyn down and led him through the scree to the base of what must be one of the first real hills of the eastern mountains. It was so dark now that Tamlyn was unable to see

231

more than a few yards in any direction, but he could still hear the river so he knew they must be close to it. Zaroth tied Tamlyn's wrists and ankles with the rope, then pulled a silk kerchief from his neck and bound it across his mouth. He was dragged across to a large rock and pushed into a sitting position in a crevice behind it..

"I will come for you when the men have gone," he said quietly, and Tamlyn heard his feet crunching away. In a moment he heard Zaroth speak encouragingly to his horse, and the sound of the animal's hoofs joined his voice.

Gradually all the sounds vanished. It was eerily quiet, as though the whole earth was holding its breath. Even the sound of the river seemed to have been muted to the merest whisper. Of course, the men must not see him; he was, after all, to be a stupid curfew breaker.

Suddenly, out of the darkness and helplessness, a bleak misery and despair fell on Tamlyn. He had never felt so totally alone and desperate, and he couldn't stop stinging tears falling from his eyes. Unable to wipe them, he felt them soak onto the kerchief that gagged his mouth. If he could have willed his death at that moment he would have done so, and he remembered Master Greenwell saying the same. He closed his eyes tightly and made himself fight against the desolation; he would *not* give in. He was still alive, and he had not been tortured as the Master had. He had to believe, until all hope had vanished, that he could survive.

He heard the sound of the keepers returning and saw the flicker of lights. They must have torches to light them on their return.

"You must hurry. I shall release the dogs in an hour, and they will follow a scent trail towards the Citadel, so I advise you to be indoors before they start." Tamlyn heard Zaroth's voice, and the nervous laughs of the men.

"Reckon we can manage that, m'lord. Don't want to be breakfast for them animals, nor get drowned in the rain as looks likely soon," one man was bold enough to say.

"Off with you then. I shall follow after, and kennel the dogs myself. Come to my man for your pay tomorrow."

The voices faded away, and Zaroth came to release Tamlyn, leading him further along to where there was a small fire in a brazier, and the dogs were shifting about restlessly in basket-work traps. Two to a trap, and five traps, Tamlyn saw. Ten tough, fast and hungry creatures, trained for the chase and to kill. Zaroth had said in an hour they would be let loose, but that was probably to speed the men. How much time would Zaroth really allow him?

"Sit," Zaroth ordered. "Near the fire if you feel a chill. Don't think to make a run for it before I tell you because I shall simply release the dogs straight away. I'll send you off in a while, and them later." He gestured at the dogs. "After that it's up to you."

He pulled a watch from his pocket and looked at it. Few could afford these except the Lords, and in another situation Tamlyn would have been interested in the delicately wrought little machine that ticked off time so cleverly. Now he simply sat as he was told and stared at his hands clasped in front of him. Zaroth went to a saddle bag and pulled a package from it which proved to have bread and cooked meat inside. He sat down himself and started to eat.

"Would you care for some?" he asked suddenly. Tamlyn looked up. He was being offered food, and he presumed it wasn't drugged as Zaroth was eating it, but his pride would not let him take anything from this man. He shook his head, and Zaroth simply shrugged and went on eating. As they sat, Tamlyn became aware of flickers of lightning in the sky in the direction of the invisible mountains. Every now and then Zaroth consulted his watch, and finally stood up. He lit a torch at the brazier and handed an unlit one to Tamlyn.

"Stand up," he ordered, and taking a small bottle from inside his cloak he sprinkled liquid from it onto Tamlyn's coat and shoes. It must be a trail scent, he thought, to keep the dogs on his track. His nose could detect very little, but he knew that dogs had a sense of smell many times better than humans.

"Come with me." Holding his torch Zaroth led him back towards the river. Finally he stopped and, reaching for the unlit torch that Tamlyn carried, he lit it from his own and returned it. "Go now," he said. "You will hear my hunting horn and at that point I shall release my dogs." He turned and strode away.

Tamlyn was so astounded at being given a light that for a few seconds he did not move. Then he set off to go down the way he had so recently ridden up behind Zaroth. Though he desperately wanted to run, he had decided as he sat by the fire that he must take the first part of his attempt to reach safety more slowly. The going was so rough there that he would almost certainly fall and might injure himself before he'd gone many yards, but if – no, when – he came to the area beyond the bridge he should be able to speed up. Must do so in fact, if he was to have any chance at all. He would make for the village and surely he would find safety there. What he would do after that he hadn't dared to think, so he just concentrated on watching the ground and going as fast as felt safe. Why had he been given the torch? Perhaps they thought it would give him a false sense of hope, but it did make this first and worst part of what he must do seem easier than he'd feared.

The flickering lightning came more frequently. With his ears already straining for the signal of the horn, he thought he could hear the thunder that trailed it. He was being pursued by a storm as well as dogs. He saw with relief that he must be nearing the bridge, and it was as he peered ahead that he failed to see and avoid a thicket of brambles. The tough, thorny branches tore at the sleeve of his jacket, through his shirt and ripped into his arm. He yelled aloud but dared not stop. His torch was more than half burnt down now, and he must keep going. The ground here was smoother and he quickened his pace. He was a walker, and knew how to maintain a steady step, step, step over long distances, but now he must run and keep running.

The horn sounded. His heart, already pounding, leapt inside him, and his legs turned his panic into ever more frantic attempts at speed. He was sure he heard forty swift feet pattering on the ground behind him and would have screamed his terror had he had breath. He tried to move even more swiftly, but his body wouldn't, couldn't respond. Just in time to stop himself collapsing, he realised that the sound was rain. Huge drops were falling, and the rolls of thunder were almost coinciding with the lightning flashes. The storm was catching up with him and maybe, just maybe, it would slow down the dogs. But it mustn't slow him. Thrusting down the fear that had almost beaten him, he went on. He tossed away his torch as it spluttered out in the torrent that was now falling, but he was nearing the place where he could turn to the village. A pain in his side was excruciating but he made himself ignore it. His legs ached and felt drained, but still he ran. His whole body told him he had to stop, but somehow he went on.

Here were the trees that marked the village road. His coat was sodden and weighing him down, so he tore it off and threw it towards the trees as still he ran. His shoes followed the coat when a small coherent thought glimmered in the darkness that was filling his mind. Coat and shoes had been scented – that might at least slow the hounds for a moment. Running barefoot on the track he scarcely noticed the pain of sharp stones on his feet because now his whole body was pain. Could he see lights or was it just the lightning? He was in the village now and dimly realised that all the windows were aglow. He was staggering, lurching drunkenly, but still he managed to go forward somehow. He veered in the direction he thought Merla's house was and his bare feet skidded on the wet grass of the green at the village centre. He cried out as he stumbled forward, knowing if he fell the dogs must get him after all. Something dark loomed in front and he pitched onto it, head first.

Tamlyn's world went black.

Chapter 28

Someone was dabbing gently at his forehead with a soft cloth. It hurt a bit, but he didn't really mind because at the same time he could smell a scent that he knew. He wasn't going to open his eyes because this might be a dream, and he wanted it to go on and on.

"Lyddy," he mumbled, tongue thick and unresponsive.

"Oops!" Water drops splashed on his face and were lightly dabbed off. "Merla, he's coming round."

Best dream yet. Perhaps it was real, but he wasn't going to look, just in case

"Kiss me," he whispered thickly.

A small pause, then soft lips gently planted a kiss on his. A warm tingle ran through him. This had to be real; he'd never managed a dream kiss before, but still…

"Lyddy! I'm not sure he's fit for that."

"But he asked me."

A chuckle from Merla. "Well in that case you'd better keep him happy!"

Tamlyn opened his eyes to find Lyddy bending over him, a small smile on her lips.

"Thought you were dream," he slurred. "Why… you here… not City…"

"I said I'd come back. Didn't you hear me?"

"Aren't you… didn't you…" Why wouldn't the words come properly?

"Yes, I am Rosanne, of all the silly names, and I do like the city. How's that for mind reading. My mother and father are lovely, but they quite understand me wanting to come back here. Now I must stop, or Merla will be cross with me. It's not that long since we fetched you in. You knocked yourself out on the mounting block. There'll be lots of time later and you need to rest now."

"Dogs coming... no... was rain... torch wet..." Frustration at his inability to say, or even think, what he wanted to say, brought weak tears to his eyes, and he closed them again. "Threw in trees..." he tried, and again failed.

A strong arm slid behind his neck and shoulders, lifting him up a little. Not Lyddy now. "Merla. I..."

"Hush. No more talking. Drink this. It tastes disgusting but I promise you'll feel better in the morning." She held a small beaker to his lips. It did taste horrible, but before he had time to complain he slid into sleep.

There was daylight coming through the window, but Tamlyn could hear it was still raining. He was thinking more clearly, and the horrors of the night came flooding back into his head, but he was here, he was alive. He'd beaten the hounds and was safe with Lyddy and Merla. He ached all over, and could feel tenderness where his fingers found a large bump high on his forehead, but he was definitely not dead or even half chewed. There was a bandage on his right arm and further search revealed he was naked to his waist. A hasty exploration below that point discovered some sort of light trousers. He felt relieved.

Tamlyn sat up, threw back the covers and swung his bare feet to the floor. He nearly yelped aloud; they were very painful, but slowly he managed to stand. Where was he? In Merla's home he knew from fragmentary memories of the night, but on previous visits he'd not seen this room. A bed, a chest with drawers beneath and a bowl and jug on top, a curtain across a corner and a chair was all it contained, but he caught a trace of perfume and realised that he must be in Lyddy's room. Lyddy! Had he really asked her to kiss him? He flushed at the thought, half wishing it might have been part of a dream. On the back of the chair he found a shirt and put it on; a bit large for him, but he certainly felt more ready to face Merla and Lyddy in it. He wondered where it had come from.

As if to answer this unspoken thought a young man stuck his head round the door and then came in.

"'Lo. You awake then? Glad ter see you again. Merla borrowed some clothes off me for you while they cleans yours. Right mess you was in. Shirt's a bit big, but better'n tight, eh?."

Tamlyn realised it was the man who'd delivered the food from Merla… when? Just yesterday; it felt much longer.

"Thank you, I'm really very grateful. Thanks for delivering that food, too. It must have been a dangerous thing for you to do."

"Not really," the man laughed. "Jared was on guard, an' he's my sister's man. He looked the other way for a bit. We can get in most places up there if we wants to, just so's we're not too obvious. I'm Riss by the way. Just on me way to work, but Merla reckoned you might welcome a hand getting to the privy as your feet's sore. Pretty wet out there."

Merla really did consider the detail of what might be needed in any situation, Tamlyn thought. Feeling a bit silly but grateful nonetheless, he accepted a lift to and from the privy at the end of the stone-set pathway across the garden, then Riss set him down in the kitchen and waved a cheery farewell. Merla was there, mixing something in a large bowl.

"Sit over here, Tam. I've made this for you to put your feet in. You can give them a soak while I get your breakfast, and you can tell me what happened if you feel well enough."

"I feel quite all right. No, honestly," he assured her when he saw Merla's doubtful glance. "Just my feet are pretty sore."

"This should help that. Here you are, put your feet in the bowl." She placed it under the table and he dabbled his feet in the warm green liquid. It did feel pleasantly soothing.

Merla brought a pan from the stove and poured thick, creamy porridge into a bowl, topping it off with a good helping of syrupy honey. "There you are. Now tell me as much as you can remember." She sat opposite him, resting her elbows on the table and propping her chin on her hands to watch him. He started to tell about riding up towards the mountains behind Lord Zaroth, but she stopped him.

"Start from when the Midnight Hounds first came into it," she said, so he went back to the High Lord's room and that last interview. He tried to remember as much detail as he could, spooning in mouthfuls of porridge between sentences.

"Do you think anyone else heard what went on there?" she asked.

"The door's very thick, but Zerac was really screaming at me, and when he called for the guards they came straight in. They probably heard something, at least that he was really angry. But it was Zaroth who mentioned the hounds, and his voice was quite soft."

"What about the man who took you to the bathing room?"

"He said that I was to have a bath because I was riding behind Zaroth, nothing else. He was silent after that, and he did have a good look round, so I don't think anyone was hiding."

"You're probably right, but you'd be surprised how many secret places there are in the Citadel, particularly in the lower levels," Merla said.

"No I wouldn't. I've lived in the Citadel all my life and explored round most of it, but I didn't have the least idea about that passage we use behind the kitchens, or the entry from the bathroom to the cell."

"There are quite a few more, very old most of them. The knowledge is passed on by The Lady, mother to daughter, and we think the passages may have started off as water channels and then been widened by hand. I'm sure I don't need to tell you that I never felt any inclination to give Zerac that knowledge." Merla gave a little laugh and then sat silent, thinking. "It's very odd though," she went on at last. "You see we were given a warning, so someone must have heard. Very vague, but it kept us watching, and that was how we saw you so quickly."

"I'm so glad you did. Even if I hadn't fallen I don't think I could have run any further." Tamlyn shuddered at the thought.

"You did incredibly well. Very few could have achieved what you did last night."

"It's amazing what you can make yourself do when the alternative is being killed by a pack of hungry hounds. My mind played horrible tricks: I was sure I could hear them; the sound of their feet, their panting, right behind me. I was... I was terrified." Tamlyn stopped, pushing back the memory of that overwhelming and nearly disabling panic.

"Enough of that now; let's see how your feet are." He lifted them from the bowl and Merla dried them. "Better?" she asked.

"Oh yes, much, much better. That really is amazing stuff. Will you give me the recipe sometime?"

"I will, I promise. Alhough I hope you never have to use it for the reason I've had to for you. I'll bind some lamb's wool on now for padding, then we must get some lunch. You can peel some potatoes, if you like. Lyddy will be back then, anxious to see you're really all right."

"Is she back in the kitchens? Didn't they ask awkward questions?"

"She told me she'd be back, and I believed her, so I said she was ill with a very bad fever. She came back three days ago, and started the next day. Mind you, she does look rather plump and rosy for someone who's supposed to have been nearly dying, but she'll soon work that off. The plumpness, I mean. I guess it was all the parties and banquets they had in her honour in the City. She's always rosy though, especially when young men ask her to kiss them."

Tamlyn groaned. "That was real then? I sort of hoped I'd dreamed it."

"Did you really hope that?"

"Yes... No! It was... it was... Was she cross?"

"I think you'd better ask her that yourself, Tam. But if you want the opinion of an old lady, I would say that a fit of the giggles and quite a few more kisses doesn't really look as though she was angry does it?"

Tamlyn didn't answer that, but he couldn't smother a wide smile.

Merla finished binding the soft wool onto his feet and looked closely at him. "We'll forget the potatoes; I think another hour or two asleep will make sure you're really back to normal. Off you go. We'll call you for lunch."

Tamlyn was going to protest, but found that it really did sound a good idea. He went and stretched out on Lyddy's bed, and was asleep in minutes.

He could hear Merla's and Lyddy's quiet voices from the kitchen and the sound of the endless rain, but that wasn't what had woken him. There was something... it was pressing inside his head. He had to go... it dragged at him, like an invisible thread, and was calling him wordlessly. Now! So important, but what...

He hobbled from the room and along to the kitchen: stood there, hand on the doorpost to steady himself.

"I've got to go. Out."

"Tamlyn, you can't," Lyddy cried, but Merla took one look at him and came across to take both hands in hers.

"What is it, Tam?" she asked softly.

"I don't know. I just know I have to. Soon… now." Tamlyn looked at her, pleading mutely because he had no words to describe this desperate need. Then he found himself once again staring into her wonderful eyes, and knew she understood.

"Yes. I see you must. But two minutes to find shoes and a coat will make it easier and quicker. Sit there a moment. Eat if you can and we'll get what you need."

He saw there was food on the table but couldn't eat. He clenched his hands in his lap and closed his eyes, trying for a clearer sense of what he must do.

"Fetch that sheepskin from the shed, Lyddy. It's old but still a good cover." Merla left the room but returned very soon with shoes and a jacket. "Riss's things are a bit big, but it means you can keep that lamb's wool on inside the shoes. There. Now the jacket." She buttoned him into it and turned back the sleeves.

"My pouch. Where…"

"Hanging by the stove." He looked inside then fastened the belt round himself under the coat. Lyddy wrapped bread and cheese in a cloth and stuffed it in his pocket, then flung the sheepskin across his shoulders. At once he made for the front door and set off into the rain.

Lyddy and Merla watched him go.

"What was it? What did you see? Is he in more danger?" Lyddy clasped Merla's hand for comfort.

"I don't know. Danger somewhere, but not there and not yet I think. Wherever he's going now, I could only see great need. That's what is calling him."

Chapter 29

Without conscious thought Tamlyn started through the rain towards the river, going in the opposite direction to last night. Then he had been running for his life; now he trudged as fast as possible, pulled by a powerful, nameless need, but no longer driven by terror. At the stand of trees where he had flung coat and shoes last night he turned towards the mountains because he knew somehow that he needed to cross the water and the only place to do that, with the river so rain-swollen, was the bridge.

The rain fell harder. Flickers of lightning and ominous rumbles signalled another storm approaching from beyond the mountains, and the river was already lapping over the banks in some places. Tamlyn's legs were soaked, but the old sheepskin which he clasped with one hand across his chest gave his body some protection. Though Riss's shoes were saturated and his feet squelched with every step, the lambswool bound round them stopped the wet leather from chafing.

By the time he reached the bridge the storm was almost upon him; lightning and thunder were seconds apart and it felt as if he was walking through a waterfall rather than individual raindrops. The river was so high that he could only see a few inches of the central arch of the three that made up the bridge; the two outer ones, which were lower, could only be guessed at by the madly swirling water where the torrent was being forced through them out of sight. Tamlyn crossed quickly and turned right along the bank opposite the one he'd just travelled. He knew that was where he must go, even though the idea of 'rocks' seemed to be echoing in his head, and he could think of none where he was now heading. The land on this side of the river was rough and hilly. No villages; farms and a few smallholdings which were scattered over this southern area grew few crops except food for the families who ran them, and they mostly concentrated on sheep rearing.

Scholars rarely went across to that side; there was really nothing to tempt them, and no flat grassy way beside the river such as that along the bank near the Citadel and village. He had to pick his way carefully to avoid stumbling among the rough tussocks, but suddenly he knew what 'rocks' meant. Opposite the vast stony outcrop that was the Citadel was a miniature version. It was so small that it had become partially covered with turf, but rough wood had been fixed in places to make some sort of shelter of it. He guessed shepherds used it occasionally, perhaps at lambing time. As soon as this thought entered his head, he was certain that was where he had to be.

Tamlyn tried to hurry, the vicious storm wind at his back pushing him forward. He came to a point where, peering through the driving rain, he thought he could make out the shape of the mound only yards away, and at that moment lightning flamed across the whole sky with a simultaneous crash of thunder that was so huge and ear-splitting the ground beneath his feet seemed to heave and tremble. He dived forwards through a gap in the rocks... and froze.

He was in a space the size of a small room, and against the far side lay a figure, head and shoulders propped against the wall.

"You!" The word forced itself from his throat like a curse. It was Lord Zaroth. For a moment Tamlyn wondered if the man was dead he was so still, but he saw the chest move and then the dark eyes opened.

"Tamlyn?" It was scarcely more than a whisper, but all the anger and loathing for this hated creature flared in Tamlyn, and he bent to pick up a rock from the floor. He would smash it into his face, crush his skull, punish him for all the hurt and evil he had caused.

Zaroth shifted with a gasp of pain, then his lips twisted into a wry smile as though he could read Tamlyn's thoughts. "You want to kill me," he croaked, a statement, not a question.

But Tamlyn didn't move. Just as suddenly as that murderous rage had risen in him it left. He knew he couldn't kill, not even this man, and the stone dropped to the ground. He realised too that the dragging insistence in him had ceased; this was where he had to be.

"How did you get me here?" he demanded.

"I? I did nothing but long for the impossible; that I could see you and talk to you before I die. I thought I was seeing a phantom."

"Did you think you'd enjoy having another try at killing me?"

"I have never tried to kill you."

Disbelieving, Tamlyn walked across the space between them and stared down at Zaroth. "What were you doing last night then?"

Zaroth looked back up at him. "Saving you," he said simply. "Tamlyn, I have been stabbed and I will die soon. Will you let me tell you the truth of my actions?"

In spite of his incredulity at what he was hearing, Tamlyn said more gently, "Perhaps I can dress your wound. It might not be fatal."

Zaroth shook his head. "The dagger that pierced me was coated with a deadly poison. Once it enters the body there is nothing to be done. I can feel it taking hold already, and I won't be able to talk for very long. Will you listen?"

"Tell me what you must, then. I can't see what I can do, but I know I had to come here. Perhaps it will ease you." He swung the sheepskin from his shoulders and laid it, dry side up, to sit on.

"It's a long story. I'll tell it as shortly as I can, but I must start at the beginning or you won't understand. My mother, Marrane, came to this land when the High Lord came. She was not adventurous or greedy for change, but she was so deeply in love with Zerac she'd have followed him anywhere. He's never cared for any woman – you may have realised that, perhaps – but I think he felt he must seem as other men and mask that which could be thought a failing, so after some time here he married her, and fathered a son on her."

"You? You're Zerac's son?" Tamlyn was surprised; he'd never heard of that relationship, though it must explain the time Zaroth spent in the High Lord's company.

"I am. Few know it now. Lord Destralion, the oldest Lord, does, because he was very fond of my mother and visited when I was young. I think he would have married her himself, and I wish he had been my father; he's a far better man. But my mother only loved Zerac, even though he was unkind to her and she hated many of his ways. As a child I loved my mother dearly and did admire my father. It was never love. I was in awe of him, and he had little to do with me as I grew up."

Zaroth paused, licking dry lips. Tamlyn reached into his pouch and pulled out Merla's water. He'd had no thought of drinking from it last night, and now he undid it and held it to the man's lips.

"Thank you. I must hurry on. My mother taught me kindness and love. She encouraged me in the things I liked doing: using my hands, carving, painting, even weaving and embroidering. They're all activities Zerac scorns for a man and he'd probably have forbidden them had he known. I made my way through the Academy as you have done, and gained my one true friend there; Lord Willard, who you saw. He is a good man, Tamlyn, and knows more about me than anyone. Remember that. Now I must tell of the time which holds the deepest sadness and horror of my life, as well as the most wonderful thing. You know my father's cruel and crazy scheme to have the men of the Citadel father children on the women of the land, by force if need be, and so breed men of what he calls 'true blood'."

"I know now. Someone told me." Though he was beginning to believe what he heard, Tamlyn wasn't ready to use Merla's name yet.

"My father told me that I must do this 'duty' as he called it. It was managed within the Citadel to keep the men from reprisals, and we were forbidden to use our real names. When I saw the woman he had sent me to I knew that I could never force her; she was so beautiful and gentle and I loved her instantly. The miracle was that she fell in love with me. That year was the most wonderful and happy of my life. We kept our love secret. It wasn't Zerac's plan that there should be attachment between his 'real' men and the Donkey women. She called me Roff and I called her Liss, and we would meet secretly, especially when she was with child, because that was supposed to be the end of it for me. It was a long, warm summer and we would wander into the countryside, mostly at night, and pretend we could be real lovers forever.

"Time passed all too quickly, but I managed to see her when our child was born. A lovely boy; I held him in my arms and for a few minutes we were a family. Then they came to take him away, and my darling gave a cry that broke my heart. I made up my mind this mustn't happen; ran to my father to plead that I might marry her and bring her into the Citadel as Lords who married Ladies did. It was the most awful mistake of my life, because he flew into a terrifying rage and had my lovely Liss taken and charged with enchanting me. I had to stand by him and hear them tell wicked and cruel lies, and I could say nothing. To have denied it would have been seen as proof that the charge was true. They took her and killed her. As she went out I could hardly bear to look, but I think she understood and forgave me, because she smiled at me and made the secret sign we had for a kiss. That was all that kept me sane, but in that moment I swore in my heart I'd kill my father."

Tears were falling from Zaroth's eyes, and he was silent for a long time. Tamlyn leant forward and wiped his face with Merla's cloth. This must be true. No one could pretend the agony he saw there. At last Zaroth gave a deep sigh and went on.

"I had to get close to my father to achieve anything. I made myself seem what he thought I should be; hard and fierce. I even thanked him many times for saving me. I hated it all, but I never hurt anyone, not intentionally."

"I saw you slash a child with your riding whip," Tamlyn accused. "That was cruel."

"The day I saw you in the kitchens! Yes, but I didn't mean to harm her. My horse was startled when she ran out, and reared almost out of my control. I tried to move the child out of the way so she didn't get trampled."

Tamlyn remembered the scene. It was possible Zaroth spoke the truth, he had to admit. "But you came down to the kitchens, really angry."

"I wished to see she wasn't badly wounded. I rode right round the Citadel buildings without seeing her and guessed the woman might have brought the child in through the kitchen passageway. You're not the only schoolboy to know that entrance, you know." Suddenly there was almost a laugh in his voice. "As you saw, I raged and ranted to keep up my facade, but all seemed well. Then I saw you there, and something in your face spoke to me. I'd never tried to find my son before; my father kept all the details of his scheme secret, and besides, I thought it would be too much to bear to know him and yet be unable to acknowledge him. But that day I started looking. In the end I found the secret record Zerac keeps, hidden inside that chair of his. No real names, but the details all fitted. That, and the Academy's birth date lists and a few other clues made me realise, *you* are my son, Tamlyn."

Tamlyn stared, his heart beating hard against his ribs and his brain spinning. His father? Could it really be possible? If he was, why had he acted as he had since that day? Had he wanted to get rid of him in case others realised too?

"Why did you..." he began, but Zaroth went on.

"It's not welcome news to you, I can see, but from that moment I determined to watch out for you. I already knew my father was suspicious of you because you spent time with Master Greenwell, and he believed the Master was plotting against him. It took very little, real or imagined, for him to fear things like that."

Tamlyn scarcely heard the end of this. "To *watch out* for me?" he gasped. "What about planning my murder when I went to the City? What about last night? What about my little fox?" He almost spat at Zaroth when he thought of Rufus.

Zaroth's face screwed up as though in agony, whether physical or mental it was impossible to tell; perhaps both.

"If I could undo what I did then I would, Tamlyn," he sighed. "Saying I am sorry is not enough, yet it did have one good outcome. It was cruel to torment the little animal, but I would have let it run, and my old Jester could never have caught it. Then you faced me and told me I was evil. I saw my darling Liss so strongly in you, and knew that you loved that animal and hated me. Such a rage consumed me that I couldn't truly be your father, and... well, you know. But as I turned away, already disgusted at what I had done, I realised I was close to actually becoming the person I'd thought I was only acting. I had done to you what my own father had done to me, killed the creature you loved out of jealous spite. Since then I have done all I could for you."

"How?" demanded Tamlyn. "It doesn't feel like that to me."

"Remember that I had to mislead Zerac about what I thought and felt or I should have been powerless. My first act though, he knew nothing about. I couldn't bring the little fox back to life, but I carved a small replica and arranged that you might get it. That day at the Scholars' disc day, your friend found it, didn't he?"

Tamlyn, totally amazed, fumbled in his pouch and brought out Rufus II. "You made this?"

"Look on his belly. I put my Z there, very small."

And there it was. "Go on," said Tamlyn. He was wanting it all to be true now. Merla and Sharkley had said there must be someone else in the Citadel who was on his side. Could it really be this man who had seemed to hate him? But Zaroth had his eyes squeezed shut and was clenching his teeth as pain gripped him. At last he relaxed.

"The poison is spreading. I must hurry; I don't know how much time I have. Zerac was becoming more and more suspicious of you and wanted to be rid of you. He'd sent young boys he didn't like to the City before, but you were different. He guessed those others simply stayed there, for his tales of the evil King and enchantments were just a useful strategy, but he wanted to be sure you died. You remember that questionnaire? It was a way to pick you out without suspicion and I made sure I was there when he called you to him. You've worked in that room; did you notice the slit of a window into the passageway?"

Tamlyn nodded. He'd thought it a useless fancy.

"It was put there to warn when people were approaching. When you went out that day I didn't see you pass, and I hoped you'd paused. I often did when I came out of Zerac's company, simply to breathe freely. I pulled the door open as though I was leaving, and stood there to discuss the real plan so that you could be warned. Mansor was there too. He hates you for beating his son, you know. Then I went back to pick up my gloves to give you time. I thought you'd heard; saw you rushing down the south stairs as though you were flying, but just in case Will kept watch the day you left and promised he'd cause a fuss near the guards if necessary. He saw you go off with that beanpole who roams around the country and we knew you were safe for a time, at least. Will knows someone near the City and passed a message that you might appear. Why did you return though?"

"Someone I'd come to like very much came rushing up to the Citadel without telling me. He thought he was on a mission to talk to the High Lord. I hadn't told him the way things are here, and I had to stop him, to save him. It was when you were all on that hunting trip."

"Ah. My father was furious that you'd come back, still very much alive. He planned to keep you under his eye, with just enough freedom that he might be able to accuse you of plotting. He also believed he could charm you into falling under his spell and becoming his body servant. He was always able to turn on a magnetic sort of attraction when he wished. It didn't work with you, did it? I was so proud that my son could take a stand against him, though I was badly frightened of the consequences. When he wanted you to be publicly executed I suggested… well, you heard, and know what followed."

"But what you suggested could have killed me just as surely."

"No. I had to make the plan as real as possible, and I knew it would be terrible for you. Terrible, but not deadly. I made things as easy for you as I could without arousing suspicion: a hint in the village so that they could perhaps get good food to you; a bath because of my pretended delicate nose; to save you from a tiring walk I had you ride behind me, and what a secret joy that was to feel you with your arms around me. Finally, when no one was there to see, I gave you a torch to set you on the way. When you'd started I returned to the dogs. I'd brought up fresh meat in my saddlebags and I fed them so much they could barely stagger. The last thing they wanted to do was run. I had to chivvy them along at a slow trot, and the storm helped. Most dogs fear thunder; they kept trying to get under the horse for shelter, poor beasts."

Tamlyn almost laughed. All that fear, running in torment, hearing the savage animals closing in; it had all been nothing, really. But it seemed to have worked so well, so why were they here?

"I found your coat and shoes, Tamlyn. Smeared them with blood and this morning went to tell Zerac that the dogs had mauled you, that you'd fallen in the river and would surely be swept away and drowned in the flood if you weren't already dead when you went in. I prayed you'd have the sense to get away, back to the City maybe. But it's… This is the end. Soon I shall have told you it all, and I can die in peace."

At last Tamlyn believed. This *was* his father, and not the figure of hate he had seemed throughout the last year. He truly had tried to protect him, his son, against the High Lord's vicious determination to destroy anyone he even suspected of threatening his all-powerful position. He laid his hand on Zaroth's, shocked at the icy chill of it, and whispered, "What happened?"

Zaroth turned his hand over and his fingers closed stiffly round Tamlyn's. "Your baby fingers curled round mine when you were born," he murmured with a shaky smile, looking down at their linked hands.

"My father did not believe me. He screamed that you were still there, waiting for him. He drew that ghastly dagger and raved that he would get you; kill you and all those who had helped you. He would rather rule a country of dead men than one with you alive in it. I looked into his face and saw what I'd suspected for some time. He'd become wildly insane and the time had come for me to keep my vow to avenge my love and save my child. I drew my dagger. For a moment I think he believed I was joining him, and it gave me time to get in close and hold him. I killed him. I stabbed him over and over. He slithered down me to the floor, but he was a strong man, and even in his dying seconds he managed to thrust his dagger into my leg. I was a dead man too."

Tamlyn felt so much that he could scarcely speak or even think. Zerac was dead and surely that was wonderful, but the man who lay beside him was dying too, and he so desperately wanted his just-discovered father to be alive.

"Isn't there something we can do… Father?" He faltered over the word, so strange in his mouth.

Zaroth's face lit up but, "Nothing. I've seen too many die like this. Those words… father… son… I've dreamt of hearing and saying them. I whispered them to you in my darling's womb in this place. We came here often those long summer nights. The river was low; there are shallows just down river and I'd carry her across. We pretended it was our home. It's why I came here now, the one place I was truly happy."

Both of them had tears on their faces. Tamlyn lifted Zaroth's stiffening hand and kissed it. "I shall remember you always," he said softly. "Is there anyone, anything…"

"If you can, tell Will I thanked him for being my friend, always."

Tamlyn nodded mutely, and Zaroth closed his dark eyes. Tamlyn thought maybe he'd never see his father look at him again, but his lids flew open and he started fumbling at his neck with numb fingers.

"Help me, Tamlyn. You must have this." Tamlyn opened his father's high collar and saw a thick gold chain. He pulled at it gently and something hanging on it wrapped in oiled cloth came out. "Look," Zaroth said with difficulty, and Tamlyn unwrapped the cloth to reveal a large golden oval locket. "I painted my darling's likeness. It was the best thing I ever did because I painted it with love. There's an empty side too where

I was going to paint you. Let me hold it once more." Zaroth's voice was so weak now that Tamlyn had to bend low to hear him. "I've worn this next to my heart, always. You must keep it; your mother, my darling."

He held the locket between his dying hands for a long moment. "Goodbye, Liss," he murmured then, as if it had given him strength, he said, "Put it on, Tamlyn. It won't need the cloth, the seal is good. It was just in case I didn't get across the swollen river." Tamlyn slid the chain over his head and tucked the locket down against his own heart.

"Now this is a place of happiness again. I won't spoil it by choking slowly to death in it. Will you help me to the river? My father won't have the last word in my life."

Wordlessly, Tamlyn helped his father up and supported his few staggering steps to the river bank and the swirling dark waters rushing close to the edge.

"Goodbye, my son," Zaroth said, giving a smile and touching Tamlyn's hand. "I am proud to be your father. Now leave me to stand alone. This I do of my own choice."

"Goodbye, my father," whispered Tamlyn, and Zaroth stepped over the edge, vanishing immediately beneath the flood. Tamlyn stood motionless, staring down into the torrent and weeping silently for the parents he had found and lost again before he could know them. At last he looked up from the river, and saw to his amazement that the rain had stopped. In the west a watery sun was pushing its way through the last tatters of the storm clouds.

Chapter 30

Tamlyn walked across the Green towards Merla's door, unsure of how he felt or even, in a strange way, who he was. How long since he'd left this place? A few hours? Half a day maybe. Yet it felt like a lifetime during which his whole world had changed. He scarcely recalled the journey back over sodden ground, which in places appeared to be steaming slightly where the late sun warmed it. He did remember having to jump over one part of the bridge span where flood water was bubbling up through loosened stones, but for the rest of the way he'd been deep in an internal turmoil, leaping between sorrow for what he had lost and rejoicing that the High Lord had gone. He was tired to the bone and so very hungry. His last food had been breakfast... A memory surfaced of Lyddy pushing a package into his pocket. He patted the place and felt it still there. Huh! Whatever it was it'd be waterlogged by now. Never mind, there'd be fresh food here. He rapped on the door.

Merla swung it open, Lyddy close behind her. Between them they dragged him inside. "Oh Tam, you're safe," Merla cried.

"We imagined all sorts of things," Lyddy added. "There's such a fuss going on in the Citadel and no one knows what's happening. We were scared you might be in trouble there."

"Zerac's dead. Killed," Tamlyn said bluntly, and they both stared, open-mouthed.

"How? I mean who?" Lyddy cried, but Merla was looking closely at Tamlyn.

"He can tell us when he's out of those clothes," she said. "And I'd guess something to eat would be welcome."

Tamlyn nodded, gratefully. He was hustled into the kitchen and left to strip and wash in a tub of hot water, then put on clean clothes. They were the ones he'd worn on that fearful run. When? He gave up trying to sort out the time; he was just glad he was here now and could share his knowledge and his grief.

When they were sitting round the kitchen table and Tamlyn was devouring dumplings in a hastily re-heated rabbit stew, Lyddy returned to the questions.

"Zerac killed? Who by, do you know that?"

Tamlyn put down his knife and fork and closed his eyes briefly to try and get things straight. "Look," he said, "I think it would be easier if I just told you what's happened to me. My head's all muddled and I'm not thinking straight. If I do that it might help me sort things out too. It'll answer a lot I promise, as much as I know anyway."

They moved to sit more comfortably in the front room. Gradually Tamlyn managed to order and relate the sequence of the afternoon to Merla and Lyddy, listening in a silence broken only by an occasional gasp or exclamation, usually from Lyddy.

"That's all I can remember now," he said at last. He didn't mind that his eyes were again wet with tears as he told them of Zaroth's death, for they were both weeping softly too. "At first I didn't believe him, didn't want to, but I do now, absolutely. Oh, I wish I'd known him sooner." He covered his face with his hands, the sorrow overwhelming.

Merla stretched her hand out and laid it on his shoulder. "Zaroth must have had great joy in your being with him at the end. People envied him I'm sure, but he had so much bitterness and hatred in his life. I'm sad for you that you couldn't know the real man for much longer than you did."

"He really saved me three times, didn't he?" Tamlyn said thoughtfully. "When I went to the City; when Zerac wanted to execute me; and at the end, when he paid with his life. It's strange; I always thought I was an orphan, and now I really am. I know my mother was… Wait!" Tamlyn got up and ran back into the kitchen. He had put the locket safely on a shelf when he stripped, and in his tired and muddled state had completely forgotten it. Such an important thing and he didn't think he'd even mentioned it in his account. Somehow his unknown mother had meant less than the dying Zaroth in those last moments there with him.

"Look," he said, suddenly excited. "How could I have forgotten? Zaroth gave me this. He said it's a portrait of my mother that he painted." He fumbled at the edge and opened the locket with his thumbnail. "Oh!" He gazed down at the face of a beautiful young woman with blue eyes and red-gold hair. "She looks lovely. Do you think you'd know who she is, Merla? It must have been eighteen years…" He stopped because Merla was gazing at him with a strangely intense look on her face. "Are you all right?"

"I'm… show me, Tam."

He handed the locket to her and she stared at it. Then her shoulders shook and her face contorted as huge tears rolled down her cheeks.

"It's Darolissa," she sobbed, as Lyddy ran to her side and Tamlyn jumped up and knelt in front of her. "It's my daughter." She couldn't say any more. Lyddy hugged her as Tamlyn gazed up at her, uncomprehending. At last Merla regained something of her usual calm.

"I'm sorry," she said, wiping her face on the kerchief Lyddy gave her. "When you told us your story, Tam, I began to think… but I didn't dare hope. There was no way to be sure, and I might have been seeing only what I wanted."

"Merla, I don't understand. Please explain. I knew you had a daughter who died, but—"

"Killed, Tamlyn. And that was unusual." Merla took a deep breath and started again. "You know about Zerac's mad breeding scheme. I told you, didn't I?" Tamlyn nodded. "We followed our decision and made no open protest, though some women did their best to get themselves pregnant with a man of The Land before they were called in, and one woman drowned herself. We cared for all of them when they were returned to us, as they usually were. When Darolissa was called she went as the others did, of course. Though the women were kept away from us until they'd given birth, Lissa and I knew the Citadel so well that we could, and did, meet during that time. She told me the man who was fathering her child was good and kind, and that they felt real love for each other, but I didn't believe her. I thought he was tricking her for his own hateful pleasures. Then she gave birth, and almost at once the child was taken and…" Merla paused, bit her lips together, and went on, "she was killed. Accused of evil enchantments and executed. I believed then that I'd been right. My thought was that Zerac had planned it especially to get at me, because he hated knowing that the people here still considered me The Lady in their hearts."

"Oh, Merla," Lyddy sobbed.

"Don't cry, Lyddy. Many people lost loved family to that evil man's twisted plans. My grief is no worse than for any of them, and time does lessen the pain. It was seeing her face there that broke me for a moment." Suddenly Merla gave a little laugh. "I can see now that he would have been doubly enraged that his own son should come to him wanting to marry a Donkey, and that it was my daughter. But I was sure his plans would work against him sometime, and see what has happened. Out of all that evil you are here, Tamlyn."

"I'm not sure I'm that good an outcome," he said, trying to respond to her surprising change of mood.

"For me you are. Think, Tamlyn. Think of the ones most closely involved in this story."

He thought, and suddenly he saw. He started to laugh, and stood up, presenting her with a bow that Mardell might have envied.

"My Lady," he said, his face alight, "I am your grandson!"

Lyddy squealed with joy, realising the link at the same moment. "We've all found family now, haven't we? Isn't it wonderful?"

It *was* wonderful. In spite of all the hatred, cruelty and death there was this amazing joy of finding living love. They sat and talked. Lyddy told Tamlyn about the people she'd met in the City, including some he knew.

"And there was one thing that really proved I was Rosanne, though the clothes pretty well did that," she said. "When I walked into my parents' house I knew exactly how to go to the room upstairs that had been my nursery. I went to see my nursemaid too, and we think we know how I became Lyddy. Her name is Lizzie but I couldn't say the zz properly then; it always came out as Liddie. When Vitsell brought me to Merla she called me that because it was all I would say. I suppose I was calling for her."

Merla told them of her daughter. "I'm so glad that I can think of her finding real love with Zaroth. It doesn't make her death better, but at least she knew that happiness in her last year," she said. "I felt such bitterness against the man, and now that has all gone. I wish I could have known him too, as he really was. He sounds good and kind as Lissa believed. She wasn't deluded."

Tamlyn had been sitting on the rug, leaning against Merla's legs, but gradually sleep overcame him and his head drooped.

"Time for bed," said Merla.

"What's going to happen in the Citadel tomorrow?" Lyddy wondered.

"Too late to think about that tonight, but if you can you must let Hallam and Sharkley know that Tamlyn is here and what he has discovered."

Tamlyn refused to take Lyddy's bed again, so they piled cushions and pillows on the hearthrug. He thought he could have slept on the stone floor of the cell again, and he was deeply asleep as Merla crept past him to her own bed. She stopped to gaze down at the young man she'd come to love. Although she wouldn't have revealed this before, now he was part of her, blood of her blood, child of the child she had lost. He was smiling in his sleep, and his fingers were curled round the little wooden fox.

Chapter 31

Tamlyn woke early, but not before Lyddy had left for the kitchens; perhaps she'd be trying to contact Hallam and Sharkley before she started work, for he remembered that she used to go later and stay till supper was cleared. Perhaps things had been reorganised since her absence with the 'fever'. It was pleasant to think about such ordinary questions after the chaos of the last few days. His heart still ached when he thought of Zaroth, but there was also the warmth of knowing who he really was. Merla's grandson! The words buzzed in his head as a truth that he knew, but could still hardly believe.

He washed and dressed in the kitchen then went outside. It was a perfect day; the sun was already warm and a light breeze had the smell of damp grass in it. He could hear a blackbird's call and a wren was piping in the ivy on the cottage wall. He whistled back, feeling peaceful for the first time in months. Something would have to be settled in the Citadel now that Zerac was dead, but it really wasn't his business. Whatever happened it must be an improvement.

He went inside to find Merla preparing breakfast, and they were about to sit down when they heard running footsteps. The door flew open and Lyddy skidded into the kitchen, swinging round the doorpost.

"Tamlyn, get out quick. They're coming for you," she panted, almost breathless.

"What on earth do you mean?" he asked.

"Oh, don't stand asking questions. Go!"

Merla ran to look through the front window, and Lyddy tried to shove Tamlyn out of the back door, but he'd decided in a moment that he wasn't running anywhere. He heard the clop of hooves, footsteps and murmuring voices. Then a single voice sounded, echoing oddly; a speaking trumpet, he guessed.

"Scholar Tamlyn, we need you to answer questions about two murders. We know you are here and ask you to give yourself up to prevent harm to the innocent if we have to use force."

Accused of two murders? How could that be possible? Tamlyn left Lyddy sobbing wildly and went through to Merla. She reached her hand to touch his face, but didn't try to stop him as he walked towards the door.

"And I thought it was a peaceful morning," he said lightly, and went out.

On the Green he saw Lord Destralion, Lord Mansor and another Lord whose name he didn't know, all on horseback. A group of guards stood near them; none of the Elite squad, he was pleased to see. A scatter of people on foot and not too close to the central group looked as though they thought maybe something interesting was going on. Tamlyn walked towards the Lords and leapt up lightly onto the mounting block. At least he wasn't going to look up to them but face them on their level.

"I am here." He was tempted to comment that they could have knocked on the door, but perhaps this wasn't the moment for that.

Lord Destralion was a little in front of the others and Tamlyn guessed he would be the senior Lord now. He seemed ill at ease, and took a moment to look straight at him.

"A charge of murder has been made against you, Scholar Tamlyn. By the laws of the land that charge must be answered in a trial," he said quietly.

"Who am I accused of murdering?" Tamlyn felt quite calm. Perhaps the range of frenzied emotions of the last few days had left him without the ability to feel the seriousness of all this; it was as though he was watching himself from a distance.

"The High Lord Zerac, and Lord Zaroth have both been killed."

"May I ask who accuses me of these murders?"

Lord Mansor could obviously stand for this polite exchange no longer. "I do, you murdering beast." He nudged his horse nearer to Destralion. "Are we standing here all morning? Get the guards to bind him and throw him in a cell while we decide what to do with him." He gestured to the guards. "Why have we got this riff-raff? Where are the Elites? They know how to deal with murderers."

258

Lord Destralion drew himself up and glared at Mansor. "As the senior Lord I am in charge here, Mansor. You have invoked the law, and we will abide by the law. As to the Elite Guard, it seems they've all found they have business elsewhere." Mansor subsided, and Destralion turned again to Tamlyn. "Are you willing to come to the Citadel? I will hold a preliminary hearing and you will be in my charge."

He put a stress on the 'my' there, and something in the old man's demeanour gave Tamlyn hope that this might be nearer to justice than so many Citadel trials in the past. The news that the Elites had vanished was hopeful too. They'd probably felt less than secure without Zerac.

"I will come with you, my Lord," Tamlyn said. He jumped down and waited for instructions.

"I'll take him and lock him in the cell," snarled Mansor.

"I have said that Scholar Tamlyn is in my charge and he will be. Will you give me your word that you will walk with the Guards and allow them to bring you to my apartment, Tamlyn?"

"I will." Tamlyn bowed to Destralion and walked to stand with the Guards; Mansor looked furious but seemed to realise another protest would be useless. Then the three Lords rode off at a walking pace back towards the Citadel and Tamlyn came after in the middle of his escorts. The onlookers drifted away, curiosity not enough to get them following.

Arriving at the Citadel, the Lords dismounted and Destralion ordered three of the Guards to take the horses to the stables. He sent another two off with messages, though what these were and to whom they were sent Tamlyn couldn't hear.

"Lord Mansor, Lord Westlea, may I invite you to my rooms while we wait for others who are necessary for this procedure," he said, and signalling to the two remaining Guards he added, "Bring Scholar Tamlyn to my rooms also." It was a long climb up through the levels, but eventually they arrived at Destralion's home; not nearly as big as Zerac's rooms, but light and comfortable. Tamlyn and his Guards were taken into what seemed to be the kitchen, while the three Lords went to another room. Tamlyn noticed that no doors were locked and the two guards seemed to feel awkward and a bit unsure what they should be doing to keep him secure. He solved their problem by sitting at a table and resting his head on his arms. He wasn't tired, but wanted to think uninterrupted.

Presently they heard a knock at the outer door, and the sound of footsteps as someone went to answer it. Then Destralion came into the kitchen. "Bring Scholar Tamlyn to the small meeting room," he ordered, and Tamlyn was escorted to an area which was unfamiliar to him and into another room. It was larger than Zerac's main room, but furnished simply with small tables and comfortable chairs. The window had no outward view but was set in the ceiling to provide a good light from above, shining at that moment on four men who were already in there and who had risen as they entered. Tamlyn almost gasped aloud; two of them were Master Jessal and Master Sharkley. He caught Sharkley's eye and saw the Master give the smallest shake of his head. It was enough; Tamlyn gave no further sign of any special recognition.

Destralion settled them all in seats, Tamlyn a little separate from the rest and just behind him. The Chief Lord cleared his throat and started to speak.

"For those of you who may not know the facts, the body of Zerac, the High Lord, was found in his rooms yesterday morning, stabbed to death. It would seem that had happened not very long before as there was still some warmth in his body. Searches were begun, and the news given to those who it was felt should be told. At this point it was discovered that Lord Zaroth could not be found and the searches were extended to find him too as he was close to the High Lord. Nothing was seen of him until the evening, when his body was found washed up on a bend of the river a mile or so west of the Citadel."

Destralion paused, as though to let this news sink in. Tamlyn wondered how many in the room didn't know it already, and what their reactions were, but nobody spoke or made any move.

"We were all shocked and trying to make sense of what had happened," the old man went on. "As the senior Lord I took charge, and it was when I was considering what needed to be done that Lord Mansor came to me and said it was his belief Scholar Tamlyn was responsible for both crimes. He gave me reasons, which I will not repeat at this meeting, as they may need to be given in a trial. I suggested waiting to see if further evidence came to light, but Lord Mansor maintained his accusations and has laid them down formally, so as the law stands I must call a trial. A public trial," he added firmly, "so that justice is clearly seen."

"How is that to be done?" one of the men who had been waiting with the two Masters asked. Though there had certainly been trials and convictions, Tamlyn could not remember any in public, and suddenly thoughts were buzzing in his head.

"There is a form. Six men will be chosen as judges, two Lords, two Masters and two of the highest position in other areas of work in the Citadel. They will hear the evidence given on both sides, and by any means they see fit come to a conclusion and decide what needs to be done beyond that. I have asked Master Sharkley and Master Jessal, both respected Masters, to be here. Are you willing to act in this position?"

The two men looked at each other and both nodded.

"Good. Tebbling here is in charge of the finances of the Citadel, and you, Beteral, are chief librarian and archivist. Are you ready too?"

They also assented. "Very well. With Lord Westlea and me that makes six."

"What about me? Don't I count?" yelled Lord Mansor.

"You Mansor? Why, you are the accuser. Your position is to present the detail of your charges and the reasons for them. That is what you implied you wanted when you brought this to trial."

"My Lord, may I speak?" The seven men all looked startled to hear Tamlyn.

"No," growled Mansor. "We don't listen to criminals and murderers." Destralion looked coldly at him.

"Nothing has been proved yet, Mansor. Until it is, Scholar Tamlyn has the right to be heard. Carry on Tamlyn."

Tamlyn took a deep breath to calm himself. He was uncertain if what he was going to do now would work, but he had to try. He stepped forward and turned sideways a little so that he had all the men in his sight, but addressed himself mainly to Destralion.

"You are aware, I think, that in past weeks I spent some time in the High Lord's rooms working as a scribe. He wished to have copies made of documents from the early years of his coming to The Citadel: I understood this was so that the originals, which had become fragile, could be stored in safety and the copies used when they were required."

Destralion nodded, and Tamlyn noticed Beteral smiling and nodding enthusiastically.

"Some of those documents related to the setting up of the systems of law here," he went on. "Of course I had to read them to copy them, and one in particular comes to my mind now." He closed his eyes and brought forward his memory of the sheet of yellowed parchment. "It said, *'Regarding those accused of crimes of such gravity that if proven they would result in a penalty of death, it is of the greatest importance that the accused is given every opportunity to prove his innocence in order that no irreversible mistake may be made in sentencing. To this end the accused has the right to speak without interruption for as long as he or she wishes, and may also choose a minimum of twelve people to listen to both sides in the trial, then consider and give their opinion to the judges. These people may be of any rank, provided they contain men and women from a wide range of life experience.'* My Lord, I claim this right now."

There was total silence as the listeners took this in, Mansor recovering first to hiss "Rubbish; that can't be right. It's his imagination," but Destralion ignored him and turned to Beteral.

"Can you tell us if this is so?" he asked.

"I can't recall the contents of all the early documents, my Lord, but I can very soon find the one in question and bring it here. If you will excuse me." Beteral rose and went to the door.

"I think, sir, that you will find it on the top shelf of the cupboard numbered three," Tamlyn offered helpfully as he left.

"You see! He's been sneaking in there. It'll all be stuff he's written, part of his plan," Mansor burst out.

Destralion sighed. "Scholar Tamlyn, as I myself know and as he has already said, was working at the High Lord's request on those old documents. I am sure there are strict rules in place about having access to them. We will check that when Beteral returns."

They waited in silence after that. Tamlyn knew the paper would be found unless it had been destroyed in the last few days, but now he was hoping against hope that this ruling was still in operation. It had obviously been completely ignored or the meaning somehow twisted since it was written, but it had still been sitting there in the dusty old cupboards of a locked room at the back of the library.

The librarian came back into the room clasping a small file of papers, a slightly bemused look on his face.

"It's here, exactly as the scholar said. This page, you see." He handed the papers to Destralion, pointing at a place on the top one. Destralion read, looked at Tamlyn and re-read.

"Can you verify for us that this is, in fact, an original document?" he asked

"Yes, my Lord. No doubt about that."

"And it has not been tampered with in any way?"

Beteral looked shocked. "Oh no, I would see that at once, and when papers are taken out and returned I always make sure they're not damaged. After that, they are kept in the room to which I have the only key."

Destralion sat, deep in thought and lightly tapping the page with one finger. He roused himself and turned again to Beteral. "And this has not been rescinded?"

Tamlyn closed his eyes and held his breath.

"No, my Lord. It would have been clearly marked and signed by the High Lord if so."

Tamlyn's legs felt weak with relief. Destralion looked at him with a small smile and said, "It seems, Scholar Tamlyn, that you can indeed claim this as of right. You quoted the law exactly, word for word. That is an extraordinary feat."

"I copied it very recently and I have a good memory, my Lord" Tamlyn replied.

"Very well, this alters things somewhat. I take it that no one has any other comment to make." Destralion looked round, particularly at Mansor. "Then can you tell us, Scholar, who you wish to have as your advisors, or do you want time to consider?"

Could he? Would it work? "I wish, my Lord, to have every man woman and child above the age of twelve who lives or works in the Citadel."

The stunned silence almost vibrated.

"What?" Mansor screeched at last. "He can't. That's impossible. He's playing games with us. Tell him…"

There was a definite smile on Destralion's lips now. "Lord Mansor, you chose to bring this to law, and the law states that Scholar Tamlyn *can* do this. There is no mention here of a maximum number he may choose, only a minimum." He tapped the pages he still held. "Betoral, I return this to your safe keeping, just in case it should be damaged."

The Librarian took the papers and Destralion went on. "It is obvious this will take time to organise. I will let you all know when we are ready, and I ask you not to talk about this affair in public until then. As I said, I will take charge of this young man, and in case you feel I may somehow help him, Lord Mansor, you are very welcome to be my guest and supervise how I behave."

He grasped Tamlyn's arm and they left the room together.

Chapter 32

It was the strangest time of Tamlyn's life. He was accused of murder, and if he was found guilty he'd be executed. He knew he had committed no crime, yet had no proof of this except his word. Everything now depended on words. Could all the people he'd called to hear him and decide his fate be persuaded by what he would say? It sounded unlikely, impossible even, yet at first his heart had felt lighter than it had done for weeks, with a certain smug satisfaction at remembering the words he'd once copied which had earned him this chance,

Now he had to think in detail what he could say, and questions suddenly flooded his mind. He'd never spoken to more than a class of his own age; twelve, fourteen people at most, and soon, probably tomorrow, he'd be confronted with hundreds, many of whom would be adults with years of experience. What would make them believe him? Would they even bother to listen? How many, like Lord Mansor, would have already made up their minds to his guilt by the time he started? Tamlyn groaned inwardly and his mouth grew dry at the thought of what was to come. Perhaps he'd stand there and find he couldn't talk at all. From his first crazy feeling of hope he was plunged into even more crazy despair.

Lord Destralion had appeared to be pleased with what had happened, but perhaps that was mainly because he found Lord Mansor very annoying. He would, Tamlyn thought, be scrupulous in keeping to the law, and he had made sure that another stay for him in that cell had been ruled out. He had to be thankful for that. Here he had food, comfort and freedom to move within the apartment; if only he could think.

His mind went to Lyddy and Merla. Unless Sharkley was able to get a message to them they would have no idea what was happening. Lyddy would be among those summoned to his trial and that might be the first she knew of it. Hallam too. He wouldn't know anything at all. What a horrible, stupid mess everything had become.

"Believe in yourself." It was almost as though Merla was talking to him, smiling and looking at him with those wonderful eyes. As the daylight faded and the constant sound of people coming to talk to Lord Destralion or taking messages for him slowed down and finally stopped, the circling torment in his head began to subside then faded and vanished. He was still alive, and somewhere inside him he felt there was the power to make that continue. When he was shown to a bed in a small room behind the kitchen he fell asleep more quickly than he would have believed possible an hour or two before.

Tamlyn woke with three words singing in his head: tell the truth. Something was giving him the sign he needed and he would listen. Truth, in the distorting mirror of life in the Citadel, had become a dangerous commodity, but he knew in his heart that it must be his weapon today. He would use it as his heart told him.

One of Destralion's servants led him to a bathroom and indicated that he might use it. Yesterday he'd washed in Merla's kitchen; today it was a Lord's bathroom. Not quite equal to Almaran's in the City, but equipped luxuriously for comfort. The servant, who was either dumb or had been told not to talk to him, pointed to a shelf above the wash-stand and Tamlyn saw his own things laid out there. Delighted, he washed and shaved, then used the last drops of Lyddy's lotion. He might never need it again if things went against him, but somehow the thought didn't send his spirits plummeting; instead the perfume, so like her own, gave him comfort. Back in the tiny bedroom a further surprise greeted him; fresh clothes were laid out on the bed and they were his own, the suit that had been so well fitted in the City! If this was to be his last day, he was at least being well treated and well dressed.

After breakfast, Tamlyn simply sat and waited, looking out of the window which from this high point allowed him to see the river. Its waters, which had been brimming over the banks in flood, seemed to have dropped, though not yet to their usual level, and it looked as though the soil swept from the banks had made the water look brown. He jumped up as Lord Destralion came in.

"We are all ready, Tamlyn," he said. "Forgive me that I didn't think it correct that either I or my servants should speak to you while you've been my guest, but I hope you were well cared for."

"I was very comfortable. Thank you for all you've done, my Lord."

Destralion nodded and regarded Tamlyn in silence. "You look… very well. Come now. We mustn't keep all your guests waiting."

They walked together until they reached the door which Tamlyn knew led onto the stage of the great hall, then Destralion handed him into the care of a Guard. Still not Elite, but the man was smartly dressed in a red jacket with grey trousers.

"Give me a slow count of thirty so that I may reach my seat, then bring Scholar Tamlyn in," Destralion ordered. "You know where he is to sit?"

"Oh yes, m'Lord." The man seemed overcome by the importance of his position, and when Destralion had entered he turned to Tamlyn with a worried look and whispered, "Did he say twenty or thirty?"

"Thirty," Tamlyn whispered back. "Shall we count them together?"

The Guard gave a relieved grin. "Thanks," and they started. When they reached thirty, the Guard put his hand on Tamlyn's shoulder. "Sorry," he said. "They've told me to do this." He pushed the door open and led Tamlyn to stand by a seat at the side of the stage. A murmur of voices sounded, then Destralion's voice.

"There will be no talking while this court is in session. Scholar Tamlyn, you may be seated."

Tamlyn bowed and sank into the chair. He was extremely glad to do this or he might have collapsed with shock. The great hall was full with more people than he had ever seen together in the Citadel. Scholars and Masters were crammed in the centre, Lords and Ladies were squeezed into the rising banks of seats behind him. The rest of the seats and benches were taken by scribes, office workers, people from the medical area and many more whose positions he had no idea about. In the aisles between and packed solid around the edges were all the staff who kept the Citadel running, most of them so-called Donkeys. To his joy he saw Lyddy; she'd put on a scarlet jacket and stood out like a flame. Lord Mansor was seated in a chair at the other side of the stage and glared at him, while Destralion with the other five judges sat at a slightly raised table in the centre behind him. Lord Destralion stood up to speak.

"I thank you all for coming to this trial. It is, I imagine, unique in the history of the Citadel but I have made sure that it is completely legal according to our laws. By now you will all know that the High Lord and Lord Zaroth were murdered two days ago, and Lord Mansor has accused Scholar Tamlyn of these crimes. You will hear him speak and explain his reasons for the accusation. Then you will hear Scholar Tamlyn speak to defend himself. Both may say what they wish without interruption. In fact you must keep silent during the trial, whatever your feelings."

Destralion paused, took a sip from a glass of water, and continued. "I would ask you to listen very carefully, because when the speeches are finished you will all be asked to show your opinion. The result of that will be considered by the judges and a decision taken about what comes next. With such a large number of you here, it will be a lengthy process so there will be a break in these court proceedings. I will ask you all to reassemble here at the same time tomorrow morning. I will explain now how you will show your wishes. You may have noticed in front of the judges table there are two large barrels, one red and one green, which both have a hole in their lids. Lord Mansor was given the choice and he has picked the red barrel, so the green one is Scholar Tamlyn's. Everyone will be given a small pebble and asked to put it in the barrel of the one who they believe has spoken the truth. This will be done behind a curtain so that you cannot be seen and everyone's name will be written down when they have chosen. If at the end you find you cannot make up your mind you are free to drop your pebble elsewhere. I will repeat these instructions when we have heard the speeches. Lord Mansor, will you begin please."

Destralion sat down, and Mansor strode to the front of the space left on the stage. Tamlyn, who had been marvelling at this choosing system, realized that his trial had actually begun.

"I am here to tell you the truth about this Tamlyn who you see there looking so meek and quiet. He is nothing of the sort. He is a stupid oaf with a violent and unguarded temper and I say this with reason. One day last year my own son Bartoly returned from the Academy looking as though he'd been set upon by a gang of brigands. He was bruised and bloody all over and his nose had been broken. He needed considerable medical treatment and time away from his studies. I discovered that Tamlyn was the cause of his distress. Bartoly is not a violent boy, but he is built strongly and yet this ruffian, in an unprovoked fit of rage, proved he is strong and vicious enough to beat him to the ground. You may say he is too much of a weakling to get the better of full grown men like the High Lord and Lord Zaroth, but I tell you now that this proves he is powered by an evil strength with which he could easily have done these deeds.

"I was for many years honoured to be a friend of both the victims we're going to avenge today. The High Lord was particularly close to me. Though older than I am, he still had the spring of youth in his heart. He was kind and generous to those he welcomed into his friendship, and I know that the cherishing of this land and the people in it was forever in his mind. Some months ago, he took an interest in this, this nobody, this upstart brat. Alhough I warned him of his hidden temper, he still chose him for a very special mission. It would be difficult and dangerous, but the High Lord said laughingly that his temper might come in useful for that reason. Tamlyn has looks, I can see, but search below that and he is a poor thing. The High Lord entrusted me with the task of familiarising him with certain monetary tasks, and I swear any scholar in Year Two could have grasped the simple workings of it more easily. However, off he went, and need I say he failed totally to do the work with which the High Lord had entrusted him, creeping back with some cock and bull tarradiddle to try and smooth over his poor result."

"I could scarcely believe it when I found that, despite all this, the High Lord had taken this thing into his own employ. He seemed to be besotted with him. He even had a desk built specially for him in his room and supervised his work personally. I saw him many times lean over to check his work, and always with a kindly 'well done' and a smile. Lord Zaroth shared my concern, I am sure, because he started to spend considerable time there, watching and noting what was happening."

"All this wonderful treatment must have gone to his self-satisfied head, for last week I heard that he had refused to do something he was asked. The High Lord was undoubtedly annoyed, but his only punishment was to be sent to spend a day or two in the cell, but with a special instruction – and I had this from the guard in question – that he must be treated well. Still he refused to obey his master. I understand that Lord Zaroth was there when this happened a second time. I wish I might have been there too, to prevent the tragedy that ensued, because both

Lord Zaroth and this animal vanished the next evening and the following morning the High Lord was killed. It is so clear what happened. He killed Zaroth first, hiding his body near the river where the rising waters swept it away. Then he crept into the Citadel and doubtless got into the High Lord's presence with pretence of sorrow and remorse at his previous behaviour. That kind and generous man would have let his guard down sufficiently for this villain to have got close enough to kill him. A coat and shoes, soaked in blood, were in the murder room. I have identified them as Scholar Tamlyn's.

"I am sorry to have had to tell such a harrowing story in front of ladies, but for their presence we have to blame this arrogant creature. This is what happened. He is guilty, and if you believe in justice, you will say so."

Mansor strutted back to his chair and sat, a satisfied smirk on his face. He certainly got a lot of details right, thought Tamlyn. Just the whole thing wrong. For one moment he wondered if he had chosen the right path, but again he heard the echo of those words, tell the truth, and he would stick to it. Was he supposed to get up and start, he wondered? No; he saw Sharkley lean across Lord Westlea to speak to Destralion and both of them nodded. Destralion got up and came forward to speak.

"Master Sharkley has reminded me that we have some young scholars here and also some of, shall we say, mature years. Before Scholar Tamlyn makes his statement we will have a short break when you may leave the room briefly or have a good wriggle." This brought a ripple of laughs. "Please do not discuss what you have heard so far, and be as quick as you can." There was some movement here and there, especially on the centre front benches, but most remained firmly in place.

Destralion came across to Tamlyn. "Do you need anything for your comfort?" he enquired.

"Some water, if that's allowed," Tamlyn said, and the old Lord fetched a cup from the judges table. Tamlyn saw Mansor glare at this.

Those who had moved proved keen to return, and in a very short time the hall was again waiting in still, attentive silence.

"Scholar Tamlyn, you may speak now."

Tamlyn got up and moved to the front. He stood quietly, taking a deep breath. Here we go, he thought.

"Thank you all for coming. I'm sorry it's such a squash. When I claimed my right to this trial I had not reckoned on the numbers. Mathematics is not my strong point, as has been noted." A giggle or two sounded, instantly stifled, but it had lightened the atmosphere. "To start with I will say this: I did not kill the High Lord. I did not kill Lord Zaroth. Now I am going to tell you a story.

"Once upon a time there lived a King and Queen in another land. They were good people and their subjects loved them, but they were sad because they had no children. Then one day the Queen found she was with child, and when the time came she brought into the world not one but two babies. Two beautiful baby boys. Everybody was delighted, and I would guess they rang the bells, had feasts and drank lots of wine to show how happy they were that the twins were born. For twelve years the boys grew up together. They were the best of friends and did everything in each other's company without a care in the world. But when they were twelve it was time for the heir to the throne to start learning about how to be a King one day, and there could only be one King; the oldest prince. He was only older than his brother by half an hour, but though both the princes protested, that was the law. The older brother tried to pass on all he learned to the younger, but the younger one was so angry about being considered as less important than his brother that he wouldn't do that. That young man made his family's life a misery, with continual rages and complaints that it was unjust, that his future had been stolen from him and he hated them all. He even began to rage at his mother, telling her she should have had him first, which of course would have been impossible for the poor lady. She was made very unhappy. Strangely, all this bad temper and hatred was only seen by his family. To everyone else the younger brother was still the bright, handsome, fun-loving young prince he had always been, and he had lots of friends.

"The royal family didn't know what to do. The older brother kept on learning to be a good King, and trying to make his brother see sense at the same time, but it was no good. In the end, the King gave his younger son a large mansion with many acres of land to try and let him see that he hadn't lost everything, only the crown, and crowns weren't really very comfortable anyway! The younger twin had a very good time with his friends on his estate, feasting, jousting, hunting, all the things that young men like him enjoyed. But he was still angry deep down inside. The only thing he really wanted was to be King, the one at the top.

"When these princes were eighteen their father died. The older brother, who was now King and so could change the laws, went straight to the younger one and suggested they should be kings together, but he would have none of it. The black anger and jealousy had taken deep root in him, and he would have all or nothing. He told the young King, his brother, that he would leave the city and country immediately and find a land where he could be the only ruler. The young King was sad that this was happening, but wished him well on his quest. He thought in his heart that maybe his brother would fail in his search and come back a little wiser. He would welcome him then, and they could once more be as they had as children, the best of friends.

"That didn't happen. The younger twin set off with several hundred of his friends who admired him and thought this would be a grand adventure. They found a small land. It was peaceful and beautiful and ruled by a woman. The people there did not like fighting, so when the young man marched in and said they must make him ruler and do as he wanted or he would start killing them, very sadly they agreed. They could see they had no hope of trying to fight all these men who were trained in using swords and bows and lances, so it was better to stay alive and hope for better things."

Tamlyn stopped for a moment and looked round. Everyone, even the youngest in the front rows, was looking at him in rapt silence; they really were listening.

"Some of you may be wondering why am telling you a story. How strange, you'll be thinking, when he's on trial for murder. In fact – and I'm sure many others of you have realised it already – this is not a made up fairy tale and there is not a happy ending to it. This is a true history of real people. The older twin is called Almaran, and he is still King of the lands and City to the west. The younger twin was called Zerac. He was High Lord of this land until two days ago."

There was a murmur especially from among the Scholars, but it was quickly hushed.

"I wasn't alive when these things happened. Zerac came to this land more than fifty years ago, but I have been told about it by some who were alive then, particularly King Almaran, and I believe him to be an honest man. I have also learned, from others who I trust, about what happened here when Zerac started to rule The Land. You would have thought he would be happy once he had got what he wanted, but the darkness of hatred, jealousy and suspicion was by then too deeply rooted in him. He had power over everyone, and I'm sure he could still be the charming young prince with those who obeyed him, but he was always afraid that someone would take this power from him. He couldn't bear to be disobeyed in the slightest way, particularly by the people who had always lived here. A year or two after he arrived those people planned to send a group of children and some older folk across the mountains in the east to a place where they could live more freely than here. Zerac discovered this, and he was furious. He took a party of his men and hid in a narrow cavern through which the children had to pass. He blocked their exit and he and his men fell upon them with their swords. Thirty seven children and fourteen old people, all unarmed, were slaughtered that day, and four who had swords but were not skilled in their use were killed also, when they stood at the cavern mouth and fought to prevent Zerac and his men from getting back through the narrow entrance and chasing those who managed to run away."

"It's all lies." Mansor screamed. "Stop him telling such wicked lies." He started running across the stage towards Tamlyn, drawn dagger in hand. It was Sharkley who intervened. He vaulted over the judges' table and barred the way. One hand moved at lightning speed and Mansor's dagger dropped to the ground.

"Sit down, my Lord. Sit down and stay quiet or you will be removed from the hall." Sharkley spoke with icy calmness, voice barely above a whisper, but Tamlyn knew his ability to control. Mansor returned to his chair rubbing his arm and Sharkley put the dagger on the judges' table. He then went back to his own seat in a rather more conventional manner.

Destralion's face was white and drawn. He looked across at Tamlyn. "Do you want a moment to recover?" he asked.

"Thank you, my Lord, I will continue." Tamlyn turned again towards the front of the stage and told of all the events that had led up to two murders. He no longer felt nervous of talking to this huge crowd. The words came to him and he used them easily, knowing that all these people deserved the truth. He mentioned no names except those that were already known and he spoke simply without bluster or exaggeration. He told of the humiliation and cruelty used by Zerac to subdue the people of The Land. He told of Zerac's plan to build a 'true blood' race of men, using the women of The Land like breeding cattle, and of his never-ending and growing fear that someone, somewhere was plotting to overthrow him.

Then Tamlyn told Zaroth's story, of the High Lord's son who rarely saw his father. A gentle boy whose mother encouraged his love of painting and carving, but she died too young, leaving Zaroth to be brought up in the Citadel Academy where very few knew his parentage and didn't enquire. After all, so many were orphans or believed they were.

Then Tamlyn came to the fateful day when Zerac ordered his son to do his duty and produce a child with a woman of The Land. He related how Zaroth unwillingly went to meet the woman chosen for him and how something magical happened when Zaroth and the woman fell in love and were happy to have a child together.

"They kept their love to themselves because they knew Zerac had no intention of allowing Donkey women any place in his world. But when Zaroth's and Lissa's son was born and taken away from them, Zaroth ran to his father and pleaded to be allowed to marry the woman he loved. It was a terrible mistake, for Zerac was enraged. He had Lissa brought before him, accused her of evil enchantment and she was killed; but in that moment Zaroth swore an oath, deep in his heart, that one day he would kill his father."

"It is now that I can tell you things that I know myself. I was brought up in the Citadel, taught and believing that the High Lord was our wonderful leader, guarding and guiding us in all the right ways and protecting us from the wicked magician-King in the City who was always attacking us with evil enchantments to spoil the happiness of the lives we had with him as our head. I repeated the oath each morning with pride and was overjoyed when I was chosen to be a Scholar in the Academy. It was a good life, and I never questioned any part of it, even the fact that so many Scholars were orphans.

"As I began my last year as a Scholar though, I did begin to have a few doubts about things like Evil Enchantment which we studied throughout the Academy, but I put them from me, feeling my worries were wrong and also fearing the consequences if anyone else was to know my thoughts. An accidental chance brought me to Lord Zaroth's attention and also into closer contact than I'd had before with some of the people of The Land. That chance made me think Zaroth a cruel bully and that the people were far from Donkeys, but I still kept it all to myself.

"Then something horrible happened. Most of you will remember Master Greenwell." Tamlyn went on. "He taught about plants, herbs, and trees and particularly their medicinal properties. It is a subject that has always interested me, so he often lent me books or told me things not covered in the set lessons. He tried, I believe, to get me to open my mind and see beyond things I was told as fact, and that was his only aim. Because it was Zerac's determination to control everything the 'pure blood' boys in the Academy learnt, he became suspicious of Greenwell, fearing he was part of a group undermining his plans and working for his downfall. Do you remember the High Lord telling us sadly of Greenwell's death because of evil enchantment, and the solemn funeral afterwards? It was all a lie. He died a broken, beaten and bloodied man, tortured by the Elite guards at Zerac's orders as he himself watched and tried to get the names of his co-conspirators from him. I held Master Greenwell's hand in the prison cell and helped him die to escape further torment. That night, I learned the reality of life in the Citadel and knew that I must try to change it if I could."

"My meeting with Lord Zaroth at this time was having consequences I did not discover until much later. Zaroth saw in me something he hadn't seen before, a face that reminded him of his beloved Lissa. He had never tried to find his child until then, but now he did. He searched and found his father's secret list of breedings and other documents like the birthday list of children born in Zerac's scheme, and he discovered that I was the child he had held on the day the woman he loved had been murdered. I am Lord Zaroth's son. I had no idea of this, nor of the fact that he made up his mind to watch over me even though he couldn't safely reveal our relationship. Over the next months I still regarded him as a cruel man, close to Zerac, but he had made himself pretend to be the sort of man

Zerac valued in order to get close to him, and he learned all of his father's plans. In fact he saved me three times when I would have been killed."

Tamlyn told the story of his mission to the City when Zerac had really meant to have him killed before he even arrived. Instead he'd got to the City another way and discovered that the evil King, the sad, enchanted people and the grey city were all made up to deter Citadel folk from going there, and it had been there that he'd learnt the truth of Zerac's childhood from his twin brother. Returning because a friend was in danger, he'd again caused the High Lord to suspect him.

"Zerac was angry that I was still alive, and planned to keep me under his eye to find an opportunity when he could finally get rid of me. He did indeed have a desk made for me in his rooms as you have been told and played the caring older man to perfection. But he asked me to do what I would not and he sent me to the prison cell. His words to the guards were, 'Do not hurt him – yet.' When I was brought before him again and still refused what he wanted, he became furiously angry and was going to have me executed at once, but Zaroth talked him into letting him play the Midnight Hounds game. It would, he said, be much more enjoyable to hear me scream as the dogs caught me and ripped me apart, and Zerac would not be blamed as I would just be an unlucky curfew breaker.

"If that sadistic game had been played according to Zerac's rules I should have certainly been caught and killed that night. It was the night the storms began, and I was terrified. I ran until I was dropping and then still ran, always believing I could hear the baying of the hounds behind me. I ripped off my coat and shoes which I believed had been scented and left them by the river as I reached the village. There I fell, hitting my head on the mounting block, and village people took me in and cared for me.

"I don't know what I might have done next, but I woke from a sleep in the middle of the next day with the certainty that I must go across the river. I followed this call and came to the rocky shelter across from the Citadel where I found Lord Zaroth, lying weak and in great pain. Although I had hated the man who I thought was evil and who had put me through such torment, I did listen to him when he begged me to. He knew he was dying and I realised that he was the reason I'd felt the call to that place. He told me all I have just told you, including the fact that he'd saved me from Zerac's fury by suggesting the run. He'd made it seem real, but after I left and started running he had fed the hungry dogs with as much meat as they could eat. They could, he said, scarcely walk let alone run me down. I did believe him. Then he told me that the dogs had found my coat and shoes so he'd smeared them with blood and taken them to tell his father that I had been killed by the dogs but my body had fallen in the swollen river and washed away.

"Zerac did not believe him. He screamed that I was still alive, that he would kill me himself and anyone who got in his way or helped me. Zaroth told me his father drew that dagger he always wore, and he could see madness in his eyes. He knew the time had come to fulfil his oath. He drew his own dagger and stabbed Zerac many times, but as his father slid dying to the floor, he found strength to thrust his own weapon into Zaroth's leg. Not a deep wound, but Zaroth knew he would die because his father's dagger was always coated with a deadly poison."

"My father had managed to cross the river to the place where I found him. It was the one place he had been truly happy when he and my mother had gone there on the warm summer nights when they'd had to hide their love. He told me how he would carry her across the shallows and how they'd dream of being together always. He gave me a locket from round his neck, a portrait of her which he'd painted and worn next to his heart every day. He called me his son as he had longed to do, and I called him Father. I helped him to get to the river's edge as he asked, then he told me to let go of him, because it was his choice to die there, not wait as Zerac's poison killed him slowly and painfully. He took one step and the water took him."

Tamlyn looked down, biting his lip to stop the tears. The silence in the hall was almost painful. At last he went on. "I did not kill my grandfather. I don't regret his death, but I am sad that somehow he went wrong and didn't live like his brother. I did not kill my father and I shall always regret that we could not have found each other sooner. What I have told you is what happened. Now you must choose which of us you believe. I'm not going to ask you to choose me. A very wise person once told me to believe in myself and I've found that is good advice, so I'm asking you to do that. Don't ask someone else what to do. If someone tells you to do as they say, ignore them. Look inside yourself and see what you really think. No one except you will see when you put your pebble in, but you will know what you did for the rest of your life. Choose what *you* think is right."

Tamlyn turned to the judges and bowed, and then walked to the guard who still stood by the door.

"Please take me where I should be. I think it's Lord Destralion's rooms," he said and went through the door as if he was sleep-walking.

Chapter 33

Tamlyn sat in Lord Destralion's home for the rest of the day, staring into space and unable to move or think. Servants put food in front of him but he ignored it, and he scarcely noticed the sound of the many feet that ran, tramped or tiptoed through the entrance hall nearby. As it grew dark, Lord Destralion came in to him and sat at his side.

"Can I not tempt you to eat, Tamlyn?" he asked quietly, but Tamlyn shook his head. "Well then, drink this. It will help, I'm sure." He put a glass of pale green liquid in front of him. Vaguely Tamlyn wondered if they knew already that he'd lost, and the kindly Lord was offering him an easy way out. If so, he might as well take it. He picked up the glass and drained it. Within minutes darkness overcame him and his head dropped forward on the table.

Then he was in a narrow bed... Where? His mouth tasted weird and his eyes felt too big for their sockets. Tamlyn shook his head, not a good idea really, but he did manage to see that he was in Lord Destralion's room. Gently he swung his feet to the floor and had stopped on the edge of the bed, trying to remember exactly how to stand up when a servant came in.

"Milord says to drink this and stay where you are."

Tamlyn looked at the thick yellow mess streaked with brown that he was being given and his stomach heaved. "What is it?" he got out.

"Is lots of things. Very good for how you feel now."

This didn't make the stuff look any more palatable but Tamlyn decided he couldn't feel much worse and swallowed it quickly. Not as bad as he'd expected, really. He put his head on the pillow again, and managed to return his feet to the level of the rest of his body. A state somewhere between sleeping and waking took over as he let things drift through his mind.

A hand shook his shoulder, the servant again. "You feeling better now?" he asked.

Tamlyn considered. "I am, actually. That was quick work."

"You have slept another hour, but now you must get up." Tamlyn really was feeling better, and memories of yesterday filtered back. The hall; all the people; talking on and on; and then the realisation that this was tomorrow and he would be expected back in the hall soon to learn his fate. He'd have liked to return to sleep but instead got out of bed and made for the bathroom.

Dressed, and his head more or less clear, Tamlyn was taken to another room where he found Lord Destralion at the breakfast table. He gestured to a seat and Tamlyn sat.

"I'm really sorry. You must have felt most peculiar this morning, but if I hadn't made sure you got some sleep you wouldn't have been fit for anything today. I had no sleeping draughts so you had one of Gènève's specials; probably too strong for you, but his morning recipe seems to have worked. Have some breakfast; that should complete the cure.

"You're talking to me, my Lord."

"I can't influence the result now, you see, and you are a guest in my home. If you would prefer being alone, do take some breakfast to a quiet place."

"No, thank you." Tamlyn helped himself to porridge and found once he started on it that he was very hungry indeed.

"We will go down together in twenty minutes." Destralion pulled one of the fascinating timepieces from inside his jacket and looked at it. "I have some work to finish, but I'll give you warning."

Once Destralion had left the room Tamlyn ate one from a dish of little pancakes stuffed with mushrooms; not as good as Lyddy's but really tasty. Thoughts of Lyddy brought back a picture of her in her red coat. He wondered if he'd be able to see her if... if the worst happened. That thought took the rest of his appetite away.

The hall seemed, if possible, more crammed with people than yesterday. Tamlyn and Lord Mansor sat as before on either side, but the table for the six judges had been pushed forward between them and had the two barrels on it with a slightly lower table in front of that. This held two large metal bowls. At the sight of them Tamlyn started to feel very sick, and wished he'd not had the little pancake. Whatever the result, he didn't want to throw up in public. Please hurry up, he pleaded silently. It all felt unreal; he simply couldn't make his brain believe that he might die in a very short while.

The six judges stood behind the barrels, and Destralion called for silence.

"We will now empty the barrels to determine their contents. The red one, which is for Lord Mansor will be first. Will you step forward, my Lord, to witness this is done properly?" Mansor came to stand by the tables, then Destralion waved his hand in a summoning gesture and two Guards appeared from the side of the stage. They went between the tables; one took the lid from the red barrel, then together they lifted it and tilted it over a bowl. There was a rattle and clatter of pebbles falling into the bowl and the guards gave the barrel a shake to be sure it was empty.

Master Jessal and Tebbling walked round and together counted the pebbles, taking each one from the bowl it was in, holding it up for all to see then placing it into the other empty bowl.

"We have counted forty-eight pebbles," Master Jessal announced clearly. "Do you agree with that, Lord Mansor?" He nodded curtly and returned to his seat, and the pebbles went back into the red barrel

"Now the green barrel, which is for Scholar Tamlyn," Lord Destralion announced. The two guards repeated their actions, removing the green lid and tilting it. A few pebbles clattered down, and the guards set the barrel back on the table. Was that all, Tamlyn thought. With Mansor's count that would hardly make a hundred. Surely so many people hadn't found themselves unable to make a choice.

But the guards had simply been changing their grip. They heaved the obviously heavy barrel up between them and pebbles began to pour out. They filled the bowl, which overflowed onto the table, cascaded over the table's edge onto the stage and some finally rattled onto the floor where they reached the feet of the youngest Scholars. As the last clatter stopped there was a breathless silence, then the hall erupted into a tumult of cheers and shouts. The six judges stood smiling but Tamlyn sat frozen with amazement. All he could think was, they believed me.

At last Lord Destralion held up his hand, and gradually the tumult ceased. "You have made your feelings clear beyond doubt, and I have to tell you that all six of the judges agree with you. Scholar Tamlyn has told us the truth of how Zerac and Zaroth died, and he is therefore free of any blame in the matter." Another roar of agreement followed, but Destralion hadn't finished.

"As I explained yesterday, it is the duty of the judges to say what should happen next, but before we do that, can we clear the stage of this litter please?"

Help came quickly to retrieve the pebbles, including the youngest scholars who scrabbled for them round their feet and enjoyed shying them directly into the barrel held steady by the guards. While that was going on, Sharkley came over and squatted down by Tamlyn.

"Well done, Tamlyn. Giving that speech yesterday was the bravest thing I've ever known anyone do. I guessed you'd be feeling very strange at this point, so yesterday evening I broke all the rules and went to see Merla. Didn't tell her anything, but she has a habit of knowing doesn't she?" Tamlyn nodded with a smile. "She gave me this," Sharkley went on, handing Tamlyn a small phial. "Destralion told us what he gave you last night. Pretty potent I believe! This won't knock you out like that, just help you to get on your feet. Merla's here, by the way, over at the back with Hallam and Lyddy." He went to join the other judges now standing in the centre of the stage. Tamlyn swallowed the colourless liquid and felt it run through him, soothing and strengthening him, and he stood, though not knowing what he should do. At that moment Mansor walked across and stopped in front of him, staring at him. The man seemed shrunken somehow; his face white and his eyes dark and blank. Tamlyn realised how awful this defeat must be for him and could almost feel sorry for him. Tentatively he held his hand out. As Bartoly had done before, Mansor looked down at it then up, ignoring the gesture. He gave a curt nod and left the stage. Nobody stopped him; perhaps nobody noticed his going.

Destralion again called for quiet, and when it was achieved looked all around the great hall, turning slowly to include those in the seats behind them.

"I must explain that it was very clear to the judges last night what the outcome of your choosing would be. We did not count in advance, but the fact that the green barrel needed two strong guards to lift it when we moved the barrels to a safe place led us to look at our future options ahead of the actual counting.

"We now have no High Lord, and Zerac's son, Lord Zaroth, who might have taken his father's place, is also dead. We do need a ruler. A country, even a small one like this, can soon fall into chaos with no one to guide it. I am the oldest Lord, but I could not deal with what we need to do here to begin healing the wounds and divisions inflicted by Zerac over the years.

"Last night the six of us discussed the problem long into the night. We realised that yesterday we saw a young man who showed both courage in telling the truth, and compassion even for those who would have killed him. I know for certain that he did not name some he could have done who were willingly involved in Zerac's schemes. Tamlyn, whose honesty shone through all the lies thrown at him, is in the blood line of Zerac, but has proved himself a very different and much better man. He is also, by his mother, one of the people of The Land. We decided to ask you, Tamlyn, if you will be our leader, wear this robe and lead us to a happier future." Destralion picked up the shimmering cloth that he'd placed on the table, shook it out to reveal a magnificently embroidered robe, and walked towards Tamlyn to lay it across his arms. A murmur of anticipation came from those listening, everyone waiting to see what Tamlyn would say.

For the fraction of a heartbeat Tamlyn saw himself in this wonderful robe, and then the inner voice he trusted told him what he really knew already. There was only one answer he could give.

"My Lord, everyone here, I can't think of words good enough to thank you for the honour you do me in offering this to me. I have always loved this land and will till the day I die, but it would be wrong for me to accept, and there are two reasons for that. Firstly, I am very young; haven't had my eighteenth birthday or even finished my schooling yet. I know I haven't got the wisdom and understanding that a ruler needs, especially where there is so much hurt that needs healing. Even if I did feel capable, the second reason would still make me say 'no'. A ruler is already here in The Land, legitimate by birth, tradition, and the loving will of the people. Please, Merla, will you come here."

Many Citadel dwellers, turning to each other with whispered questions, strained to see who Tamlyn was talking to. People of The Land knew, and held their breaths in amazed excitement. Tamlyn could see Merla come forward down the crowded aisle, everyone there pressing back to make room for her. She reached the stage and stopped in front of Tamlyn. Many Ladies in the banked seats behind were dressed in coloured silks and satins, bedecked with jewels, but Merla made them look gaudy. She had a plain dress of deep blue and her only jewel was the locket that Tamlyn had insisted she must have. Her richly deep auburn hair was not, as usual, tied up or covered with a shawl, but hung loose to her shoulders.

Tamlyn went down on one knee and held the gown towards her across his outstretched arms. "My Lady, will you take this which is already yours by right?"

Merla looked quietly down at him for a moment, and then round the crowds surrounding them.

"If it is the wish of those here, I will," she replied, and the cheers echoed from everywhere in the hall. There must have been many there who knew nothing of her, but they were still drawn towards this woman whose calmness and beauty seemed to speak to them, even without words, of comfort and love. Just a few who maybe could not bear to face her slipped out; perhaps the forty-eight whose pebbles had been in the red barrel Tamlyn thought, though one of that number had already gone.

Sharkley and Beteral stepped forward and held the gown while Merla put it on and now she looked truly wonderful and Queenly, but her first action was to fling her arms round Tamlyn and kiss him, an embrace he returned with a will. There was a pause, as though no one was quite sure what to do next, then a voice rang out from the centre of the hall.

"Oy, Tam, can I have a kiss too."

Of course it was Hallam. Tamlyn felt it was time for something light-hearted after all the solemnity so he walked to the front of the stage and said, "Scholar Hallam, I believe. I'll give you a kiss if you really want one." There was a ripple of laughter, especially among the scholars.

"Not from you, you idiot. From The Lady." This caused a slightly horrified intake of breath.

Tamlyn stroked his chin, pretending to consider the proposition. "Well, I'll have to think. I can kiss The Lady because she's my grandmamma, you see: I'm not sure about you. You'd better come up here and ask her nicely."

Hallam landed on the stage and produced a creditable bow. He started to speak, but Merla grabbed him and kissed him soundly, which, Tamlyn noticed with amusement, actually caused him to blush.

Merla then took charge. "Gentlemen," she said addressing the six judges, "I think it would be a good idea that we should talk, if you agree. Somewhere a little less crowded perhaps." When they all bowed their assent she turned to the rest of the assembly.

"This is a day when life here has changed. Anyone who wants to live in The Land, my Land, is welcome as long as they remember that all who live here are equal. Not perhaps equal in what they are capable of doing – we're all born different – but in being allowed and encouraged to make the best they can of their lives. It may take some getting used to, but I know it is right. People of The Land, we've had hard times and great sorrows; most of you have known nothing else, but that is now in the past; not forgotten, but put away in our hearts. If you go on bearing grudges in the present, you will hurt yourselves the most, as I believe Zerac did. People of the Citadel, all of you are welcome too, if you can do all you can to learn new ways, so that we may become one people. It will take time, but it will happen.

"Now, it's a lovely and a very special day; I feel we should all be able to enjoy the happiness of it as much as we can. May I ask that all school and Academy students have the rest of the day free. I know some of the rest of you have work that can't be ignored, but make it as light as possible. There is a beautiful stretch of grass down by the river. It would be wonderful if we could all gather there later to have a picnic supper together and start to know each other. Bring whatever food you can, and I'm sure that any help from Citadel folk in the preparation will be very welcome."

She waved cheerfully and blew some kisses to the children in the front. Then she held Tamlyn close again and whispered, "Enjoy today, Tam. You've given it to us and I think that will be remembered as long as people live here. More importantly in the present, Lyddy will be longing to see you. Go and be just Tamlyn for a while; no worries and no more dangers." Then she joined the six judges and went with them to start being The Lady for all in the Citadel and The Land.

Chapter 34

Tamlyn sat by the river, waiting for Lyddy who'd gone round by the kitchens to collect some food for them. She was probably chatting to Ysalle, he guessed. Ysalle, who'd gleefully cast off her title as a Lord's daughter on the day after everything had changed, and come to ask Lyddy if she could work in the kitchen. She'd proved she could match even Lyddy's high standards and the two had become close friends. Tamlyn didn't mind waiting. It was a beautiful spring evening and there was no need to start yet.

He watched a family of ducklings bobbing along behind their mother, and his mind drifted among memories of the last months, since Merla had become the ruler and the Citadel was no longer Zerac's stronghold, kept fast by fear, cruelty and suspicion. Swift messengers had been sent to the City after the trial, and Almaran with Veranne and Mardell had come to The Land at once, closely followed by Lyddy's parents, Belsanna and Daven. Tamlyn remembered Almaran visiting the bodies of Zerac and Zaroth in the chilled chamber deep below the Citadel. He'd stood in silence, looking at the brother he had lost more than fifty years before and the nephew he had never known, his face white with grief and regret. Only Tamlyn and Merla had accompanied him, and afterwards the King had spent a long while talking with Merla. Tamlyn knew by Almaran's face later that Merla had been able, in her wonderful way, to help him understand everything that had happened and to release his feelings of guilt about his own inaction. All the same, he'd promised whatever help the City could give, a promise that was being kept in countless ways now.

Hearing that Zerac's brother was coming probably caused some who had suffered over the years to be fearful, but the sight of the King on his knees in the nursery, playing growly bears with the children, must have soothed their anxiety, as did seeing the Queen in the kitchens with her sleeves rolled up and washing dishes. That had also been a powerful lesson for some of the Citadel Ladies who, unlike Ysalle, were slightly less anxious to give up the easy life they'd been used to.

Tamlyn had his own special moments to remember. Almaran had taken Zerac's body back to the City for a quiet and private burial. He understood that the people of The Land would want no reminder of his years of misrule. Zaroth's funeral had been quiet too, but Merla and Tamlyn had watched as he was laid to rest with Darolissa.

"They're together now," Merla had said softly, and she and Tamlyn had planted a rosemary bush above them.

Now Tamlyn's mind drifted among other more cheerful pictures. Merla and Destralion laughing at a shared joke as they walked through the Citadel together; Master Garrid, released from teaching something in which he didn't believe by the removal of whatever fear the High Lord had used to force him. Evil enchantment no longer featured in the Academy timetable! With a grin, he recalled Hallam, growling with disgust when he heard that Almaran was sending a woman to assist him and Tebbling in their efforts to produce an efficient and fair financial system out of the chaos Zerac had left.

"Bet she'll be an old hag who can't even count on her fingers," he'd grumbled, but Tamlyn had heard about Shalanna and laughed.

"Wait till you meet her," he'd told his friend, and when the young and remarkably attractive mathematician had arrived and fallen on the numerical mess like a hungry lioness finding fresh meat, Hallam had soon admitted he'd been wrong.

One memory still made Tamlyn cringe with embarrassment, that of being told by Almaran and Merla that he had, in law, inherited his grandfather's wealth.

"I don't want it, any of it," he'd yelled at them both, feeling sick at the idea. "I won't touch it." He'd turned to storm out of the room until Merla recalled him in a voice that he'd rarely heard from her, and he'd returned to listen as his grandmother and his great uncle talked quietly to him. In a sense, they'd explained, it was Zaroth's fortune as Zerac had died first. They understood how he felt, but if he didn't want it himself he could surely find worthwhile projects to use it on. He'd been ashamed and apologised: now he was making a list of possible projects, and he'd decided the first would be to build a library that everyone was free to use.

He'd call it the Greenwell Library, and Beteral had almost wept with pleasure at the idea. Tamlyn and Hallam had retrieved Greenwell's books from their hiding place, creeping in alone and at night. Secret passages should remain secret until really needed they agreed, but Tamlyn decided to keep the volumes for himself, to remember the man and to start the personal library he'd long dreamed of having.

"Thought you'd gone to sleep." Lyddy sat down beside him and dropped a quick kiss on his cheek. She'd got a satchel with her and a small package wrapped in a soft cloth. "You can put this in your pouch; less likely to get broken," she said, handing the parcel to him. He took it and stowed it away carefully. He knew what it was.

"Lyddy, are you quite sure you want to come?" he asked her, a worried expression appearing on his face.

"Of course I am. I'm not letting you go off anywhere on your own again; not anywhere that might turn out dangerous that is."

Tamlyn smiled at her. "It's not going to be dangerous, just a bit… well, you know."

"Yes, I do know. But I don't feel it like you, do I? It's dark and creepy, but I don't see and hear those awful things. I want to be with you so you're not alone."

"Oh Lyddy, thank you." Tamlyn grasped her hand and kissed the palm, then stood up quickly to hide his tears.

He'd realised a few days before that the spring equinox was nearly there. It was the day when, every year since she'd become The Lady on her parents' death, Merla had visited the cavern through which the river ran into The Land to flow down past Citadel and City to the sea. Every year except last year, when Tamlyn had gone and experienced something of the horrifying slaughter Zerac had carried out there. It had been the moment when he'd realised the depth of the High Lord's evil and cruelty, and learnt too that he had a close relationship to the people of The Land. Part of him shied away from repeating the experience, but he knew it was very important to Merla that the names of those killed should be spoken on that day, so in the quiet of her house he'd told her he'd go. He reminded her he could also look to see if any of the strange water plant, tache de sang, had survived the floods of last year.

"Are you sure, Tam?" she'd asked.

"Of course." He'd tried not to let his voice quiver.

"I'll go with you." Lyddy had come in from the kitchen. Though Tamlyn and Merla exclaimed and tried to refuse her offer, she insisted.

"It'll give us a chance to hold hands for a bit without half the population gossiping about it before bedtime." She wasn't being trivial, they knew, just making it easier to say yes.

So here they were. As the sunset faded they set off under a moon that wasn't full, but shed enough light to help them walk easily on the first part of their journey. Their eyes accustomed themselves to the growing darkness so they felt safe enough, and when they'd passed the bridge they stopped to eat some of the food Lyddy had brought. The next part of the journey would be slower over the rough miles towards the cave.

Tamlyn found himself remembering his previous journeys this way. Last year, not knowing what lay ahead in the cave, he'd been excited at the adventure of it and the thought of a plant he'd never even heard of. Riding behind Zaroth it had been much quicker, but his mind had been veering crazily between anger at what was happening and fear of what was to come. Tonight he could think of Lyddy by his side and be glad that life had become so wonderfully different.

And yet that cave... he could feel it pulling him and repulsing him at the same time. They did hold hands, helping each other over the roughest places, and pausing now and then to rest legs that were beginning to ache with the increasingly steep gradient. I'd never have got down here running without that torch, Tamlyn thought, and wished, as so many times before, that he'd understood the truth of what was happening that stormy night.

On and on they trudged. The dim presence of the dark cliff face began to loom ahead of them and they decided that the almost imperceptible paling of the sky really was the pre-dawn light and not their imagination. Eventually, they stood with their backs to the high rocky wall just before they had to find their way along the narrow path that curved inwards beside the dark waters of the river; the place where four had held Zerac and his men pinned in the cave just long enough to let a few of the children escape.

"Let's wait here a moment," Tamlyn said. "Don't want to be too early, its dark enough even when the sun is shining in. Then we'll go in and... I don't know. Can we tell them that Zerac is dead and The Land is a happy place again, do you think?"

"That's just what we'll do," whispered Lyddy, giving his hand a quick squeeze before dropping it and moving half a step away from him. Did she know he needed a moment to calm himself before he went in?

"I'm going to shut my eyes and count to forty. It'll be easier to see."

Tamlyn counted, at each number telling himself this was fine, he was going to be all right. "... Twenty-seven... twenty-eight... twenty..."

"*Tam!*" Lyddy's voice screamed. His eyes flew open and he realised she wasn't beside him. He couldn't see her. In terror he ran towards the entrance, imagining he didn't know what horror.

But she came back round the corner, not frightened but with her face alight.

"It's all right Tam, I think they know already. Come and see." She grabbed his hand, pulling him into the cave, and it wasn't the black and fearful place he'd been dreading. Where last time the waterfall had dropped, high and straight like a huge steel blade from the small gap in the cavern's roof, the water now bubbled and splashed down a long, shallow slope of rocks and boulders that reached far back into the distance beneath the open sky. The cavern roof had disappeared except for a small arch of rock under which they'd just passed, and the sunlight glowed behind a distant peak, outlining its shape with silver, ready to burst upwards with the new day.

The floor of the cavern was littered with rocks, and the waters of the dark pool were no longer eerily still but rippled around others that had fallen into it. There was a scattering of rubble on the huge bridge stone, but it could still be used to reach the far shore.

"What's happened?" Lyddy asked, but Tamlyn had no answer. He stared round in amazement, wondering the same thing.

"I'll see if the plant has survived," he said. "Stay here, Lyddy, it won't take long." He picked his way across and down the southern shore. It was easier to see his way than last time. He bent over, peering carefully until at last he saw the red, globelike leaves nestling behind a boulder that in falling had created a sheltered inlet. The survivor looked strong enough but was too small to be divided. Tamlyn straightened up to return to the bridge and stopped there, staring at it. This was where the horrifying vision had come. Zerac slashing his sword across a screaming child, and cackling with laughter as he kicked her body into the pool.

He could see Lyddy gazing at the water that splashed and bubbled whitely between and over the rocks like an ever-changing pattern of lace until it was channelled beneath the bridge. She's my reality, Tamlyn thought, whatever happens now. He stepped onto the bridge, watching carefully where he put his feet, clenching his hands, scarcely breathing.

In a few short steps he was over, and standing beside her. Nothing! The fearful images had been dissolved into the openness of the new cave, the new Land.

"The horror's gone. Zerac's gone. Those who died are at peace." Tamlyn knew this as a certainty, but he called out their names and it sounded more like a song of triumph than a remembrance of death. As he ended Lyddy pulled at his arm, pointing.

"Look. Up there... and there... everywhere." The sun had risen over the river in its new rocky valley, and between the stones at the water's edge green shoots were showing with here and there a glimmer of yellow. "I think they've turned into flowers," Lyddy whispered. "It'll be beautiful instead of sad. We must tell Merla."

They made their way out into the dawn and Tamlyn felt as though he could float down the hillside. That haunted place had been transformed. Suddenly he remembered the storm on the day he'd found Zaroth, and the earth-shaking thunder just before he'd dived into the shelter.

"I think I know what did that, a thunderbolt," he said, and told Lyddy about it.

"I'm sure you're right. It had to be something really tremendous."

"And the river. When my father stepped into it the water was dark, yet later when I saw it from the Citadel it was muddy, full of earth. Washed from up there, I'm sure."

They walked on in silence for a while, and then Tamlyn took a deep breath.

"When shall we get married, Lyddy?" he said, as calmly as he could around his beating heart. She stopped and turned to him, and Tamlyn could see her lips curving and her eyes sparkling.

"Are we getting married? I don't remember being asked," she said.

Tamlyn stared at her, and then realised what she was saying. Right! He'd show her! He gave a bow and dropped on one knee in front of her.

"My Lady Rosanne, will you do me the honour of being my wife?"

Lyddy looked at him, face struggling to stay solemn.

"My Lord, I'm sorry but there is no Lady Rosanne in this land. Will I do instead?"

Tamlyn reached up and caught her, dragging her down to him so that they were kneeling together, face to face. He leaned into her, drew her closer, buried his face in her hair and felt her warmth, smelt her perfume.

"Marry me, darling Lyddy. Please, *please* say 'yes'."

"Oh, yes, yes, yes, yes, yes," she laughed. "Yes, please. When?

"Tomorrow."

"Can't do that."

He held her away from him to see her face. "Why?"

"I've got to make the bridal cake. I'm not letting anyone else do that. But you can stir it; for luck."

"Don't need that. I've already got all the luck there is." He kissed her over and over, never once wondering if he was doing it right, and she joined in, her lips closing on his and on every part of him she could reach without breaking their embrace.

At last they realised they must go back and tell Merla everything. A slightly panicky thought came to Tamlyn

"Have I got to ask your parents?" he asked.

"They know, and quite approve. They're still in love themselves, so they understood why I had to come back."

"Merla?"

"Oh, I told her after that first day in the kitchen with Fliss."

Tamlyn laughed. "Was there anyone but me who didn't know?"

"Well you were a little slow coming round to it, my darling."

"Oh I was there all right. I just thought you'd find someone better than me, especially when you went to the City. Mardell perhaps."

"Mardell?" she spluttered. "He's an idiot. Charming, but an idiot. Anyway, he's marrying Dee."

"Is he? I didn't know."

"They don't know either yet, but they will, you'll see. Oh, I've just thought. You'll have to tell Vitsell. He thinks I belong to him."

Laughing and hand in hand, almost dancing down the spring-green river bank, they went to share their happiness with all The Land. It was no more perfect or trouble-free a place than anywhere else, but it was free now, and their home in which to love and make their lives together.